The Wedding Wager

SARA ORWIG

D0785880

Published in Great Britain 2014
by Mills & Boon, an imprint of Harlequin (UK) Limited,
Eton House, 18-24 Paradise Road, Richmond, Surrey, TW9 1SR

THE WEDDING WAGER © 2014 Harlequin Books S.A.

Dakota Daddy, Montana Mistress, and *Wyoming Wedding* were first published in Great Britain by Harlequin (UK) Limited.

Dakota Daddy © 2009 Sara Orwig
Montana Mistress © 2009 Sara Orwig
Wyoming Wedding © 2009 Sara Orwig

ISBN: 978 0 263 91177 0
eBook ISBN: 978 1 472 04472 3

05-0314

Harlequin (UK) Limited's policy is to use papers that are natural, renewable and recyclable products and made from wood grown in sustainable forests. The logging and manufacturing processes conform to the legal environmental regulations of the country of origin.

Printed and bound in Spain
by Blackprint CPI, Barcelona

DAKOTA DADDY

BY
SARA ORWIG

Sara Orwig lives in Oklahoma. She has a patient husband, who will take her on research trips anywhere from big cities to old forts. She is an avid collector of Western history books. With a master's degree in English, Sara has written historical romance, mainstream fiction and contemporary romance. Books are beloved treasures that take Sara to magical worlds, and she loves both reading and writing them.

With love to Hannah, Rachel, Ellen,
Elisabeth, Colin, Cameron and Maureen

Prologue

"May the best man win!" Jared Dalton declared as the three cousins stepped out of a limousine into the bright Houston sunshine. Waiting on the tarmac were three sleek jets with each man's logo proclaiming ownership.

"One year from today, whoever's net worth increases the most wins our bet." Chase Bennett said, rehashing their agreement.

"Yes, the deadline for our bet is the first Friday next May," Matt Rome confirmed. "We each put five million in the pot, so whoever wins gets a fifteen-million-dollar prize."

"Right," Jared nodded. "On top of poker winnings, Chase."

Chase grinned. "I was lucky this year. Guys, it's been great to be together again."

"Still best friends, still bachelors—maybe forever bachelors. This weekend together is necessity," Matt said.

All three shook hands. "So long, my two best cuz," Jared said, grinning.

"If nothing else, we'll see each other next at the family Christmas get-together," Jared added. "Stay cool." He boarded a white plane and sat by a window, watching his cousins' planes taxi, one Houston-based cousin heading off to Paris, the other returning home to Wyoming. With mothers who were sisters, they had grown up close, even competing in football in college. All were wealthy and owner-CEOs of vast enterprises.

Jared intended to win the bet Matt had dreamed up. It would add some spice to work, akin to the thrill of success when he'd started out. Waiting until they were airborne, Jared withdrew his BlackBerry to send out messages that would start his staff searching for possibilities for solid moneymaking deals. He mulled over current projects and realized the bet gave him an opportunity for payback.

Excitement gripped him. He'd offer to buy the Sorenson ranch in Dakota. If Edlund Sorenson would sell, Jared could make money. Whether or not Edlund would sell, Jared knew he would have the satisfaction of letting an old enemy know he could buy him out. Making money was great. But best of all was revenge.

One

June

That old saying about a woman scorned was too damn true, Jared Dalton thought.

He thought back to when he'd first learned that old man Sorenson had died and that Megan had no apparent interest in keeping the family ranch. Jared assumed he could buy it easily. To his surprise, the minute Megan had learned who intended to buy the ranch, she'd withdrawn it from the market. Now he was here to get her to sell.

With a disturbing skip in his heartbeat that overrode a simmering anger, he saw Megan emerge from the Sorenson barn, carrying a saddle to the corral. She was too far away for him to see if her looks had changed. Her red shirt was as noticeable as her long-legged, sexy walk, which still revealed the years she had studied dance before she'd left for college. Her black hair was in a thick braid that lay on her back. Setting the saddle and blanket on the fence, she turned to the approaching horses to give each a treat. Within minutes she had saddled and mounted a sorrel.

The sight of her brought back too many hurtful memories. Vengeance was sweet. He just wished her father had lived to be part of the intended payback.

Jared intended to encounter her out on the ranch, where she would have to talk to him. He'd spent the night in a comfortable log guesthouse on her ranch without her knowledge in order to watch for her this morning. Before dawn he had dressed in jeans, a blue Western shirt and a wide-brimmed black Stetson.

Now he went to the barn to saddle a bay to follow her without haste.

The vast, grassy land made it easy to see in all directions except along the river, where trees could hide a rider from view. He knew he could catch her when she stopped at the river to let her horse drink. Until then, he didn't want to alert her that he was trailing behind. Thunder rumbled in the distance, and a glance at gathering clouds told him rain seemed imminent.

As soon as she reached the line of trees, she vanished from view. Watching, he could remember meeting her at the river—and their steamy kisses. Since their split, he rarely thought of her without bitter feelings surfacing.

Unwanted memories enveloped him. He had known her all his life. Even as their dads battled over water, he'd paid no attention to her because she had been six years younger—the skinny little kid on the neighboring ranch. The first time he'd ever noticed her was when he was getting his master's degree and she'd entered his same university in Chicago.

Too clearly he could recall that initial encounter. Her black hair had cascaded in a cloud over her shoulders and her startling turquoise eyes sped his pulse. She filled out a white cotton blouse that tucked into the narrow waistband of a tan skirt. When she'd smiled broadly at him and said hello, he'd thought he was looking at a stranger. If a beautiful woman greeted him, however, he had no intention of not responding.

"You don't know me, do you, Jared?"

Surprised, he'd stared at her and frowned, trying to recollect. "Did you go to UT?" he asked, referring to the University of Texas, where he'd gotten his undergraduate degree.

She laughed and stuck her tongue out at him and he sucked in his breath. All her pink tongue had done was make him think about kissing her. He was getting turned on and he didn't have a clue how he knew her.

"Jared, for heaven's sake!" she said. He shook his head, touching a lock of her soft hair.

"Okay, I give. I can't believe I don't remember a gorgeous woman. Where have we known each other?"

"I'm Megan Sorenson," she'd said, laughing at him. He stared in astonishment, seeing it now in the turquoise eyes. But that was all. Gone was the skinny little kid, replaced by a luscious, curvaceous woman.

"You grew up," he said, and that sparked a fresh burst of laughter.

"I didn't know you're going to school here," she said. "I thought I'd heard you'd graduated."

"MBA," he said slowly. "Have dinner with me tonight."

She tilted her head to study him. "You know how our dads fight. You and I should keep a distance."

"C'mon, Megan. Their fight isn't our fight. I've never in my life had anything against you."

"Oh, liar, liar!" she accused with amusement again dancing in her eyes. "You thought I was a pest. You wouldn't even say hello if you saw me."

He felt his face flush. "I'll make it up to you. I promise to give you my full, undivided attention," he said, and saw a flicker in her eyes. The moment between them sizzled and his heart raced.

"Dinner it is," she said breathlessly.

"About seven," he'd replied. And from that moment on, he'd thought he was in love. He'd hoped to marry her. They'd talked about it and planned on it, and then that summer after her freshman year, when Megan had gone to Sioux Falls to stay with her aunt and uncle, Olga and Thomas Sorenson, her dad sent one of his hands to summon Jared.

The old man had run him off by threatening harm to Jared's dad. He'd always wondered how much Megan had known about what her father was doing. For over a year he'd hurt, pain turning to anger that had grown when she wouldn't answer his letters. It pleased him enormously to buy her ranch. This payback was long overdue, and again he wished he'd offered to buy the ranch when Edlund Sorenson had still been alive, just to watch the old man's face.

Most obstacles weren't insurmountable, he'd discovered. Not with the wealth he had accumulated. He didn't expect this one to be, either.

He heard her horse before he rode into a clearing at the river's edge, and then he saw her. His insides clenched. Longing, hot and intense, rocked him. He rarely spent time on regrets but briefly, the thought that he never should have left her tore at him. Surprised, he shook aside his uncharacteristic reaction as she whirled around.

Color drained from her face. Her eyes widened until they were enormous and she swayed, making him wonder if she were about to faint. "Jared!" she exclaimed, as if he were an apparition.

"Megan, I didn't intend to startle you." He dismounted, dropping to the ground.

She drew herself up. As abruptly as she had looked on the verge of fainting, she pulled herself together.

Jared's heartbeat quickened at the sight of her. "You're more beautiful than ever," he said, and cursed himself with his next breath. Anger flashed in her turquoise eyes, those crystal-clear blue-green eyes that were astonishing when he first looked at her.

"Why are you trespassing?" she asked, her composure obvious. He'd surely imagined her terrified reaction to the first sight of him. "This isn't your ranch, nor will it be. You get off my land."

"Whoa, give me a chance," he replied in amusement, reassessing changes in her. "Seven years was a long time ago."

"Not long enough. Your people were told this ranch is no longer on the market. I'm not selling. You'll never own this land." While thunder rumbled overhead, she withdrew a cell phone. "I don't know how you got one of my horses, but leave it where you found it and go. You're trespassing, and if you don't get off this ranch, I'm calling the sheriff."

"Don't be so emotional," Jared said, wishing he could unfasten her thick braid. "At least listen. You have nothing to lose."

Thunder boomed again, and she glanced skyward.

"I think, unless you don't mind getting soaked, you'll have to ride back to the barn with me," he added.

Without saying a word, she glared at him and then turned to mount her horse. Observing her tight jeans that pulled across an enticing bottom, Jared swung into the saddle as well, and waited for her to lead the way through the trees.

As the first large drops hit leaves overhead, they rode into the clearing. A jagged bolt of lightning flashed, and Jared knew they should get out of the open field and back to shelter.

He urged the bay he'd chosen, Jester, hoping she could keep up. Drops were coming faster by the time the barn loomed in sight.

As they galloped into the barn, the heavens opened. Jared dismounted, dropping to the ground while both horses shook their heads, sending drops flying.

To the accompaniment of the steady hiss of rain, they

unsaddled and rubbed down the horses. Once the animals were in stalls, Megan strode to the open door and watched the rain.

"Probably a summer shower. It'll move on," Jared said, standing close enough to catch the scent of an exotic perfume, not the rose perfume she once wore. "Why don't you listen to my proposition? I know you don't intend to retire to the ranch."

"You don't know that," she said, glancing up at him with hostility simmering.

"So you are?" he probed, and saw another flash of anger, knowing he had been correct.

"I am not selling my ranch to you," she said slowly and clearly. He looked at her mouth, remembering their kisses. She'd been eighteen years old then. What would it be like to kiss her now? "Why do you even want it? There are other ranches."

"I have a bet with my cousins, Chase and Matt, to see which one of us can increase his net worth the most during the coming year."

"My ranch is to help you win a bet?" she asked, glowering at him.

"That shouldn't make any difference to you."

"One more thing that you want for your own purposes," she said in a clipped tone.

"Whoever buys the place will purchase it for his own purposes," Jared said.

"I don't see how acquiring my ranch can put you over the top," she observed.

"That alone won't. It'll be one of several projects," he answered easily.

"How'd you get here and where did you get my horse?" she asked.

"If I had called you, I didn't think you'd take an appointment to talk to me about the ranch, so I sent one of my lawyers, Trent Colgin," Jared answered, and she compressed her lips.

"I should have known," she said. She rushed to yank up a horse blanket. "I'm going to the house. It could rain all day, and I don't intend to stay here. You get off the ranch however you got on it. Don't spend another night here, or I truly will call the sheriff."

"You're going to get soaked."

"That's better than staying here with you," she said and turned to dash for the sprawling ranch house. Jared ran easily beside her, not caring if he got wet as long as he could try to convince her to listen to him. They rushed up the back steps and across the wrap-around porch. While she draped the dripping blanket over a rocking chair, he pushed his hat to the back of his head.

In spite of the blanket, her jacket was soaked in the front and she shed it to hang it on another chair. Her damp shirt clung, revealing lush breasts that stirred erotic memories of kissing her as he caressed her breasts.

As she started to turn away, he looked into her eyes and suspected she guessed what he was thinking. His gaze trailed leisurely over her. Her quick breaths made her breasts thrust out more. When he looked up again, sparks flashed between them.

Raising her chin defiantly, she placed her hands on her hips. "I'm not inviting you inside."

"Megan, listen to what I have to offer. You may be losing a huge fortune. One you could make easily by getting rid of something you don't want anyway. You're letting emotion get in your way."

"I know what I want," she said with a frown.

"Try to keep an open mind. Come to dinner at my house tonight and let's discuss the sale."

"In this weather? I think not, thanks," she said, shaking her head.

"According to the paper, this rain is supposed to stop before noon and it won't rain again until tomorrow afternoon. Now quit spiting yourself and come have dinner with me. Why don't we discuss a deal? You have nothing to lose."

"I won't sell to you at any price," she snapped as she yanked a key out of her pocket and put it into the door.

"Scared to eat with me?" he asked softly in a taunting voice.

Her head came up and she faced him with anger blazing in her eyes, making them look more green than blue. "I'm not the least bit afraid of you," she replied in a haughty tone. "All right. I'll come to dinner, but you should know you won't change my mind."

"How's seven?"

"I'll be there."

"You know the way," he said, and her cheeks turned a deeper pink. "See you then." He left for his cabin, fighting the urge to glance to see if she stood watching him. He hadn't heard any door slam, but then in the rain, he probably wouldn't have.

* * *

She was coming for dinner, so there was hope. When hadn't he been able to talk a woman into something he wanted? She was beautiful, more poised than she'd been as a teen. Then, she had been friendly and warm as a kitten. Now she was a hellcat. Despite her anger, her self-confidence showed. She was not the naive, starry-eyed eighteen-year-old he had fallen in love with years ago.

Anticipation bubbled in him. How long before he could seduce her? he wondered. He planned to keep a clear sight on his goal of acquiring her ranch, but this new Megan was an unbearable temptation.

He packed his few things and drove back to his ranch to make arrangements for dinner. As if nature were cooperating, the rain ended by noon and sunshine broke out with a magnificent rainbow arching in the sky.

When he caught some news on the television, he went to his office to make a phone call to his cousin.

The minute Chase Bennett answered, Jared could picture his green eyes and easy smile. "Hi, Jared here. Just caught you on the news about oil you've found in Montana."

"Hope to find," Chase corrected. "If it pans out like I expect, it's going to be a tidy discovery."

"A bonus that it's in your home state," Jared remarked dryly.

"Yeah, but I don't spend much time back on the ranch," Chase replied.

"I'll wager you think you're going to win our bet," Jared joked, rubbing his finger on his knee as he talked.

"I hope to. You guys are going to have to get busy."

"I'm working on an interesting project. Remember Megan Sorenson? I plan to buy her ranch."

"Nice! That'll crush her dad. It will be satisfying to let him know you can buy him out."

"I wish I'd done this sooner. The old man died. As soon as Megan discovered I'm the buyer, she pulled the ranch off the market."

"Too bad. Making the offer should give you a bit of satisfaction. That would be a good purchase, a prime pheasant-hunting ranch, even though it won't help you win."

"Wait and see," Jared replied, chuckling, unwilling to reveal his plans to Chase. "Better go. Just called to offer congrats and tell you I still intend to collect."

"Dream on," Chase replied in a good-natured tone.

"I will," Jared said, and broke the connection, trying to be the one to get in the last word, a habit of the cousins since childhood. Jared gazed out the window. What to do about the Sorensen ranch…

The day seemed an eternity long, but eventually Jared showered, shaved and dressed with care in a tan knit shirt, chinos and hand-tooled leather Western boots that added to his six-foot-six height.

Promptly upon her arrival at seven, Jared met her on the porch. Watching her get out of her SUV and walk toward him, her slim column of a navy dress swirling around her shapely calves, he sucked in his breath. A large bow held the dress on her left shoulder, leaving the other shoulder bare. The material split as it fell from her shoulder, revealing her long legs as she walked. Her hair was rolled and fastened at the back of her head, giving her a sophisticated, self-possessed appearance. Had they gone out in public, she would have turned heads anywhere—the men in appreciation and speculation, women in envy and admiration.

Jared's pulse skipped, and he wondered if that bow on her shoulder released the front and back of her dress. He desired her with an intensity that shocked him. She was gorgeous, and momentarily he forgot the ranch, his purpose, old hurts, even anger. He saw a ravishing beauty whom he intended to seduce.

"Evening, Jared," she said. Her greeting brought him back to reality.

"You're stunning," he said in a deep, raspy tone, gazing into the cool, thickly-lashed turquoise eyes. "Welcome to my ranch," he added. "Come inside."

Without a word, she swept up the steps past him. When she passed, he caught that same exotic scent, a perfume he couldn't identify. Watching the slight sway of her hips, he followed her through the flagstone-covered entry into the wide front hall with its polished plank floor. She took his breath away with her beauty. He was reminded again that the open, outgoing warmth of the eighteen-year-old had deepened into the fieriness of a beautiful woman.

"I'm grilling steaks. Let's go to the patio," he suggested as he caught up to walk beside her.

She strolled in silence beside him outside to the patio, where smoke came from a large state-of-the-art stainless steel cooker. "You have all you need to live out here," she said, glancing around.

"Can I get you a glass of wine, tea, a soft drink? What's your preference?"

"White wine, please." She followed him to the bar, and he turned to hand a glass of pale wine to her. Even though their fingers brushed lightly, the contact was electrifying. He could feel the sparks, as close as he stood to her.

She tilted her head to study him. "You'll be returning to Texas soon, won't you?"

"It depends on what happens with you. I'm not in a hurry to go after seeing you again."

"Stop flirting, Jared. Or is that impossible?"

"Not impossible, but infinitely more interesting when you provoke it. How can I be with you and remain all business?"

"You might as well. The personal touch will get you nowhere."

He gave her a mocking smile. "Watch out, I might prove you wrong." He saw her gazing up at gray clouds streaking across the sky.

"When I crossed your river, the water was almost up to the bridge."

"Scared you'll get stranded with me?" he asked in amusement.

She whipped around to give him a level look. "No. I'll leave before I let that happen," she remarked.

"Here's to the future and forgetting the past," he said, ignoring her remark and raising his drink in a toast, even though he doubted he would ever lose all his bitterness toward her.

"This is pointless, Jared," she said, sipping her drink.

"Megan, we both did things that hurt. I left here and you married someone else two months later," he said, hoping he kept his tone casual enough to hide the stab that memory always brought.

"I'm sure you know my marriage didn't last much more than a month before we filed for a divorce," she replied with anger in her voice.

He recalled his fury and pain when his parents told him about a reception her father had for her and her new husband shortly after the marriage, and then the next thing he'd heard was that she was divorced, which gave him a degree of satisfaction.

"Where's your son from that marriage?" he asked, wondering about her child.

"With my aunt and uncle in Sioux Falls," she replied. A shuttered look had come over her features and he could feel a wall of coldness between them. She looked half angry, half afraid. He tried to curb his emotions and not let his bitter feelings interfere with his goals.

"At the time I couldn't stay to tell you why I was doing what I was doing," he said. "I never meant to hurt you like I did," he admitted quietly, refusing to get into it now, knowing she wouldn't listen to the truth about her father.

Twisting her shoulders out of his grasp, she strolled farther around the patio while he walked with her. "Jared, let's not rehash the past. As you said, it's done. Let go of it."

"I will if you will. But I know this is why you backed out of the deal we had for the ranch. Admit it, you were ready and willing until you discovered that I was the buyer."

"I'm not arguing with you about it. My dad would have despised selling to you. I'll not do it—I promise you," she said, her eyes wide and almost green again.

"Wait and let me talk to you about it, and what I'm willing to pay," he said, fully confident he would win her over.

"I agreed to tonight only. In the next hour over dinner you can make your offer and then I'm out of your life." Her gaze slid away from his, as if there were more she wasn't saying. She'd hardly been reticent before. He had a suspicious feeling there was something he was missing, but he didn't know what.

"As far as leaving you alone—I don't know about that. There's unfinished business between us."

"I can promise you, we won't renew it," she said with such force he was taken aback. She walked on and he stared after her. Again, he had been mystified by the venom in her quiet tone. Why would she be that bitter now? They had planned to marry, but he hadn't left her at the altar. He'd never gotten that far—they'd talked about marriage and getting engaged, and he was looking for a ring for her when her father ruined their plans. Her reactions were still strong enough for it all to have happened last week instead of seven years ago.

"I'll check on dinner," he said, and went to the cooker.

Jared turned the steaks, watching her between glances at his cooking. He wondered whether she was truly interested in her surroundings or simply trying to avoid him.

After turning the meat, he went into the house to get things ready. Because of the threat of rain, they would eat inside. If they had a real downpour, his bridge would be underwater and the ranch cut off.

Jared hoped to avoid any threat that would send her home early before he could convince her to sell. Revenge was his goal. He didn't want to return to Texas empty-handed, so he planned the kind of offer she couldn't turn down. This was a battle he wanted to win. And he hoped to have her in his arms tonight.

As he returned outside to get the steaks, she continued to circle the expansive patio. He observed her for a moment, aware how easy it was to watch her, letting his gaze drift slowly over her, recalling her passion and fire the night he had taken her virginity.

Pushing aside memories, he plated the steaks and joined her. "Dinner is served. I thought we'd eat inside— it's cozier."

"Fine," she said, smiling. "Although, 'cozy' isn't necessary to discuss business."

"You haven't smiled much. I like it."

"A smile changes nothing," she said, falling into step beside him.

He caught her arm and turned her to face him, holding both arms lightly. It was on the tip of his tongue to blurt out the truth to her about her father. Instead, Jared held back, knowing it might be a misguided sense of honor. Or not wanting to sound like he was making excuses. "Megan," he said solemnly, "admit it, all your hostility is a grudge because I walked out seven years ago. If that weren't between us, your father's fight with my father would no longer matter. It's solely about us. Right?"

Two

As Megan looked up at him, her heart drummed. "Yes, I hate you for that, Jared," she admitted reluctantly, hoping to get him out of her life with a desperation that was making a wreck of her nerves. This morning had shocked her beyond belief. She had almost fainted. She hated the light-headedness and queasy stomach the sight of him caused.

Even worse, she loathed the jump in her heartbeat, the unwelcome reaction he could still evoke effortlessly. He was more handsome and appealing than she remembered, and that cleft in his chin was even more noticeable to her now. Tall, dynamic, sexy—too many qualities that she couldn't ignore.

"I'm astonished you're even here. You have your chain of successful restaurants and you have high-rise

condos. I'm sure you have investments galore, plenty
to keep you busy."

"I'm interested in your ranch, and now in you. I'm
amazed you haven't married again," he said.

"Not so surprising," she replied carefully, her palms
growing sweaty with nervousness that she prayed she
hid. "I'm a divorced single mom. I'm young—six years
younger than you, if you recall. I haven't met the right
person. I've pursued a career."

"Why do I think you haven't touched on the real
cause," he broke in, and her pulse accelerated.

"I've given you all the explanations you'll ever hear,"
she said. In a taut moment, she was lost in his dark gaze.
When his gaze lowered to her mouth, her lips parted.
She hated the reaction she had to him, but she saw the
faint, mocking smile on his face. He knew what he
could do to her.

He ran his finger slowly along her jaw. "You know,
we could go at this a completely different way. We can
renew an old, solid friendship."

"Solid until you walked out without a word!" she
said, and yanked her head away, stepping back.
"There's nothing between us now. Jared, I—" she
began, tempted to get into her SUV and go.

"Let's eat," he interrupted, as if he guessed she was
on the verge of leaving. He walked away in long strides.
Distraught, with her heart pounding and her insides
churning, she watched him. Why was the past being
flung back in her face, when she had found some peace
and thought she was safe from having to deal with Jared?
If only he would leave. She couldn't wait to get through

dinner. The minute it was over she was going home, and, hopefully, he would go back to Texas forever.

In minutes, they were seated inside at a table, where thick, juicy steaks, steaming potatoes and crisp green salads awaited.

"Tell me about your life in Santa Fe. You have gallery now."

She smiled and sipped her water. "I suspect you already know a great deal about my life at home. I'd guess you have staff check on all pertinent details. Admit it, you could write a dossier on me. And you know what my home looks like, what my income is, what I drive. And you've seen pictures of my gallery."

"Actually, no," he replied, as she had his full, undivided attention. "Only pertinent facts. You're a potter living in Santa Fe with your son. You're single. You have your own gallery."

"That's about it," she said quietly, sipping ice water. "Santa Fe is an artists' colony, actually. It's a peaceful, thriving place, where someone can have a degree of privacy while maintaining an artist's public lifestyle. I prefer to keep it that way, Jared. You don't have to know about my life. Of course, you're in papers and magazines and the news often enough for any six people."

"That means nothing," he said.

"In the meantime, you've built a fortune on delicious dinners, with your exclusive Dalton's steak houses."

"I've been lucky. That first restaurant in Dallas was a far bigger success than I ever dreamed. You have to make reservations a month ahead at a Dalton's."

"Sounds impressive. You've had a spectacular rise."

He shrugged. "My dad bankrolled me with a huge sum of money, telling my brothers he would do the same for them when the time arrived. That hasn't been necessary. I made enough of a fortune that I brought my brothers into the business and we've never looked back."

"So what about your life and your offices and homes?"

He looked amused by her refusal to discuss herself. In spite of the polite conversation, they were sparring. She could feel the tension in the undercurrent, with his constant, unwanted appeal. So much about him was agonizingly familiar that it tore at her. Guilt, anger, desire pulling at her with increasing force. Dinner was eons long already, and they hadn't even gotten to the true purpose. She had lived with a secret for over six years now. Was she staying silent and committing a sin beyond measure?

She tried to focus on what he was saying about himself.

"I'm not anywhere half as interesting," he said. "I work and I play. The usual way. Mostly, I'm at my headquarters in Dallas, in meetings or on the phone. Depending on what's happening, I go out in the evening. Nothing exciting. I travel a lot, have no serious love life. Any men in your life right now?"

She wished she could answer yes and put another wall between them, but if he'd had staff check into her lifestyle, even minimally, Jared already knew the answer to his question. She shook her head. "No. I lead a busy life and my days are dedicated to my son first and my pottery second. They fill my hours."

"You're a beautiful, desirable woman," Jared remarked, his words slowing and his voice growing husky. "I find it difficult to think there's no one. It has to be your choice."

"Thank you," she replied, intending to answer briskly and move on, but her words came out breathless, far too revealing. "I suppose it's my choice, but my hours are taken. As it is, there aren't enough hours in the day."

Even though the steak was delicious, she had little appetite. Each bite was an effort. She was aware the evening had darkened early given the thunder, but she sat with her back to the windows.

"Tell me about Ethan," Jared said, startling her to hear him say her son's name.

"What's to say? He's a normal six-year-old. He plays soccer and T-ball. He has a mind for numbers, even at this age. He's tall and has my black hair."

"Where is he tonight?"

"In Sioux Falls with Aunt Olga and Uncle Thomas. Every summer when school is out, he stays with them for several weeks. You must know my parents died, but Uncle Thomas and Aunt Olga are like grandparents to him."

"Do you have joint custody?" he asked, startling her. She shook her head quickly.

"No. Mike wanted out of our marriage as much as I did. When he learned about a baby on the way, we were already divorced. He gave me full custody. He had no interest in Ethan. Ethan doesn't even know him."

"I can't imagine a man not wanting to know his own

son. Sorry," Jared said. "At least Ethan was too young to know what happened."

Thunder growled, rattling the windows and she glanced back. "I'd like to head home while it's not raining." She turned to look into Jared's dark eyes. "Let's get this over with. We might as well get to the main topic. My ranch is not for sale."

"Look at options," he said easily, leaning back in his chair. "You plan to stay in New Mexico, don't you?"

"Yes, I do, but as long as my aunt and uncle are alive, I have Dakota ties. They're close to Ethan, as I am with them."

"If you sell the place at the price I'm offering, you can afford your own plane and pilot, or charter a plane whenever you'd like to see them. That's not any reason to hang on to something that will be a burden. Your place will go to ruin if you don't care for it constantly."

"I'm aware of the problems," she said.

"Your uncle and aunt won't move out here?"

She shook her head. "No. They're city people and they have no interest in the ranch. I said I'd pay them to run it and give them a share in it, but they prefer to stay in Sioux Falls. Uncle Thomas and Dad never got along, and I don't think Uncle Thomas wants any part of the ranch. Their only son, Ralph, lives in D.C., and his wife's family is from Virginia, so he'll never come back here."

"So, why spend your money maintaining the ranch?" Jared asked. "Surely not out of spite. That's expensive and impractical."

"Our ranch is a profitable place, as you know. Which is exactly why you'd like it."

He shook his head. "It's profitable if it's run right. But you know your dad invested hours and money into it and made it what it is. You can't work in Santa Fe and maintain the ranch the way your dad did."

She knew Jared was right, but she wasn't going to admit it. She couldn't keep from feeling that if she refused him, he would go on to other things, and she could quietly find a buyer later in the year and sell without Jared knowing until it was a done deal.

"Are you willing to close your gallery and move back here?" Jared asked. He sounded as if he were asking a casual question. His quiet voice and easygoing manner were deceptive. Even though she hadn't been around Jared in years, she knew better. He had to care, and with his wealth, she suspected he was unaccustomed to rejection.

"I don't think I'll have to," she answered, with the same lightness of tone that he maintained. "If it turns out more of my time is required, I'll hire someone to run my gallery."

They both had stopped eating and she could feel the tension increase. She also realized the thunder was more frequent. "Jared, I have to get across your bridge."

"You have time," he said dismissively, and with as much certainty as if he controlled the weather, which, under other circumstances, would have amused her. "Here's what I'll do," he said. "I'll pay you one million more than your asking price of thirty million," he said flatly. "That has to be a figure that you have to consider."

Stunned, she stared at him. One million more was

huge. On top of her asking price, it was fantastic. "That's impressive," she said, studying him. "Why would you possibly want the Sorenson ranch that badly?"

He nodded. "Plus, I'd like the water rights."

"The river runs through the Dakotas, far north of us. You can't control all of it."

He smiled as if they were discussing the weather. She knew he expected her to jump at his spectacular offer. "No, I can't, but I'll feel better about it if I control more water than I do now. That's what our dads fought over. Plus, you have a thriving ranch. I would fully expect to make back my investment, or I wouldn't want it. There would be no point.

"I've made you a damn fine offer, Megan, and you know it. Think about it. Whatever you do about the ranch, I don't think you're going to spend a lot of your time in South Dakota."

"That's not the only consideration."

"You're hanging on out of anger, not because of a business decision. I know you don't run your gallery this way."

"I've never been emotionally involved with anyone the way I was with you, so it's difficult to view objectively," she admitted, hating to reveal the depth of her hurt. His eyes widened as if in disbelief, and she wondered what he was thinking about. Just being with him was opening doors to more problems and hurt. Thunder boomed again, as if a reminder to terminate the evening.

Staring at his supreme self-assurance in consternation, she knew he was right, but she wasn't going to let him win. "You're a ruthless man, Jared," she said flatly.

"No, I'm not. At least not in this case, and you know it. That's a fabulous bid, more than you'll get from anyone else. More than the place is worth. You've admitted that yourself. There's nothing ruthless about it. Most people wouldn't even be discussing the matter." He reached out to touch her hand, startling her and causing an unwelcome jump in her heartbeat. "But then, you're not 'most people,' and you never have been," he added in a husky voice that made her draw a deep breath. His gaze lowered to her mouth and her lips tingled. "You think about it," he suggested quietly, continuing to hold her hand. His hand slipped down to her wrist lightly, finding her racing pulse.

Satisfaction flared in his eyes, and she knew he could tell that she still had a strong physical reaction to him. The moment became taut, as his dark eyes probed hers. She should look away, move, speak—anything to end this electricity that intensified with each second; but she was held by his mesmerizing gaze. Memories rose to haunt her, tormenting moments of the past and their lovemaking. She could remember his kisses in exact detail, recollections she'd tried to shake.

"Stick to business," she said, the words bubbling up in anger even as her soft tone sheathed the steel in her voice.

She became aware of rain, wondering when it had begun, because she had been engrossed by their conversation. To her chagrin, she discovered it was a downpour, barely heard inside while sheets of water beat against the windows. She stood abruptly. "I'm going. I've stayed until it's pouring and I didn't intend to."

"Sit and wait it out," he suggested. "We can be civilized with each other. If you prefer, we can stay off the topic of business."

"The only thing I have to talk to you about, Jared, is business," she said, praying that was all she had to discuss with him and that he never learned the truth of why she was so unhappy to see him. The whole day and evening had turned into a nightmare, and she tried to hide her nervousness over seeing him again.

"You'll have a rough drive home. Let me take you and you can send a couple of your hands for your SUV tomorrow."

"No," she said, going to get her purse. Jared strolled behind her, his long legs eating up the distance with ease.

"Do you have a raincoat or umbrella?" he asked, and she shook her head.

"I didn't think about it. I have an umbrella in the SUV."

"I've got an extra. Wait a moment and I'll get it for you."

She watched him walk away, her gaze drifting over his long legs and through the memories of their bare strength against hers. Annoyed, she turned to the darkened window, watching rain beat against it. She wanted out of his house. Clearly, she recalled the muddy, rushing river nearly brushing Jared's bridge. She had to be able to get through. She couldn't stay the night with him.

To her relief, he reappeared with an umbrella and raincoat.

"Take both. I have others."

"Thanks. Where are you going?" she asked, as she watched him yank on a second raincoat.

"I'll follow you and see that you get across the

bridge. I intended to have it replaced, but I forget about it in the dry spells. We can go years without it being underwater."

"I can manage by myself. Thanks for dinner, Jared. I'll consider the offer and get back to you," she said over her shoulder, but he caught up with her, reaching ahead of her to open the door. His car was nowhere in sight, and she knew he would have to go back through the house or make a run for a garage. She didn't care what he did. Her focus was on crossing the river.

As she started the SUV and drove away, she peered through the watery windshield that couldn't be completely cleared by the wipers, even set on the highest speed.

Each flash of lightning increased her concern. Brilliant light illuminated fields that were turning into ponds, water running in the bar ditch. Occasionally, thin streams crossed low spots in the graveled road, and she knew the saturated ground was not soaking up the rain.

She couldn't be cut off. Not here and not now. Why had she let him goad her into this dinner? He would have made his pitch whether she showed up to eat with him or not.

Rounding a bend, she topped a rise when lightning flashed. She gasped as the streak of light revealed a river ahead. The instant display vanished, leaving driving rain and darkness, but the image was indelible in her mind. There was no bridge in sight because it was underwater.

She glanced in the rearview mirror and received another surprise. Headlights were a quarter of a mile behind and gaining on her. It had to be Jared. How fast was he driving in this storm?

She forgot about him as the next bolt lit up her surroundings, and again she saw the river with only the top of the bridge rails showing.

With a sinking disappointment, she knew crossing it would impossible. Jared pulled close behind, honked his horn and stopped. He climbed out of his black pickup, dashing to the passenger side of her SUV. Reluctantly, she unlocked the door to let him in out of the storm.

"You can't cross the bridge. Sorry, Meg," he said as he slid in, slamming the door.

"Megan!" she corrected. It was the first time he'd called her Meg since he'd walked out on her.

"You'll have to come back to the house. I've got plenty of room."

In another flash of lightning, she looked at the river that spread out of its banks.

"I promise you this night will pass and be only a memory," he said quietly, and she turned to find him watching her. "If you'd like, I'll turn your SUV around for you."

"Of course not, but thanks," she answered. "I've gotten along on my own," she said, unable to keep her resentment from showing.

Her cell phone rang, and she pulled it out of her pocket and answered, only to hear her son's voice. She glanced at Jared, fear and guilt returning as she said hello to Ethan.

Jared waved at her and climbed out of the car.

Relieved to have him go, she let out her breath. A tense evening was now turning into a grim night. She talked briefly, promised she would call again when she was out of the storm. Then she turned her SUV around in water that lapped over new ground.

Still, the rain came in thick sheets, drumming on the SUV and shutting the world from view except what was caught in her twin headlights. Jared's pickup had faded from view quickly in the rain. The thought of being under the same roof with Jared through a stormy night frazzled her nerves. She didn't care how large his house was—it could never be big enough, being thrown together through the night and morning until the rain stopped.

She wasn't going to worry about tomorrow. Just get through tonight and resist his dark eyes. Their midnight depths held blazing desire, a continual hot-blooded look that made her tingle from head to toe. There was nothing circumspect, businesslike or remote about what she saw smoldering in his appreciative gaze.

When he was younger, he went after what he wanted with a single-mindedness that was fierce. She knew that intensity was focused on acquiring her ranch, but she didn't care to have it turned on seduction.

Squaring her shoulders, she promised herself to keep barriers between them and try to get him out of her life before he discovered what she never wanted him to know. The SUV slid on the wet road and she turned her full attention to driving.

As she expected, when she reached his house he was waiting on the lighted porch. He stood by the railing, one booted foot propped on the rail. If he weren't so handsome and sexy, it would be far easier to remain cool toward him. Too many shared moments that, at the time, she had thought the best of her life, made it impossible to deal with him objectively. She cut the motor and sat a minute. The wind was blowing, a thorough storm lashing the earth as if a mirror of her emotions. Taking a deep breath, she stepped out with the umbrella and dashed to the porch and into the house, where she kicked off her impractical pumps. She left her umbrella on the flagstone entryway. "I'll leave them so I don't track water," she added, walking along the wide hall with him, trying to block memories of being in this house years ago. Her simmering anger crushed conversation and she walked in silence.

"Remember any of this?" he asked.

"Of course," she answered in clipped tones, and he glanced at her with his head tilted and one eyebrow raised in a questioning glance that made her heart thud. She knew that look only too well.

"You haven't changed much here, if my memory is correct," she said, looking at potted palms and gilt-framed seascapes.

"Not in this part of the house. I've left this part alone. Otherwise, I had an addition built to the kitchen, as well as a new bedroom for me. I'll show you later. How's this room?" he asked, switching on a light and entering a room with a king-size four-poster bed and maple furniture that stood on a polished oak floor.

"Fine," she said, following him into the room and seeing the adjoining bathroom.

"Let's go back to the kitchen for something warm to

drink. What would you like—hot chocolate, hot tea or something cold?" he asked while they walked down the hall again.

"If you have some, I'd prefer hot tea," she answered. "I told my son I'd call him back. If you'll excuse me," she said, getting her cell phone from a pocket in her skirt. She went to the living area to stand at one of the floor-to-ceiling glass walls and watch the rain while she called Ethan. She missed him and just wanted to wrap her arms around him. Reassuring herself he was safe and happy with her relatives, she tried to quell her anxiety. Next she talked to her aunt to tell her she was marooned at Jared's ranch.

With each jagged streak of lightning, she saw that the drenching rain hadn't let up. The puddles had spread, increasing her concerns that she might be stranded in the morning.

Assuring her aunt she was fine, Megan put away her phone and rejoined Jared in the kitchen. Asking about his work, she perched on a bar stool and watched him set yellow china mugs on a large tray. Her gaze traveled over his features, so familiar to her. If he ever saw Ethan…

Her heart did a flip at the thought. With brown eyes and black hair, Ethan looked as much like his dad as a child could, even down to the cleft in his chin.

Another clap of thunder boomed and lights dimmed. Jared glanced toward the windows. "I'll get candles, in case," he said, crossing to disappear into a walk-in pantry.

"All I need," she mumbled softly, hoping she didn't

spend the evening in candlelight with him. He had too many things going for him already.

Still focusing conversation on his work, she followed him into the living area, where she curled up in a chair. Lights were low and Jared had switched on soft music, while rain still drummed outside and poured off the porch roof. He took the nearby sofa and placed a tray with their steaming cups of tea and coffee on the glass table in front of both of them. Usually, such surroundings would lend a cozy intimacy to the evening, but she planned to have her drink and get back to the bedroom and close the door on Jared for the night.

As he answered her inquiries about his Dallas and Paris offices, his traveling and his houses, she wondered if she had made the mistake of her life. Should she have revealed to Jared long ago that he was the father of her son?

Had she erred by never contacting Jared through the intervening years? The minute the question came, she knew if she had to do it all over again, she would do the same. Jared had walked out on her without a word, never contacting her until their encounter this morning.

The simmering resentment boiled momentarily as she remembered her joy and his declarations of love, the wild passion between them and then…desertion. He didn't contact her, give her any indication that anything was wrong—he left, and when she began to look for him, she discovered from his parents that he'd gone to Texas, where he'd taken a new job. They gave her his phone number, but she had no intention of calling him.

The hurt had been monumental, compounded when she'd learned she was pregnant.

To forgive and forget was impossible. Tonight, he wanted something from her, and therefore was flirting and charming once again; but there was a solid, lasting bedrock of pain that he'd caused.

Still, guilt nagged and worry plagued her. Had she cut her son out of a relationship that would have enriched his life? Yet, how could a man who left like that have been that role model? He might not have paid any attention to him, which would have multiplied hurts.

Again, she hated the painful memories—agonizing ones of Jared, hurtful moments with her father, who was enraged when he discovered her pregnancy. Jared had been gone two months by the time her father learned the truth, and from the first moment when the doctor had given her the news, she'd known that she would be alone when she had her baby.

It hadn't turned out that way, thanks to her aunt and uncle in Sioux Falls, who stood by her through Ethan's birth.

Jared tilted his head to give her another one of those quizzical looks that was so familiar. How often had she seen the same look from her son?

"I think I'm talking far too much about my life. Tell me about yours," Jared said. He sat back with one foot on his knee. A brilliant flash was followed by a window-rattling clap of thunder, and the lights dimmed and then went out.

"Sit tight," Jared said in the darkness. "We're ready for the emergency."

With the next flash of lightning, she saw him standing, holding a candle. He began to light candles and place them in holders on the table.

The hiss of rain could be heard clearly, since music no longer played. Candlelight flickered and bathed Jared in a golden glow, highlighting his prominent cheekbones, his thickly-lashed eyes, the cleft in his chin and the sheen in his well-trimmed black hair. Unbidden thoughts came, of running her hands through that thick hair which had a tendency to curl, particularly in damp weather. Most of the time, Jared fought the curls and kept them combed out as much as he could, taming them into slight waves. He sat again, closer to the end of the sofa and her chair. "You look gorgeous, especially in candlelight."

"Thank you," she answered, hating the stab of pleasure his compliment gave her. "In candlelight everyone looks appealing. And on another topic—do you work more in the U.S. or abroad?"

He looked amused as he answered. "A safer topic, as you wish. Far less interesting," he said. "I'm in the U.S. the majority of the time. Did you move to Santa Fe when you started making pottery?"

"Not right away," she answered. She couldn't imagine that he really cared what she'd done. "I worked for a decorator in Sioux Falls as well as on my own," she continued. "I marketed through a Web site, and through the decorator. I thought it would be good to work in Santa Fe, so I moved and eventually went out on my own."

"I doubt if your dad liked you leaving here."

"No, he didn't, but he decided it would be a good experience for me. I think he thought I'd fail and come home, despite the fact I'd even bought a house," she replied, remembering how frightening it had been to move and go on her own with a small son. She had worried about Ethan and if the change would hurt him. The early years she'd lived with constant worry.

"Did he ever recognize your talent?"

She smiled. "Once I began to make sufficient money, my dad's attitude changed."

"It usually does," Jared said. "Nothing succeeds like success. It's difficult to imagine you working in clay, though," he said, taking her hands in his warm ones. "These hands don't look like you're a potter."

He turned her hands in his, intensifying a smoldering desire that she couldn't extinguish with either anger or logic. Drawing a deep breath, she pulled her hands away.

"I liked holding your hands," Jared said in a husky voice.

"It's the storm and candlelight—and wine you had with dinner. I suspect you like holding the hand of almost any woman you spend the evening with."

He ran his finger along her cheek and studied her with a somber, intent look as he shook his head. "Perhaps, but this is different. I didn't know when I came back here and saw you that it would be this way."

Her heart drummed along with her annoyance at him. She had no intention of letting him rekindle an unwanted physical attraction. To her dismay, he still held appeal, but her emotions battled it.

Beyond her physical response to him, there was not only her smoldering rage over the hurt he'd inflicted by leaving but also icy fear over what he might discover about her now. To be in close proximity to him set her nerves on edge.

"Jared, this isn't a special moment, other than we may be having the rain of the year. Don't pour on the compliments because I have something you want. You have a captive audience tonight, but don't overdo it," she said, thankful she could sound detached. Anything to keep an emotional distance between them. Yet her heart raced and his words weren't going to be easily forgotten.

He gave her a crooked smile. "That wasn't the reason for the compliments, I promise you. Buying your ranch was the last thing on my mind," he added, in that same husky voice that was a caress in itself.

She finished her tea and stood. "I'll turn in. I rise early."

He stood. "It's early to turn in, Megan."

"Times change, Jared. We're different people. I'll take a candle." When she reached to pick up her dishes, his hand closed around her wrist. The touch was light and casual, but the outcome was an unwanted skip of her heartbeat. Warmth suffused her beyond anything the hot tea had accomplished. Startled, she glanced up.

"You know that's not true. Leave the dishes," he said, his husky voice revealing his reaction to the contact. She was bending over the table and he had leaned close to take her wrist. Now they were only inches apart, closer than before. Candlelight flickered with pinpoints of light reflected in his brown eyes.

Once again she was captive, as she'd been beneath his volatile kisses—those kisses that had always set her ablaze.

"Megan," he said softly.

"No," she answered with little force. A pang of yearning tore her, instantly followed by anger that he could still have such an impact on her. Worse, she knew he was on the verge of a kiss she very much wanted. "No," she repeated more firmly. She straightened and he dropped his hand, still watching her with searing fire in the depths of his eyes.

"We could declare a truce," he suggested softly. "That was long ago, Megan."

Holding back a seething retort, she glared at him. "This is a useless discussion," she said, hating that she couldn't appear more poised. Appear as if what he'd done years ago no longer mattered. She reached to light another candle, but he steadied her hand and they lit a candle together.

Once more, he was holding her wrist. His slight touch increased her awareness of him more. And he was taking his own sweet time getting the candle burning. She was tempted to yank away from his grasp, but she'd already been foolish enough to reveal how much she reacted to the past. Over the flickering light, she looked up to meet his hot gaze trained on her mouth. She couldn't get her breath. Her lips parted and she wanted him in spite of what was sensible.

"Light the candle, Jared," she whispered.

His thumb moved back and forth slowly, a feathery touch on her wrist, until he paused and she knew he was fully aware that she always reacted to the slightest contact.

Desire magnified, pounding with each heartbeat. Setting aside the candle, he slid his hand behind her head.

"Jared," she whispered, a protest that came out a breathless invitation.

He drew her the last few inches and his mouth covered hers.

His warm lips moved caressingly, his tongue touching hers and then sliding deep into her mouth. Longing, physical and emotional, tugged at her even as she returned his passion. His other arm went around her waist and he stepped around the corner of the table to pull her body against his.

Once again, she was in his arms. How often had she dreamed of this moment, only to wake and discover it had been a fantasy. That Jared had still broken her heart so ruthlessly. Amazingly, here she was, actually kissing him, held in his strong embrace, finding him even sexier than she'd remembered.

Heat became fire. She fought the urge to wind her arms around him and press closer against him. Half of her longed for him desperately and the other half screamed to step away, to prevent what was happening.

His kisses burned wisdom to ashes. She kissed him hungrily, aching for more, knowing she was tumbling to disaster. Each second compounded her years-old need. Finally, she pushed against his chest.

He released her slowly, opening his eyes to study her in a heated silence.

"We're not going back there, Jared," she declared

with a gasp. "I didn't want that to happen. Don't make anything of it. It meant nothing, except I haven't kissed a man in a long time."

"Don't be so angry, Meg. I like kissing you," he said in a husky voice that held such warmth she tingled from head to toe. "No harm intended and no damage done," he added in unruffled assurance.

"Don't!" she cried. "I'm turning in," she said, circling the table in the opposite direction from Jared.

"You don't have to escort me to the bedroom door," she said, when he started toward her.

"Good night, Jared," she stated firmly.

"I wish I could take away your anger. We were young, Megan." His dark shirt was open at the throat and locks of hair had fallen over his forehead. Because of the rain, the natural curl in his hair had tightened and black curls framed his face.

She shook her head. "Good night," she repeated.

Emotionally exhausted, she entered her bedroom.

Her lips were still warm from his kisses and she was on fire with craving. The manner in which she had responded to him tore at her. He had opened Pandora's Box for her. She blamed it on not dating, but she kept busy and didn't miss having a man in her life. Between work and taking care of Ethan and his activities, her life was full, busy, so she fell exhausted into bed at night. But with a kiss, Jared had effortlessly demolished all her defenses. One touch, one kiss and she had been mush, melting and kissing him back. He'd made her yearn for his kisses and the feel of his warm, muscular body.

All yearnings she didn't want.

Crossing the room, she tried to forget that Jared was close, that he was soon to be undressed and stretched in bed. He used to sleep in the nude and she suspected he still did. Images plagued her, driving any chance of sleep away.

Why couldn't she have remained aloof and showed him that he couldn't stir her? Instead, she had responded passionately. She couldn't stop going over it, even though thinking about it made her hot. How could she have responded like that to a man whom she despised?

And his one million…

Sell him the ranch and she'd never see or hear from him again. Logic said to sell. She would get an incredible price, be rid of something she didn't care for anyway, She would sever most ties with South Dakota and only run a risk of seeing Jared when she visited her aunt and uncle. She would narrow the chances of Jared discovering what she had done.

On the other hand, she couldn't bear to deed the ranch to him. Fury over the hurts he'd inflicted tempted her to strike out at him in any way she could. Retribution was too enticing, something she had dreamed about for the first years after Jared's disappearance.

Plus, her father would never sell Jared the ranch. Her dad had hated the Daltons, despising Jared's father because of their continual fights over water. Each one had accused the other of taking too much. Water fights had always spilled over into every other contact. If a fence went down, each man blamed the other.

She knew, too, her father had viewed Jared's dad's simple background with disdain, as if he were a peasant. When Jared had walked out on her, her father had hated him for hurting her, even though he had been doing his best to talk her out of marrying Jared when Jared had vanished. Many issues fueled the family feud.

Both sides of her argument were strong. Money versus emotional satisfaction.

When her father's health began to fail, he had deeded the ranch to her. Upon his death, that decision became a safety net for her. It saved her time and money to have the ranch already in her possession, and left her free to sell it.

Each time she thought about Jared walking out on her and now coming back to buy the ranch, she felt as if she couldn't bear to sell—at any price.

Was she harming herself and Ethan by her refusal to let Jared buy the ranch? The money would be more than enough to provide for Ethan's education and a comfortable lifestyle they could never have otherwise. If she refused Jared, she might not get anywhere near her asking price from other buyers.

She was certain she would sell, but it could take a while—time she really didn't want to devote to the care of the ranch. It took money to keep it running smoothly, and with her father's failing health the past year, there were areas that had been neglected. The sensible business and professional approach was to sell to Jared or counter for an even higher amount—something she suspected he would agree to, to get what he wanted.

She knew she would pore over the arguments all night long. So far, the only person interested in the ranch had been Jared. She curled up in a chair near the window, watching the rain and flashes of lightning. Hopefully, once the rain stopped, the river would drop rapidly.

She rubbed her temples. Sleep would likely elude her for hours. To sell or not to sell? Stop remembering his touch and being aggravated with herself for succumbing to his slightest touch.

She paced to the window to stare outside, blowing out the candle to depend on lightning flashes for illumination.

If she would agree to sell the ranch, it would be the quickest way to get Jared out of her life. She stood at the window watching rivulets of water zigzag their way along the glass. Flashes of lightning revealed small rivers running through the yard and large silver puddles. The river would be high and impossible to cross, and the rain hadn't slacked off any.

She returned to a chair to stare outside while her thoughts churned over her predicament. Far into the night, she fell asleep in the chair.

Dawn was streaked with rays of the rising sun, lifting her spirits and giving her hope that she could leave soon.

She still struggled with her decision. Because of her fury at Jared, and her father's memory, she didn't want to sell. Keeping the ranch when Jared wanted it would give her immense satisfaction and a bit of revenge.

At the same time, the argument to sell couldn't be dismissed lightly.

She fell asleep in the chair, and woke undecided in the morning. Gathering her things, she headed to the bathroom to shower and dress in what she had worn the evening before. After combing her hair, she went to the kitchen, where she found Jared with a cup of coffee on the table in front of him. Dressed in jeans and a short-sleeved, gray Western shirt and boots, he looked irresistible.

"Good morning," he said easily, walking over to her, his gaze roaming over her appreciatively. "You're gorgeous—as you were last night," he said, curling a lock of her hair around his fingers. "This is the way I like your hair best." Catching the scent of his masculine aftershave, she felt her pulse kick up.

"Thank you for your compliment," she replied, wishing she had done something else with her hair. She didn't care to wear it in the style he liked best. "I'm a little overdressed for breakfast, but so be it."

"I could loan you my jeans," he said, with a twinkle in his eyes.

"No, thanks," she answered quickly.

"I didn't think you'd accept, but they wouldn't fit you anyway. I cooked breakfast—help yourself to whatever you like," he said, waving his hand toward covered dishes and pans on a stove. "Fruit is on the table. Would you like orange juice or tomato juice, milk, coffee—you can have all if you'd like."

"Orange juice and coffee please," she said, picking up a plate and looking at the many dishes. She helped herself to scrambled eggs, slices of kiwi and a bowl of blackberries. She had lost her appetite. As she watched him serve her juice and coffee, she knew she couldn't bear to sell him the ranch, no matter how much refusing him cost her. She would get a bit of satisfying retaliation here.

"This is a huge breakfast. Do you cook often?"

"Not unless there's no alternative. This morning we're cut off from my kitchen help."

"Looks like I'm here longer." She carried her plate to the table where he sat facing her.

"There are all sorts of things we could do to fill the day," he stated, causing her to look up sharply. When he gave her a disarming smile, she shook her head, smiling in return.

"I think simple conversation is the most likely. Or if you have business you can transact, you go right ahead."

"I wouldn't dream of it. If you don't sell your ranch to me, we'll be neighbors, so we might as well get reacquainted."

"I see no point in that," she said quickly.

"You surely don't plan for us to go through the future fighting, the way our fathers did."

"No…but reacquainted—I don't think so."

"So what's it going to be? To sell or not to sell?" he asked.

Three

Jared's pulse drummed as she faced him. Intuition hinted she would refuse him. Using logic, he couldn't imagine her rejecting his money.

"You made me a generous offer. One that kept me up almost all night," she said.

"A shame. I can think of other ways we could have spent the time," he said, unable to avoid flirting in spite of the tension between them. She was breathtaking, and he wanted to reach for her. Sunlight spilled through the windows and highlighted strands in her cascade of black hair. Her eyelashes were a thick, dark fringe that were a startling contrast with the crystal turquoise of her eyes. He waited in silence until she shook her head, dismissing his remark.

"I won't sell the Sorenson ranch to you," she answered.

His insides knotted and he curbed the urge to swear, instead remaining impassive, smiling at her as he shrugged. "That's what you want to do. You're turning down an extra one million."

"You received that well, Jared. Too well. I pulled the ranch off the market and decided to keep it."

"Even with your son to consider?"

Her face flushed and something flickered in her eyes and he knew he'd hit a nerve. "Yes, Ethan and I will get along without your money. We have thus far."

He was disappointed, but the world held countless opportunities. "Win some, lose some," he repeated the old saying. "Maybe you'll change your mind about selling after you spend a few years going back and forth and maintaining the ranch and your Santa Fe home."

"I'll manage, Jared."

"Well, I'm disappointed, but if you're not going to sell to me and go hurrying back to New Mexico," he said, approaching, "there's a bright side." He placed his hands on her shoulders, sliding one hand under the large bow that fastened her dress over her shoulder. "We'll be neighbors," he said in a warm voice. Undeniably, he wanted her more than her ranch. "You'll have to come home more often… I'll certainly spend more time here."

Drawing a deep breath, she frowned. "We'll be neighbors, not *seeing* each other."

"You opposed anything concerning me, Meg," he said in a husky voice. "We're bound to see each other, and why not? Why cling to the past? I told you I was sorry. Your refusal to sell guarantees I'll be around," he said.

"That wasn't my intention," she said. Her words were unfriendly but her tone wasn't. Her protests were light, almost halting, and contradictory to what she was saying—an unspoken invitation to him. "Not at all, Jared."

"Well, that's the result you've achieved. You've put me back into your life. I'm looking forward to being your neighbor."

"Go back to Texas, Jared. You know this is going nowhere."

"If you really want me out of your life so badly, maybe you should think some more about this answer you've given me. I can't help but feel that there's some part of you that wants to keep me here."

She twisted out of his grasp as his cell phone rang. He took it out of his pocket. "Excuse me, Megan," he said, answering his phone and talking briefly.

"That was one of the hands," he said when he was finished. "The river is still as the bridge level—some water washing over, but you can get through."

"Great!" she cried. "I'm going home."

She was clearly combating the physical attraction with all her being, a battle he felt she would eventually lose. He knew how to be patient, and the bet had been the most exciting thing he had going. Until she came along.

"I'll go first, Megan," he said as they walked to the door. He took a wide-brimmed, black Stetson off a hat rack and put it on. They stepped out into warm sunshine and a day that was crisp and clear, with a deep blue sky. A vast difference from the stormy night.

At her SUV door, he paused. "Wait and let me go ahead. I'll cross the bridge to make sure it'll hold. After I get to the other side, you can cross."

"I know I'm wasting my breath when I say you don't have to accompany me."

"Stop cutting off your nose to spite your pretty face, Megan."

"I'll try, Jared," she said with sarcasm lacing her voice.

"Keep your SUV doors unlocked so you can get out or I can get in to help you. Let me clear the bridge before you follow. If it shifts or anything indicates it's weakened, I won't motion to you to proceed. Okay?"

"Yes, thanks. I'll follow you."

"Megan," he said in a deep voice, "I'm glad you were here last night. It's good to see you and be with you again. Better than ever," he said, thinking about their kisses and her eager response. If she reacted that much in anger, what would it be like if he could melt those hurdles she kept between them?

"It was meaningless, Jared. The result of my not dating enough and a turbulent night. And you know you hold a certain charm for me, whether I like it or not."

"I think there may have been a left-handed compliment somewhere in there. I certainly hope so," he said.

She shook her head and he held the door, assessing her long, shapely legs as she climbed into the SUV. He closed her door and hurried to his pickup. As he got in he caught her watching him. Once again, he had the feeling that he was missing something with her and he couldn't fathom what.

* * *

Passing her, he worried about the safety of the bridge.

He topped the rise and looked at the muddy, rushing water that was tumbling and flowing as rapidly as the night before, sending rivulets over the bridge. It was standing, but the force of the water could have taken a big toll on it. He slowed and saw she was only a short distance behind him. Stopping, she waited while he proceeded.

As soon as they had crossed, he stopped and walked over to talk to her through her open window. Leaning closer, he pushed his hat to the back of his head. "Would you like to go to dinner tonight?"

She shook her head. "No, Jared. Business between us is finished. There's no reason for us to get together again. I meant no sale. And it's good-bye."

He slid his hand behind her head, leaned down and kissed her hard, thrusting his tongue into her mouth, aware of her soft hair tangled in his fingers and spilling over his hand.

He'd caught her by surprise, but she kissed him back, arousing him instantly. He was tempted to open the SUV door, slide inside and take things further, but he knew that would end the kiss.

She pulled away. She was breathless, her eyes filled with longing, her mouth red from his kiss. "Good-bye, Jared," she whispered, but her inviting expression contradicted the farewell.

He stepped back. "Call if you change your mind. Otherwise, I'll see you soon," he said, knowing he was annoying her.

Without a word she drove away and he watched, standing in the road with his hands on his hips, until her beige SUV disappeared from sight.

She was more beautiful than when she'd been eighteen. More poised, infinitely more sexy. He wanted her and didn't intend for her to go out of his life until he had seduced her.

He suspected that might take awhile, but he wasn't a marrying man and he wasn't the green twenty-four-year-old that he had been.

And he still expected to buy her ranch. It would be ridiculous to refuse to sell to him because of old hurts. He didn't see how she could possibly mean no.

He climbed into his pickup to cross the river and drive back to the house, lost in thoughts about Megan, about making love to her when she'd been eighteen, naked and passionate. He stirred uncomfortably. He wanted her in his arms in his bed. With a groan he tried to get the erotic images out of mind.

If he could get past her smoldering anger, she could be seduced. Even as she burned with indignation, she hadn't rejected his touch and his kisses. Attraction was still alive between them. It was only a matter of time, he felt certain, until seduction. Everything in her cried out to him.

The future didn't hinge on Megan selling the ranch to him. He could move on to the next lucrative deal. This had looked like an easy one that could have been handled quickly, made him some easy money and cinched the bet.

A jingle interrupted his thoughts. He answered his cell phone again, to hear his cousin's voice.

"Hey, Matt here. Chase said you're in South Dakota. I wanted to see if you've been washed away. The rain is making national news."

"Thanks for call," Jared replied. "I'm fine. Bridge was underwater last night, but we have sunshine today and the water's receded."

"That's good news. I hear you're buying the Sorenson place—that's sweet payback!"

"The old man died, but it's still sweet payback with Megan," Jared said, thinking about her refusal and feeling certain he'd get his way eventually.

"Good luck with it. It doesn't matter, though, I still intend to win our bet."

"Wishful thinking. Thanks for your call," Jared said, smiling and remembering a pugnacious look Matt often had when he wanted something that was difficult to acquire. Beneath the curly black hair was a brain that clicked constantly.

"Go back to work. You'll need to do all you can," Matt teased, and was gone. Jared chuckled over the good-natured teasing and the competitiveness that had been present since as far back as he could remember. He glanced at his calendar, Matt's call fading from his attention.

Monday morning, he was scheduled to see his attorney in Sioux Falls before he headed home to Dallas and now he had a lunch appointment with his real estate agent. As Megan invaded his thoughts again, he forgot about a schedule.

Monday, the eighth of June, he dressed in a charcoal

suit and tie and drove himself, leaving behind his bodyguard and chauffeur, feeling secure in South Dakota.

In Sioux Falls, he drove downtown to his attorney's office. It was another sunny June day.

As soon as lunch was finished, he parted with the real estate agent and headed to his car, his thoughts already turning from South Dakota, as he mentally ran through projects for the week. He paused to call his pilot to be certain his plane would be ready. As he talked, he glanced up the wide main street and saw an unmistakable dark head of hair.

His pulse speeded—it had to be Megan. She stood in front of a restaurant talking to two people with a boy beside her. He had his back to Jared and wore a ball cap.

Jared recognized her aunt and uncle and guessed that Megan had her son with her.

Impulsively, he crossed the street in long strides. Megan was dressed in red slacks and a red, short-sleeved cotton shirt and her back was to him. Her hair was caught up in a clip high on her head.

It had been years since he had seen Olga or Thomas Sorenson, the older half-brother of Megan's father, Edlund.

"Hello, there, Megan," he said cheerfully. They all turned to face him, and once again Megan's face drained of color.

"It's been years," he said, extending a hand to Thomas Sorenson, who hesitated a few seconds and then reached out. In that first moment, her uncle and aunt had looked as shaken as Megan.

Under Thomas's solemn, half-angry gaze, Jared realized something was amiss. Tall and graying, Thomas Sorenson gave him the barest possible handshake. Jared smiled at Olga Sorenson, Thomas's diminutive blond wife, who merely nodded with tight lips. His sudden departure seven years ago resonated badly with all three adults even today. Jared turned to Megan who was frowning at him.

"Sorry, if I interrupted you folks, but I saw you and thought I'd say hello. I didn't intend to intrude," he said.

When his pleasant comment was met by awkward silence, his curiosity grew. He glanced at the boy, who was looking at a bright red toy rocket he held in his hands. "This must be your son, Ethan," Jared said, holding out his hand in greeting. "Ethan, I'm Jared Dalton."

The boy looked up and shook hands with Jared.

"I'm glad to—" Jared's words died, as if he had been punched in the stomach. With midnight eyes, a cleft in his chin and black curls escaping from his cap, the boy staring back at him was his own image, a face that would match childhood pictures of Jared himself.

His own son!

Four

Jared glanced at Megan and her expression confirmed that Ethan Sorenson was his son. For an instant, he forgot the others as Megan's terrified gaze captured his. Her wide-eyed mixture of fear and anger put all the reactions this past weekend in place for him.

The moment would become permanently etched in Jared's memory—sun shining brightly, the three adults facing him with a mixture of unfriendliness and guilt in their expressions. And Ethan, who was looking at his rocket once more and unaware of the undercurrents.

The boy seemed not to have recognized Jared. All these years, Jared had had a son. The enormity of it overwhelmed him and for a moment he was at a loss. Megan had never told him. By all indications, she wasn't going to tell him now, either. She had been planning to let him go back to Texas without ever knowing about his son.

Astounded over his discovery and her duplicity, his gaze shifted from Ethan to her.

"I need to see you," he said to Megan. "We have to talk now."

She nodded and turned to tell Ethan good-bye and hug him.

"It was nice to see you," he said to the Sorensons. "Ethan, I'm glad to meet you," he said.

His *son!* When would he grow accustomed to that? He longed to pull the child into his arms and just hold him for a minute. Instead, he smiled.

"How old are you, Ethan?" he asked.

"Six, sir," Ethan answered politely, an unnecessary confirmation. Jared had left seven years ago and Ethan must have been born nine months later.

The Sorensons bade Ethan come with them and they strolled away.

Jared thought about where they could get some privacy as quickly as possible. He wasn't waiting to drive out to her ranch or his own to talk. Questions spun, anger was like wildfire consuming him.

Why hadn't his staff unearthed the parentage of her child? The marriage. A marriage on the rebound—or to give an excuse for the pregnancy?

"They know the truth, don't they?" he asked Megan.

"Yes, they do. I'm close to them, closer than I was to my dad," she said.

Jared placed his hand on her arm. "We can't discuss

this on the street. Let's go to the hotel and I'll get us a room where we can have privacy."

"Hotel? We can go to the ranch."

"No," he said flatly. "I'm not waiting through a long drive. I have questions, Megan, and I want answers now." In the taut silence, she gave him a stormy look; the clash of wills crackled between them.

As she clamped her mouth closed, he escorted to the tall, remodeled hotel.

She slanted him a look. "I thought you were leaving town today."

"I had planned to fly out at one," he said, and she turned away while he left her to step to the desk to get them a suite.

In silence they rode the elevator to the fifth floor, where they entered a large suite decorated in muted earth tones of umber and green and deep red. Sunshine poured through floor-to-ceiling glass windows and doors, giving a sunny glow to the room and sharply contrasting Jared's icy rage.

She crossed the sitting room, putting distance between them before she turned to glare at him defiantly. "You walked out, Jared. You have no claim. Absolutely none."

"The hell I don't!" he snapped, shedding his coat to drop it on a chair. "That's my son. Why didn't you call me?"

"Call you?" she raised her voice, her cheeks flushing a deep pink, shaking with anger. She leaned forward. "Why would I call you when it was obvious that you never wanted to see me again?"

He crossed the room to clasp her shoulders. "You should've let me know that I was going to be a father. You damn well know it," he said, grinding out the words, shaking himself.

"Get your hands off me!" she ordered, jerking away from him. "You asked for whatever happened."

"Is that why you married, or did you have some kind of rebound relationship?"

She looked away and bit her lip before turning back to him. "The marriage was solely because I was pregnant."

"You were never in love?" he asked in surprise, feeling glad even through his rage. "You didn't marry to get even? Wasn't that guy furious when he discovered what you'd—"

"No, he wasn't, because our marriage was a business arrangement. My father negotiated it to cover up the paternity of my baby!" She flung the words at him.

"Negotiated?" Jared asked in disbelief. "You went along with that?"

"Damn you, Jared! You crushed me and left me and I was pregnant. My control freak father was enraged. He said horrible things. Then he contracted for the marriage and it was all settled beforehand."

His anger toward her father returned full force. How the bastard tried to govern everything. "Your meddling father—what did he do exactly?" Jared asked, unable to stop prying, yet knowing he was going to hate what he would hear.

"He arranged or, rather, bought my marriage," she said, pronouncing the words slowly and distinctly as if Jared were unfamiliar with English.

"Where did he find the guy?" Jared asked while his hurt multiplied.

"Mike was the son of a Montana rancher. By then, he was an engineer, living in Phoenix. My father paid him to marry me."

"And you went along with that?"

"What was I supposed to do? It was a paper marriage, a business arrangement to give the baby a father."

"He wasn't our baby's father. Did you even live under the same roof?"

"For a little over a month. The marriage was never consummated. We had separate bedrooms and each of us went our own way. Mike had no interest in me. He only wanted the money to open his own firm. But under that guise of respectability, my father would pay for the baby and my care."

"That bastard!" Jared exclaimed, rage eating at him. He had thought when he'd left South Dakota that the Sorensons could never hurt him again. How wrong he'd been! To discover she'd hidden the most important thing in his life from him—his son—cut to his soul.

"Who are you to say that?" she answered. "You walked out and left me pregnant! Damn you, Jared! I was uneducated, young and dependent on my dad."

It was on the tip of his tongue to reveal her father's duplicity, but he wasn't going to get into that now, or hurling accusations would be all they would do. He wanted to know about Ethan.

"So go on—tell me what you did. You married Mike and moved to Arizona."

"That's right. Under the circumstances, I was less than pleasant. Mike was interested in his career and I think there was someone in his life, but he was kind enough to keep her out of our lives. We got a quiet divorce after seven weeks and I left."

"You came home once for a reception, I heard."

"Yes, so Dad could convince people that Ethan was Mike's son."

"How could anybody believe that lie after Ethan was born?"

She shrugged. "I don't know what gossip flew, nor did I care by then."

"I got a degree of revenge on your father in Ethan, since he looks exactly like me. Your father had to be constantly reminded of me," Jared said. No one who knew both him and Ethan could mistake the connection. "Do you ever see Mike?"

"No. We went our separate ways and I haven't talked to him since," she said, and Jared was surprised by the relief he experienced over her answer. "My dad used to tell me about him occasionally. I think he'd even hoped we'd stay married. Mike established his own firm and married. That's the last I heard about him."

"Damn it," Jared said. All they had both gone through because of her father. "And in all that time, it didn't occur to you to let the father of your baby know about his son's existence?"

"Don't, Jared! Don't accuse me—"

He grasped her shoulders again, fighting the urge to shake her. "I'm the father, and in this day and age I have rights. Yes, I accuse you. You know damned well you should've let me know we were having a baby."

"I never once when I was pregnant thought I should let you know," she said, the words tumbling out in a rage.

"When I first spoke to you last Saturday, you went white as a sheet and looked as if you might faint." His voice was low, and he leaned closer with anger white hot. "You were filled with guilt for keeping silent. Admit it, Megan! Admit that you know you should've told me about Ethan."

Her eyes were wide and green with anger as she shook her head, adding to his fury. "No. You gave that right up when you walked out without a word. You cut all ties with me in the cruelest possible way."

When he flinched because what she accused him of was true, he still couldn't bring himself to reveal to her that it was her father, because it would sound weak, as if he were making excuses. "Maybe I deserved for you to keep me out of your life, but when Ethan was born, you know you should have informed me. If you'd told me you were expecting a baby, I would've come back here."

"Oh, please, Jared! Don't stretch credulity to that point! You know you wouldn't have. You would have run all the more, if I'd called you and said you were about to become a father. Or you would've asked if I was sure it was your child."

"That's not true," he said in a voice that was low and vehement. "I damn well would've come back."

"You'll never, ever convince me of that. It's a moot point now," she said, glaring at him and he noticed she was breathing as rapidly as he was.

"Even so, I can't believe that in all these years you haven't told me. I can't understand why my own parents didn't tell me, but they moved from here two years later."

"I didn't see your parents. I didn't come home to live for a year and a half. People here met Mike at the reception, so they accepted the story that he was the father. Your parents moved shortly after I returned."

"I still say you should have told me. You know you should have. When you moved back here, you could have faced dealing with letting me know. We'd put enough time between us—"

"Enough time between us that I no longer hurt from what you did?" she flung the words at him as he clamped his jaw closed while he clenched his fists.

"Even so—"

"All right," she said, her voice suddenly sounding restrained. "When Ethan was one, I should've informed you. But I always thought I would when he got a little older, or if you came home and we crossed paths. Or if you tried to contact me, which of course, you didn't until you wanted something I have. Whenever a year rolled by, I put off telling you again." His anger was mirrored in the depths of her eyes. "What was I to do? Pick up the phone and call the man who walked out on me and say, 'Oh, by the way, we had a baby'? You left without a word—that means you wanted to sever all ties with me. Why on earth would I call you?" she cried. "Can't you get it?"

"I deserved to know, Megan, simply because I'm his father," Jared said. "I guess you don't know a parent's rights, but I do have rights. Where was Ethan born?"

"In Chicago, where we had gone to college. It's a large city and far from here."

Jared's pain over the past intensified. "You were alone in Chicago? Did you have any friends?"

"I'm sure you care!" she exclaimed bitterly. "Jared, this is all past."

"I want to know what happened. Answer my damn questions."

"If you must know, my aunt came to stay with me the last two weeks. My dad never came. After Ethan was six months old, he told me to come back home."

"Well, I got some damned revenge there. Ethan looks like me. What a blow that must have been."

"It was to all of us. I prayed he wouldn't look like you—and that you'd never know," she said, the coldness and anger clear in her voice.

"Damn it, Megan!"

"Damn it is right! I prayed my baby wouldn't resemble you in any way and that you'd never know as long as you lived. How can you act like you care now?"

"It's a shock to discover I have a child. I have questions. And frankly, Megan, I want to know my son."

She looked as if he'd hit her. And then he could see her pull herself together in that manner she had. She stood taller, a coolness coming to her features.

"Was it difficult for you when you came back home? With one look at Ethan, I'd think anyone would've known who his father was."

"How much gossip there was, I don't know," she admitted. "In the course of months, other scandalous things happened around this area, so interest shifted. It didn't matter after we moved to Santa Fe and it never has again, I'm sure you and I were a major source of gossip until I married Mike. You couldn't tell who Ethan's dad was by looking, until after the boy got a full head of hair. While he was a baby, people thought that he was Mike's child. Dad was smart enough to find a guy who bore a physical resemblance to you—black hair, dark brown eyes, tall. It was inevitable that Ethan would have black hair. No one would give that a thought."

"I'll bet my folks never laid eyes on him. One look at him, hair or no hair, and my mom would've known."

"As a matter of fact, they didn't."

"Damn it, even if I did walk without telling you good-bye, you should've let me know about our baby. I know now, though," he said coldly. "We're going to have to work something out," he said.

She walked away to stand by the floor-to-ceiling glass door before she turned back to face him. "You keep your distance. You forfeited all rights to Ethan when you walked out on me. You're not coming into our lives now, Jared. Forget that one. I don't see that you have any rights in the matter."

"I damn well do. You're not going to pack and go and take him away from me."

"I'm going home. You know what happened after you left me, and this is getting us nowhere."

"How the hell can you walk out of here and try and say good-bye? Understand me, Megan, I intend to get to know my son," he declared, his temper rising. He clenched his fists and inhaled deeply.

He stood with his hands on his hips and they glared

at each other, the clash fierce between them. In spite of all his fury, he wanted her. She was as beautiful and enticing as she was infuriating. Long strands of her black hair had come loose from the clip and fell around her face. Her cheeks were flushed and her eyes wide, and she was enticing in spite of the struggle between them. He desired her and he wished she would cooperate with him—both impossibilities.

"All right, we'll go back to the ranch and discuss it," he said. "You come to my place or I'll go to yours. The sun is shining, no rain is predicted and the river has lowered enough that the bridge is definitely above water."

"I see no point in arguing further," she said.

"Megan, I will get to know Ethan. That's a fact, not a wish," he stated, trying to control his temper, pushed to his limit. "We can discuss what we're going to do in the future. Your ranch or mine will be more comfortable for both of us and this may take a while."

She clamped her lips closed for a moment. "I know you've had a shock. The drive to the ranch will give you some time to adjust to your new status and to think about all that's happened. Don't tear up Ethan's life. You think about it when you drive home. You're being selfish again. I know you're accustomed to thinking only of yourself, but you'll hurt him if you come into his life. And you'll raise a hundred questions."

"You should have thought of those questions," Jared said. "You should have known that this day would come."

"It wouldn't have happened if you hadn't wanted to buy the ranch," she said bitterly.

"You might have slipped by if you'd sold it to me.

My attorneys would have handled the deal, and I doubt if you and I would have crossed paths except at the closing, and then you would have left for New Mexico and I would've gone on my way. Big error, Megan, if you'd really hoped to keep me from Ethan."

Her face flushed and he knew he'd been correct in all he'd stated.

"Perhaps, but I couldn't bear the thought of selling to you. You get what you want in life too easily."

"Well, now you pay the price for that refusal."

Frowning, she picked up her purse and hurried to the door. "If you insist, I'll see you at my ranch. I'm not taking any chance of getting marooned at yours again."

Grabbing his coat, he caught up to hold the door and walk out with her. "We'll start another flurry of rumors by this little interlude in the hotel."

"I can't worry about that. I don't plan to live here," she said. "I don't have many close friends here any longer. The few that I have are close enough to understand and to know that there will never be anything between you and me again."

"You can't foretell the future," he said.

"I can predict that much with certainty. There's too much bitterness on either side for it to vanish."

He didn't answer, his mind reeling with his discovery and what he'd learned from her. He escorted her to the street where she motioned with her hand. "My car is parked right there. I'll see you at home."

"All right. This will give you time to think, too."

She nodded and walked quickly away. His gaze traveled over her, looking at the sway of her hips and her leggy stride while he thought about their future. He hurried to his car and in minutes he was out of town.

As he drove to the ranch, he pored over their conversation. His mind kept going back to that startling moment when Ethan looked up at him. Jared vowed that he wasn't going to be out of Ethan's life. Megan wasn't thinking straight, and he knew he had rights. He'd heard too much about a birth father's rights. He'd never let her cut him out of Ethan's life now.

Damn her bastard father. Now Jared could understand her bitterness and anger. Why hadn't she called and let him know? No undoing the past now—but he wasn't leaving here without settling up when and how he could have Ethan with him and be talking to Ethan as his father.

Now he could understand her frightened and unhappy aunt and uncle's reactions. Only Ethan was oblivious to the emotional tempest swirling around him.

Realizing how fast he was driving, Jared eased his foot and set cruise control while his mind was still on Ethan. All the years of Ethan's life he had missed, babyhood, toddler—it hurt, and he vowed that this distance was going to end as soon as possible.

He tried to think of ways they could share Ethan's life. They needed solutions, not accusations and anger. How could they work it out to share their child, when they had such disparate lives, and while she was so furious with him?

In front of Megan's ranch house, he spotted her car outside her garage. As he crossed the porch, she opened the door. "Come in, Jared," she said.

He entered a wide hallway that he hadn't seen for the past seven years, recalling the last time he'd walked along the hall and out the front door. He'd been hurt, his life had changed and he wouldn't see Megan again—until this year. All because of her father.

He followed her into a spacious living area that was just as he remembered, with a huge stone fireplace, animal head trophies on the walls, a large gilt-framed portrait of her father, Edlund, on one wall and a smaller picture of Megan beside it. Leather-covered furniture filled the room, along with a wide-screen television and ceiling fans that slowly turned overhead. The polished wood floor held Navajo rugs. Window shutters were open. Memories crowded him—some not good.

She turned to face him. "Let's get this over with. I hope you've done some thinking and that you've calmed. Jared, your life is too busy to give much attention to a child."

"Your life isn't busy?" he asked with cynicism.

"Of course it is. But I don't travel the world or have much social life or have any lifestyle like you do, and my kiln and studio are at home, and my gallery is attached to the house, so I can be with him when he's home."

"I'm glad to hear that."

"Oh, please!" she replied. "You have an interest in him because of the novelty of discovering you're related to him."

His anger climbed. "Megan, I want my son part of the time, and I'm going to have him. Now, what can we work out?"

Frowning, she shook her head. "I can't think of any feasible plan. You live and have your headquarters in Dallas. You travel the world. I reside and work in New Mexico and here. That makes it impossible for him to see you often."

Jared clamped his mouth shut and jammed his hands into his pockets, turning to walk to the window and gaze outside while he mulled over possibilities of what they could do.

"I don't see any hope for this, and I worry that you're going to upset his life," she said.

Jared whirled around. "I'm his *father!* If you'd told me, I'd have been in his life from the day he was born. If I upset his life, it will be only initially. Kids adjust. I expect to win him over, Megan. Can't you see that it will be good for him to have a father around?"

She turned away, but he'd seen her frown and her teeth catch her lower lip. He walked up behind her and tried to speak quietly. "It'll be better for him to have a dad who's interested in him. There are things I can do with him that you can't. Stop depriving him of a father."

"Don't act like I'm hurting him by keeping you out of his life!" she snapped, whirling around to face him, tears in her eyes.

"Megan," he said, grasping her shoulders gently.

She twisted free and walked away from him. "Don't, Jared!"

"We were in love seven years ago," he said quietly, following her to stand close behind her. "We both were present when Ethan was conceived. I was in that bedroom, too."

She turned again to face him, green fire flashing in her eyes. "Next, you'll be telling me you love me," she said.

"No," he admitted, placing his hands on her upper arms and rubbing them lightly. "But I know we can be compatible, we have been, and we have some kind of electricity between us. You can't deny it. I think you and I can find a common ground once more," he said, trailing his fingers lightly along her soft cheek. "Our lives became irrevocably bound with Ethan's birth, so let's put our heads together and see what solutions we can find."

"That's because you're the one searching for the answer to your dilemma," she said, glaring at him.

He was tempted to kiss away some of her stubborn refusal. Her passionate response earlier seemed to let all her barricades crumble. His gaze went to her mouth and he battled the urge to kiss her and stop the arguing.

As if she sensed his intentions, she walked farther from him.

"One way or another, Megan, we're going to work this out," he said.

She turned to perch on the edge of a leather wingback chair. He sat in another, facing her. "I thought of several things when I was driving here."

"I can well imagine," she remarked dryly.

Annoyed with her steady refusal to cooperate with him, he tried to hang on to his tattered patience. He was unaccustomed to people saying no to him, unaccustomed to a woman being so unyielding with him. Knowing he had to work this out with her, he sat back in his chair and took a deep breath. "A large percentage of problems have solutions if people pursue finding them," he said. "And *want* to find them," he added. Megan wanted him out of her life and that of his son, but that wasn't going to happen. There was no way he would stay out of Ethan's life now.

"Have you even tried to think what might work out?" he asked.

"Frankly, no, because nothing would."

He considered the possibilities he'd mulled over in the car while driving to the ranch. "Fine. You have him during the school year. I get him for most of the summer."

"No! He spends one month with my aunt and uncle, who are like grandparents to him."

"He can do that, and I get him the other months and during spring break."

"I won't do it, Jared. Ethan's been so close with me. The first years of his life, I was home with him constantly. It's just the two of us. He won't want to go off next summer for two months and live with you." She crossed her long legs.

"Not next summer, *this* summer," Jared corrected emphatically, and she shook her head.

"I don't want to share Ethan with you."

"You're going to," he said lightly, knowing he would never give up. He felt certain the law would be on his side. Her stubbornness was driving his anger, and he tried to calm down and think of what they could do that would be acceptable to both.

"Here's another idea, Megan. See if this is palatable. A marriage of convenience."

Five

"A marriage of convenience. You've already had one before," Jared said, and Megan's temper shot up.

"You're only after Ethan to get my ranch," she replied. "A marriage of convenience or any other kind would give you access to the ranch." She shook her head. "Never!"

He stood and approached her, stopping only yards from her, his brown eyes harboring anger that buffeted her in waves. She raised her chin to meet his gaze.

"I'm not doing any of this to get your damned ranch!" he declared gruffly, and she knew he was fighting to hang on to his temper as much as she was. "I want my son!" he said. "Can't you understand that?"

"Frankly, no! You don't strike me as the daddy type. Not at all. You're a well-known society playboy, a jet-setter, and I think you want Ethan to help get you access to my ranch, either because of the novelty of it or because you can't stand to not control your world just like my father," she said and his face flushed and she'd clearly pushed him to the edge.

"Don't you ever lump me in with your father!" Jared ground out his words. "Megan, you'd better think about an answer to this."

"I'll fight you, Jared," she declared, walking away before she turned to face him. All the old pain rushed back, memories of panicked days after he left. "I don't care how much money you have! I'm Ethan's mother. I've raised him. You walked out on us. You go ahead with your lawyers and your threats."

They glared at each other and she knew they were locked in an impasse. In spite of anguish and anger and their battle over Ethan, Jared still made her heart race. She hated herself for wanting him, when he had hurt her so badly and was trying to do it again.

"No judge will take Ethan from me," she declared, fighting her rising terror of a court battle with Jared over Ethan. "Your lifestyle will work against you, too."

"A judge has to consider my rights. I can provide Ethan with far more opportunities than you can." His words chilled her. She could never give Ethan what Jared could.

"If I walk out that door, Megan, I'm calling my attorney and I will get him started on my custody of Ethan. In the future, you'll never be able to bargain with me to the degree you can right now, so you better rethink your refusal."

"Go ahead, Jared. Bullying only makes me more certain."

"Bullying? I think I've been damn cooperative. I'm trying to find something we can both live with. You're not. You refuse to consider any arrangement."

"None are feasible. All your suggestions will hurt Ethan."

"A marriage of convenience wouldn't," Jared replied.

"I don't want to be locked into a loveless marriage with you."

Again, his face flushed and she knew his fury was increasing. "Then I know one solution. I'm calling my attorney and you'll hear from one of us, probably tomorrow morning, and the court can determine how much time each of us gets Ethan."

"Fine. I'll call my attorney now, too," she said, growing frightened and uncertain. "You're a ruthless man, Jared. I learned that too late."

"In this situation, you're forcing me to be."

"Go ahead and contact your attorney or your whole law staff. You'll have to take me to court to get your son."

"You check that out," he repeated, and strode out, not waiting. He slammed the door behind him. She stepped to the front window to watch him, his long legs covering the distance to his car quickly. He climbed into his car and sat a moment without driving away. She could see he was on his cell phone and she turned to look up the phone number of Rolf Gustavsson, her family attorney, whom she had been seeing often lately because of her father's demise.

Relieved to hear his pleasant hello, she related her problem. He said he would do some research and get back to her. Ethan's tire swing moved back and forth under a black walnut tree. It caught her eye and she ended the call.

She rubbed her temple. She knew Jared had rights. Rolf might be a nice man who had always been helpful to her family in dealing with their legal matters, but Jared had access to the world's best legal talent.

A marriage of convenience? That was impossible. Not one of his suggestions was workable. She put her head in her hands, hating that Jared had discovered Ethan.

As much as she loathed the thought of letting him have the ranch, that was better than losing Ethan to him. No way could she think of Ethan as *their* son. She had always thought of Ethan as her son only.

Now she regretted not selling the ranch to him quickly and putting as much distance as possible between them. If only—but it was too late now. The damage was done and she was going to have to live with it. She had made too many wrong decisions in her life. Was she making another one concerning Ethan?

Her head throbbed. Any joint custody she'd ever have to agree to would be ghastly to her. The fact that Jared had walked out on her had to count as a strong factor.

Halfway through the night, she decided she would offer to sell the ranch to Jared if he would forget about Ethan. It was her only hope and she hated the thought, but that would be infinitely better than having to share Ethan with him.

The rest of her sleepless night was filled with apprehension. At dawn she showered and dressed, but even sitting with a cup of coffee did nothing to shake her mood. It was too early.

When she received a call from Jared, vitality seemed to ooze from the phone.

"Good morning," he said. "I thought you'd be awake. I'd like to talk to you in person."

"Come over. I've been up for a couple of hours," she answered, hoping she sounded as upbeat as he did. She wondered what he had on his mind.

"I'll be there soon," he replied.

All too soon she heard Jared's car pull up. She went to the porch as he climbed out. Dressed in a long-sleeve, charcoal Western shirt, jeans and boots, he hurried toward the porch. Wind tangled locks of his black hair above his forehead and he looked refreshed, filled with energy, and eager—all dire implications. She smiled despite the inner turmoil that kept her stomach churning.

"Good morning," he said solemnly, studying her.

"Come inside to talk, Jared." She turned to lead the way. He closed the front door and caught up to walk with her to the family room. "Have a seat."

He nodded and they sat facing each other. The blanket of silence did nothing to soothe her raw nerves. She could tell little from his expression.

"I've heard from my attorney. Have you heard from yours?"

She shook her head. "Not yet, but mine doesn't have the resources or staff yours do, so I'm not surprised.

Jared, if you'll drop all this, I'll sell the ranch to you and you can forget the bonus one million," she said and held her breath.

He shook his head. "That wouldn't begin to take the place of getting to know my son."

Disappointment swept her and she locked her fingers together, knowing he had bad news that she didn't want to hear.

She put her hands on her face as she tried to keep from making a sound, but she couldn't prevent tears.

"Megan, don't," Jared said gently, his arms going around her. He pulled her close against him while she sobbed, letting go. "Stop crying. Plan with me and let's get an arrangement we can both live with," he said in the same gentle tone.

She knew, without waiting to hear from her lawyer, that she was going to have to do what Jared wanted.

Unable now to control her emotions after the worry of the past twenty-four hours and a sleepless night of anxiety, she sobbed and his arm around her waist tightened. He tilted her chin up and pulled out a clean handkerchief to wipe her eyes. "Stop crying," he ordered in the same quiet, gentle tone. He brushed her tears away.

He tilted her chin up to look into her eyes. "Look, you're off work anyway, and so am I. Ethan is with your relatives. Come fly with me to the Yucatán coast. I have a home there and we'll get away from interruptions for a couple of days. We're going to have to establish some kind of truce."

While she couldn't imagine spending a couple of days with him, she had to work something out or he would do as he warned. She knew Jared well enough to know that any threat he made he would carry out, if he had to.

On the other hand, they weren't going to court. He wasn't taking Ethan away. Or so he said. "I guess I don't have any other choice," she said.

"That's better. I can have a plane ready in an hour. How long will it take you to wind things up here to leave for two or three days?"

"I've never been away from Ethan, except when he's here with my relatives and I'm in Santa Fe."

"He's with them now and he'll be fine."

She nodded, becoming aware of standing in his arms. His look was heated, and under his deep focus she realized his concern was no longer about Ethan. Jared's torrid gaze made her heart drum.

She pushed against his chest and distanced herself. "All right, Jared," she said. "I can probably leave in an hour."

"I'll come pick you up. Do you have a pen? I'll give you a phone number at my house where they can reach you."

"I'll have my cell phone."

"Give me a pen. Your cell phone might fail. This way you'll have two possibilities for contact." She handed him a pen and watched him, looking at the familiar handwriting that she still could remember. When he handed a business card back to her, it had two numbers, his house and a cell phone. "Is your plane at the airport?"

"No, at the ranch," he answered.

"Then I'll drive to your place. It'll be more convenient."

He crossed the room to her, to slip his arms around her waist. "Stop worrying, Megan. We'll work something out and I'll do my damnedest to win his love and to get to know him. I want what's best for Ethan, too."

If he really wanted what was best for Ethan, he would stay out of Ethan's life. But she knew she had to stop fighting Jared, because it was hopeless. The law was on his side. "I'll work on it," she whispered.

"No, you stop worrying," he ordered, but his voice was gentle and quiet. "I promise, I'll try if you will to find a viable solution."

Unable to speak, afraid she would start crying again, she nodded. "I had better get ready."

"Okay, but I wish you could smile." He knelt slightly to be on eye level, smiling at her, and teased a half-hearted smile from her. "That's better. I'm going to try to get a real smile out of you while we're together."

She didn't want to go away with him. She wanted to tell him that she still thought he was ruthless and arrogant and had to have his way, but it was useless. She followed him outside, and the minute they parted she rushed back into the house to call Rolf.

"Rolf, thanks so much. I'll deal with Jared. He is willing to work something out."

She finally got off the phone to put her head into her hands and cry. She didn't want any of this.

In minutes, she called her aunt to tell her what had happened and that she was going with Jared for a few days. She choked back the tears when she talked to

Ethan, but he never noticed. He'd gotten a new electronic game and when she told him she was going away, he accepted it with barely a pause in his chatter about the game.

Knowing he was in good hands, she said good-bye and hurried to change and pack.

She dressed in brown slacks, a matching sleeveless top and wore high-heeled sandals. Brushing her hair, she clipped it high on the back of her head.

She was going away with Jared to one of his secluded homes. She could well imagine what he had in mind. Along with arranging custody plans was a plan for seduction.

She didn't want to return after several days with him, not only losing rights to her son, but in love with Jared—twice in her life.

And Jared might be the sexiest, most charming man she'd ever known.

She would have to keep up her guard. So far, she had failed miserably in all dealings with him.

By a quarter past eleven, she was airborne, flying over Jared's ranch and headed south. To avoid conversation with him, she gazed out the window, looking at his ranch spread below. She turned back to find him watching her. Dressed in chinos, a charcoal knit shirt and loafers, he looked commanding, as if satisfied with all facets of his world. And why wouldn't he, she thought. He'd won the first part of their fight.

"This is a hopeful start, Megan," he said, leaning close to touch a wispy lock of hair that had come free from her tie.

"You're an incredible optimist," she said.

"If we work something out, then there's no problem."

"I know you already have something in mind," she said stiffly.

He shrugged. "Not necessarily. Let's let it go for today and get back on better footing with each other," he suggested.

"If we can," she said, looking out the window while fighting the urge to scream that she hadn't planned on a better relationship with him, but she knew she had to now. Getting concessions from him on the custody front could be impossible otherwise.

"Of course, we can," he said, taking her hand. "I've got three days with a beautiful woman, who I intend to get to know."

"You know me well enough," she said, gazing into his dark eyes that hid his intentions and thoughts.

"No, I don't. I knew an eighteen-year-old. You've changed. You're far more poised, more self-assured and much more unattainable."

"I suppose that comes with growing up, although, when I met you, you had all the confidence imaginable."

He gave her a crooked smile. "Does that mean arrogance? That's what it sounds like."

She had to smile in return. "Definitely. But I'd like to stay on your good side as much as possible on this trip, so I'm trying to be polite."

"Don't be polite with me. But staying on my good side—that's fine. What are your plans for the future,

Megan? Do you intend to always keep your gallery in Santa Fe, even if you divide your days between there and the ranch?"

"Yes. Santa Fe is home and perfect for us," she said, aware her hand was still in his, as he ran his thumb back and forth over her wrist. His touches added fuel to the lust she battled.

"I love Santa Fe," she continued, "and I never want to move from there. I always hoped Ethan would grow up and stay nearby, but that isn't realistic, I know. Now that he'll have time with you, heaven knows what he'll do when he's grown."

"That's far away," Jared said. "Do you like to swim?"

"Actually, I love to. I guess because there was little chance to when I was growing up, and then there aren't many opportunities in Santa Fe. I don't have a suit, though. There's no need to keep one at the ranch."

"We'll stop and I'll get you one."

"I'll buy my suit," she said, laughing.

He smiled. "That's better," he said, touching the corner of her mouth and running his finger lightly along her lower lip, building a warmth in her. "I promise to get a real laugh out of you before the night is over."

"Stick to why we're here, Jared," she said quietly. "This is an interlude to work out a plan for our future concerning Ethan. It's not to get reacquainted all over again. Not at all."

"What's wrong with renewing a friendship?" he asked.

"It was more than a friendship, and I don't want a

broken heart twice," she said, hoping she never hurt again as badly as she had the year he left.

"I promise, I don't intend to hurt you," he said.

"Then keep these few days relatively impersonal. I'm working at this, Jared. Don't make it complicated and more difficult," she instructed briskly.

"I wouldn't think of it," he said, once again leaning back in his chair. "So, tell me about a typical day in your life. What do you and Ethan do?"

"Through the school year, Ethan is in a private school and I spend most of the day in my studio. I have someone who runs the gallery for me, except on Wednesdays and Fridays, when I run it myself. I have three salespeople who work in the gallery for me at different hours, not all at the same time, but there are always two of us present. It's easier that way."

"I haven't been to Santa Fe in years. Not since you moved there. What's the name of your gallery?" he asked, locking his fingers behind his head and stretching out his long legs. Looking totally relaxed, he reminded her of a leopard or tiger, some large cat lazing and half asleep, yet able to pounce in a flash. Except Jared would never physically pounce. His methods were emotional and mental. "Wait, let me guess," he said. "Sorenson Gallery."

"Am I that unimaginative?" she asked, smiling at him. He smiled in return. "I toyed with some less ordinary names, but when I opened it, it was all new and exciting, and I was trying to get established and make a name for myself, so it became Sorenson Gallery. That was about the same year you opened your first restaurant in Dallas—Dalton's, I believe."

"I used my name for the same reason you did," he said quietly. "You kept up, did you?"

She shrugged. "My aunt and uncle knew people who knew your family, so word got around. In some ways we're in a small world."

"One that got far more interesting when you came back into my life," he added.

"Jared, is it possible for you to avoid flirting?"

"Not with you," he replied with an enticing smile. He leaned forward. "You look elegant, but there's one flaw."

"Oh, what's that?" she asked, trying not to care, yet aware how close he was again.

"You would look much better," he said and reached up to remove the clip holding her hair, "without this." Her thick curtain of black hair tumbled on her shoulders and back. "There, that's perfect," he said.

She smiled and shook her head to get her hair away from her face. "You may like it better, but it's not as convenient."

"I definitely like it better. Sacrifice convenience to please me. I'll appreciate it."

"How's the weather where we're headed?"

"It's beautiful. Perfect, too."

"Enough of that!" she retorted, his compliment pleasing her.

She settled back and listened, chatting with him, laughing at some of his stories. The day passed surprisingly fast, and she realized she was enjoying his company, even though each minute with him brought back memories of being together. Too often, she dreaded when they got to the point of this trip.

"We must be getting close." The deep blue of the Gulf caught her eye. "Are you in town?"

"No. I have a villa on the coast. We'll have total privacy."

"I don't think we'll require total privacy, but it'll be nice."

It was a long trip, but eventually they landed and deplaned, and Jared escorted her to a limo where his chauffeur and bodyguard stood waiting.

Within minutes, Jared and Megan were driven into town to a small, exclusive shop to look for a swimsuit. While Jared stood near the front window and talked on his cell phone, she was shown a variety of suits. Selecting a half dozen, she tried them on without showing them to Jared. She made her selection and dressed again, emerging from the dressing room.

"I didn't get to see you model the suits," Jared said with a twinkle in his eyes.

"You'll see me soon enough when you swim with me."

"I'm counting the minutes," he said, and she smiled.

"Always flirting, Jared. If we aren't fighting," she amended.

"I hope to be done with the latter," he said, and there was a solemn note in his voice that made her feel he was sincere in wanting to work something out in cooperation. She remembered he was a master at convincing people to do what he wanted, and wondered if his words were shallow or really held meaning.

For a moment she gazed into his brown eyes and had a pang of longing for what could have been between them. Shaking off the wishful thinking, she started to open her purse.

Stopping her, Jared took the suit from her hand. "I'll get this," he said in a tone that ended her argument.

As she watched, Jared purchased two more identical ones.

She laughed. "Jared, I'm not in a swim contest. I only need one suit."

"You never know. Always be prepared. Why not?"

"Because it's a waste of your money," she said, wondering about his extravagant lifestyle, and how much Ethan's life was about to change. And perhaps her own.

"Then let me worry about it," he said, smiling at her. She stopped protesting.

They drove out of town and thick trees and bushes crowded the narrow highway until they turned into iron gates and Jared waved at a man who returned the greeting.

"How often are you here?" Megan asked.

"A few weeks out of the year. He's a gatekeeper, and I let him know we were coming. The staff is here now."

Curious about Jared's life, she wondered if he was showing her this home to prove that he could do more for Ethan than she could. Yet it didn't feel like a jab. His pride in his home shone through. They drove through more thick vegetation and then through another set of gates that swung open at the limo's approach. A high plaster wall glowed pale yellow, with patterns of shade from tall trees close by. Past the gates, the surroundings transformed into a garden paradise. Palms, other tropical trees and plants dotted the emerald grass.

Beautifully landscaped lawns led to a sprawling white villa with the brilliant blue water of the ocean as a backdrop. Blue trumpet-shaped blossoms of tall jacaranda trees were bright in the sunlight.

"Jared, it's fantastic!" she said, awed. She was certain now that he wanted to impress her with how much more he could do for Ethan than she.

"I enjoy it. I hope you do, too. How about a swim first thing?"

"That sounds wonderful." She conceded. "A swim after the long flight is exactly what I need." In the flash of pleasure she released her hold on their problems momentarily.

"Swim it is," he said. "Unpack later, or I can have Lupita do it for you."

"I'll unpack myself, thank you," she replied in amusement. "I really can't wait."

"I can't wait, either," he said in a husky voice that registered with her, and she glanced at him.

"You don't swim often?" she said, as if deliberately missing his meaning.

"I want to see you in your suit."

"Oh, stop!" She turned back to look at the house and its porch, with pots of lavender orchids. Yellow and scarlet bougainvillea ran up the walls and onto the roof. "Jared, this is magical." Feeling a pang when she thought about Jared bringing Ethan to see it.

"I'm glad you think so."

As soon as they parked, a uniformed man emerged from the house. Jared introduced her to Adan, who took their bags. Inside, she met Lupita, who smiled broadly and listened to brief instructions from Jared.

As Megan walked through the front door, her breath caught. The entry was wide and open with columns. Extended beyond the entrance was a large living area she could see through open, floor-to-ceiling glass doors and bamboo furniture.

Beyond the room, through the open doors, was a veranda that extended to a sparkling, aqua pool with a fountain and waterfall. The deck over continued to a glistening white beach and on to the ocean.

"Jared, this is incredible."

"I told you, I think so, too," he said, walking up to her. "Get your suit and I'll meet you outside."

She looked up to meet his gaze, and the air between them crackled from the attraction. Her nerves were raw, her desire hot. Drawing a deep breath, she stepped away. "Where's my room?"

He escorted her along a hallway and his fingers rested lightly on her arm.

He led her into another room that opened onto the veranda and had a view of the ocean. He paused. "How's this?"

She looked at the rattan furniture, with its yellow-and-white-chintz cushions, and at a ceiling fan turning lazily overhead. "This is beautiful, Jared. It looks like a house staged for a movie."

"Nope, it's ready for living. I'll meet you at the pool." He traced his knuckles along her cheek. "This is good, Meg. We don't have to be at odds with each other. I know we can find common ground and be friends."

"That's what *you* want," she reminded him, her pulse racing from his touch. With a twist of longing, she wished she could drop her guard, trust him again and be friends.

He flashed her a smile and left, stepping outside through the open doors.

She looked at a king-size bed with a white spread, and then she explored a spacious bathroom with a sunken tub, potted palms and a wall of mirrors. She returned to the bedroom to open her sacks of purchases she'd made in town.

After she changed, she studied herself in the mirror with a critical eye. She'd known she would swim with Jared and she didn't want anything skimpy. Without encouragement of any kind from her, he came on strong. He'd spent the day flirting, yet no matter how casual his touches, each contact sizzled.

She had bought a navy one-piece that covered her as much as possible and still looked nice, because she wouldn't be wearing it with Jared after this week. Also, she'd bought a navy cover-up and flip-flops. When she was dressed, she went out through the open doors, stepping onto the veranda and heading toward the pool.

Watching Jared swim to one end of the pool, she kicked off her flip-flops and shed her cover-up. He paused to shake water off his face and rake his hair back with his fingers. As always when damp, his hair curled and short locks sprang back, curling on his forehead. As soon as he saw her, he swam across the pool, causing a big splash of water when he lifted himself out on the side of the pool.

Water glistened on his shoulders and chest and body. The thick mat of black curls on his chest was covered with drops of water. At the sight of his lean, muscled body, even more fit than when she'd known him in his twenties, her temperature climbed. His swimsuit was a narrow strip of black that covered little. Too well she remembered exactly how he had looked aroused and nude. She realized how she was looking at him and glanced up to see his gaze roaming slowly over her. And she knew she'd made another colossal miscalculation by traveling here with him.

Six

As he walked to her, her heart pounded.

"Jared," she whispered. There was some dim protest echoing in her thoughts, but she paid no heed.

He walked up to take her into his arms and draw her to him. The scanty clothing they wore was nothing. She was pressed against his muscled body, his warm, wet chest, his strong thighs. Every inch she touched was hard and firm. When his gaze lowered to her mouth, her lips parted.

"Jared," she repeated softly.

He leaned down and she raised her mouth to his, his lips covering hers and then his tongue slipped into her mouth as he kissed her. Her insides clenched while insistent need swept her, pooling low. She wound her arms around his neck and clung to him, kissing him hungrily, beyond caring about the danger to her feelings. He was temptation and excitement and sizzling sex.

As they kissed, she ran her fingers through his thick hair and along the strong column of his neck, savoring, exploring every inch of him.

His arm tightened around her, pressing her intimately to his firmness and her heart pounded.

Holding her, he caressed her nape before sliding his hand down to push away her suit and cup her breast. He rubbed his palm lightly in circles over her nipple.

Moaning with pleasure, she arched against him, tingling and wanting more. Running her hand along his smooth, bare back, she pressed her hips against him.

"Ah, Meg, so fine," he whispered. Lowering the top of her suit fully, he held both breasts in his hands. His thumbs circled each taut peak and his hot gaze was as scalding as his touch. While she slid one hand to his waist, her other hand gripped his broad shoulder.

Desire was explosive. She knew what they could do to each other, and she wanted to rediscover him. When her hand skimmed along his thigh, drifting up over his hip and down his flat belly, she heard his intake of breath.

Stirring a shower of tingles, his hand played lightly on her stomach and between her legs, his fingers inching beneath the suit to touch her intimately.

"Jared! Yes!" she cried, thrusting against his touch, clinging to his upper arms as his fingers created a tantalizing friction.

She was lost, spiraling into a vortex of hunger and memory. She couldn't stop. All her being cried out for him. Searing need burned like wildfire. He traced circles around her nipple with his tongue, as dazzling sensations showered her.

"Jared!" she cried, unaware she'd spoken.

Gasping for breath, she pushed away his suit, freeing him. Bending to take him into her mouth, her tongue circled the velvet tip of his manhood.

His fingers wound in her hair and he groaned. She hoped to make him as desperate for her as she was for him.

Stroking him with her tongue, she caressed his inner thighs, running her hands between his legs. He groaned again and then his hands went beneath her arms and he lifted her to her feet and plunged his gaze into hers, his broad chest expanding with his breath.

He scooped her into his arms and carried her to a chaise lounge to place her on it and sit beside her, tracing feathery kisses along her collarbone to her breasts, sucking and biting each nipple lightly, an exquisite torment for her.

"Oh! I want you. Heaven help me, how I want you!" she blurted.

His hand was between her legs, caressing her, rubbing her and starting to build tension all over again. Then he moved between her legs to place them over his shoulders and give himself access to her, his tongue re-tracing his fingers' path.

She squeezed her eyes closed tightly, as she was bombarded by sensations. She was open for him, eager, intensity building with each stroke of his tongue.

"Love me," she cried as he lowered her legs to the chaise.

"I'll get protection," he said, picking her up. He carried her with him through open doors and laid her gently on the bed.

She watched as he retrieved a condom from the bedside table. Caressing her inner thighs, he moved between her legs. Wanting him with increasing urgency, she stroked his strong legs.

While he opened the packet and put on the condom, she drank in the sight of him, storing the moment in memory, relishing looking at him and touching him. Virile, muscled, and bronze except for a pale strip across his groin, he was masculine perfection. Thick black curls spread on his chest, tapering in a narrow line to his waist. Short crisp hair curled on his thighs. Locks of black hair fell over his forehead. His body was marvelous.

As she looked up into his dark eyes, magnetism sparked between them from a mutual feeling of attraction and something deeper, a tenuous bond held for the moment, created by sheer physical longing.

In a silent welcoming, she held out her arms. While he kissed her, she wrapped her arms around him.

Jared was in her arms again, consuming her. Time didn't exist. How she had hungered for this moment!

Driven, she pulled him toward her. When he entered her, she arched her hips to meet him. Making love with him enveloped her and smoothed over problems. She wrapped her long legs around him and ran her hands over his smooth back, and then his firm buttocks.

For this brief moment, their union seemed right, incredibly necessary for her. She held him tightly, running her hands over him again, relishing the feel of his body and that he was in her arms.

Moving her hips against him, she groaned with pleasure. He filled her slowly, withdrawing and then entering her again, in a sweet torment that heightened her need to a raging inferno.

His powerful body was spectacular. She clung to him, mindlessly raking his back with her fingers, moving faster beneath him.

"Jared!" she cried his name, unaware of anything except his loving. She moved frantically.

His control vanished and he moved rapidly, pumping deeply into her. They were locked together—rocking, intimate and close, and she sobbed because she wanted him with all her being.

"Meg, darlin'." He ground out the words in a husky voice. His endearment made her heart leap, and she knew she was vulnerable in too many ways. His words were as seductive to her as his lovemaking. Physically and emotionally, she wanted him.

She climaxed in a shattering release. Lights exploded behind her closed eyelids while her heart pounded violently. Ecstasy enveloped her as spasms rocked her. He pumped faster, and then groaned, reaching his own finish, still pleasuring her.

He inhaled deeply and slowed and she could feel tension winding up once again. She tightened her arms and legs around him again.

"Jared," she cried softly, "don't stop loving me," she whispered as he thrust slower, and as it commenced another building, sweet torment. Impaled on his thick rod, she moved her hips faster. And then another climax rocked her with rapture.

She hugged him, feeling the sheen of sweat on his back. They held each other tightly, returning to earth from a distant paradise.

Reality was a wolf at the door, and she didn't want to face tomorrow's problems.

He turned on his side, untangling his long legs from hers. She pressed tightly against him, her face against his throat with her head on his shoulder. Deliberately, she kept her mind blank, relishing the euphoria and lethargy after lovemaking.

He shifted, then tilted up her chin so he could look into her eyes. "Loving you is fantastic, Meg."

"Shh." She put her finger over his lips. "Don't talk. Don't do anything for a few minutes," she urged. She agreed privately, but she wasn't going to confess what she'd experienced.

He was quiet, gazing at her solemnly while she traced his jaw with her fingers, letting her hand caress his chest lightly. He sucked in a deep breath and gently combed her hair away from her face while he showered light kisses on her.

"You're fabulous," he said in a husky voice, shifting away again to brush his fingers across her bare breasts.

She caught his hand in hers, trailing kisses over his knuckles, still refusing to think about anything except the present moment.

Rolling onto his back, he drew her close in his embrace, remaining quiet, as she had asked. She tangled her fingers in his chest hair and then let her hand slide over him to his waist. His body was in peak condition, a marvel to her.

As she shifted, starting to sit up, his strong arms held her. "Where are you going?" he asked.

"To shower," she said.

He sat up. "I'll shower, too," he said and she shook her head.

"Jared, we've—"

His arm circled her waist and his mouth covered hers, taking her words. He kissed her deeply, lowering her to the bed. Once again, she knew now was the moment to stop him, but she was already responding to him as if they hadn't just made love.

When he raised his head, she opened her eyes to find him watching her. Standing to pick her up, he was hard again, ready for love. While he gazed into her eyes, he carried her into the shower and turned on warm water.

As he lowered her feet to the floor, he leaned forward to kiss her. Desiring him more than ever, she wrapped her arms around his neck, leaning into him. Their bodies were wet, warm, pressed against each other while her heart raced. Desire rekindled, quickly reaching a raging fire.

Jared's arousal was hot against her belly. She moaned softly. It had been so long since she had been loved by him, and he was the only one, something she never intended for him to know. Worse, she couldn't get enough, now that she had let go.

He picked her up, stepped back to brace himself against the glass wall of the shower and then lowered her onto himself.

She cried out with pleasure, throwing her head back,

running one hand over his shoulder as she moved with him and he thrust fast, taking her quickly.

She squeezed her eyes closed, gasping for breath, holding his shoulders tightly now while he kissed her.

"Love, this is good," he whispered, but she heard him as she had before.

"Love me," she whispered, wanting him.

In ecstasy once more, she climaxed as he climaxed. She draped herself on his shoulders, kissing his neck and caressing him, running her hands lightly on his shoulders and back.

He would break her heart again. She knew that clearly. She couldn't refuse to face the truth. Fighting all the tender feelings toward him that surged in her, she turned away.

"Meg, darlin', this is fine. So fine," he said in his deep voice. "You're magic, pure seduction, beautiful."

His words were golden, taking her heart as he had once before. She raised her head to meet his gaze. "Put me down, Jared."

He set her on her feet and pulled her against him to kiss her until she responded fully. "You don't know what you do to me," he said.

She would lose any battle with him, she realized. Why had she ever thought she could successfully contend with him and win? She was consumed by his lovemaking—boneless and unable to think straight.

He showered light kisses on her shoulder, drawing his tongue over the curves of her ear. Still kissing her and holding his arm around her waist while he caressed her, he walked her backward beneath the spray of water. He smiled. "This is perfect."

His smile softened his features, lending a warmth to his expression that had been missing too much since he'd come back into her life.

She smiled in return, a part of her responding, a part of her knowing she was flying into disaster at the speed of light.

"You're a charming devil," she said, shaking her head.

"And you're a seductress. Pure temptation." He took one step back and his hands rested on her waist while his gaze slowly traveled over her.

She couldn't keep from studying him as thoroughly and intently as he was her. His body was magnificent, radiating vitality and energy.

"I know something better," he said, switching off the water. He opened the door to grab thick, soft terry-cloth towels off a shelf. He handed her a blue towel and began to dry her with his towel. In turn, she dried him, running the towel over his broad shoulders, his muscled chest.

His strokes were light, a slow, sensual friction rubbing her nipples. Then he dried her belly and the insides of her thighs, then he ran the towel between her legs lightly.

She gasped, pausing in her task, grasping his arms. "Jared!" she whispered.

"I'm only drying you," he said, continuing. "Come here." He picked her up and carried her easily out of the shower and set her on her feet in front of the mirrored wall. He gazed over her head. "We look right together. You're more beautiful than ever," he whispered, standing close behind her and letting his hands play over her stomach and breasts. As he watched her in the mirror, he cupped her breasts and began to tease her nipples. Longing flared, and she wanted him again.

She started to kiss him, but he held her. "Wait," he whispered. "Look at us. Look what I can do to you," he added, cupping her breasts as he ran his thumbs in circles over her nipples.

"You can do too much to me," she whispered. His hands were tan against her pale skin. His caresses were torment and she wanted him inside her again. She spread her legs, her heart pounding, while she tugged at his arm and hand, but he wouldn't stop what he was doing.

He continued to caress her breast with one hand while his other drifted between her legs to touch her intimately. While she moved her hips, she reached behind her to touch him in any manner she could, knowing she was violating all her promises to herself.

"Jared, you have to…" she began, but he leaned closer, kissing her shoulder and ear, and her words ceased.

His hand between her thighs was torment. She spread her legs wider, giving him access to her as she moved her hips and as tension wound as tight as a spring.

"Wait!" she said, clutching his arms. "We can't do this!"

"We're doing it," he whispered into her ear. "You're setting me on fire, Meg," he added in another harsh whisper.

She wanted him inside her now more than ever.

He kissed her, then picked her up and carried her to bed to love her slowly, tantalizing her until her climax was more dazzling than before.

Afterward, as they were locked in each other's embrace, she was quiet until she started to ease away.

He held her tightly with one arm. "Where are you going?"

"To my room, Jared."

"Stay here awhile," he said. "I want to hold you close. I need you here, Meg," he said.

She did as he asked and lay quietly while he turned on his side to look at her and brush her hair away from her face. "I want to look at you," he whispered.

Unable to answer him, she ran her hand lightly across his chest. Regrets grew, threatening to overwhelm her. Finally she sat up and pulled a sheet up over her. "Jared, I've been too vulnerable."

He lay on his back to study her. "Don't regret what happened. It was fantastic, and no harm to either of us."

She shook her head, looking away so she wouldn't have to gaze into his dark brown eyes that seemed to see right into her thoughts. "Don't say anything, Jared. It's over. I haven't been with a man in a long, long time. You're incredibly seductive and I have a weakness where you're concerned, which you know. Once we started, I wanted it as much as you did. I'm not blaming you for our lovemaking, but it's done. Really ended. We're going to have to work something out about Ethan, but we're not going to become bed partners or marry for the convenience of it."

"Why not? We're good in bed, and you said it yourself—we enjoy each other. An understatement when it comes to the sex. It's the best."

She was struggling to get distance back between

them, knowing too well how easily he could overcome her opposition. But she intended to declare her feelings and let him know what she wanted the most. And it wasn't his lovemaking.

"I told you, I succumbed today, when I really didn't intend for that to happen between us. It complicates life."

"It simplifies it immeasurably, and it adds a spectacular dimension to living."

She turned to look into his eyes. "Don't you get it? You broke my heart—and I won't go through that again. We made love today because I've never *had* another man in my life, only you!" She flung the words at him angrily and saw his eyes widen in surprise.

"There was never anyone who could measure up. Even when I planned to sleep with someone—I couldn't go through with it. You know Mike and I never consummated our marriage, but there wasn't anyone else, either. That's why I was so damned vulnerable to your kisses today. It won't happen again, so don't plan on it. We're here to work out something about Ethan. Nothing else, in spite of what's happened today."

Breathing erratically, she stood and yanked the sheet off the bed, wrapping it around her.

He got off the bed, but she shook her head and backed away. "Don't touch me," she said, and he stopped, frowning as he watched her.

"Megan, when I left, I hurt and I hated it."

"Oh, you hurt, too?" she said, shaking her head. "Cry me a river. Let's not dredge up even more anguish. I'll shower and then I'm going for a swim."

As she hurried out of the room, tears stung her eyes and she didn't know whether she was crying out of frustration or anger.

Hopefully, now she no longer would, and she could deal with him on a more rational basis. She knew, in spite of her admonitions, he would continue to caress and flirt, because that was as natural to him as breathing. If only she could get this trip over with and something tolerable worked out!

As she went outside to retrieve her cover-up and her suit, she wondered where his staff was, but at the moment she barely cared. She'd never see them again after these few days.

She hurried to shower and in minutes jumped into the pool to swim laps, hoping to work off her emotional turmoil and restore her normal perspective.

Seven

"Let me help you out. We can swim in the ocean. It's warm and buoyant, and if you see fish, they're tropical and beautiful." Lost in the rhythm of her laps, she'd missed Jared's approach.

She gave him her hand and he pulled her up easily onto the side of the pool. He placed his hands on her waist. "Let me really look at this suit. It's great, but it covers a lot."

"Jared, we're getting far away from working out our problems. They're still present."

"Lighten up, Megan," he said easily. "It won't hurt to drop them for tonight and get back on friendlier footing."

"I can's shut off my worries the way you can," she replied swiftly, thinking about Ethan and the prospect of having him cut out of a big chunk of her life. "Kisses and moonlight swims don't gain us anything."

"Yes, they do," he argued solemnly, stepping closer. "If we can get some kind of friendship and cooperation, it'll help. We're in this together, to some degree, for a long time to come. Tonight, let go of your worries. Ethan's safe and happy. You won't help him by staying aloof and worrying. C'mon. Try to be friends."

"That's a strange thing to say after making love to me," she said, yet she realized he had a point, and her worrying tonight wasn't going to solve her problems. "It's just hard to let go when I'm filled with concern."

He caressed her cheek. "I'm sure it is," he said gently, making her want to plead her case again, but she knew that was pointless.

"You win for now. I'll try, but I can't let go of my anxiety."

"I'll try to help. Come on. A good swim will remove a little stress," he said, leading her toward the beach.

"There's someone's yacht anchored not far out," she noticed, looking at the sun splashing over a dazzling white boat.

"It's mine, and right now no one's on it. It's wired with alarms, so it doesn't have to have someone there constantly. That's two things money can buy—security and privacy."

"Race you to the floating dock," he said, while he tossed their towels onto the warm sand.

She ran with him and knew he was keeping pace with her, because he could easily outrun her. He released her hand when they were in knee-deep water and she continued to splash on, surprised how far the shallow water extended. When it deepened, Jared jumped in to swim.

She followed, knowing he would easily reach the dock first. When he did, he gave her a hand and pulled her up beside him and she raked her wet hair back from her face.

"The water is perfect and so beautiful."

"What's beautiful is you," he said, turning to place his hand behind her head.

"Jared—"

"Shh, Meg. One kiss isn't catastrophic," he said, his gaze lowering to her mouth. Her pulse drummed as he leaned down to cover her mouth with his.

"Not to you," she whispered, before his lips covered hers. Then he kissed her and she wound her arm around his neck and kissed him in return. Finally she pushed away.

"Stop—and remember what I told you."

With a hungry look that was filled with desire, he released her and sat beside her. She wrinkled her nose at him.

"Besides, I don't want you to interfere with my swim."

She expected one of his light remarks. Instead, he gave her a somber look, and she couldn't imagine what he was thinking.

"Jared, today has been unique, a temporary truce and lull, and I love your home and I love swimming. But all this is simply postponing the inevitable."

"I know, but I thought it would be best if we got on better footing with each other."

"We've done that, all right," she quipped.

"It's better than arguing," he said quietly. "Also, it gives each of us more of a chance to think things through."

She knew she would remember this day the rest of her life. She'd remember Jared sitting beside her, drops of water glistening on his bronze shoulders and body, the warm sun shining and cool water lapping around them, the beach and house in sight—a dream that was real.

"After dinner, we'll give it another go."

She nodded, knowing this was an illusion of peace and compatibility. In spite of the past few hours, their relationship was stormier than ever.

"Well, I came planning to swim, so I'll swim," she said, turning to look at the yellow buoys bobbing several hundred yards farther out. "It's safe to the buoys?" she asked.

"That's right."

She jumped in and swam, and in seconds he swam beside her, eventually swimming back to shore. She walked out and spread a towel to sit cross-legged in the sand, and he did the same.

"That was fantastic. The water is perfect. I may have to think about some kind of place like this for myself. It would be good for Ethan because he's not much of a swimmer, but he likes the water."

Jared stood and extended his hand. "If you're ready to go in, we'll dress and I'll tell Lupita to put on dinner."

"Where is Lupita? I haven't seen anyone since we first arrived."

"The staff knows how to stay out of sight. She'll get dinner on and then go for the night. They have homes in this compound, but beyond the security walls. There's nothing inside the walls except my house, its outbuildings and us."

At the veranda, he paused. "I'll go find Lupita and meet you here in half an hour and we can have a drink before dinner."

She nodded and headed for her room.

Finally clad in a black knit shirt and black slacks, Jared looked dark, handsome and dangerous. He was a threat to her future and he wasn't going to go away and let her live her life the way she had before.

Jared crossed the veranda to take her hands while his gaze drifted lazily over her. "You look beautiful. Far more tempting than dinner."

She waved her hand dismissively. "Thank you, Jared."

"What would you like to drink?"

"A piña colada, please, if that's possible."

"Quite possible," Jared replied, moving around behind a bar to get bottles of light and dark rum that he poured into a blender, adding other ingredients and mixing them with crushed ice. He poured the drink into a hurricane glass and handed it to her, getting a cold beer for himself. Taking her chilled glass, she moved to a chair to sit and gaze at the ocean. The sun was a huge fiery ball, low on the horizon.

"Will you bring Ethan here?" she asked.

"I'll take him everywhere," Jared said. She felt the hurt again.

"I always thought about taking him places, but I thought I should wait until he's older. I suppose I waited too long."

"Nonsense. You can still go where you want with

him," Jared said. "You can come with us, if you want to," he said.

She turned to him. "Jared, today was lust. It was sexual, meaningless, nothing more. It didn't bind us together in any manner except physically. My feelings toward you haven't changed. And your feelings are no kinder toward me than mine are toward you."

He set his drink on a table. "That's not so. I think there was more to this afternoon than you'll admit or recognize because you're still angry with me. We can both come here and bring Ethan with us and have a wonderful escape," he said.

She shook her head. "No. That won't work, Jared. Not really. Today was no indicator of the future."

He looked annoyed, and then he seemed to visibly relax. "You're cutting yourself out of some good moments," Jared said.

"I'll manage."

"Dinner is served," Lupita announced, her voice cutting through the tense moment.

"Thanks, Lupita," Jared said, standing to take Megan's arm to stroll to another section of the veranda where it curved around a wing of the house. Tall palms lined their patio, and potted palms and banana trees gave the appearance of being in a garden by the sea.

With candles burning despite the daylight, the glass-and-iron table set with colorful china and sparkling crystal was ready for a photo shoot. On the table was an appetizer of escargot, while steaming, covered dishes waited next to it. Jared held her chair, his hand drifting lightly to her nape and then he sat himself across from her, smiling at her.

"I don't know how you ever leave this and go back to Texas."

"It's too quiet except for a few days at a time. I'm too active and like to work. I imagine you'd feel the same if you were here for weeks. The first visit, I stayed a month. I haven't lasted that long since."

She could well imagine that he always brought a woman with him. Just as he had with her. Trying to avoid the subject burning inside her, she chatted with him over dinner of jambalaya, fluffy golden asiago biscuits and melons, mango and kiwi with Gorgonzola cheese. Dessert was thin slices of cheesecake flown in from Miami. Pale slices were drizzled with chocolate and raspberry sauce. Dinner was delectable, their conversation innocuous, but his gaze clearly conveyed smoldering desire.

"Dinner is delicious. Are you trying to soften me up in all possible ways?"

"You're soft and warm now, each luscious inch," he said, smiling at her.

"I walked into that one. Thank you, Jared. Those compliments come so easily to you, you must not even think about what you're saying."

"Not so, Meg," he said, caressing her hand. "Being together is good. I see great hope for the future."

As the sun vanished and darkness enveloped them, lanterns and outdoor lighting automatically came on over the veranda and along the beach. The flickering light highlighted the planes of Jared's face, his straight nose and prominent cheekbones.

"Let's move where it's comfortable," he suggested, and she nodded.

While she chatted with Jared, Lupita and Adan cleared and said good night.

"It's difficult to imagine that you require a body-guard."

"I think I should hire one for you, and I know Ethan is going to have to have one." Jared leaned forward. "His life is going to change and you can't stop it. There are things that go along with my wealth. Paparazzi, the possibility of kidnapping."

She flinched and looked away, hating everything that was happening to her life and to Ethan's. "If only I had sold the ranch to you. You would never have known about Ethan," she said bitterly.

"It's too late for that now."

"Jared, try to understand. I've told you before and I'll say it again—you have an extravagant lifestyle that doesn't make you good daddy material."

"I won't be that way with Ethan. Give me some credit here," he replied with a stubborn just of his chin.

"You do wild things like mountain climbing. I know you used to do bronc riding in rodeos," she said, elic-iting a brief smile from him.

"I haven't ridden in years. I gave that up when I graduated from college. And I won't take him moun-tain climbing."

"I don't want him jet-setting all over the world with you."

"I'll be reasonable about travel, too, but there are places I'll want to take him, like where I'm taking you now."

"Some places I can get used to," she said, locking her fingers together. "Jared, I've been so close with Ethan. I guess I hover, and I may be overprotective, but I love him with all my heart. Except for my pottery, he's my whole world. And he comes first. It just hurts to think I have to share him. As much as I hate to admit it, I feel I'm losing him."

Jared nodded. "I understand, Megan. That's why I've suggested things like the marriage of convenience. And remember, you willingly shared him with your aunt and uncle."

"That's part of the problem. I share him with them, and now I'll have to divide my time with you. I'll lose being with him a lot."

"Yes, you will, but let's try to find the most workable way—and I'm not averse to having you around when I'm with him."

"It's just incredibly difficult to give up my child," she said.

"You won't have to give him up if you'll work with me. There are some things that come with the territory, though, and I know you want to keep him safe. How you've managed to hide his paternity from the world all these years, I'll never know. Whose name is on the birth certificate? It can't be that ex-husband of yours, because he never adopted Ethan."

"It is Mike's name. My dad paid to get that taken care of by some doctor in Chicago. It may be illegal, but I have a birth certificate claiming Mike as Ethan's father."

"Well, we'll get that straightened out, but the minute

word gets out about his tie to me—and you become part of my life again, even if we're not on the best of terms—you both will be vulnerable. You might as well have a chauffeur—"

She laughed in this first truly humorous moment since Jared came back into her life. "A chauffeur! In Santa Fe!"

He grinned. "I finally got a laugh out of you, and that's great, Meg. It's good to hear you laugh again."

"I'll become the town oddity."

"No, you won't. There are more people chauffeured around Santa Fe than you think. Famous and wealthy people live there. You don't pay attention to things like that."

"He'll want to tell his best friend."

"Tell away. His friends will meet the guy. Give a thought to schools, too. I can afford whatever you want."

"I'm not sending my six-year-old away to school. He's in private school now, and I do schoolwork with him."

"I can afford tutors, too, if you want them. Same with lessons. I'll pay for all that. As for the bodyguard, you'll be on the ranch part of the year, so you're incredibly vulnerable there because of the isolation. I'll get someone who'll be discreet. You should also have a guard on the premises."

"You're being generous," she said. Every suggestion tore at her. Even if it was best for Ethan, it would change his life.

"Now, what can we work out about his visitation?" Jared asked.

She glanced at him. "What about if you get him Saturdays and Sundays and we alternate holidays," she finally suggested, hating the thought of losing Ethan on weekends. "Though I don't know how he can play on the soccer team or basketball or baseball or anything else if he goes out of state with you," she added.

"Of course I don't want to destroy Ethan getting to play soccer or any other sport. But he's surely not into all those yet."

"No, but he will be soon. He played soccer and T-ball this year."

"You can give me schedules and we'll work it out so he can play. But Saturdays and Sundays and alternate holidays won't be enough time. That's not sharing him equally."

His words were quiet but held that same note of steel. She looked away again, thinking about how she could divide Ethan's time to Jared's satisfaction. "I don't know. You move your headquarters to Santa Fe," she suggested. "Then we can work this out much more easily."

"I can't do that," he answered patiently. "It isn't the air hub that Dallas is, or the oil center. Dallas is far more accessible. If either of us is going to move, it would be less of a hassle for *you* to move. Fort Worth is filled with museums and Dallas and Fort Worth both have art galleries. You could work in either place and be close at hand."

She laced her fingers together and thought about her peaceful life in Santa Fe that had been simple in so many ways, and about how Jared was going to demolish all of it.

"Move to Dallas, live in a big city with all the traffic and hassle."

"There are quiet housing sections, both inner-city and suburban, old and new, with their own shopping areas and galleries. I can look into the best locations, Megan. I can buy the house you want or build it for you," he offered.

She closed her eyes and shook her head, tempted to cry out that she didn't want his money or support or interference.

"I don't know, Jared," she replied finally. "Leaving Santa Fe and all I've established and have there seems monumental. What about Ethan's friends?"

"Megan, he's six years old," Jared reminded her gently. "He'll adjust to anything you do."

Agitated, she stood and walked away from him, gazing at the flaming torches on the beach that shed bright circles of light on the white sand. She could see the tiny whitecaps washing on the shore's edge, the vast dark ocean beyond. Could she bear to move? If she didn't, she would have to pack Ethan up and send him off a great distance, whenever Jared saw his son.

If only she had sold Jared the ranch—what a bad decision she'd made!

Jared turned her to him. "If you move to Texas, it'll be much easier for us to share him. You know that. And there's no way I can move my headquarters and all my people to Santa Fe. Be realistic."

"Realistic! Give him up and tear my heart out is what you mean!"

"No, it's not," Jared replied firmly in a quiet, patient voice. "I keep telling you to share him with me. Megan,

I want what's good for him, too. You act as if you're sending him to some terrible fate."

"I know," she admitted. "I know you want what's good and you want to get to know him, but moving to Dallas is an idea I have to adjust to."

"That's the most workable solution. He could still participate in all the activities and you and I'd both be there to see him."

"What happens to him if you marry someone?" Megan asked. "She'll want to have her own children with you. She'll never love him like a mother."

"I'm not marrying anyone. That's not remotely on the horizon. Unless it's you."

"No. I'm not marrying without love. You'd be getting Ethan and convenient sex and I'd get my emotions too tangled up in a relationship."

"Look, just take life as it is now. Let's not take on additional problems.

"Stop fighting me, Megan. I can see it in your expression." His hands squeezed her shoulders lightly, kneading and massaging. "You're as tense as a spring that's wound tightly."

"There's no way this is something I can take lightly," she insisted. "Would a month in the summer work and maybe a week in the winter?"

"Not at all. Equal division. That's what I want," he replied and she took a deep breath, her mind running over possibilities and rejecting them as quickly as she thought of them.

"Let me consider it, Jared," she said, twisting away from him and walking farther out onto the veranda.

She stared out at the ocean and the silvery moon reflected in it while she pondered.

Jared's hands closed on her arms. "Megan, you're making this so damned difficult," he whispered, leaning near to trace kisses across her neck.

She turned to protest and looked up into his eyes. "No," she whispered.

"You don't mean it," he answered and leaned forward to silence any further protests with a kiss.

They died the minute his mouth covered hers. In spite of her intentions, all she could think was she wanted to make love once more with him.

She wound her arms around his neck and stood on tiptoe and kissed him fervently. With a groan, his arm tightened around her waist and he shifted to stroke her back, twisting free the few buttons.

"Meg, darlin', you'll never know how I want you," he whispered, pausing to frame her face with his hands and look at her. "With all my being," he whispered and kissed her again.

Faint tugs at her back made her realize he was unfastening her top. He peeled it away and leaned back to pull it free and drop it. He unclasped her bra, taking it off, and then he cupped her breast and rubbed his thumb lightly over her nipple.

Desire was a storm, as impossible to refuse. He was enticement, forbidden dreams, a danger to her peace. But he'd already destroyed that. Her hips rubbed against him in invitation. Her kiss caused his groan. There was no stopping or going back. She was as helpless as a leaf carried on a rushing current.

His fingers touched her waist, and in seconds her skirt fell around her ankles. She stepped out of it and her shoes as he leaned back to look at her, his leisurely gaze made her tingle. Eagerly, she tugged off his shirt and unfastened his belt and slacks to let them fall. As soon as he'd kicked them off along with shoes, she peeled away his briefs to free him. He knelt to pull a packet from his trousers and then he picked her up.

"Jared, this is a dream," she whispered, more to herself than him.

"It's a dream come true, Meg."

Clinging to him, she kissed him as he walked a few yards to place her on a chaise lounge. He moved between her legs and paused to put on the condom. Then he lowered his weight and she wrapped her arms and legs around him as he entered her slowly, driving her wild.

"Jared, love…" His kiss smothered her words and he kissed her as he eased out and then entered her slowly again, teasing and building need, until she arched against him and was writhing with urgency.

Perspiration beaded his shoulders and his forehead as he continued, and finally his control vanished and he thrust hard and fast. She crashed with a climax and rocked with him as he reached his, rapture enveloping her in a golden glow.

Sex was fantastic, but the wrong thing to happen in her life. She lay in his arms as he turned on his side and kept her with him. She caressed him, stroking his back, kissing his shoulder lightly.

"Meg, I want you here with me," he whispered

between the light kisses he showered on her temple and cheek. "Give us a chance and see what develops."

In a tropical setting, it was more difficult to cling to logic and remain cool and remote. She knew she couldn't trust him with her heart a second time. She had to go home.

He shifted, holding her close with one arm while he caressed her shoulder and brushed her hair away from her face. "You're beautiful. And this is the best."

She caressed his shoulder, kissing him lightly, momentarily enveloped in euphoria and wanting to stay that way a little longer. She wondered whether she would remember this moment all her life. Both of them nude, wrapped in each other's embrace on the sandy beach. A faint breeze came off the water and she could hear the splash of breakers as they rolled into shore. Lantern light flickered over Jared's face, illuminating his prominent cheekbones, leaving his eyes in shadows.

"We should shower," she said.

"How about a quick, moonlight dip? Pool or ocean?"

"Ocean," she replied and he stood to take her hand. They ran into the water, and when it was over their knees, both fell into it to swim. After minutes, he caught her and stopped, standing in waist-deep water to pull her to him and kiss her again. Their bodies were wet and warm, tantalizing to her. Her heart thudded and she was certain she had to go home to put distance between herself and Jared and get out of this magical dreamland setting where problems lost all reality.

Wrapping her arms around him, she kissed him. He

picked her up and waded out to the beach to carry her back into a bedroom.

They made love in bed, and afterward he held her close while he caressed her and murmured endearments that she barely heard. Her mind raced over what to tell him and when, deciding to let it go this night, and to deal with it in the light of day, which would restore a semblance of normalcy.

She wrapped her arms around him to hold him and kiss him again.

They loved through the night and finally slept in each other's arms, as sunlight began to tint the world with pink. In his arms, she thought about the future, deciding she would go home, mortgage the ranch and hire the best lawyers possible to fight Jared. That would throw it into the courts where the best lawyer usually won.

She woke to an empty bed and left to shower and dress in blue slacks and shirt.

As soon as she was dressed and ready, she sat by the open door to gaze at his tropical flowers and the ocean while she called the family accountant to get him to look into the best rates to mortgage the ranch. After a brief argument, he acquiesced and made plans, saying he would be prepared when she returned home.

Next, she called her South Dakota bank to check on the savings left to her by her father. Then she called the Santa Fe bank to check on savings there, then talked with her stock broker about what she could get from stocks and bonds.

She would have to find new lawyers, the best she

could hire. Jared would know the most competent, but she couldn't ask him. There was that billionaire client—he'd bought her pottery. He could probably give her sound advice. When she was back at the ranch and knew how much she would have available for a court fight, she'd get in touch.

She would have to go home and tell Ethan about his father. There was no avoiding that, so it might as well happen her way.

And she wanted Jared to have a day or two of full responsibility for Ethan, because as a confirmed bachelor, Jared might discover he didn't want to be burdened with a child after all, and all her problems would be solved. She couldn't imagine him enjoying being tied down to his son to the extent that he talked about.

Finally, she brushed her hair and put it in a thick braid. She found Jared in the kitchen with breakfast waiting.

He wore khakis, a white knit shirt and deck shoes, and he paused to look at her thoroughly. "Good morning. Come join me," he said, strolling to her.

She put up her hand and shook her head. "Last night was magic, Jared, but it's daylight, and reason rules now. I want to go home as soon as possible."

"Why? I thought we were gaining ground. We've talked about some options, developed a relationship, eliminated some possibilities—what's the rush?"

"I never intended seduction and lovemaking."

"You can't say it's been bad," he remarked.

"Of course not. But it isn't what I want and it isn't

doing my future any good. And I told you, I can't separate it from my emotions the way you can. I don't want to fall in love again."

"If falling in love occurs, I'd think it would be the best possible development. It would solve our problems."

"I don't trust you. At home we're in a regular setting, with a normal routine. Logic is not swept away by tropical breezes and magical nights. I want to be back where I can weigh the options for the future. And so far, I haven't found any I like, even if you have. This may have to get settled in court, Jared," she said.

His features hardened and a glacial look came to his dark eyes. She didn't care if he didn't like her answer. She hadn't liked any of his.

"Megan, don't make me take you to court. That could get really ugly and cause a world of hurt for all three of us," he said in a tone of voice that she suspected had made more than one grown man quail.

She shook her head. "You don't frighten me. I'll tell you what I want to do first. I want to go home and tell Ethan that you're his father. Then I want you to come stay a couple of days at my ranch and begin to get to know him. After that, if it looks feasible, and I approve, I want you to take him home with you and see how you like having responsibility for him all on your own," she said.

Jared's expression changed instantly. He came around the table and placed his hands on her waist. "Megan, absolutely fantastic! Now that's more like it.

I can get to know him and Ethan can get to know me and you can see us together. That's a terrific suggestion!"

"I thought you'd like it," she said, wondering if he thought he would win her over to doing things his way completely.

"Thank you, Megan. That's grand. It will give us time to bond. I'll call to get the plane ready and we can be on our way in about two hours. How's that?"

"It's fine with me, Jared."

He smiled at her and her pulse raced. He looked so damned appealing and sexy, and in spite of all her anger with him, she wanted his arms around her and she longed to kiss him.

But she had the wisdom to not do anything personal. Yearning and anger conflicted; she wanted him to back off. She knew she was in love with him a second time.

"We'll work this out to everyone's satisfaction. You'll see."

"It would be miraculous if it happened. I just don't see how."

He moved away and got his cell phone out of his pocket to make calls. She left him to get ready for the trip home, carrying her bag to the front door and sitting on the veranda to wait.

"Tell me about Ethan, and remember, I want a picture. I'd like to see your scrapbooks about him," Jared said as they flew home.

"Of course," she said, "although most of the scrapbooks and that sort of thing are in Santa Fe, not South Dakota."

"When I come to Santa Fe, I'll see what you keep there."

"Jared, you may find you don't want the responsibility of a child," she said, receiving a stormy glance and feeling their clash of wills that had returned full force.

"If you're counting on that, you might as well forget it. I'm going to try my damnedest to get along with my son and be a father to him."

"That's different than being a chum."

"I know that much. How soon will you get him home from your uncle's house?"

"I'll drive to Sioux Falls when we get back. I called while I was waiting for you," she said. "I told them I would pick him up today and take him to the ranch. You can come tomorrow."

"Did he mind the change in plans?"

"No. You said it yourself—kids adapt. He's looking forward to seeing me, and I'll be glad to see him. This has made me miss him twice as much."

Jared nodded and reached over to take her hand. "Thanks for what you're doing. I know you don't want to, but it's inevitable and much better this way, when you smooth the introduction. Anything we can do to make this transition easier will be better for Ethan, and I appreciate it."

"I might as well try to do things the best way for him," she responded, aware of her hand in Jared's, his dark eyes resting on her.

"I still want you," he said, sliding his hand behind her head and leaning forward to kiss her long and slowly.

She kept reminding herself to resist him, but she kissed him back instead. And each kiss forged a tighter bond, would be a bigger heartbreak and more of a struggle for her.

He raised his head. "Stop fighting me, Meg. You want this, too."

"No, I don't. I will contend with you as long as you kiss and flirt." She withdrew her hand from his. He stretched out his long legs and crossed them at the ankles.

"Tell me about Ethan," he said.

They talked about Ethan over a light lunch, and then Jared tried to charm and entertain her the rest of the way home with stories from his life.

Finally, she told him good-bye and headed to the ranch, anxious to see Ethan. And she wished with all her heart she didn't have to face her son and tell him that his real father wasn't who he'd thought all these years, but another man—one he had met only recently and briefly.

That evening, she pulled her son onto her lap. He was big enough that his legs dangled almost to the floor, but not quite. "Ethan, I want to talk to you about something important."

Eight

Thursday morning Megan opened the door and stepped back to let Jared enter. For the first time since he was in his early twenties, he was nervous. He held a package in his hand wrapped in plain gray paper. He also had a junior-size football and a paper sack. Even with all his thoughts on the event ahead, he noticed Megan. He wished they'd stayed at his Yucatán home another day or more, because he wanted more nights with her, and he'd already missed her badly. It was a surprise that he would want her with him so much because he had thought he was over her and she would no longer be so important to him. She had her hair in a braid today and she wore tight jeans, a green T-shirt and boots.

"I left my things in the car. I can get them later,"

Jared said and she nodded. "He's okay with all this?" Jared asked.

"Yes," she answered. Her eyes were wide, a clear turquoise, and she looked pale and somber. "He's curious and I think he likes the idea of having a dad, but he's shy."

"Where is he?"

"He's waiting in the family room. Jared, after I introduce you, I'm going to leave the two of you to get acquainted. I may go riding. It's a pretty June day and he likes to play outside, so that's good. You can take him out or you can stay in the family room. If you want to call, I'll have my cell phone. I'll stay out of the way for the next two hours."

He nodded. "That's great, Megan. I want to take both of you to dinner tonight."

"Thanks, but I already have steaks. We'll eat here and it'll be easier."

They entered the family room and he saw Ethan dressed in jeans and a T-shirt. He sat on the sofa playing with toy cars. As soon as they walked into the room, Ethan assessed him with a mixture of shyness and curiosity. He stood and waited.

"Ethan, this is Jared Dalton. You met in town last week. He's your real father. I told you about him."

Jared held out his hand to shake Ethan's. "I brought you a present."

"Before you open it, Ethan," Megan said, "I told you earlier, I'm going to leave so you and Jared can get to know each other. I have my cell phone and you know how to call me. I'll be back after a while." She leaned down and he ran to her, holding up his arms and she swung him up to hug and kiss him. He held her tightly until she leaned away to set him on his feet. "Be a good boy."

Ethan looked solemn and worried as she glanced at Jared. "I'll be back in a bit."

"Thanks, Megan." He turned to his son. "Ethan, I also brought you a football," Jared said. "We can throw it a little if you'd like to. First open your present."

Ethan nodded solemnly.

"Ethan—thank him," Megan prompted.

"Thank you, sir."

"You're welcome," Jared said, smiling at him, wishing he knew a way to make this easier for Ethan.

"I'll leave now." Megan walked away and Jared wondered whether she was crying or not. He looked back at Ethan. "You can open your present, Ethan."

Ethan slowly tore away the wrapping paper and opened the box to stare at the contents.

"It's a model airplane and it has a real motor. If you want, I'll help you put it together and then we can take it out and fly it."

"Sure," he said, glancing at Jared with a faint smile, and Jared let out his breath, thankful that it appeared he'd bought the right gift. Ethan looked in the box again and sat on the floor, starting to pour the contents out.

"Wait a minute, Ethan. I brought some things we'll use. Let's go out on the porch and work out there."

Ethan picked up the box and ran outside and Jared followed. "Ethan, I also brought a camera. May I take your picture?"

"Sure," he said, immediately halting and waiting.

Jared pulled a camera out of the sack and took three pictures.

"Can I take your picture?"

"Of course, here's the camera. Do you know how?"

"Yes, sir. Mommy showed me." Jared watched Ethan turn the camera in his small hands and hold it out, clicking a picture. He smiled and handed back the camera and Jared showed him the picture he had taken.

"Good job. When I get home, I'll print out copies and send them to you." Jared began to empty his sack, withdrawing a newspaper to unfold it. "Now, let's build the plane and fly it."

Ethan plopped down and helped Jared spread the newspaper. Next, Jared pulled out an instruction sheet and glue and a sheet of stickers from the sack and sat on the floor of the porch beside Ethan to work with him, letting Ethan do all that he could by himself.

He was surprised how well Ethan took directions, soon losing his shyness and working happily with Jared as if they had known each other for years.

"Mr. Dalton—"

"Ethan," Jared interrupted gently, placing his hand on Ethan's shoulder. "I'm your dad. Call me Daddy or Dad, whichever you like, but I'm not Mr. Dalton to you."

"Daddy," Ethan said shyly, staring at Jared, and Jared reached over impulsively and picked up Ethan to hug him.

"Ethan, I already love you. You're my son, my child, my baby even if you're not a baby any longer. You're part of me and my love is yours."

Ethan put his thin arms around Jared's neck and hugged him. "I'm glad you're here, Daddy. I've wanted a daddy because my friends have daddies."

"Well, you have one and I'm here to stay. If I had known I was going to be a dad, I would have come back immediately, Ethan. I won't ever leave you again except for short times when I go to work or you go to school," Jared said, feeling tears well up, surprised he was so emotional about Ethan. He hugged the boy's small, thin body and closed his eyes, holding his son close. "You'll never know how much I do love you, Ethan, but someday, when you're a daddy, you'll begin to understand."

Ethan laughed and wiggled to get free, so Jared set him back where he had been, beside the toy plane that was almost complete.

"We have to let this dry for about thirty minutes," Jared said. "Then we'll go fly it." He watched, helping when necessary, as Ethan did the finishing touches and then picked the colors he wanted and lined up the small pots of paint.

Ethan picked up a paintbrush, dipped it in green paint and began to apply it to the fuselage.

Watching as Ethan concentrated on painting his airplane, Jared marveled at how easily a child accepted life. Jared watched small fingers put on a coat of bright green paint, with orange flames along the cowling.

"Great plane, Ethan!" Jared praised his son as he rose to step back and take a picture of Ethan painting his toy model.

"Now, Ethan, we wait for it to dry," Jared said,

closing the pots of paint. "We'll clean up. And since I brought a football, we can go toss it, if you'd like."

"Yes, sir. I want a drink of water first."

"Okay, come with me to the kitchen."

Jared held the door and went inside the quiet, cool house, feeling Megan's presence even though she wasn't there, seeing her touches in a vase of cut red roses, seeing a book she was reading that was on the table beside a chair. If only she would agree to the marriage of convenience, or at least to move to Dallas, they could so easily share Ethan's life. Instead, from all she'd said, she was preparing to go to court, and Jared dreaded it. It would hurt all of them—a bitter, damaging battle. One he expected to win, which would hurt Megan even more.

If they went to court, though, he vowed to fight for full custody. She'd regret not cooperating with him. He could get better lawyers than she could, and more of them, he was certain. The whole prospect was dismal and distasteful. And so unnecessary. They'd had a wonderful night in the tropics. Megan was the most exciting woman he'd ever known, and since their return to South Dakota, he'd missed her terribly.

He poured Ethan a glass of water and watched the boy's small hands encircle the little glass. He was totally fascinated with his son, and thankful Megan had suggested they get to know each other right away.

As Ethan finished and handed the glass back to Jared, he cocked his head to one side. "Where's the football?" he asked, running toward the porch. Jared followed, stepping out to see Ethan already in the yard, tossing the ball up and then running to get it when it fell in the grass.

He turned to throw it to Jared, who had to leap to one side to catch it. Jared moved closer and threw an easy toss underhand, which Ethan caught with both hands. He beamed with pleasure, throwing it back toward Jared.

After ten minutes, Ethan tired of catch and ran to climb on his swing. "Come push me."

"How about a 'please'?" Jared asked, strolling over to swing Ethan.

The morning passed and they were flying the plane when Megan emerged from the house carrying a platter with sandwiches, which she put on the table on the porch. She came out to join them as Ethan called to her.

"Look, Mommy! Look at the plane I built. And it flies!"

"Good job, Ethan!" she complimented him, walking up to Jared. He watched her approach, and he longed to go take her into his arms and kiss her and thank her for the morning with Ethan. Instead, he stood quietly waiting, wanting her in his arms and in his bed again with an increasing urgency.

"Looks like you've won his friendship, which I knew you would," she said solemnly.

"Don't sound so disappointed," Jared said, annoyed with her tone—even as he desired her.

"I'm not. I know he needs a father in his life. I brought lunch, if either of you are hungry. Looks as if I may not be able to tear him away from flying his plane."

"He can come back to it," Jared said, turning to Ethan. "Ethan, land your plane and let's go eat lunch."

"Watch, Mommy. Watch my plane. Look at this," Ethan called, pressing buttons and toggling a switch on his remote control, bringing the plane to the ground with a bounce. Jared and Megan both clapped and she smiled.

"That's great, Ethan," she said.

He dropped the remote control and ran toward the table.

"Go wash your hands," Megan called after him, and he disappeared into the house.

"I think I'll do the same. We've had an assortment of activities this morning, and I feel dusty," Jared said, heading into the house behind Ethan.

They all reconvened on the porch to eat lunch, which Ethan wanted to escape after only a quarter of a chicken salad sandwich. Megan excused him and he ran off to play with the airplane again.

"So you bonded instantly. I'm relieved to see that you get along and can communicate with him."

Jared smiled at her as he sipped ice tea. "You're surprised and I would guess you're disappointed."

"Not really. I'd be unhappy if you couldn't."

"He asked me why I didn't marry you. I told him I asked you a few days ago and you didn't want to change the life you have with him right now. You may get questions yourself."

"I have, and I expect to get more. I try to be as up front with him as I can. Your answer was a stretch, because what you proposed was a marriage of convenience. Of course, that's the only kind it could be, because we're not in love."

He leaned forward to touch her cheek lightly. "It

doesn't mean that love isn't going to happen. It could occur if we both try to be friends."

"Forget it, Jared. I'm not marrying you and we're not going back to the way we were."

"I thought we got along great at my Yucatán home," he said.

"The time in the Yucatán was a rare moment that won't happen again. Let's drop it. Here comes Ethan."

Jared straightened and turned to watch Ethan, who came to sit with them and talk about his airplane. "Daddy, will you come fly it with me?"

"Sure will," he said, looking at Megan, who was frowning. "If Mommy will excuse us."

"Of course," she said, and Jared left with Ethan, who ran to jump off the porch steps, half-stumble and keep running to his plane. Jared watched him get the plane in the air. He thought about going back to help Megan clean up, but decided to stay out of her way.

After Jared had grilled dinner, they spent the evening in games with Ethan. Megan finally stood. "Ethan, it's bedtime. Say good night."

"Mom! School's out and I'm not sleepy."

"Give me a good-night hug, Ethan, and do what your mother says. The first thing you know, it'll be morning and we can fly your plane again," Jared said, pushing his chair away from the game table and standing to hold out his arms and pick up Ethan, who put his arms around Jared's neck in a hug.

"Will you come kiss me good night?"

Jared looked over Ethan's head at Megan.

"He can come kiss you good night in about thirty minutes. You have to have a bath and then I'll read a story to you," Megan said, reassuring him.

"All right. I'll be there in about thirty minutes from now. For the moment, good night, Ethan," Jared said, kissing Ethan's forehead. He set him on his feet. "Now go and get to bed so you can get up."

Ethan turned to scamper away ahead of Megan. "Well, thanks. Tonight he's cooperating fully with you and that makes my job easier." She left the room and Jared hoped she would return and sit with him in a while. He wanted to be with her. He missed her and their night together had been paradise. But the future wasn't going to be rosy if she was going ahead with what she'd threatened.

He moved to the porch and sat, propping his feet on the railing and staring out into the yard. Light from a lamppost shed light on a flowerbed, and faded into darkness beyond.

He glanced at his watch and headed toward Ethan's room. As he approached he heard the sound of Megan's voice. At the doorway of Ethan's room, he paused. Megan was stretched out in bed with Ethan beside her, and she held a child's book in her hand. She read quietly to Ethan, who was curled against her, his eyes barely open. One hand held his toy airplane and another held a frayed blue blanket that he fingered as she read. A battered white bear lay in Ethan's lap.

Jared entered and sat quietly in a rocking chair. She glanced at him, though Ethan seemed too sleepy to notice. Jared rocked and watched her. A small lamp burned and showed Megan beautiful in the low light. Her midnight hair spilled forward, glints shining in the cascade of thick, straight strands. Jared wanted her, but he was also held captive watching her, hearing the love and tenderness in her voice.

He knew whatever happened in the future, he could never take Ethan from Megan. All afternoon and evening love radiated between them constantly. When he'd been around her, Ethan had hovered next to her, touching his mother as if to reassure himself she was there. And she watched him with obvious love and pride in her gaze. Sadness swamped him that they were caught in a dilemma that could so easily be avoided if she would drop her bitterness over the past.

Jared realized he'd let her father intimidate him. He should have stayed.

In the end, right before he'd left, he had gone to his own father to let him know about Sorenson's threats. Jared could remember his father's rage and insistence that Jared stay and try to talk to Megan, but at twenty-five, after growing up watching the two men fight over every ranch problem that involved his neighbor, Jared had no doubts that Edlund Sorenson would carry out his threats.

At the time, deep down, he'd felt Megan probably had known what her dad was doing. He was her father, after all. If she didn't, Jared figured they would get back together, and shortly after he had gone, he wrote her the first letter. All his letters went unanswered, which to him, at the time, seemed an answer in itself.

She must have known some of what her father had done. He couldn't imagine Megan would condone her father harming his neighbor, but she had to have been aware of his acts throughout the years. Too many times, Sorenson had tried to take their water by damming up the river.

Both men always shot the other man's animals when they roamed on either of their properties after fences had gone down—his own father in retaliation. Occasionally hands from the Dalton ranch had had tires slashed in town, and they'd always blamed Sorenson's hands.

Also, Jared had known there was no use going to the police and telling them about the threats. Edlund Sorenson was respected in the community and it would be his word against Jared's.

His dad had been ready to fight, and wanted Jared to stay, but Jared was afraid for his dad, who was getting older and wasn't as strong as he'd once been. He didn't want his family hurt, so he'd left.

Waiting, Jared thought about the future. When she finished the book, Ethan had fallen asleep.

She picked him up and Jared stepped up to turn back the covers. She tucked Ethan into bed, gently moving his plane beside him on the bed before kissing him good night.

"My turn," Jared said. He kissed him, still marveling that he had a son and how easy it had been today to get to know him. He turned to walk out with Megan.

"He's great, Meg, and today was the best. He accepted me."

"I figured you'd charm him. He's happy to discover he has a dad. Part of it is simply envy, but so far, you're winning him over. Don't get too chummy, because it could hurt him later."

"That's in your hands," he said, as they returned to the family room and she crossed the floor to sit in a wingback chair. He sat nearby, facing her.

"I might as well tell you, Jared, I'm hiring a legal firm in Chicago. You'll get to see Ethan sometimes, but not half. I'll fight for that until the court takes him away from me."

"Megan, damn it, don't do this! It'll tear all three of us up. Ethan will be torn between us. I don't want to fight you over him. We can work things out if you give it half a try."

She shook her head. "No. Pack and go if you want to avoid a fight."

"I promised him I would never leave him. And I told him I didn't leave him the first time, that I didn't know about his birth."

"He told me what you said. Why don't you simply tell the truth? Admit that you got cold feet about marriage and walked out. He can take that as easily. It didn't involve him."

"I didn't get cold feet, Megan," Jared said with force.

She tilted her head to study him. "I don't even want to hear about it," she said, getting up and walking away. "I told you to come spend a few days to get to know Ethan, but I don't know that my nerves can take this, Jared. Tomorrow, take him home with you for a couple of days overnight and then bring him back. By then you two should know each other better."

Jared fought the urge to take her into his arms and

kiss away her protests. Instead, he crossed the room to put his hands on her shoulders and turn her to face him. "I want to take him home with me, but, Megan, drop this going to court. Rethink it…give us a chance to develop a workable relationship. Stop hanging on to anger from seven years ago," he said.

"That's easy for you, Jared. You're the one who wants all the changes."

"Yield an inch or two here! Try to cooperate," he said. He could feel the clash of wills, but desire was just as strong. Standing this close to her, looking into her thickly lashed turquoise eyes and at her full red lips that he knew were so soft, he was on fire with want. He pulled her to him, winding his hand in her hair and claiming her soft mouth. Fleetingly, he wondered if he was going to fall in love again with Megan, head for heartbreak twice himself.

Angered by her stubbornness, desiring her with all his being, he poured his raging emotions into his kiss.

Her hands shoved against his chest, but the push was brief and feeble, stopping as she slid her hands up and around his neck. And then she was in his embrace, pressed against him as he shook with eagerness.

He wrapped his arm tightly around her, leaning over her as he kissed her, thrusting his tongue deep into her mouth.

She kissed him in return, setting him on fire.

He wanted to pick her up and carry her to a bedroom, but he was afraid to break the tenuous moment; and holding and kissing her was better than having her tell him good night and send him on his way.

To his gratification, she responded, setting him ablaze. Finally she pushed forcefully against him and turned her head, ending their kiss. "Jared, you stop."

"You like me kissing you, Megan. Heaven knows, I like to kiss you more than any other woman I've ever known."

"Oh, Jared, please stop the shallow comments."

He wound his fingers in her hair as the other arm banded her waist, and he pulled her head back so she looked up at him. "There's nothing shallow about what I feel for you, and I meant exactly what I said. There's never been a woman in my life like you," he said solemnly, realizing that it was the truth.

"Jared, we're not going to sol—"

"A visit to Dallas is all I'm asking," he said, cutting her off and releasing her hair, then caressing her nape. "Bring Ethan with you. Will you come right away?"

"I'm going to regret it."

"That's a yes," he said with a jump in his pulse, because he saw a glimmer of hope of Megan cooperating with him. If she would come look at the Dallas-Fort Worth metroplex, with all the diverse lifestyles there, he thought he could win her over. Little by little, maybe she would work with him. "I can fly you there."

"I don't know about that," she replied cautiously.

"Nonsense. I'll fly us there. Plan to spend three days."

"Jared, I haven't said yes. I'll think about it."

"Bring Ethan with you and you'll see the possibilities."

"You're always a charmer, talking people into doing things the way you want them."

"And you're a seductress, setting me on fire." He

framed her face with his hands. "I want you, Megan. I want you and I want to work out things between us."

"I don't think we can," she answered.

"I know we can if we both try. Megan, are you scared I'll hurt him?"

"Heavens, no! Not physically, anyway."

"Then what are you afraid of?"

"I'm frightened you'll find him a fascinating diversion in your life for a while and then tire of the responsibility and care of a child and disappear out of his life. Children can't cope with that like adults can."

"No, I'll never do that," he said solemnly. "I love him too much to hurt either of you. I don't want a court fight over him."

"Words are easy," she said.

"I won't tire of him, either." Jared took her hand. "Come sit out on the porch and let's talk," he said, taking her hand.

She went out with him, sitting, watching him in the semidarkness as he pulled his chair close to hers. Light spilled through windows and the open door, dimly illuminating the porch.

"I'll show you Fort Worth. I can drive across Dallas if I have to and if you don't want to live close. Of course, close would be more convenient for both of us and make it easier."

"Easier for you," she said.

"Megan, I'm trying to find something workable," he reminded her.

"If I'd move to Dallas, would you back off having custody of him?"

Jared gazed at her. His first inclination was an immediate no, but he waited, considering what she was asking, but knowing that unless he was given legal custody, Megan could easily keep him from seeing his son.

"No, because I don't think you'll always let me see him otherwise. Let's not argue 'what ifs'. Just visit Dallas."

"I'll think about it," she said, standing. He stood at once.

"Jared, be honest with Ethan. Don't tell him we're thinking about moving to Dallas, because at the moment, I'm not seriously entertaining the thought. Santa Fe is home, and I have roots there now. Don't tell him you want to marry me unless you think you can make it clear to him that it's a business arrangement. You'll get along better if you're up front and truthful."

"When haven't I been truthful with you?"

She shrugged. "When you declared you loved me."

"I did love you, Megan," he said, grinding out the words, knowing his patience was stretching thin. He caught her arms and pulled her closer and her eyes widened as she placed her hands on his forearms reflexively.

"Megan, I left because your father threatened my dad if I didn't go!"

She closed her eyes and rocked back on her heels.

Nine

"Jared, don't! Don't lie to me," she said, hurting and angry at Jared.

"I'm not lying to you," he said in a tight voice, scowling at her. "Your dad warned me that he'd cut off water to our ranch and hurt my dad. He said he'd disown you and you'd be harmed in other ways, too. I may have made the wrong choice, but I still believe he would have injured my family terribly and you worse."

"If that's true, why didn't you contact me later and try to let me know?"

"We were threatened, Megan. I was a kid, and I left. I've paid for it a thousand times over."

"I don't want to hear this pack of lies, Jared!" she cried, jerking away from him. With every word he said, her fury intensified until she was shaking. "If he'd done that, you would have come to me," she said, certain Jared was lying and doing a poor job of it. "My father was in such a rage about your disappearance—there's no way he could have been the reason you left. Not possible. I won't listen to such garbage!"

"Megan, I swear I'm telling you the truth," he said quietly.

"I know my father better than that. You were headstrong. Dad was a control freak and he interfered with my life, but he wouldn't be that cruel. I know our dads did dreadful things to each other, but neither ever did bodily harm to the other. If he'd threatened you, you wouldn't have listened," she said, disgusted with him. "There's no common ground for us. This is hopeless. I told you that you could take Ethan to your ranch and I'll stick by my promise. Ethan can go home with you tomorrow night. You leave with him early in the morning and bring him back the day after tomorrow, on Saturday, by dinner. Is that clear?"

"Megan, he threatened you. I don't know what else to say," Jared said, clenching his fists. "I loved you and it hurt to leave—"

"I will never believe you," she declared. "I don't want to hear about it. Not anything. I'm going inside, Jared. I'll see you in the morning." She walked past him and into the house without looking back. She hated the lies he'd told her. There was a dark side to him she knew nothing about. She was surprised he would come up with such a lame excuse. Yet she did know he could be ruthless when he wanted something.

She prayed the legal firm she was hiring would get

what she wanted in a court battle. If they didn't, then she would try to bargain with Jared. If she lost badly in court, she'd look into moving to Dallas, but only as a last resort.

If only her pulse didn't still race with Jared's every look and her heart skip beats with his slightest touch. Right now, her nerves were raw and desire was a tormenting flame.

Ethan would be with him for two days. He had been good with Ethan, and they bonded instantly, which hadn't surprised her. When Jared was his charming best, he could easily win someone's affections. And Ethan wanted a daddy. Tears stung her.

She wasn't going into any marriage of convenience—one convenient only for Jared. She was already in love with him again. A marriage of convenience would devastate her emotionally. And he'd get the sex he wanted because she just couldn't resist.

He was in Ethan's life now, so she couldn't try to cut him out. Nor would she be able to legally, but hopefully, she could limit how much Jared would get Ethan.

She closed the door to her room and changed for bed, pulling on a robe, knowing sleep wouldn't come.

She left her room, stepping through the connecting door to Ethan's to look at him sleeping, serene and quiet. How she loved him! She could never regret knowing Jared, because he had brought her Ethan, the joy of her life. She smoothed locks of his black hair from his forehead, assured he would sleep through her light touches. Her love for Ethan had no measure, and she had to admit that Jared would make Ethan happy.

As he got ready for bed, he'd talked constantly about his daddy and what they had done today. His toy plane was still nestled beside him as he slept.

Was she being a fool to believe Jared again, when he had broken her trust completely once before. He had promised her that he wouldn't take Ethan from her, and he'd promised Ethan he'd never leave him. Would he really honor those promises? Tears stung her eyes once again and she knelt and kissed Ethan.

"I love you so," she whispered, and then she turned.

Jared leaned against the doorjamb, watching her.

Glaring at him as he crossed the room to her, she scrubbed her eyes furiously. Her emotions were in an upheaval.

"Don't cry, Meg," he murmured. He picked her up and carried her into her bedroom, shoving the door shut behind him before setting her on her feet. He brushed her tears with his fingers. "Don't cry. I don't want to hurt you. He was happy today and you didn't lose a lot of time with him. You let your aunt and uncle have him for weeks."

Nodding, she firmed her lips, gazing up at him. He had unbuttoned the first few buttons of his shirt and she was aware of his bare chest, conscious of his hands on her, memories of their lovemaking tormenting her.

Jared framed her face with his hands and gazed at her intently. She couldn't keep from looking at his mouth and wanting to kiss him.

His gaze lowered to her lips and she inhaled, her lips parting and tingling. "Stop fighting me at each turn," he ordered. "You're making this damned difficult, and it doesn't have to be." Jared's mouth covered hers and he kissed her. His arm slid around her waist and pulled her tightly against him as he kissed her, passion heating between them.

She ran her hand over his chest, feeling his groan.

He shook as he kissed her as he had before, and she was astounded by his need for her. She wanted him with an urgency that shocked her.

Reason prevailed and she pushed against him, finally leaning back. "Jared, we're not going to make love. I'm going to sleep alone tonight."

He raised his head and his eyes opened slowly. "I want you, Meg. I want you more than you can imagine."

"I'm not the woman for you. There's too much unhappiness between us. I can't tell you to get out of my life, but I'm not going to bed with you again."

When she pulled out of his embrace, he let her go. She walked away, going to the window. "Good night," she said.

In a moment she heard the door close and she turned to see that he had gone.

She put her head in her hands in frustration and anger. His story about her father had been appalling. She had never expected Jared to come up with such a lie.

She sat in a chair and gazed outside. Moonlight splashed over the yard, lighting broad areas, while beneath the trees was darkness. Near dawn, she dozed. And when she went into the kitchen for breakfast she found a note from Jared saying that he and Ethan had left for his ranch.

She wasn't hungry and went to her office to take care

of details regarding the new law firm, making arrangements to fly to Chicago overnight while Ethan was with Jared.

Saturday, early in the evening, she waited on the front porch with mounting excitement. She had missed Ethan more each day. Worrying about him in a way she never did when he was with her aunt and uncle, she had tried to reassure herself often that Jared loved Ethan and would take good care of him.

All the time they had been gone, she had promised herself that as soon as Ethan was through with his visit to Jared's, she would pack and return to Santa Fe. She wanted to get back to the home that was a haven, and far from Jared Dalton.

She saw the car approaching before she heard it. Her eagerness mounted as she watch his black car wind along the drive and finally stop. Ethan unbuckled and climbed out, running to her and waving his arms, his hands filled with toys.

She swung him up and kissed him while he hugged and kissed her.

"Look what Daddy got me! I have another plane and a car that will really run and I have a bigger car at his house that I can ride around in on the patio. I have a new game."

"Good heavens! It's not even your birthday or Christmas," she said, laughing at his exuberance as Jared strolled up the steps. Looking too appealing, he wore boots beneath tight jeans that rode low on his hips. His navy Western shirt was partially unbuttoned, revealing the thick mat of his chest hair. As his gaze drifted over her, she became aware of her cutoffs, her red T-shirt and her hair in a braid. His unhurried gaze was as warm as a caress, and she tingled from head to toe.

"Thanks, Megan. We've had a great visit."

"I can tell."

"Want to go to dinner tonight? Or I can take you both to my place," he asked, as Ethan sat on the porch playing with his car.

"Thanks anyway, Jared, but we have plans."

He nodded. "I'll call you in the morning."

He looked at Ethan. "Ethan, tell me good-bye," Jared said, and the child jumped up to hug Jared, who scooped him up. He hugged and kissed him and she turned away to go inside the house. Tears threatened, and she hated that she got emotional so easily, where Jared and Ethan were involved.

In minutes, Ethan came running inside and she heard Jared driving away.

"Why couldn't we go eat dinner with Daddy?" Ethan asked, his brown eyes as intense as Jared's.

"We're going to get ready and go back home to Santa Fe," she said, something that usually Ethan was eager to do. To her surprise, he frowned.

"Is Daddy coming?"

"No, he's not."

"Can't we stay here so I can see him?"

"We'll be back here."

"Soon?" he asked, looking worried now. Megan frowned. Jared had already won Ethan's affections.

"Soon, I promise," she said. "If you want to."

"I want to. I want to see Daddy and he said he likes to be with me."

"I'm sure he does. So do I. Now let's get packed. It'll be for a week, Ethan, and then we'll talk about coming back here."

He nodded, but he didn't look any happier, and she wondered if her life was going to be in a perpetual turmoil because of Jared.

Jared drove away. The last two days with Ethan had been a delight with one flaw—he missed Megan. He'd hoped she'd come home with him tonight, or at least spend the evening with him, and he wondered what she was doing.

Each day that passed, he missed her more and he thought about her constantly. When he'd taken Ethan home, it had taken all his control to keep from crossing the porch and kissing her.

He wanted her badly. He thought about the marriage of convenience. It would be more than that, definitely no cut-and-dried business arrangement.

With his thoughts on Megan, he drove automatically, wondering what her plans were for the evening and why she couldn't go with him or if that had been merely an excuse. One certainty, she always responded when he kissed her.

At the thought of their kisses, he was aroused, tempted to turn the car around and go back.

She was important to him, necessary again. Years ago, after he'd left and she wouldn't answer his letters, he'd tried to get over his hurt. He'd wanted to drive her out of his mind as much as she was out of his life. Most of the time he'd succeeded to the point he felt she didn't matter. She was merely a part of his past. All through those years there had been a simmering anger. Maybe he actually had still been hurting. At the time, revenge had been a sweet idea. Had it really been revenge, or wanting to get her back in his life?

He realized he was in love with her again.

The truth shocked him, but then as he considered it, he knew it was love. He wanted to spend the rest of his life with her. Was there any way he could ever get past her anger? Perhaps there was one thing he could do. It could backfire or it could make a difference, but he was desperate with wanting her.

Megan waited until Sunday evening, when they were back in their home in Santa Fe, before she called Jared. The walled patio gave her complete privacy. Pots of bougainvillea and hibiscus bloomed in a riot of orange, pink and yellow. Potted palms and banana trees added greenery, and it made her glad to be in Santa Fe. Ethan worried her though, because he'd been uncustomarily glum.

Along with Ethan's, her own spirits had sunk. Had she made another mistake leaving South Dakota? She hated to admit that as furious as she was, she missed Jared.

She heard Jared's deep voice on the line. "Jared, it's Megan. I wanted to tell you that Ethan and I are in Santa Fe."

"You didn't give me any warning that you were leaving. Are you returning to South Dakota soon?"

"I don't know. I'll let you know if we do."

"I'd like to talk to Ethan. I was going to call him tonight."

"You can talk, but you won't be doing him any favors. He wasn't happy about leaving the ranch, because he wants to see you. You've managed to charm him, which I knew you would, and of course you've showered him with toys."

"Don't resent it, Megan. I have some years to make up—and I love him."

"You don't even know him!" she cried, and there was a long silence. "Jared, I'm sorry," she apologized. "That was uncalled for. I'm glad you love your son. My nerves are shot over this."

"You're causing a lot of trouble for yourself that's unnecessary, and you're going to cause yourself even more. Try to avoid catching Ethan in the crossfire."

"You're one to talk!"

"I've never deliberately hurt him. I didn't know about him, but then we're both aware of that."

There was another long silence and she started to say good-bye.

"Megan, write down this number." She picked up a pen and pad from the table beside her, figuring he was going to give her his Dallas office or home number.

"Go ahead," she instructed, then wrote the number, repeating it back to him. "Is this your home in Dallas?"

"No, it's not. Do you remember when your dad bought the ranch that adjoins yours to the north? I don't know how old you were."

Puzzled, she frowned. "I remember. I was a junior

in high school. The McGinnises moved away after their son's car wreck."

"That's right. Give Dirk McGinnis a call and ask him what prevailed on him to sell out to your dad and move out of state."

"Why…" she started to ask, but then bit off her words, going cold all over as she looked at the number on the pad in her hand.

"Megan, let me talk to Ethan. Please."

She barely heard what Jared said as her head swam. "Megan!"

His shout broke through, and she called Ethan, who came running and took the phone, walking away to talk to Jared. She stared at the number in her hands, knowing there was only one possible reason Jared would give her the McGinnises' number.

If her dad had made them move—threatened them or worse—then Jared had been telling her the truth.

She didn't have to make the call to have an answer, and she wasn't certain she wanted to hear the answer anyway. But if true, then it had been her father behind the breakup after all.

His treachery had been monumental. All along, it had been her father behind Jared's mysterious disappearance. Jared *had* left to protect his family.

She felt weak in the knees and had to sit quickly, as a light-headedness swept her. Through childbirth and the months of her pregnancy, her father had caused Jared to leave, and she'd been alone. Jared deprived of knowing his baby, their marriage plans in shambles, her heart broken—all because her father hadn't liked Jared or his family, and needed to control her life. She put her hands over her face and sobbed. Her own father hurting her so badly, being so cruel to them. She couldn't blame Jared for leaving.

"...*I may have made the wrong choice, but I still believe he would have injured my family terribly, and you.*"

She hadn't known what her father had been capable of doing. She shuddered, shocked that she had been so incredibly wrong.

Error after error piled up with Jared, yet how could she have suspected her father's duplicity?

Her wrecked marriage plans, having Ethan alone, without Jared present at his son's birth or even knowing about it, her financial struggle, which had been unnecessary, a paper marriage—her father's cruelty had been monumental. And she'd cut Jared out of knowing about Ethan all those years. She owed him terribly to make up for all he'd suffered because of her father's unscrupulous ways.

Stunned, she barely heard Ethan when he came inside after he'd finished talking to Jared. Ethan seemed to sense something amiss and grew quiet through dinner. When Amy Brennan, his best friend's mother, called and asked Megan if Ethan could come to their house and sleep over, a rare treat, so Ethan and William could catch up, it seemed a blessing to Megan, and Ethan brightened immediately.

As she drove him to William's house, she glanced in the rearview mirror at Ethan. He sat buckled in the back, in his seat, with his new toy plane he'd brought to show William.

"Ethan, I think we'll go back to South Dakota sooner than I said. Would you like that?"

He brightened instantly. "Yes, I want to go. When?"

"Tomorrow, if we can get a flight."

"Awesome!" he cried, clapping and waving his arms, making her laugh for the first time in days. "Can I call Daddy and tell him?"

"Yes, but wait until you come home tomorrow," she said, suspecting she should have told him later. But he'd been glum since they'd left South Dakota.

Unable to stop grinning, he wriggled with eagerness. "That way, you can tell him when we'll arrive. I have to get our flight before we can tell him exactly when we'll be there."

Driving home she passed the red adobe buildings, turning into her quiet house. Pink, red and white hollyhocks bloomed in the yard and tall cottonwoods shaded her home and its double-thick adobe walls. She could see people milling on the porch to her gallery.

She returned to her house, to call Dirk McGinnis. She listened to how her father had threatened him and his family if he didn't sell. He'd refused to sell to her father, ignoring threats. Shortly afterward, his son had had a car wreck. The brakes had failed on his truck and he'd almost been killed. The young man still walked with a cane. There was nothing they could prove, but it had been her father, and she might as well know.

Weak-kneed again after she'd finished her call, she sat staring into space in the silent house. She owed

Jared the most profound apologies. There was no question she would share Ethan with him now.

Over breakfast, as the sun spilled over the thick adobe patio walls, she listened to birds sing, yet she felt as if the world would never be the same peaceful place she had known before.

As she cleared the table, the doorbell rang.

She glanced at her watch and frowned because it was only seven in the morning, and she couldn't imagine who would be ringing her doorbell.

She hurried to glance out the front window and saw a sleek, dark-green car in her drive. Anticipation churned in her as she rushed to the door to open it.

Ten

As if her wishful thinking had become reality, Jared stood holding an enormous bouquet of roses, lilies and daisies. Under his arm was a large box wrapped with a big bow.

"Jared! Come inside," she said, her excitement mounting. He looked handsome, solemn, fabulous and she wanted to throw her arms around his neck. Instead, she closed the door.

Jared turned to hold the flowers out. "I was going to send you flowers and then I decided I'd bring them myself. Megan, go to dinner with me tonight."

She laughed, feeling giddy in spite of a sleepless, worried night. "You surely didn't come to ask me to dinner." Her laughter faded. "Jared, I have to apologize to—"

He placed his fingers over her lips, and the instant he touched her, her heart thudded. He took the flowers from her and tossed them aside and dropped the package, taking her into his arms and leaning over her to kiss her.

Her heart missed beats as she wound her arms around his neck and clung to him.

While she kissed Jared, the walls she'd kept around her heart crumbled forever. She loved him and she wanted to work out whatever they could. And she had to apologize to him for doubting him and accusing him of lying.

"Where's Ethan?" he paused to ask.

"At a friend's house. Sleepover. We're alone."

Jared kissed her again and all else no longer existed.

He paused, framing her face with his hands and tilting her head up as he gazed into his eyes. "I had this planned differently, but I can't wait. Meg, I love you. I've missed you terribly and I love you."

"Oh, Jared!" she exclaimed, tightening her arms around his neck and standing on tiptoe to kiss him, stopping his words. His arm banded her waist and he leaned over her, kissing her fiercely, curling her toes and melting her knees.

Her heart pounded and she moved her hips against him, wanting him with all her being. He picked her up, still kissing her, finally raising his head. "Where's a bedroom?"

She pointed and pulled his head down to kiss him. Jared headed in the direction she'd pointed, and in a moment set her on her feet beside a bed as he pulled off her T-shirt and unfastened her cutoffs.

She fumbled with his clothing, peeling it away, and in a few seconds he was putting on a condom and moving between her legs.

She arched to meet him, hugging him and closing her eyes, already in ecstasy over his declaration of love. "I love you, Jared. Maybe I always have, and that's what made finding solutions so difficult."

He kissed away conversation, loving her until they both climaxed and finally lay locked in each other's embrace.

"I love you, Megan. The happiest times of my life have been with you," he said. "I made a mistake when I left. I should have listened to my dad, stayed and talked to you. I was hurt and angry and afraid for my family."

"Shh," Megan said. "We both made mistakes. I should have let you know about Ethan, because you would have come home. I had more wrong judgments than you did, Jared. I called Dirk McGinnis, but I knew when you gave me the phone number what I would hear. Actually, it was worse than I'd imagined."

"I'm sorry. I debated telling you, and I haven't all these years because I didn't want to turn you against your dad, and I didn't want to hurt you."

"It's all done. We've both erred and suffered for it."

"I'm not making a mistake now," he said, getting out of bed and picking up his trousers to come back and take her hand. "Will you marry me, Meg?"

Her heart thudded and happiness enveloped her. She threw her arms around him. "No marriage of convenience?" she asked with laughter.

"Hardly," he responded dryly. "Unless you call the past hour merely convenient."

"Oh, yes, I'll marry you, Jared."

He slipped a ring on her finger and she gasped in awe. "Jared, that's enormous!"

"You can select something else if you don't like it."

"Don't like it! Oh, Jared, this is so wonderful," she said. "This means you'll get me to move to Dallas after all."

"We'll see what we can work out so that we're both happy. I hate to take you away from here, if you love this. How about keeping this home, and you can come here when you want to?"

"When you come with me, you mean. I'm not letting you get far for long ever again in my life."

"I hope not," he replied solemnly. "Damn, I hope not. I love you, and you've made me the happiest man on earth."

She laughed. "I think that's my line to you."

"I'm getting you and Ethan, Meg. That's irresistible!" he said, pulling her to him for a scalding kiss, and all talk of marriage was gone for the next hour.

Later, she lay in his arms, their legs entangled while she looked at her ring, turning it so the light hit it at various angles. "Jared, are you sure you aren't marrying me to get my ranch?" He chuckled and she laughed, turning on her side to look at him. "Now it'll be yours, too."

"I told you I wanted it for a bet I have with two of my cousins."

"I remember. You bet Chase and Matt. I read about them in magazines almost as much as I did you. And if my memory is correct, they're each worth a fortune. I hope all of you made that loot honestly."

"And I hope you're joking."

"Of course I am. I'm deliriously happy. Tell me more about your cousins and your bet."

"We made a bet that we'd each put five million in the pot, and whoever makes the most money during the year will win the pot."

"Good heavens! You each bet five million dollars!" she said, sitting up to stare at him. "You didn't mention the amount."

"That's right," he said, caressing her bare breasts, and she grabbed the sheet which he promptly pushed away. She caught it once more.

"I need this or I won't hear one word you're saying. You expect to turn around and sell my ranch for a huge profit?" she asked in disbelief.

"Probably. It's one project of several that would bring a quick profit. What do you think about remodeling your ranch?"

She laughed again and shrugged, stroking his thigh. "Darlin', you can do anything you want to with whatever concerns me," she said in a sultry tone. He inhaled, pulling her to him to kiss her.

It was another hour before she sat up again. "Jared, I can't believe some of this. It isn't real."

"It's happening for sure," he said, rolling over. "One more item of business—plan this wedding as soon as possible. Money is no problem, so get the staff you need. I don't want to wait," he said, smiling at her.

She smiled in return, touching the corner of his

mouth. "I can't believe how happy I am. I agree. We'll have this wedding so soon that your head will spin."

"Let's get Ethan home to tell him," Jared suggested. "Isn't he young for a sleepover?"

"This is only the second time. His friend's mother and I are really close. And the two boys are, too. I thought it would cheer him up because he's been so glum about leaving you."

"I hate to say I'm happy about that, but I can't keep from being pleased that he's missed me."

"He's missed you, all right. We both have." She wrapped her arms around Jared's neck, clinging to him happily. "But first," she said, "there's some more loving to do here. We have years to make up, Jared."

"I'll try," he said, lowering himself to kiss her.

Epilogue

Megan gazed at her reflection in the mirror and felt as if she were in a dream.

"You look gorgeous!" her aunt said, smoothing Megan's cathedral train.

"Thank you, Aunt Olga," Megan replied, smoothing her pinned-up hair.

"I still can't believe you've pulled this all together in just weeks."

"Saturday, June, the twenty-seventh," Megan said, glancing at her watch.

"I need to go. The wedding planner called me in minutes ago. Jared said he'd watch Ethan. That child is so excited. I hope he doesn't lose your wedding ring."

"Ethan won't lose it," Megan said with a laugh, thinking about Ethan being their ring bearer. She walked over to pick up her enormous bouquet of white roses and white orchids from Jared. His simple note had read, "I can't wait…all my love."

"We'll be fine," Megan said, looking at her plain satin dress that was simplicity itself.

"Megan, it's time for you," the tall, brunette wedding planner, Stacy Goldman, said, opening the door. She helped Megan with her train as they walked to the foyer. Her hand rested on her uncle's arm as the wedding planner gave her the signal to start.

Megan's gaze went to the tall, handsome man who would soon be her husband. Her heartbeat quickened, racing with joy and love for Jared. He looked incredibly handsome, his black hair neatly combed and the black tux emphasizing his dark hair and eyes.

She loved him with all her heart—the lost years seemed nothing now. Jared was here and he loved her. In minutes he would become her husband. He was already Ethan's daddy, and they'd had the birth certificate changed to state the true parents.

As she drew closer to the altar, she glanced at Ethan, the ring bearer, standing beside his daddy. She smiled at Ethan and winked at him and he smiled in return, looking up at Jared with a big smile.

And then she was standing beside Jared, and her uncle placed her hand in Jared's. His warm fingers closed around her hand as the minister began to speak, but she barely heard the words. She glowed with love for Jared, so happy, knowing she was the most fortunate woman on earth.

Together, they repeated their vows, and finally they

took Ethan's hands and the three of them walked up the aisle together. They went out the door to go around to the back entrance to come back in for pictures..

"I love your mommy, Ethan," Jared said, swinging his son up into his arms and giving Ethan a hug and a kiss on his temple. "I love you. I love both of you with all my heart," Jared said, holding Ethan with one arm while he put the other around Megan's waist to hug her.

"I love you," Ethan said, hugging Jared's neck and then looking at his mom and reaching out to give her a hug.

They returned to the sanctuary to pose for pictures. Jared's dad was his best man, and his cousins, Chase and Matt, were groomsmen, plus Tony, a close friend from Dallas.

The reception was at Jared's ranch, where tents had been set up and tables were covered with food, including a six-tier wedding cake decorated with rosebuds and small pink orchids.

Jared took Megan into his arms for the first dance and she smiled up at him. "I can't believe I'm finally your wife."

"Believe it. I'll make it real for you if we can ever get away from here. I love you, Meg, darlin', and I'm going to tell you every morning and every night."

She laughed. "No, you won't! But if you do just some of the time I'll be happy. I think Ethan is as happy as I am."

"I hope so. God knows, I'm happy, Meg," he said, gazing at her with warmth. "Let's get out of here soon. They can all party without us."

"We will," she promised.

* * *

When the music stopped, Jared's dad claimed her for the next dance. Later Megan danced with Ethan, and halfway through Jared joined them, and the three held hands, smiling and dancing together.

"Here comes Chase," Jared said, and she glanced around to see his cousin approaching.

"May I have the next dance?" Chase asked, stepping up to take her hand. Jared and Ethan left and she danced away with Chase, his green eyes sparkling. "You've made him one happy man," Chase said.

"And he's made me a happy woman, Chase. And Ethan loves his daddy beyond measure."

"It's good for all of you, then, but I know it's good for my cuz. Megan, I don't want to bring up a bad time except to say one thing—Jared was brokenhearted when he left here. You'll never know."

"I can imagine," she said, looking toward the sidelines and seeing Jared watching her while he talked to Matt and friends.

"But that's over, and now he's so happy, he's goofy. And since it was our bet that got you two together again, it's even better, because he's too in love to win. He's so muddled right now, he's probably letting all kinds of deals slip through his fingers."

She laughed. "Don't count him out yet, Chase."

Chase grinned at her. "It's amazing how much Ethan looks like Jared. He's the spitting image."

"Yes, he is. He's so happy with Jared. Jared's already a good dad."

"He surprised me there. He's nuts about Ethan. I'm

happy for all of you," Chase said, gazing at her. "This is really great." He looked past her. "Here comes Matt for his turn to dance with you."

Megan turned, seeing thick black curls and blue eyes as Matt sauntered up to them and the dance ended. "You're rushing us," Chase said as Matt jerked his thumb.

"You've had your dance." He smiled at Megan. "May I have *this* dance?"

"I'd be delighted," she said, smiling in return. "Thank you, Chase," she said.

"My pleasure, Megan. Best wishes. And take care of him," he said, brushing her cheek with a light kiss.

"I intend to," she answered. Wind caught locks of Chase's straight brown hair and tumbled them on his forehead. He combed them back in place with his fingers as he walked away.

While a ballad commenced, she turned to Matt and they began to dance. "I hope you're both happy," Matt said. "Jared is, I know."

"Thank you, and I am, too. I love him."

"I'm glad you're in the family now. Of course, you know, now you'll have to attend Dalton family reunions and Christmas gatherings."

"That sounds wonderful. I like all the Daltons I know so far."

"Good thing. You're stuck with us now. Take Jared on a long, long honeymoon, and keep him out of Chase's and my hair. We've got unfinished business, and if you'll keep him busy, we can get a lot done without him."

"Could you be referring to a bet you made?"

He grinned. "Dang! He told you about our bet?"

"Yes, he did. Knowing Jared, he'll compete, honeymoon or not."

"Speak of the devil," Matt said and they stopped as Jared stepped up to take her hand from Matt.

"You guys go away. You've danced with her long enough, and Chase has had his turn."

"How you got her to marry you, I'll never know!" Matt teased, and Jared shook his head, taking her hand to dance away from his tall cousin.

"At last, I have you to myself again."

"Your cousins are charming," Megan said.

"You bring it out in them. Have I told you that you're gorgeous?"

"Yes, but I don't mind hearing it again," she replied, looking into his dark brown eyes and feeling the current that spun between them.

When the dance ended, they posed for more pictures and then cut the cake, and shortly after, she was separated from Jared as friends crowded around to talk to her about the wedding.

In the afternoon, Jared found her and took her hand and led her to the dance floor for another dance.

Jared danced her away from the crowd and around the corner of the house, then stopped. She was surprised to see her aunt and uncle standing there with Ethan, and she glanced at Jared.

"I told them to meet us here so we could tell them good-bye," he said.

She turned to hug her aunt and then her uncle. "Thank you both for all the help you've been. Thank you for everything and for keeping Ethan for us."

"You enjoy your honeymoon. Ethan will be fine," Thomas said, kissing her cheek.

Her aunt hugged her. "I'm so happy for you, Megan. I hope you have the joy that Thomas and I have had. Now don't worry about Ethan. We'll take good care of him."

"I promise, I won't worry." She kissed her aunt and then turned to pick up Ethan. "Give me a big hug," she said and hugged him in return.

He leaned back. "You'll come back and get me?"

"Yes. We'll be gone two weeks and then we'll come get you and take you with us for two weeks."

"Wow!" he exclaimed.

"Be a good boy."

"I will," he promised, and Jared lifted him to hug him. Jared reached into his pocket and pulled out a box that was wrapped in blue paper. "Here, Ethan, this is for you."

"Thanks, Daddy!" Ethan said, taking the box and ripping into it to pull out something folded up. Jared helped him unfold it, and a wire frame covered by a nylon net popped up.

"It's a bug cage, Ethan. Now you can catch a bug and put it in there and watch it. You'll have to feed it something or put some grass or flowers in the cage. After a day or two, let it go so it can go home."

"Thanks!" Ethan repeated, his eyes shining.

"We'll get going before we're missed," Jared said, taking her arm with another flurry of good-byes.

"Jared, what about your family? And I have to change clothes."

"I've already told my family good-bye, and I told

them we're slipping out. You can change on the plane. Your aunt gave me your dress and your things, and they're on the plane. Let's go." Holding hands, they ran to a waiting limo where Jared's chauffeur held the door for them.

She fell into Jared's arms, turning to kiss him, aware he had closed the partition to the front of the car and that they had privacy, with darkened windows.

"I love you," she finally said, raising her head. His hair was tangled over his forehead and he opened his eyes slowly, gazing at her with warmth in his expression.

"I love you, Mrs. Dalton."

"That sounds wonderful, Jared. I can't ever hear that enough," she said, smiling at him and tracing his lips with her finger as he smiled in return. "Now, where are we going?"

"To the airport. I have a seaplane that will fly us to Minnesota, to a cabin I bought on a lake there. We'll spend two days there and then we'll fly to my home on the Mediterranean. You'll like it. In two weeks, we'll come back and get Ethan, and we'll all go to Switzerland."

"Jared, this is a dream."

"No, it's real. I'll convince you of that today and tonight," he said in a husky voice.

"And how long before we get to that cabin in the woods?" she asked, running her hand across his chest.

"About two hours."

She groaned. "That's forever, Jared."

"I agree, but it's the best I could do, short of going to the hotel in town. We'll think of some way to make the time fly," he said, leaning down to kiss her again.

* * *

They finally were on the last approach, and the pilot landed on the ice-smooth surface of a brilliant blue lake. A man came out in a small boat to take them to the dock. Nestled in tall pines was a sprawling two-story chateau with a corral, barn and outbuildings.

"Jared, how many people live around here? And a cabin? This is a mansion in the woods!"

"There are a lot of people who work for me who have homes up here, and there are a few people who live around here all the time. It's an elegant cabin, I'll admit, but I don't care to rough it for my honeymoon."

At the door, Jared scooped her up to carry her over the threshold and set her on her feet.

She barely saw the house, glancing at polished oak floors, lots of pine and dark wood walls, but the minute Jared set her on her feet and closed the door, she turned to slide her arms around his neck. "Are we finally alone?"

"Yes," he said, drawing her to him. As she kissed him she could feel his fingers tugging free the long row of tiny buttons to her dress.

"Jared, you'll never know how much I love you and want you. I want to make up for all we lost. I want to kiss every inch of you, caress you, drive you wild," she drawled in a sultry tone, running one hand over his hip and winding the other in his hair. "You've always been the only man in my life."

"Ah, Meg, love. I've loved you since that moment on campus when you said hello to me. I don't think I ever really stopped loving you. I tried, but there was never anyone else I loved," he admitted, kissing her throat and ear, turning to cover her mouth with his until he paused. "I just didn't recognize what I felt for you."

His kisses were passionate, his lips warm on hers, and he shifted to caress her with one hand while he held her with his other arm. He pushed away her dress and inhaled, running his hands over her.

He raised his head. "You've made me the happiest man on earth, Meg."

She stood on tiptoe to kiss him, finally leaning away, "I love you and I want to make you happy always. Jared, this is so good," she whispered and then placed her mouth on his.

Her heart pounded with joy and she held him tightly, knowing they were a family now, and she would love him with all her heart for the rest of her life.

* * * * *

MONTANA MISTRESS

BY
SARA ORWIG

With love to Hannah, Ellen, Rachel,
Colin, Elisabeth and Cameron

Prologue

"This is August, and next May the time is up for our bet," Chase Bennett said, gazing at his two favorite cousins as they relaxed at a table in the VIP lounge of the busy Chicago air terminal. "Hope you guys have been productive."

"Don't worry about us," Matt Rome replied easily with a twinkle in his blue eyes. "You take care of yourself."

"Our newlywed here probably can't think, much less get out and earn a dollar. He's in love," Chase teased, drawing out the last words as he raked his dark brown hair away from his forehead.

"I think he just married to get her money," Matt added, glancing at his watch.

"None of us would go to that length to win," Jared said. "I didn't expect to marry, and I know neither of you do. Life is full of surprises. Money wasn't why I married Megan, but it's a nice plus on the side. When we made our bet to see who could make the most money in a year, I had no intention of losing, marriage or no marriage."

Chase swallowed the last of his coffee. "I'm glad we were all in Chicago at the same time. You fellows are difficult to catch. If you'd get out of Wyoming more, cowboy, we could get together."

"I'll get out of Wyoming. Just let me know when and where," Matt said, finishing his drink and standing. "My plane is ready and waiting. We'll leave as soon as I'm on board, so I better go. Good to see you guys."

Jared stood, dropping bills on the table. "That's for the drinks. I'll see you guys at Christmas. In the meantime, keep working. Or give up. Either way, I'm going to win in May."

"You may be in for a slight surprise," Chase said, smiling.

"You think your new oil discovery is going to flow liquid gold into your coffers. You have to get it out of the ground first, and you're not absolutely certain it's as big as you think. In short, you don't have a sure thing," Jared said with a good-natured lightness.

"Dream on, cuz," Chase answered, unruffled because the three had competed since they were small boys. He held out his hand to shake with each cousin. "It's been great to see both of you. We're doing better about seeing each other this year, but having a wedding helped."

"Don't count on me for another one," Matt said. "I think both of you know better than that."

"No wedding in my future, either," Chase said. "Jared, you have our sympathy, you poor sap."

"Neither of you know what carnal delights of marriage you're missing," Jared said, and both Chase and Matt rolled their eyes.

"Go on back to the little woman," Chase instructed. "Matt and I will take our single life." They paused in the hallway. "I've got an appointment soon, so I have to run. I'm spending two more days here before I go on to Montana."

"See you, Chase. Take care," Matt said and waved as he walked away with Jared, who called goodbye again.

Chase headed toward the front and his waiting limo. In spite of the good-natured teasing, he intended to win the bet with his cousins. He thought he had the best chance of winning, but he knew it would be stiff competition. He thought about Jared's recent marriage, a surprise. No marriage loomed anywhere in his future. He was never falling into that trap.

One

"Be nice to the man." Laurel Tolson repeated the words of her red-haired hotel manager, Brice Neilsen. She gritted her teeth. "Be nice, be nice, be nice." She recited the litany to herself, glancing at her bare ring finger but seeing the 14-carat diamond that Edward Varnum had given her. She pictured Edward's flashing blue eyes, remembered being in his arms and then she clamped her jaw shut.

Today, the first week in August, another wealthy playboy, the oil magnate Chase Bennett, was coming to her hometown of Athens, Montana. She wanted no part of him, but over the next few weeks she was going to have to feed and entertain him and his executives, and she would have to be as friendly as Brice had cautioned.

Glancing at her watch, she planned to return to the hotel in less than two hours, since Chase Bennett should arrive later and she wanted to be present to greet him. She imagined he would travel in the same manner that her ex-fiancé had, in a limo with a staff at his beck and call.

As she drove along a wide street of Athens, she reflected on how she had grown up in a friendly place. The small town had none of the bustle and traffic of Dallas, her current residence. Tall black walnut trees and pines shaded the street, and wide lawns surrounded the two-story frame houses that always meant home to her.

She inhaled the crisp, fresh air and turned into the hospital parking lot, saying another prayer that this day her father would come out of the coma. Each time she thought about him, her insides clenched. How it hurt to see him lying immobile in the hospital, because her dad had always been strong and filled with vitality.

Taking another deep breath, she squared her shoulders. She loved her father—as did everyone who knew him. He was an elegant charmer, full of fun before his stroke last month.

When she turned into an empty parking place at the hospital, the roar of a motorcycle interrupted her thoughts. Glancing over her shoulder, she watched a deeply tanned man race past her, his dark brown hair ruffled by the wind. He wore a red bandana around his forehead, a tight T-shirt and jeans. She frowned slightly at the noise he created in a hospital lot, but then she forgot him as she climbed out of her car.

Inside the hospital she greeted front desk attendants and hurried through an empty corridor to enter an elevator. She pressed the button for the fifth floor, but before the doors closed, a booted foot stopped them.

The doors opened automatically, and she recognized the biker when he stepped into the elevator. She couldn't stop staring. He was strikingly handsome. Tall and broad-shouldered, he dominated the small space with a commanding air as if he were in charge of the entire hospital. The thought crossed her mind that few women could keep from noticing that his snug T-shirt revealed muscles and the tight jeans hugged narrow hips. Adding to his rugged appeal was his dark brown hair, a tangle from the wind with locks falling over the red bandana. His sunglasses were pushed up on his head. His thickly lashed, startling green eyes were his most breathtaking feature, and she could imagine how easily women succumbed to them.

As he turned to make eye contact with her, she was held immobile in his riveting gaze. Electricity crackled between them, and she wondered if he was aware of the aura that surrounded him. She suspected he was fully cognizant of his effect on women.

He smiled, revealing creases that bracketed his mouth and softened his features. It was an enticing, coaxing smile and had probably melted feminine hearts as easily as his bedroom eyes.

"Hi," he said in a deep voice.

"Good morning," she replied. She couldn't recall ever seeing him before, and no female could possibly forget him or avoid noticing him.

"Can you tell me where the Tolson Hotel is located?"

Startled by his question because she had come from the hotel, she nodded. "Yes, you're almost there now. Two more blocks to the west and one block to the east. You're not from here, but you're visiting someone?" she asked, wondering aloud why he was in the hospital.

"I have a friend who flew in last night and had emergency gallbladder surgery. I'm here for a visit. You can come with me and meet my friend if you want to verify my story," he said with a twinkle in his eyes, and she could feel heat flush her cheeks.

"Sorry. It's not often you find solitary strangers in this hospital, because people know each other throughout the area—whether they live on a ranch or in town." As soon as the elevator stopped at the second floor and the doors opened, the stranger didn't move. When she glanced at him, he merely smiled.

"You're going to miss your floor," she remarked.

"I've decided to ride up and back down again so I can talk

to you. I didn't expect to meet a beautiful woman, and I have a few minutes. I don't see a ring on your finger."

"No. You're observant," she said, not caring to discuss herself with a stranger.

"After you finish your visit, it would be nice if you'd show me the downtown area because I've never been here before. I don't know anyone, and my friend won't be getting out and around. I'd like to take you to dinner afterwards."

She smiled back at him. "Two blocks beyond the hotel is the Athens Chamber of Commerce and the tourist bureau. If you'll go in there, you can arrange for a walking tour and they will answer your questions about our town."

"That is definitely not what I had in mind," he said, looking more amused. "If you're worried because we're strangers, I can give you some of my background and you can meet my friend. If you show me around, we won't be alone. We'll be on foot in public. Where's the danger in that? Unless you have a better place to suggest, I'll take you to dinner in the hotel later—still very public."

"Thank you, but I have commitments. Try the Tourist Bureau."

"So, when this elevator stops on the fifth floor, you're going to walk out of my life forever?"

"I'm afraid so," she said, smiling at him while she stepped closer to the door. "You'll get over it," she added lightly. He moved closer to her and she inhaled, catching the scent of an enticing aftershave.

"You're breaking my heart," he said in a lower tone. "And your name is?"

"I think we'll remain anonymous strangers. And I'm sure you won't have any difficulty finding someone to show you the town."

"What makes you think that?" he asked with great innocence.

She laughed. "We're a friendly place, and you're not

bashful," she replied instead of answering truthfully that she was certain he could find several women who would be more than glad to escort him around Athens.

He smiled in return. "If you live here, I suspect I'll see you again."

She nodded. "Perhaps you will," she answered, half tempted to toss aside caution and show him the downtown. She gazed up into his eyes and knew she was making the right choice, but she had regrets. This stranger might be an antidote for Edward and their breakup.

The elevator stopped and she stepped out.

"Goodbye, until we meet again," he said.

She waved and went on her way, her thoughts on her father, and the stranger ceased to exist.

Feeling helpless and hurting, for the next hour she sat at her father's bedside, relieving the private-duty nurse the family had hired. As machines regularly pumped and an IV dripped, she watched the monitors steadily charting his condition, which wasn't changing.

"Dad," she whispered once, touching his hand. "I'm here. We want you to come home," she said, tears filling her eyes. "I'm selling the hotel and a potential buyer is arriving in town soon," she said quietly.

Knowing her dad couldn't hear her, she stopped talking. A charmer, her dad had a huge weakness that she had learned about in college, two years after her mother had died—he loved to gamble. But she hadn't known the full extent of it, that it was a compulsion and that he owed large sums of money.

She mulled over the shocks and changes that had occurred in the past month. First the devastating stroke, and then before he had lapsed into the coma, he had held her hand and, with tears in his eyes, confessed to her that he'd had huge gambling debts he had covered by mortgaging the hotel and getting a smaller loan from the bank with their family ranch as collateral. Sounding anguished and so unlike himself, he had told her that he didn't know what they would do if something happened to him.

Laurel had promised him she would take care of the others and told him to not worry, that they would be all right. Then he'd lapsed into a coma and the future had changed.

Except for family, very few people in the area knew about their finances. Their banker, a lifelong friend, and his staff had been privy to the confidential information about her dad's loans. Yet no one but the bank president knew the loans were for paying off gambling debts.

The hotel had been mortgaged to the hilt, and if she sold the Tolson, she would use the money to pay off the mortgage. When she sold the Tall T Ranch, she could pay the smaller loan against the ranch and hopefully, have enough left to buy a home in Dallas for her family and help her sisters go to college. She intended to make as much profit as possible on both the hotel and the ranch.

Her father's secret about the gambling debts was safe with her, and she prayed that the bank would keep their business confidential.

Glancing at her watch, she picked up her purse and stood. "I'm going back to the hotel. I love you." She bent to brush his cheek with a kiss.

Wiping her eyes, she went out the door, talked briefly with the nurse and hurried to her car. She ran a couple of errands, then called the ranch to talk to her grandmother and younger sisters. Next she spoke to their ranch foreman and finally headed back to the Tolson Hotel, which had been built more than a hundred years earlier by her great-great-grandfather. The six-story honey-colored Montana limestone structure was ornate, clearly belonging to another era. As she walked through the lobby, she noticed with satisfaction the oriental rugs on a highly polished chestnut plank floor, potted palms and deep red leather furniture. Hurricane glass fixtures added to the turn-of-the-century ambience. In the hall to her office, she spotted the tall, blue-eyed Brice and motioned to him to join her in her office.

She put away her purse in the antique, hand-carved mahogany desk as the manager knocked and entered her office, crossing the room to take a chair facing her. Brice was nattily dressed in a charcoal suit for the arrival of the VIPs later in the day.

"I take it His Highness hasn't arrived," she said.

"I know you're stressed, Laurel, but remember, be nice to the man." Smoothing red hair that already was parted with every hair in place, Brice shook his head. "They say trouble comes in threes, and you've had your three, so maybe the arrival of Chase Bennett will turn out to be a blessing and solve some of your problems if he buys the hotel."

"I know," she said, sitting behind her desk and tapping her finger. "I expect another Edward and I didn't see any limos out front when I arrived."

"He may be another Edward. Don't hold that against him. Chase Bennett is worth a billion and he's intent on buying property here because of his new oil field, so smile at the man. He's a handsome bachelor and you're single and pretty."

"Thank you, Brice, but believe me, the last thing on this earth I'm interested in is another playboy." She shuddered.

Brice made a steeple of his hands. "You're sincere about that, aren't you?"

"Yes, I am. What's so difficult to understand?"

"Don't bite my head off. If you're so worried about the girls and your grandmother and your dad's health and medical bills, a rich friend or husband would solve your financial problems."

She shook her head. "Sorry if I snapped at you, but another Edward wouldn't be worth the money. I'll take my responsibilities as they come."

"How's your dad?"

"He's the same. Thanks for asking."

"Your dad is a strong man. I think he'll come through this."

"Thanks for the encouragement," she said, knowing Brice was always the optimist. "Do you think everything in the hotel is ready?"

"As we'll ever be. The hotel looks marvelous—and it's summer, so we have it almost totally booked through August, although that part may not interest him. I'm sure he'll have no problem filling rooms. A lot of his people are here because they've already started working on the new oil field." With a glance at his watch, Brice stood. "I'll be in the kitchen, making certain all our supplies have arrived."

"Thanks for all you're doing." She nodded and stood.

"You're welcome. It's my job. Please remember—"

"Be nice to the man," she finished for him. "I'll try my best. After all, I need to sell this place desperately. If I do, I want to tell Dad even if he won't know it."

"I understand," Brice replied, smiling and giving her a look filled with sympathy.

When they parted, she rode the elevator to the suite she occupied on the top floor. Chase Bennett had reserved the other two suites, which included the largest suite that ran along the entire south side, plus half of both the east and west sides of the hotel. She guessed he would take the larger suite of the two he'd booked and assumed his closest associate would take the other.

She stepped out of the elevator and was surprised to see the biker from the hospital emerge from the second elevator. Dark locks of his wind-blown hair still fell over the red bandana wrapped around his forehead, and his aviator shades hid his eyes. He had no luggage with him.

"I see you found the hotel," she said, wondering what he was doing and if he had followed her.

Removing his sunglasses, he turned to her. The moment their gazes met, the chemistry that had sparked earlier between them ignited again, even hotter this time.

"Yes, thanks," he answered easily, walking toward her to stop only yards away.

"I'm sorry, but this floor is occupied," she said. "These are suites and they're all booked."

One corner of his mouth lifted in a grin. "The desk clerk said I'd be on the sixth floor."

She smiled. "What's your room number? You're probably on the fifth floor," she said, realizing he might work for Chase Bennett.

He fished in a pocket. "Believe it or not, I have a suite on six."

"I believe you," she said, reassessing him and guessing he was in Bennett's company. Red flags of warning went up in her mind. This handsome, sexy stranger was too appealing. He was probably almost as wealthy as his boss and someone she should guard against getting to know well, even though she suspected few women wanted to shield their hearts or anything else from him.

"Do you work for Chase Bennett?" she asked.

"Indeed, I do. I think it's time we introduce ourselves," he said, holding out his hand, his green eyes dancing with wicked mischief. She wondered if she had offended him earlier by turning down his invitation to show him the downtown—a legitimate request if he was one of Bennett's employees.

"I'm Chase Bennett," he said as she extended her hand and his closed around it.

Two

Shocked, she stared at him while his warm hand enveloped hers, sending tingles spiraling through her.

"Oh, my! You don't look like your pictures. I think I made a dreadful mistake this morning," she blurted, feeling her cheeks flush.

"You can make up for it," he replied in a deeper voice that filled his words with innuendo and stirred another sizzle.

"And how can I do that?" She couldn't resist flirting in return, speaking in a sultry tone that made one of his dark eyebrows arch. Desire was obvious in his expression.

"Have dinner with me tonight," he said.

"I'd be delighted and I'll show you our town," she replied, aware of her hand still held in his while his thumb ran lightly back and forth across her knuckles. Her emotions churned because he was another moneyed womanizer, and distaste curled in her with a sour urge to keep as much distance as possible between them. On the other hand, she wanted to win him over in hopes he would like the hotel and buy it.

"Deal," he said. "And your name is—?"

Her cheeks flamed again as she realized she'd forgotten to introduce herself. "I'm sorry. I'm doing everything wrong with you."

"Not at all," he drawled. "You shouldn't be expected to recognize me from my pictures," he added, combing his hair back from his face with his fingers. Now she could see the resemblance, but she realized she never gave a thought to the possibility of a biker being Chase Bennett.

"I'm Laurel Tolson," she said.

"Of the hotel?" he asked, waving his hand to take in his surroundings.

"Yes. You reserved two of the suites on this floor."

"I thought I had the entire floor," he remarked with surprise in his tone.

She shook her head. "There are three suites, one large and two smaller, and I live in one of the suites. If you really need this entire floor—"

"Ah, that's even better," he interrupted. "You and I will have this floor to ourselves," he said, his voice once again becoming deeper.

"You have both suites for yourself?" she asked in surprise.

"Yes. I like privacy. Look, I have to clean up. Are you free in about half an hour to show me around the hotel?"

"Certainly. I'll be happy to do so," she answered briskly, withdrawing her hand from his. "We can eat in the hotel's main restaurant, and it'll be complements of the house."

"I believe I asked you to dinner, not the other way around," he said, looking amused again.

"Maybe we'll do that another time. Let me show off my hotel tonight," she coaxed, smiling at him as he flashed a smile in return that made her knees weak.

"That's also a deal," he said. He glanced at his watch. "Let's make it three o'clock. Which door is yours?"

"Give me your keys and I'll show you your suites," she said, holding out her hand.

As he placed two small plastic cards in her hand, his fingers brushed hers, a light touch that she noticed. She crossed the hall, aware of him beside her and then holding the door for her to enter after she unlocked it. "Does this look satisfactory?" she asked, turning to him.

"Beyond my wildest hope," he replied, his gaze on her. She realized he was again flirting.

Trying to hang on to her patience, she smiled. "I'm referring to the suite."

"Ah, the suite," he said as if he had forgotten anything else existed except the two of them. When he looked around, she did also. She noted with satisfaction the chilled bottle of champagne in an ice bucket along with the large platter of hors d'oeuvres she'd ordered to be sent to his suite the moment he checked into the hotel.

Two baskets of fresh flowers from the local florist lent a festive air, and she decided everything was the best she and the hotel staff could possibly achieve. He glanced around at the marble and mahogany tables, the red velvet upholstered chairs and camelback couch, the paintings in gilt frames and the hurricane lamps, the fireplace and its granite mantel. His gaze returned to her.

"Very attractive," he said politely.

"Thank you. Even though this is an old hotel, we try to stay first-class and have attempted to maintain the historical ambiance. I can imagine the luxurious places you've stayed."

"This is excellent. I know there are meeting rooms downstairs. Is there a desk anywhere in my suite?" he asked, prowling the room like a cat in a new home.

"Yes. It's in the bedroom," she replied, leading the way. "If you want it moved, we can do that easily." She stopped in the center of the bedroom and motioned toward an antique rosewood desk, which was less ornately carved than the one in her office. She was suddenly very aware of the high-backed cherry wood king-size bed.

Looking around, Chase stood with his hands on his hips, and he dominated the large bedroom as much as he had the small space of the elevator.

"The desk is fine in here," he said.

"Good. If you'll come with me, I'll show you the other suite."

He stepped close and held out his hand. "You don't need to bother. Give me the key. Is there an adjoining door?"

"No, there aren't any adjoining doors between the suites. You'd better let me show you which of the other two suites is yours, so you don't try to get into mine."

"And that would be bad?" he asked.

"I'm not worried, Mr. Bennett," she answered with a smile.

He stepped closer and ran his finger along her shoulder. She could detect his aftershave again, and her nerves tingled from his proximity, but it was his finger touching her shoulder that stirred desire.

"No 'Mr. Bennett,' please. It's Chase," he said in a warm tone. "You and I are going to get to know each other and not on a professional basis," he said. "We'll start today, even though the first hour will be business."

"We'd be much better off to keep things impersonal and on a business basis," she stated briskly, wondering if she was saying that for her own benefit.

"I can't think of one good reason why we'd be better off on an impersonal basis for our friendship." He caught a lock of her hair that had come loose from its clip. He toyed with the blond strands, winding them around his finger. "I hope it's up close and personal and business has nothing to do with what happens between us as a man and a woman. A beautiful woman whom the man wants to know."

She laughed. "I find that a real stretch, but I'm looking forward to dinner tonight."

He touched the corner of her mouth, tickling her slightly. "Ah, I'll have to make you laugh often. You have a great smile."

"Thank you," she said, heading for the door.

"Show me which suite is yours, so I don't try to get into the wrong place."

She stepped into the hall, getting out her own key. "Right there," she said, pointing. "How's your friend in the hospital?"

"He's doing fine, and if he were home, he'd be released today, but since he's here, I've made arrangements for him to stay in the hospital another two days at least. Once he's released, he'll fly home in my company plane with someone accompanying him."

"That's good. I'm glad he's recovering."

"May I see where you live?" Chase asked.

"Of course," she said, thankful she had picked up her things earlier. She opened the door to her suite and they entered a smaller living area with blue-upholstered mahogany furniture instead of red.

He turned to look at her. "You realize I'll know where you live and what it's like."

"They're all similar with a few variations in decor."

He walked up to her again, stopping close. "I'm looking forward to this afternoon and tonight. When you stepped off the elevator at the hospital, I thought it might take me days to find you."

She smiled at him. "You were going to search for me? I'm flattered."

"Yes, I was. A fabulous-looking woman. A chemistry between us—which I know you feel," he said in a raspy voice. "A woman who was a challenge to me. How could I resist trying to find you?"

"I'm not a challenge, Chase," she said, aware of saying merely his first name. Already they were on a personal, first-name basis and had scheduled an evening together. She knew she wasn't exercising the caution she had intended to use

when she met him. It could easily be Edward all over again
except Chase Bennett did not seem the type to get engaged.

"You turned down my invitation in the hospital," he
reminded her.

"And you're not accustomed to getting turned down or to
hearing 'no,' are you?"

He shrugged. "I hear it, but if it concerns something I
want, I go after it anyway. Unless it's a woman who doesn't
want me around. I won't intrude. But if there's a fiery chemistry that both of us feel, I'm not going to back off that one,"
he said and ran his fingers lightly across her hand.

"Well, I haven't said no this time. I don't go out with
strangers, so that was why I refused earlier. You come with
all sorts of credentials. We've got an afternoon and evening
together, so I'll get ready."

One corner of his mouth lifted in a crooked smile. "I can
take a broad hint like that. I'm leaving and I'll be back at your
door at three."

He closed the door behind him and Laurel let out her
breath. She had done everything wrong with him, but he
hadn't seemed bothered that she had turned him down at the
hospital or had assumed he couldn't be the occupant of one
of the suites.

She went to find something to wear and to shower again.
Even though her pulse raced when she was around him, she
didn't want to spend the evening with him; she had to keep reminding herself of the purpose behind all this—it was an opportunity to promote the hotel. So far she had to admit that in
most ways he wasn't another Edward. She expected to find that
arrogant, "I-own-the-world" attitude manifest itself soon
enough. And there were similarities: Chase was brash, filled
with all possible self-confidence, as determined to get his way
as Edward had been. Chase happened to like motorcycles and
Edward liked limos. Each could afford whatever he wanted, and
she guessed they felt the same where women were concerned.

Also, she suspected the limos would appear before long. And she was certain he was far more of a womanizer than Edward, who had none of the sexy charm of Chase Bennett. She'd read about Chase in tabloids, in the Dallas paper and in magazines, and he'd always had a beautiful woman at his side—but she'd never noticed the same one twice.

Searching through her closet, she selected a simple burgundy linen dress that was sleeveless and ended above her knees. She laid out high-heeled sandals. After taking down her hair, she shook her head to let it fall freely across her shoulders and then pinned it high on each side while her thoughts were on Chase Bennett and his fabulous smile. He was getting ready to spend the evening with her. What were his plans for the night?

Chase let the warm water pour over him, closing his eyes and raising his face into the spray. In minutes he turned his back to the gushing water. His thoughts were on Laurel Tolson. He had been surprised when he'd learned who she was. His staff had researched the town, the properties for sale and the hotel, but no mention had been made to him of the owner except that Radley Tolson had had a stroke and was in the hospital and his daughter was handling the hotel in the meantime.

She was a stunning willowy blonde with luscious curves, and she had flirted briefly with him this afternoon, although it was after she'd discovered his identity and not before. This always sent warnings that the woman might be far more interested in his fortune than in him. She wanted to sell him her hotel, and from what his staff had told him, the hotel had a large mortgage, while the Tolson ranch was three-fourths paid off. She wasn't without funds, but whatever she had would be paltry compared with his worth.

He had first noticed her as she was walking into the hospital and he'd hurried across the parking lot to catch up. He'd been intrigued by her blond hair, which looked fantastic in the sunlight. That and her enticing walk and long legs.

Maybe he'd spent too much time without a woman, but he'd been caught up in work 24/7 for more than the past month.

He had rushed to avoid losing sight of her, barely stopping the elevator doors from closing, and then had met her gaze and been riveted. They had a chemistry between them that he hoped to explore.

She had been cool and unreceptive, yet in spite of her aloof manner, she had sounded breathless.

He grinned, remembering how she'd seen him as a biker and discounted that he could be Chase Bennett. To her own embarrassment. She said she had done everything wrong with him, but it had merely amused him and he had not been offended. When she had flirted, his interest had escalated.

He wanted her in his bed. Soon. As he shaved, he continued to think about Laurel. She was single, which surprised him. Friendly toward him, once she knew who he was. She wanted to sell the family hotel to him—that would give him some leverage—and he suspected that was why she'd accepted his dinner invitation. He could still picture her standing in the elevator, trying to remain cool and aloof but exuding an air of awareness of the chemistry between them. While still wearing his sunglasses, he had looked her over carefully, starting with her silky blond hair clipped behind her head, her thickly lashed blue eyes and her creamy skin. Her plain white blouse had clung to full curves and then was tucked into a narrow waistband of a tan skirt ending above enticing knees. He could envision her long, shapely legs wrapped around him. From that first moment he had been interested in her. Then he'd removed his shades, looked into her eyes and received an electric jolt that held the heat of a lightning bolt.

Just thinking about it aroused him. He wanted her naked, pressed against him, beneath him in his bed. Why hadn't she married? he wondered, yet he didn't care. He just knew that while he was here, he intended to seduce her.

It had been awhile since the last woman in his life. And he'd been happy to tell Carole goodbye. He recalled the tall blonde he'd had the last affair with. She'd been sexy, cooperative, enticing at first. But then she'd become too clingy, and he'd been happy to break it off permanently. Work had easily replaced her, and he'd all but forgotten her. Maybe that's why Laurel was having such a strong effect on him—because he'd gone too long between women.

Beautiful, sexy women were easy to find, but when it began to get serious, he wanted out. No getting locked into a life of routine for him. Seven or eight months with one woman and he began to get edgy and want his freedom. Often much sooner.

Chase raised his face to the water and then shook his head. Tonight he would be with Laurel. Anticipation heightened. He turned off the water, stepped out and wrapped a towel around his waist. Picking up his cell phone, he called Luke Perkins, his Senior Vice President of Land Administration, to come upstairs so they could talk.

Chase walked into the closet, which had already been filled by his staff. He chose a navy suit and tie and a white shirt. As he dressed, he realized that Athens was small and since everyone would know everyone else, he'd be able to find out Laurel's history easily if she didn't tell him tonight.

At a knock on the door, Chase called out "Come in," and Luke Perkins strolled into the room. His tall, black-haired vice president had been with Chase from the earliest days, and Chase could always count on Luke's judgement.

"Have you looked over the hotel?" Chase asked as he stepped into loafers, combed his straight brown hair and put on his watch, glancing at the time to see he still had twenty minutes before he was to meet Laurel.

"Yes. This hotel is overpriced for its age. Of course, it's probably priced that way as a point to start bargaining from, and I'm sure she doesn't expect to get her asking price. Her father, Radley Tolson, is in the hospital in a coma, but she has power of attorney and has been appointed his guardian, so she can do what she wants and it's all legal. The grandmother and Laurel Tolson's two sisters live on their ranch. This family settled this area in the territorial days in the nineteenth century. The family ranch is for sale also."

"Know why she's selling their property?" Chase asked.

"The real estate broker and the banker both think she's selling because of her father's health," Luke replied, stretching out in a wing chair. "He oversaw running the ranch and the hotel. Now even if he survives this stroke, his health is gone. She's made a life for herself in Dallas. There's the grandmother and younger sisters to care for. From what I've heard, it's a close family and this daughter is in charge now."

"A real family person," Chase said with coldness. He tried to avoid getting involved with anyone into commitment or family, which amounted to the same thing. They wanted to extend that commitment to him. He valued his bachelor freedom, and he wasn't getting into the marriage trap his parents had been in, tied down constantly. He'd watched them grow older without ever getting to do anything except farm and raise their family.

"That's right. She's a landscape architect with her own business in Dallas. She was engaged to Edward Varnum."

Chase stopped combing his hair and turned to look at Luke. "Edward Varnum? I know who he is, but I've never really been around him. He inherited a fortune that his grandfather made and his father increased. His grandfather patented some kind of equipment that goes in every plane ever made. That was the start. Now he has multiple international enterprises. They're no longer engaged?"

"No. I think it's a fairly recent break, but from what I understand, Edward is definitely out of her life."

"So, she's on the rebound. Know whether she did the breaking up or Varnum?"

"No. I haven't heard any rumors yet. I'm sure I will."

"I'm meeting her at three and she'll show the hotel to me," Chase remarked, and Luke headed toward the door.

"I better clear out. We have an appointment with her in the morning, and she's taking five of us on a tour. I'm surprised she didn't wait and lump you in with us tomorrow, but maybe this is a personal, individual tour where she can try the hard sell."

"Have you met her?"

"Oh, yes," Luke replied, grinning, his gray eyes twinkling. "She's a real head turner. Don't forget, this is a business deal."

"I'll remember. Did you leave the folder with all the figures in it for me to read?"

"I did," Luke answered, motioning toward the desk.

"Are we still set to drive to the field Wednesday morning?" Chase asked, putting his billfold into his pocket and picking up keys.

"Yes, we are. I'll see you later, Chase." As Luke closed the door behind him, Chase crossed to the desk to retrieve the folder and read the figures for the hotel. Gazing out the window, he thought about the new oil discovery and the land and mineral rights he'd acquired. His fortune was going to grow. Here in this quiet, sparsely populated state, oil would flow and money would be made. His thoughts jumped to the bet he had with his two closest cousins: whoever could make the most money by next May would be the winner, with each man putting five million dollars into the pot. With this oil field he hoped to win. Forgetting about the bet, Chase envisioned Laurel's blue eyes and her smile. He closed the folder and left his suite, crossing the wide hall to knock on her door.

When the door swung back, his pulse accelerated. She'd let down her blond hair in the back in a silky fall. The simple lines of her dress were perfect to emphasize her beauty.

"You're gorgeous," he said in a husky voice.

"Thank you," she answered, smiling at him. "Come in and let me switch off my computer."

He stepped inside and watched the sway of her hips as she hurried away from him.

The burgundy dress was straight and hugged her hips. He imagined her without it, noticing the long zipper down the back of the dress and wishing he could take her into his arms right now to pull down that zipper.

She smiled at him as she approached. "Is this strictly business tonight, or part business, part pleasure?"

"Definitely pleasure with you," he said.

"If you'd like, we can go downstairs to the bar and have a drink first, complements of the house. This will be an informal evening as far as business is concerned."

"Forget work other than showing me around," he said, the purchase of her hotel the last thing on his mind. He could worry about that later and let his efficient, reliable staff get the pertinent facts.

As he held the door for her, he inhaled a whiff of an exotic perfume and noticed the slight swing of her shimmering blond hair. Taking a deep breath, he fell into step beside her.

"Tell me about the hotel," he said when they were in the elevator.

"My great-great-grandfather built the original hotel in 1890. Billings was founded earlier than Athens, and the railroad went through there. Later a line was laid from Billings to Athens, and we're also on the river," she said, gazing up at him with wide blue eyes that captured his concentration. "Then the hotel burned and this one was constructed on the same spot in 1902," she continued. "Two years ago my dad had it remodeled and refurbished. So with that, you have our history."

"The hotel's history. Not Laurel Tolson's. I intend to learn that, too."

"It's not nearly as colorful and nothing out of the ordinary. I grew up in Montana."

"We have that in common. So did I."

"Did you really?" she asked, sounding surprised. "I thought you were a Texan."

"I live in Houston now, but our family home is a ranch near Dillon. That's where I grew up."

"It's a pretty part of the state. So we do have things in common. I grew up here in town and also on a ranch. That same great-great-grandfather is the one who acquired the land we have. He managed to keep the hotel and ranch going, and the generations since have been able to do the same."

"Do you live in the hotel all the time or on the ranch?"

"Actually, like you, I live in Texas. I have a landscape business in Dallas, and I did the landscaping for the hotel."

"Later, we can take a walk outside and I'll see what you've done."

When they emerged from the elevator, she led the way to a darkened bar with large mirrors, low lighting, walnut paneling and dark walnut booths and tables. A small dance floor was at the opposite end of the room from the ornately carved bar. So far, all he had seen of the hotel had exceeded his expectations. He hadn't anticipated anything terrific in the small ranching town.

Sitting at a corner booth, Chase faced her and thought about the coming month. When they'd discovered the rich oil field where he held leases and mineral rights and owned the land, he'd thought good fortune had fallen in his lap. After meeting Laurel, he considered himself doubly fortunate. From that first moment he had been captivated by her.

A small light glowing on the table threw a warm, rosy glow on her and was reflected in her crystal-blue eyes. His gaze traveled down to her mouth, and he wondered what it would be like to kiss her. He vowed he would know before the night was over.

"I saw a dance floor as we entered the bar. What time does the music start?" he asked.

"After eight every evening. We have a small band that

plays, so it's live music and mostly old favorites with some rock and western thrown in."

"Then we'll come back later tonight and dance. In the meantime, tell me more about the hotel and the town," he said, leaning back and opening his navy jacket.

Their waiter arrived, interrupting the conversation. "Chase, I want you to meet Trey, who's been with us for a long time," Laurel said, and Chase greeted the waiter. "Anytime you're in the bar," she continued, "he will see that you and your staff are well taken care of, so let him know what you want." She turned to her employee. "Trey, this is Mr. Bennett, who'll be our guest."

"Welcome to the Sundown Bar," Trey said. "Here is a wine and drink list." He placed a thick black folder in front of each of them. "I'll give you a moment to look it over."

Chase nodded, and she looked at hers although he suspected she knew it from memory. She shoved aside the menu at the same time Chase closed his. "Now, back to your interest in the hotel and the town," she said.

"Where do your guests come from? People driving through town, people on vacation? Is there anything that draws people to this town specifically?" he asked, looking at the V-neck of her dress and wanting to slide his fingers beneath it and caress her.

"The hunting and fishing and dude ranches draw tourists. We have a rodeo that attracts people."

"I'm interested in a comfortable place for my employees to stay and in seeing to it that they can get good food while they're here," he said. The hotel was comfortable and held a degree of charm, harking back to another era, but he was far more attracted to the owner than the hotel.

"I think you'll find this a well-run and well-staffed hotel. We have excellent dining, which you'll taste tonight and can make your own decision," she said. "My dad always made a special effort to get and keep superb chefs."

"Good sales pitch," Chase said, leaning forward. "Now tell me about yourself."

"I already have," she replied, and he shook his head. "There's not much to tell. My dad's in the hospital, and my grandmother and two younger sisters live on the family ranch."

"Do you mind my asking why you're selling?"

She glanced away and he reached across the table to take her hand, feeling another jump in his heartbeat the instant he touched her. "I can tell that question caused you pain, so ignore it because the only thing I need to know is that the hotel is for sale."

When she smiled again, he realized he could get addicted to her smiles, which warmed him each time.

"No, if you're considering buying it, you have a right to ask because for all you know, there could be rumors floating around that it's haunted."

"Are there rumors?"

She shook her head. "Not at all. I'm selling for my dad's benefit. He's in a coma in the hospital, and even if he recovers, he won't be able to manage the ranch and the hotel the way he had in the past. My grandmother cares for my two younger sisters, but my grandmother is getting older."

"So you're a family person," Chase observed coolly, remembering his conversation earlier with Luke. Laurel Tolson was the kind of woman he usually avoided getting entangled with. She was the type for marriage. He always thought of all the years he'd watched his parents locked into responsibilities and cares that had turned them old ahead of their time. That kind of commitment wasn't for him and gave him chills. "You're making sacrifices in your own business to take care of your relatives."

"Yes, as a matter of fact, I'm very much a family person," she said with a bite to her words. Anger flashed in her blue eyes. "I've taken responsibility for my family in my dad's place. I intend to take care of them financially as well as otherwise."

The last was stated with a chip-on-her-shoulder attitude, and he wondered about the breakup of her engagement. Had Ed Varnum offered to take over the finances and she had refused to let him, creating a wedge between them? She seemed highly independent, and he could imagine her turning down less than acceptable offers. He tucked away the question, determined he would get the answer.

"That's commendable," Chase said, looking at her full mouth and knowing he wasn't going to back off getting to know her better. He always made it clear he wasn't into commitment, but this was one woman he wanted to make love to in spite of her apparent opposing views on relationships.

"What I'll do depends on Dad's recovery, but eventually, I hope to either get my grandmother and sisters settled in town here or move them to Dallas. My business is good and growing, and I don't want to leave it. I can have a much better business in a big city like Dallas than here."

"True enough," Chase remarked and then paused as Trey returned for drink orders.

When they were alone again, Chase leaned forward to take her hand once more, compelled to touch her if he possibly could. He glanced at her bare ring finger. "How long ago did your engagement end?"

"It's been a month now."

She looked surprised. "I see you've done some research on me."

Recent," he said. "I hope you're not sour on all men."

"Hardly," she replied, smiling at him.

"Good news. There's no other man in your life?"

"Heavens, no! Actually, I've been too busy for anything else. I try to spend some time each day at the hospital with my dad. We've hired a private-duty nurse to stay with him, but all of us go to see him often, even though he doesn't know it."

"Sorry to hear about him," Chase said.

She held his gaze for a moment and nodded. "I've been overseeing the hotel, and I get out to the ranch for the weekends. I live here during the week. Right now, with you in town, I'll be here at the hotel."

"Selfishly, I'm glad, but I'm sorry to take you away from your family," he said, brushing her hand lightly with his fingers. "I had no idea I'd find Montana so fascinating."

"Let me introduce you around. If you'd like, I can have a reception here at the hotel so you can meet the locals."

"That would be good because we plan to be here off and on for most of the coming year and while I don't wish your father ill, I hope you don't go back to Dallas soon."

"There's no danger of that."

"Who keeps shop there while you're away?" he asked, looking again at her lips and wondering about kissing her. He wanted their dinner to be over so they could dance and he could hold her in his arms.

Trey returned with a bottle of chilled Chenin Blanc to uncork, and she withdrew her hand from Chase's. After tasting the wine, Chase gave his approval; he waited until the wine was poured and they were alone again to raise his drink.

"Here's to Montana's spectacular ladies, particularly the one I'm with right now."

"I find that difficult to drink to—a toast to myself," she said with amusement. "Here's to Montana's economy growing through your efforts," she said, lifting her glass. "That's what I'll toast."

"If you sell the hotel, since it's been in your family so long, won't that be a heart-wrenching sacrifice for you?"

"I can't look back or cling to the past. I doubt if you do either and I'm sure your life has changed a great deal, hasn't it?"

"Sure. I don't recall anything that was a big sacrifice in mine. I was happy to get off the ranch and into the world of finance," he answered, admiring her for what she was doing to take care of her family. Because, in spite of her answer, selling the hotel had to hurt.

"You must enjoy the career path you've chosen, too," he said. "I guess when you were engaged, you'd planned to give it up when you married."

"Actually, no. I don't have to be present constantly to keep it running—that's what I'm doing right now. I'm sure you can juggle yours when you're away."

"That's right. I just figured you would want to let it go."

"Not at all. Everyone here is excited about your Montana discovery. You'll see how happy when you meet people."

"With you to introduce me, I'm sure they'll be friendly." He paused. "So where did you go to college?"

"K-State for a degree in landscape architecture. I wanted to go farther south, but still some place I could get to and get home, something that must not have mattered to you," she replied.

"Nope, and I had a great scholarship offer from Texas A&M."

"So was Edward your first love?"

"Actually, no. There were boys in high school, but I wasn't really serious with them, and one in college, but we never got engaged. I don't even need to ask you because I can guess— and you have far too many pictures that showcase your life."

As they chatted, he noticed she continually shifted the conversation to either an impersonal topic or a focus on him, trying to steer away from talking about herself; yet little by little he gleaned tidbits about her.

When they finished their drinks, she said she would show him around the hotel. He walked beside her, inhaling her perfume and wishing he could link her arm in his or better yet, put his arm across her shoulders, but he didn't want to rush things, because she had a definite barrier in place.

They circled the attractive grounds in front, which had thriving plants that were well suited to the northern climate, and he was impressed with her landscaping. The patio with a heated pool was equally inviting, and he could imagine how appealing it would be year-round if it had a retractable roof.

Finally they went to the dining room and were seated for dinner, where Chase met more of the wait staff.

"I suppose you know what you want for dinner," he said.

"I have favorites, but I'll look at the menu again," Laurel replied.

"Tell me what you recommend," he said as she skimmed over the listings of entrées.

"The steaks are delicious. I particularly like the rib-eye. I like the roasted pheasant, and I think our fish is tasty. The cedar plank salmon is a favorite of most regular diners."

They lapsed into silence for a few minutes while they read menus. Chase closed his to see that she had already put hers aside. "So you grew up on a ranch, too," he said, eager for more personal information.

"Part of the time. Otherwise, we lived at the hotel so we could go to school here."

Their waiter returned and as she gave her order, Chase was able to look her over slowly, mentally peeling away the burgundy dress, his imagination running riot with erotic images. He was impatient to hold and kiss her, yet he was enjoying getting to know her. So far, his first impressions had been accurate, and he was still intrigued by her and wanted her more than ever. He tried to stop thinking about how long it would be before they could dance and he could take her into his arms.

After she ordered the Madeira-roasted pheasant with mango sauce, he was aware of her watching him when he ordered the rib eye.

The minute they were alone, he took her hand in his; she glanced down at their hands. "This isn't a big city or even a large town. Everyone knows everyone else, and you'll start wild rumors by sitting here and holding my hand or if we dance tonight."

"First, is that bad? Do you mind?"

Smiling, she shook her head. "Not really because it means nothing to me. It will be forgotten fast enough, and I don't mind the questions."

"Maybe it means a little more than 'nothing,'" he remarked, and her eyebrows arched as she shook her head.

"It can't possibly. We don't know each other, and there isn't anything between us," she said with emphasis, and his suspicions strengthened that she was sour on relationships. Only a month ago she had been planning a wedding, so her attitude was no surprise. And no real hindrance as far as he was concerned. If she was sour on relationships, that would make life easier for him, because she wouldn't be focused on wringing a commitment from him. This was actually good news.

"I thought there were women, or at least *a* woman, in your life," she continued.

"Currently, not at all. You said no men in yours, either, and I take it your fiancé is definitely out of the picture?"

She nodded. "Positively, and he won't be back in it."

"So, we're both free and can enjoy getting to know each other. I know I am now," he added softly, wondering what she was thinking and what her expectations were for the evening.

She smiled at him, yet he felt a coolness and that she was merely being polite. The waiter returned with a basket of freshly baked rolls, their iced teas and tossed salads, and she withdrew her hand from his with another smile at him. He wished it promised something more later, but he knew better. Their entrées arrived, and his juicy steak looked cooked to perfection the way he had ordered, and her pheasant appeared equally enticing. After the first bite, he took a sip of his iced tea. "My compliments to the chef."

"We budget extra to get one of the best chefs in this area— as far as I'm concerned, he is the best chef. He's from St. Paul and had enough of city life. Dad has been delighted with him, and if you'll notice, the dining room is filled and there is a line of those waiting. People come from the surrounding area to eat here—the customers tonight aren't hotel patrons exclusively."

"Good recommendation for your hotel."

"The pièce de résistance is the Chocolate Sin dessert, which I've already ordered," she said. "You'll see when it arrives."

"An enticing dessert named 'Sin' in your hotel? Intriguing. What other sinful things will I find here?" he asked, dropping his voice and leaning closer over the table.

"I can tell that you're hoping the owner is, but alas, no one would describe me in that manner."

"It doesn't mean I won't, does it?" he asked. She inhaled and something flickered in the depths of her eyes.

"Chase, darlin', maybe I should change my lifestyle and add a little excitement to it," she drawled, slanting him a look and licking her lower lip.

"Laurel," he whispered, suddenly burning in the cool dining room. He knew she was flirting and had replied to him in fun, but as he drew a deep breath, he had to fight the urge to take her hand, get out of the busy dining room and go where they could have privacy.

She winked at him. "Calm down, Chase, I'm teasing," she said in a brisk voice, but that didn't wipe out the past moment and her flirting. He couldn't wait to get through dinner—his appetite for food had fled.

Twenty minutes later their waiter appeared and set a dessert in front of each of them. Chase gazed at the mountain of dark chocolate, ice cream, chocolate syrup, brownie, sprinkles of walnuts and whipped cream with a red cherry on the top. "Absolutely luscious," he said, looking directly at her and not considering the dessert when he made his remark. "And before the night is over, I'll see how sinful," he added in a deep voice.

Again, something flickered in the depths of her eyes, and he suspected her pulse was racing as fast as his.

"What's sinful," he said softly, "is what we do to each other. Only I intend to do more and I hope you do, too."

"Eat your dessert, Chase. That's all that is wicked here," she instructed, picking up her fork.

She ate little of hers and he ate only half of his even though it was fabulous. He was more interested in dancing with her now that the band had begun playing.

Finally, they stood, and this time he linked her arm in his to return to the bar. "Now we'll dance."

"I believe I promised to show you our town after dinner," she said.

"I'll take a rain check on the tour of Athens. I'm interested, but I want to dance with you now."

"Whatever you'd like," she answered without hesitation. "Your real estate agent has probably already taken you around more than once."

"Actually, no. Anyway, that would be entirely different from you showing me," he said, smiling at her as they entered the darkened bar.

They sat in the same booth they had occupied earlier, because she had told Trey they would return and to reserve it for them. As they waited for her iced tea and his cold beer, Chase glanced around the packed room. "This has to be more than hotel guests."

"It is."

"Good music, nice place—you have a great hotel. I'm impressed."

"Why do I think you're being polite?" she asked. "I suspect it takes much more than our century-old hotel to really impress you," she said.

"Not when the owner is a stunning blonde," he replied and took her hand as he slid out of the booth. "Let's dance, Laurel."

Three

With mixed feelings of caution and a bubbling excitement, Laurel walked to the dance floor with Chase for an old ballad. As they threaded their way through the crowd, she gazed at him. Handsome with enticing eyes that would melt ice, he was too hot-blooded, too charming, and she could feel the barriers around her heart crumbling. And she was certain he was aimed at seduction.

Why wouldn't he? He knew the effect he had on women. He liked women and he was charming and wealthy, a combination that made him totally irresistible.

Yet she intended to withstand his appeal and keep up her guard because she was certain that there was nothing long-term in his intentions. She would be a temporary fling to entertain him while the new oil field was being developed.

And he was absolutely another Edward, one more jet-setter who wanted life on his terms and thought only of himself. Never again would she be so gullible.

Chase definitely desired her and was coming on strong, but

then he had leverage because he had something that she wanted—she hoped he would buy the hotel.

She wouldn't let herself think about the possibilities, but he could afford her asking price and he was going to buy property here anyway, although there were other places and he could afford to get what he wanted.

Every time she thought about him making an offer, she focused on a different subject because she didn't want to have to deal with the enormous disappointment if he didn't make an offer.

Even so, it was difficult to keep from speculating and hoping. Equally impossible to withstand his charm.

He was magnetic and sensual, and something inexplicable stirred a fire between them. She'd never had that before with any man and couldn't understand it. Nor did she want it. Not with this man, of all people. Why couldn't it be Frank Durbin or Kirk Malloy or one of the other locals who was reliable and so much like her that any of them could have been a brother? But maybe that was part of why there were no fireworks with any of them.

On the dance floor Chase drew her close into his arms. His aftershave was enticing. He was warm and his crisp cotton shirt smelled fresh, but it was their touching each other that took her attention. She was aware that their slightest contact stirred physical needs.

Sex had never been great with Edward. He had wanted her and pursued her, pouring attention on her and showering her with gifts, dazzling her until she had been blinded and thought they had something solid together.

How wrong she had been! She didn't intend to fall into the same trap twice, although she couldn't imagine Chase ever marrying or pursuing her in the manner Edward had. Yet she knew Chase had seduction on his mind and wanted her in his bed. He had made that obvious, and while her intentions to resist seduction, as well as falling in love, kept up emotional barriers, her body responded and she succumbed to the fun of flirting with him.

As they danced, she became acutely aware of their legs brushing and their bodies lightly pressed together.

Then the number ended and a fast one started. She watched his enticing moves. He loosened his tie, his heated gaze traveling slowly over her, and she tingled from head to toe.

Circling him, she wondered whether she could maintain his interest in purchasing the hotel yet stay out of his bed. She intended to try to sustain that balance and keep her body to herself. As she watched him dance, she reminded herself that she was flirting with disaster. Chase's narrow hips gyrated to the heavy beat, and she imagined him in bed and realized she was going to be incredibly tempted. With every move the man was sexy. He flirted, he charmed and his green eyes beguiled. How was she going to hold him at arm's length while flirting and dancing and soon…kissing him?

The thought of kissing him made her heart race. Looking at his full, sensual lower lip, she wondered what it would be like. The room warmed and she became breathless, more so when she glanced up to meet his knowing gaze.

One lock of dark brown hair had fallen over his forehead, reminding her of that slightly wild look that he'd had when she'd first seen him.

At the end of the dance, he took her hand to go to their booth. "I have to shed this jacket," he said, pulling it off and hanging it on the side of the booth before turning to take her hand and head back to the dance floor for a slow number.

By midnight, she was wrapped in his arms, dancing close against him, and he had talked her into going out with him tomorrow evening.

"What time does the bar close?" he asked.

"Not until two in the morning. Two more hours," she answered. "But we won't be here that long because I have to get up early."

"This is enjoyable, but let's call it a night as far as the dancing is concerned and go up for a nightcap." He leaned back. "How does that sound?"

"Fine with me," she replied. If only he were an ordinary Montana cowboy, she would be excited and happier to be with him. As it was, she was on edge, wondering if they would each be working to get what the other wanted.

As they left the bar, he draped his arm across her shoulders. In the elevator he watched her with a smoldering gaze. Certain that kisses were inevitable, she wanted him to kiss her. Otherwise, she was afraid he would vanish out of her life and her hotel. His kisses should be reasonably harmless and a good antidote for Edward, she thought, knowing she intended to kiss Chase tonight.

When he looked at her mouth, she couldn't catch her breath. The elevator stopped and still watching her, he took her hand and they stepped off.

"Want to come to my place for a nightcap?" she asked and he nodded. He took her key card and opened the door.

Only one small lamp burned in her suite. Chase placed the key on an entryway table and turned to look at her. His eyes filled with fiery, blatant lust as he reached for her and drew her to him.

Her heart thudded when she walked into his embrace, winding her arms around his neck and raising her mouth to his as his head came down and his lips, his tongue, met hers. Setting her ablaze, he kissed her while she pressed against him and wound her fingers in his hair. His sizzling kiss, deep and thorough and demanding, was so much more than she'd expected or ever known before.

With a desperate urgency, she clung to him and met his fervor. As he held her, desire increased enough to destroy reason and control.

Chase swept her up into his arms and carried her to a couch to hold her on his lap. His arousal pressed against her hip, and her body arched in response. She wanted him.

His hands moved to her zipper, and then he pushed her dress off her shoulders. With the rush of cool air on her bare skin came lucidity.

"Chase, wait—we're going way too fast," she gasped, glancing up to find his gaze on her breasts, which were covered in a lacy pink bra. Pulling her clothing back in place and gathering her wits and caution at the same time, she tugged up her dress.

"Zip me, please," she whispered. "We've just met. This is too soon for me."

Nuzzling her throat, he trailed kisses to her ear. His warm breath and lips dissolved her protests. Holding him, she relished his mouth grazing her throat, until she realized how easily she had succumbed again.

She grasped his upper arms to push him. "Chase—" she whispered. "Just wait a little. Let's catch our breath."

He raised his head to look into her eyes and she trembled. His desire was unmistakable, blazing in the depths of his eyes. "You're fabulous, Laurel," he replied, his words melting her.

He ran his index finger across her lips, adding to her longing.

"Chase," she said, "let's get something to drink and cool down."

He gazed at her intently, and she wondered if he'd even heard her. He wanted her and it showed as much as if he'd announced it.

"Laurel, come here," he said and slipped his hand behind her head to pull her closer as his mouth came down on hers for another kiss.

Her toes curled and her arms wound around his neck, and in spite of the brief pause she kissed him as passionately as before. Time spun away while he held her close against him.

She had no idea how long they kissed, but she knew when he ran his hand over her hip and along her thigh, and then beneath her skirt. She took his hand and pushed against his chest, breaking away and wriggling off his lap.

"You go so fast that you take my breath."

"Your kisses are what take my breath," he declared. He stood and placed his hands on her waist. To keep him at a distance, she put her hands against his chest, but that wasn't what she really wanted to do. She longed to wind her arms around his neck, stand on tiptoe and kiss him again.

She put her finger over his lips to quiet him. "Stop saying things like that, because you know that's as seductive as your kisses. Let's get something to drink and put some distance between us."

"Why?" he asked, nuzzling her neck.

She moved away and took his hand. "Come with me," she said, gazing into his eyes. Her heart drummed and she wanted him more than she should.

With a solemn expression, he followed her. Still on fire from his kisses, she dropped his hand as she led the way into the small kitchen, where she switched on lights and motioned to him to sit.

"I'll help," he said, getting glasses while she got a pitcher of tea she'd made earlier. He filled glasses with ice and she poured tea, all the time aware of him moving around her, brushing against her lightly, keeping her breathless. "Lemon or sugar?" she asked.

"Neither," he said, shaking his head. "I don't even want tea," he added, and she glanced at him. "I want you, Laurel." He set both glasses on the table and turned to take her into his arms, and she couldn't protest any more than she could walk away from him.

"Let's start the evening early tomorrow. How about four? You can show me the town and then we'll eat afterwards," he said. "This time I'll take you somewhere."

"Chase—"

"A few extra hours—that's all. Let's get to know each other."

She wanted to kiss him, and dinner tomorrow night was a distant appointment that she barely gave thought to. "Yes," she whispered, slipping her hand across his nape. She craved his kisses, something she had intended to avoid. Instead, she was hopelessly lost with wanting him.

Standing on tiptoe, she kissed him ardently and once more was swept away by heart-pounding kisses she wanted to continue all night.

Finally, she paused. "Chase," she gasped, trying to get her breath. "You either go or we sit and drink our tea. We can take our drinks into the other room."

While they stared at each other, she wondered what he debated. "Is this a problem? Are you that unaccustomed to hearing a woman say no?"

A smile briefly flitted across his features. "Actually, maybe I am. I was wondering if I ought to walk out and leave you alone from now on, but that isn't what I want to do. I like a woman in my life, but I want her to choose to be there."

"I'm happy to get to know you, but we were moving into a more intimate relationship too fast for me."

"Get to know each other, it is," he said. He picked up his iced tea and walked back into the living area.

Sitting and talking, they sipped tea until two in the morning, when Chase stood. "I better let you get some sleep."

Keeping distance between them, she followed him to the door. "I'm scheduled to meet with your staff at ten o'clock. I'll show them the hotel. Will you join us?"

"If you're there, of course," he said. He reached out and slipped his arm around her waist and drew her to him. "This has been a fabulous evening, but it's your kisses that are sensational. You know you've killed all chance of sleep, unless—"

"Don't even say it," she whispered. "You go and you will sleep."

"Have breakfast with me," he said.

She hesitated a moment and then nodded, thinking breakfast wouldn't be filled with temptation and she could talk some more about the merits of the hotel.

"The whole evening was fantastic," he said.

"I agree, Chase," she replied softly, and they locked gazes again, yearning building with each heart-pounding second and then his head lowered and his mouth met hers.

She held him tightly, yet at the same time she remembered that this was the road to disaster. Finally, she stepped back. "Enough for tonight," she whispered. "See you tomorrow, Chase."

"How's seven for breakfast?" he asked.

"Fine."

He smiled and touched her cheek with his fingers before releasing her and leaving.

As she shut the door behind him, she took a deep breath, crossing the suite to turn off the lamp and carry empty glasses to the kitchen.

"He's Edward all over again. Don't for one second forget that," she lectured herself aloud, her words sounding hollow in the empty suite, trying to convince herself to use her good sense where Chase Bennett was concerned, yet her mouth tingled and her body clamored for him and his loving. "There's only a few degrees of difference in the two moneyed executives, Chase and Edward," she argued aloud, knowing her lectures were useless. Chase set her on fire with longing and need.

When she was ready for bed, she turned off the lights and pulled on a cotton robe, picked up a throw and stepped onto the balcony, where she curled up on a chaise and looked at town lights and rooftops while trees were dark shadows in the night.

Chase was far too appealing. She would have to maintain a balancing act—resist him yet keep him interested. Chase was by far her most likely prospect to buy the hotel, so she couldn't drive him away. Tomorrow she and Brice were showing Chase and some of his executives the hotel. Later her real estate agent would take Chase's staff again, to look at the hotel and answer any questions.

Sell him the hotel and combat his attraction. The latter was going to be the most difficult, she knew.

She stretched back in the chaise and closed her eyes, thinking about Chase's tempting kisses and mulling over the evening until she realized she would never get to sleep if she didn't get him out of her thoughts.

Impatiently, she tossed aside the throw and went to bed, running over chores involving the hotel until she finally fell asleep, only to dream about Chase.

Determined to be professional the next morning, she dressed in a tailored, seersucker, pale blue and white pin-stripe suit and white blouse, looping and pinning up her hair. She wanted to appear serious, hoping to look like the owner of the hotel and a businesswoman and keep that image in front of Chase so he thought of her more that way than the woman he'd flirted with, danced with and kissed last night.

Promptly at seven, she heard a knock at the door and hurried to meet him.

Dressed in a gray knit shirt and slacks and western snake-skin boots, Chase stepped inside her suite, closing the door behind him. His brief scrutiny made her acutely conscious of her appearance, and her pulse speeded.

"You look luscious this morning," he said in a husky voice. He placed his hands on her shoulders.

"Thank you. You look quite handsome. I'm trying to be a businesswoman, and you know how you can help," she said, attempting to sound brisk, yet her voice came out breathlessly.

He grinned. "I don't have a clue."

"Oh, yes, you do," she said, tapping his chest with her fore-finger, losing her struggle to sound all-business, because his aftershave was as enticing as it was the night before. Fresh and filled with energy, he looked as appealing as ever.

His disarming smile added to her defeat. "I've been looking forward to breakfast and being with you again."

"Thank you—that's nice," she answered politely.

"Most of all, I've been looking forward to one good morning kiss to make the world right," he said, sliding his arm around her waist and causing her heart to skip a beat.

"Chase, you can't—"

"Oh, yes, I can," he whispered and placed his mouth on hers; her protests died.

He kissed her fiercely and she forgot the morning schedule or even why he was there. She wound her arms around his waist and held him close as she kissed him back. Her heart thudded while she forgot every resolution she had made in the night and early morning hours.

"Chase," she finally whispered, twisting away from him and stepping out of his embrace. "We have to stop."

"I don't know why," he said, caressing her nape and moving closer again.

Shaking her head, she placed her hand against his chest, feeling his racing heartbeat and realizing it probably matched her own. "Let's go to breakfast, act sane and remember a business meeting is the aim of the morning."

"That comes later," he reminded her with a cavalier manner that dismissed all her protests. "This is a private breakfast together, only us, and I can't resist you."

She wanted to say that was mutual, but she had no intention of confessing her reaction to him, although he obviously knew it. "We need to stay on schedule," she persisted.

"We are," he replied and kissed her again, and this time their kisses lasted longer before she finally stopped him.

"Now we have to go," she said, stepping away from him quickly.

He held the door and she walked out ahead of him. "Thank

you," she said. "I think you'll enjoy our breakfast buffet, and as usual we attract diners who are not guests of the hotel, but you'll see why."

"Everything I've seen here so far is impressive," he said, and she smiled at him.

Returning to the main dining room, which was filled with morning sunlight, she moved ahead of him in the breakfast line that held glasses of various fruit juices, freshly cut melons, bright red strawberries and slices of green kiwi, yet all the tempting food couldn't take her attention from the man with her. Along with omelets, biscuits, sausage and strawberries, they chose steaming cups of coffee and chilled orange juice.

Leaving the line, they strolled outside on the patio, deserted in the early morning. As she set her tray on the table, she remembered the last time she'd had breakfast with a man on the patio—it had been Edward. And she was with another Edward this morning.

"Nice out here," Chase remarked, holding her chair and caressing her nape with his fingers, fueling the fire he'd kindled with his kisses.

"When few people are around, I love the patio," she said. "Early morning is the best time because the rest of the day and the evening, the place becomes busy and crowded."

"We agree on that. I like solitude."

"Are you an only child?" she asked, thinking she could look into his bedroom eyes all day.

"Hardly. I have five siblings, three brothers and two sisters."

"So there were six of you, and you're the oldest," she said.

"How'd you ever guess?" he asked with a grin and they both chuckled.

"Do you return home to Montana often?" she asked.

"Not during the past few years. I have a brother, Graham, who stayed on the ranch and a sister, Maggie, who lives in

Montana, so they have family. There are four grandchildren, so far." Chase's prominent cheekbones left his cheeks in slight shadows. Wayward locks of his dark brown hair fell over his forehead, with the faint breeze ruffling them. He looked as if he belonged on the Harley more than in a boardroom, but she knew that first impression she'd had of him had influenced her. She might as well be seated across from Edward, she reminded herself, feeling that familiar curl of distaste; and in spite of Chase's torrid kisses, she hoped to maintain distance between them.

"My family is still on the ranch. My mom would like to sell and move to Florida, or let me take it over so they could live in Florida, but my father can't exist without work. When I was growing up, we took few vacations, except to get together with family. Mom has sisters and I have cousins. We could afford to take trips but didn't because my dad couldn't imagine letting a day go by without working. Nor would he turn his jobs over to another person."

"I'm afraid that doesn't run in my family," she said, smiling. "My dad loves a good time. He's a people person and everyone in the next six counties, plus here, knows him. That makes his stroke so difficult to accept," she said.

"Sorry. That's tough," Chase said, touching her hand lightly and sounding sincere, but she suspected that was part of his ability to convince people to do what he wanted. "You said last night you expect to be here in Montana for a while?" he asked.

"Yes. While I'm away, business will move along without me because I have a competent manager in Dallas and a great staff. Right now my family needs me and I want to be closer to them."

"When you sell the hotel, will you move to the ranch?"

She shook her head. "Actually, if I sell, I hope I can make arrangements with the new buyer to let me stay here as long as I need to, so I can be close to the hospital and my dad. If not, I'll rent a place in town. I don't want to drive back and forth from the ranch to the hospital, and I try to go see him often. If Dad rallies, that will change because they will move him to a physical therapy center in Billings. We had already started making plans for the move but stopped because he lapsed into a coma."

"Sorry. You have the ranch for sale, too."

"We can't run the ranch without Dad, and I don't want the responsibility for it, therefore it's for sale. My grandmother and sisters live there now."

"And if it sells, will you move them here or to Dallas?" he asked.

"Well, it depends on my dad. I told him I'd like to move them to Dallas, but I don't know if any of them will want to go. Ashley is seventeen and can drive now, and Diana is fifteen. They may want to stay here. So may my grandmother. We'll have to see what we can work out for care for Dad." She smiled at him. "Now you know my family history and situation."

"And I've told you mine. So, what do you like to do? Swim, hunt, travel, movies—what?" he asked, reaching across the table to take her hand and run his thumb across her knuckles. She should withdraw it, but her reluctance crumbled in his presence, as usual.

"I swim. No hunting or fishing. Because of starting my own business, all my time is taken by my job."

"Not all," he contradicted. "You were engaged," he said. "Not that I care to delve into your past relationship, except to say that frankly I'm glad it's over. But that's a selfish view."

She thought that in addition to selfish, it was typical, knowing Edward would have been the same way had he been interested in her.

Chase's appetite seemed as poor as hers as they ate only a few bites, and she tried to avoid thinking about their morning kisses.

"If I'd known you were running this hotel, I would have come to Montana more often than I have and stayed here," he said.

She smiled at him. "I find that difficult to believe. I know there have been women in your life recently because I've seen a picture somewhere. Maybe more than one picture if I remember correctly."

"Whoever she was, she's been out of my life quite a while."

"You always end the relationship, don't you?"

"Obviously, or I wouldn't still be single. I'm not a marrying man. I don't want to be tied down like that."

"In other words, you've never met a woman you couldn't live without," she said, thinking he was coldhearted. "You sound scared of commitment."

"Terrified by it," he replied easily. "I'll admit it. I don't want to be in the trap my parents were in. Not ever. No relationship is worth being tied down all your life the way they have been. So am I alarming you?"

She smiled. "No. I have no intention of losing my heart to you. You've given plenty of warnings about the dangers of loving you."

"Maybe I've overdone it," he said, with a sparkle in his eyes. "I'll have to make up for that. I'll bet I can show you a good time if you'll give me a chance."

"I think I'm already doing that," she answered lightly, knowing they were moving away from his admission of fear of commitment. And now she understood a little more about him and his past. It actually was a valid warning to avoid emotional entanglements with him. Her brain was clearly on target. If only her heart was.

Soon he had her laughing over stories about starting in business, and she shared some of her experiences until she glanced at her watch.

"Chase! We're going to be late. It's time to meet the others."

With a smile he came around the table to hold her chair, and she noticed that he was undisturbed about the time and didn't hurry. She realized that everyone would wait for Chase's arrival regardless of when he showed up.

In the main lobby his staff already had gathered, along with Brice.

"Laurel, this is Luke Perkins, Senior Vice President of Land Administration," Chase said upon joining the group. As she shook hands with Luke, she noticed a wedding band on his finger and was grateful for the married men in Chase's party who would be able to keep focused on business. "And this is Dal Wade, Vice President of Marketing for our northern division," Chase added, and she shook hands with a stocky, blond man who also had a friendly smile. She greeted Brice, who stood between the two vice presidents.

Next, she met a vice president of Purchasing, an executive accountant and a Billings real estate broker, Sam Kilean. She introduced Chase to Lane Grigsby, her real estate agent, who had already met all the others.

Finally, when all the introductions were over, she led them to one of the smaller meeting rooms, where they had coffee and a continental breakfast, which neither she nor Chase touched. Aware of Chase's steady attention, she took turns with Brice telling the group about the hotel and answering questions.

She glanced at her watch. "We'll break for ten minutes and then meet again in the main lobby. Brice and I will give you a guided tour of the hotel. Any more questions?"

There were none and as the men stood to leave, Chase strolled around the table to her. "Appealing presentation. Maybe I should try to hire you."

"Thank you. If you have an interest in hiring a landscape specialist, we might have a discussion, but for anything else, I'd be out of my field," she said, smiling and realizing they were alone in the meeting room as she gathered up folders and papers, placing them in a neat stack to retrieve later.

He ran his fingers across her nape. "We'll get into the landscape possibilities later. That would be in Houston, not here."

"I have a capable staff."

His gaze bore into her. "I promise you, if I hire you, it won't be your competent staff I want."

She smiled. "I'll remember that and I'm sure you'll make it clear."

He grinned and ran his hand along her high collar, tracing it down to the vee of her tailored blouse until she captured his hand. "You've figured out that much about me, so far," he said.

"I've discovered a lot about you," she snapped, for a moment letting her animosity show and thinking about his wealthy persona that would want to have his way constantly.

One dark eyebrow arched and his eyes filled with a curiosity that made her cheeks heat. "I touched a nerve," he said. "We hardly know each other. You're not getting me mixed up with Edward, are you?" he asked with a shrewd perception that disturbed her.

"In many ways, I'm certain you're really quite different," she said coolly. "Your ten-minute break is vanishing, and I think I should run to the ladies' room before the next segment of our schedule."

"Of course," he said, and she hurried away, feeling her back prickle and suspecting he was watching her and speculating about what had rankled a few minutes earlier. She didn't have to stop in the rest room, but she had wanted to end the conversation between them that had taken a bad turn.

Starting at four, she would be alone with him again. She would be spending most of the day and evening with him. This was going to be an incredibly long week, perhaps a month or more, and already she was edgy from dealing with Chase.

Emerging from the ladies' room, she hurried to the lobby, where Brice was talking with several of Chase's men. As she strolled toward them, Chase turned to watch her, and beneath his gaze she tingled from her head to her toes.

"I see everyone is here," she said after taking a swift count. "Gentlemen, we might as well get started with our tour of the hotel, and we'll begin with the kitchen."

It took an hour to complete the tour, and the entire time she was aware of Chase's undivided attention. As they viewed the kitchen, he had questions and she answered them, aware he was also paying attention to business. Finally, they gathered for a lunch in a private room, where he sat beside her. Afterward they had a break and then met in a conference room, where she and Brice answered questions until they broke up at two o'clock.

As everyone left and Lane promised to call her, Chase strolled to her side. "Thanks for so much information. That was a good presentation."

Inordinately pleased, she thanked him, aware of Brice moving around nearby. "Brice and I will be happy to answer any further questions. Your people have some appointments with various hotel staff that should give you more information."

He nodded and touched her wrist. "I'll come to your suite at four," he said quietly.

"Fine," she replied, smiling at him. As soon as the door closed behind him, she sat in a chair and kicked off her shoes. "What did you think?" she asked Brice.

"I think Chase Bennett is interested in you."

She gave Brice an exasperated look. "Let's stick to business. Did we influence them?"

"They seemed impressed by our presentation and the hotel, but I can't tell whether they're interested in buying or not. I suspect that they don't know and are waiting to hear from their leader to decide what he wants to do. After all, it will be Chase Bennett's decision, not theirs."

"True enough. Brice, I don't even want to think ahead about selling to them beyond what we have to do to present the hotel. It's like counting your chickens before they hatch. The money from the sale would be a miracle for me and help in more ways than anyone knows," she said, tapping her finger on the arm of her chair and thinking about her dad. "I'm scared to count on it until I have the signed contract in my hand."

"For your sake, I pray we get the sale," Brice said.

"If we do, do you think he'll let all our people go?"

"Who knows what he'll do, but it's difficult to imagine he won't come in here with his own crew."

"It would be easier to keep who's here. Do you think he'll tear down the hotel?" she asked, mulling it over in her mind and knowing Brice had no more clue than she about what Chase would do.

"I don't know him and I have no idea. He's friendly and easy to talk to and best-buddy type, but it's only skin-deep. He's got all his plans locked away in that head of his. I hope for your sake he buys."

"Even if it means you work for him? That's what I hate. That and a few other things."

Brice smiled. "Word gets around in a town like this, and I've had four offers from various places, the closest being the new motel out on the highway and another was from the new hotel in Billings. I'll get along and you know the kitchen staff will survive the transition. Someone is trying to hire one of them away from us constantly."

"I know," she agreed with a sigh. "I'm going out with Chase tonight."

"Why do I feel there's no enthusiasm in that statement, while more than half the single women in the United States would turn green with envy and jump at the chance?"

She smiled. "You're right. If I expect to get the sale, I can't tick him off and I have to be nice, but it's already a struggle. In fairness, sometimes it's not. He's a charmer, but that's what makes it difficult. I don't want another heartbreak."

"You won't have one. I've watched you grow up, and your dad always said you have a head on your shoulders. Get a nap and go enjoy yourself and give him another sales pitch tonight."

"Thanks, Brice, and thanks for all your help today," she said.

After he left, she sat quietly for a few minutes, staring at the door and thinking how fortunate she was to have Brice, who had worked for her dad for twenty-four years, starting when she had been three years old. Level-headed and thoroughly familiar with the hotel business, Brice kept the place running smoothly without any seeming effort, but that was the result of years of experience and handling problems before they got out of hand. With a sigh, she stood to gather her things and go to her suite to stretch out and sleep for ten minutes and then shower and dress for the evening.

She selected a black dress with a dramatic draped neckline and a straight skirt that ended above her knees. Stepping into high-heeled black sandals, she wondered where he planned to take her. She left her hair down, parting it in the center and combing it so it fell in a cascade across her shoulders.

When he arrived at four, she gave him a quick perusal. He wore a gray sport coat, charcoal slacks and a white open-necked shirt and was as stunningly handsome as ever. With each passing hour she knew him, his good looks made a bigger impact on her.

The moment he entered her suite, his gaze drifted down over her, and his eyes revealed his approval. "You look gorgeous," he said.

"Thank you," she answered politely, conscious of how much his compliment pleased her, even though she was certain it was probably said without thought.

"Laurel, let's go to my suite and have a drink. I'd like to talk a little before we go."

"Fine," she said, instantly curious. Her heart skipped and she wondered if he had an offer for the hotel. She banked all speculation immediately, terrified about getting her hopes high.

He held the door, closed it and looped her arm in his to walk beside her. His aftershave was enticing and his touch light but enough to make her tingle. In his suite she set her purse on a table and walked across the spacious living area, noting that new bouquets of flowers had replaced the others. She also noticed that he had a bottle of champagne on ice.

"Champagne?" she asked, surprised.

"Yes. I thought we'd celebrate," he said, shedding his coat and folding it carefully to lay it over the back of a chair.

"What are we celebrating? Our new friendship?" she asked with amusement, her curiosity increasing by the minute.

"Of course, along with your successful hotel presentation and your sales approach."

"Thank you," she answered. Inordinately pleased, she smiled, even though common sense told her that her casual presentation, occasional sales pitches and tours couldn't possibly have sold him on the idea of buying the hotel. He peeled away the wrapper around the bottle and popped the cork, picking up a flute to pour bubbling champagne and hand it to her.

When she accepted her drink, her fingers grazed his. "Thank you again," she said. "Both for the champagne and for your compliments about the sales presentations."

He poured himself a glass of the pale liquid, and she looked at the delicate flute in his well-shaped, tanned hands. "Let's talk about the hotel and what you expect and what I hope to get."

"I think you know all the particulars and what I want," she said. "We've been over that, with you, with your staff and with your real estate agent," she added, her heart starting to race with the realization that he was actually talking about buying the hotel. Maybe she was going to make the sale!

"Yes, you have," he said as walked to stand by the mantel. Turning, he raised his flute of champagne. "Here's hoping we can work out a fabulous deal for both of us."

"I'll drink to that," she exclaimed, moving close to touch her glass against his as their gazes locked and the tension wound tighter. Her heart raced and excitement simmered in her. While he watched her, his eyes darkened with desire. Her mouth went dry and her breathing became erratic.

Dimly, she was aware that he set his drink on the mantel and took hers from her hand to put it beside his. Then he turned to her, placing his hand on her waist. Sensibly, she wanted to protest, yet the words wouldn't come. Instead, she looked into his eyes and felt consumed by them as he drew her closer. When he leaned down to place his mouth on hers, her heart slammed against her ribs.

She slid her arms around his neck and clung to him. His kiss carried more than the knee-melting jolt of earlier ones. There was all the fire of a streak of lightning. What was worse, his sensuous kisses fanned flames more than ever. Never before had she experienced kisses like Chase's, and she didn't want him to be special or unique, yet her fleeting thoughts were easy to ignore. She wanted his kisses.

Finally, wisdom and caution nagged and she pushed against him, causing him to raise his head. Both of them were breathing hard, and for seconds they stared at each other.

"I want to make you an offer," he said.

Her heart missed beats while excitement shook her. Trying to gather her wits and at the same time thinking he was taking unfair advantage by kissing her senseless before launching into business, she inhaled and struggled to regain her composure. Stepping out of his embrace, she picked up her champagne flute to take a sip and give herself another moment before she listened to him. "Go ahead," she said, the moment becoming etched in her memory.

"You want to sell your hotel," he stated.

"Yes, you know that. That's what this is all about."

"Partially," he replied. "That's what you want. Are you able to make a decision about selling, or are your grandmother and your dad or even your sisters part owners?"

"It's my sole decision," she said and couldn't see any change in his expression. "Two years ago my grandmother deeded her part of the ranch and hotel to Dad. After his stroke, the first opportunity he was able Dad insisted I be appointed his guardian and be given complete authority over everything."

"Shrewd moves by both of them," Chase said. "Do you need to confer with your grandmother out of courtesy?"

"Not really. I'll tell her, of course, when I have an offer, but the decision is all mine. Do you want to buy the hotel?" she asked, unable to stand the suspense of waiting.

He watched her intently and for the first time, she wondered what he had on his mind. "I want to make you an offer."

Curious, she became concerned with the roundabout way he was leading up to what he planned. She wondered if he was going to quote her some ridiculously low figure. Or something else entirely, or to work for him and keep her hotel? "All right, Chase," she answered in a subdued voice. "What or how much do you intend to offer?"

"Half a million more than your full asking price," he answered.

Stunned and perplexed, she stared at him. All her senses sharpened, and she realized he had been building to this moment. Barriers rose, caution enveloped her and she perceived a threat to her well-being. At the same time, her curiosity mounted.

"I don't understand. You'll pay a fortune—so what is it you want?" she asked.

He took her champagne glass from her hand, setting it on the mantel beside his and holding her hand in his. "I want you. I've told you I'm not into commitment or permanent relationships, and I don't think you're into temporary relationships or a relationship without a commitment."

"I'm not," she answered flatly, going cold.

"I want to make you an offer we both may be able to live with. I'll buy your hotel, Laurel, for your full asking price plus half a million, if you'll agree to be my mistress for a month."

Four

She stared at him while her heart slammed against her ribs. Her fury ignited and swept over her with the heat of a raging fire.

Starting to answer, she yanked her hand away from him. Before she could state, "No," he placed his finger on her mouth, stirring a sensual awareness of him.

"Wait, before you refuse," he urged. "You think about it. No strings, no ties. My mistress for a month and then it's over. You'll get the price you asked for and then some, which you're not going to get from anyone else. Don't answer me now. Let's have our evening together, and you think about your answer and sleep on it. I'm not into marriage, now or ever, and at this point in your life, I suspect you aren't either. This arrangement would be perfect. You'll get what you want and I'll get what I want."

"Perfect for you perhaps," she snapped, anger brimming. "I can give you an answer, Chase—"

"Don't," he commanded quietly. "Keep your options open

and think about it and your future and your family. I'm offering more money than you will get anywhere else, and it will solve some of your problems."

"There's a name for that. In short, sell my body to you." She flung the words at him with bitterness.

"If you want to put it that way, but not really," he answered in a tone that held a note of steel, and for an instant his friendly facade slipped, revealing the strong-willed man that he really was.

"A month is fleeting and temporary," he said. "I can court you and perhaps seduce you and have my month without buying your hotel or paying anything extra."

She tilted her head to study him. "Why don't you? It would save you half a million and maybe get you what you want, where this way isn't likely to."

"I don't want to wait, and you've already given me refusals—the day we met, remember?" he asked, one corner of his mouth lifting. Her fury increased, but this time it was at her own physical reactions to him, which she couldn't control.

"You don't want to invest any of your valuable time in a relationship, do you?" she countered, and he arched one dark eyebrow as his index finger traced the curve of her ear.

"You can put it that way, but it's more that I don't want to wait to make love to you," he answered in a husky voice. "I'm not that interested in your hotel, but it'll serve my purposes because I need something for my employees as fast as I can get it."

"They can rent the entire Tolson Hotel immediately, so that part of your argument isn't valid. You want what pleases you without waiting," she said with contempt. The wealthy, arrogant playboy had surfaced, as she'd expected. He sought instant gratification and was accustomed to getting what he wanted regardless of the means.

"Perhaps so. The whole idea isn't so preposterous—and think of the rewards. You aren't giving them consideration.

Imagine having the hotel sold. I can pay cash for it. You're not really thinking about that aspect of my offer."

"I find it difficult to contemplate selling the hotel when it's my body you want."

He smiled and put his hands on her shoulders. "You concentrate on the prospect of selling your hotel and drop the other temporarily. That may change some of your thinking here."

"No, it—" His head tilted and he bent slightly as his mouth covered hers and stopped her argument while he kissed her again. His arm banded her waist, pulling her close to him. She started to push away and protest because she didn't want to kiss him, but as his tongue stroked hers, her arguments vanished. Sensations rocked her and she put her arms around his neck. In spite of being furious with him, she kissed him in return. She wished his kisses weren't fantastic, mesmerizing, erotic.

As she kissed him passionately, she suspected she was already spinning off into a world of heartbreak, but at the moment she didn't care.

The thought dimly crossed her mind that seduction was inevitable.

While he kissed her, he leaned over her and her arms around his neck tightened. Time and problems vanished. With his arm banding her waist tightly, his other hand caressed her throat, roaming down over her breast, rubbing her taut peak. Even through the fabric of her dress, she burned from his caresses, moaning softly and losing caution. Desiring him, she wanted barriers between them removed. She ran her hand down his back, then lower along his hip, conscious of his arousal.

Abruptly, he raised his head. "You want this, too," he reminded her. "Say yes, Laurel," he urged.

Her mind spun as she attempted to focus and think and ignore the clamoring of desire. Either way, he would seduce her. She knew that without any doubt, because beneath the onslaught of his hot kisses, her caution always faded.

With a shiver that ran from her lips to her toes, she stepped back and pulled herself together.

"You know you make me want you, but it's lust. Absolute lust."

"You think about our future and your hotel," he repeated softly. "C'mon. We'll go to dinner and get to know each other a little better."

Feeling as if she had lost round one in a fight, she silently picked up her purse and left with him. Waiting at the curb was a sleek black limo and she thought of Edward. Only Chase was not Edward. Chase was sexier, more charming and a shark. He went after what he wanted with less subtlety than Edward but with even more determination. And even more assurance he would get it.

Her thoughts churned over her dilemma and her decision. He had presented his offer and then shown her why she might as well accept it.

Half a million above her asking price! The amount dazzled her, and she tried to avoid consideration of what she could do with the money for her family. Half a million versus becoming his mistress. Weighed against the temptation of his offer, her distaste and anger simmered over his arrogance.

She studied his handsome profile, which kept her pulse racing. No matter how hard she tried or how annoyed he made her, it was impossible for her to see him any way other than sexy and appealing. One month of intimacy with him. The mere thought took her breath. His strong hands held the wheel and he watched the road, but she suspected he was aware of her gaze on him.

He was irresistible, yet at the same time he was another billionaire who lived by his own rules and thought of the world in relation to himself. She longed to fling her refusal at him, yet wisdom held her back. There was too much at stake to do that, and she knew she would eventually accept or hate herself forever; yet each time she was on the verge of saying yes, every principle in her screamed no. She admitted to herself it was his high-handed, presumptuous attitude that aggravated her.

As she studied his profile, she tried to think of any conceivable way to avoid accepting yet not lose what he had offered. She couldn't come up with any possibility. To get the money and sale, she had to become his mistress. Live with him starting immediately! She might as well accept his proposition, yet the prospect was dizzying. Her gaze ran down the length of him and desire was hot, intense. And could she possibly be his mistress for a month without having her heart shattered far worse than the hurt she had suffered from her broken engagement?

At the restaurant she barely noticed the linen-covered tables or heard the soft piano music in the background. In the flickering candlelight all she could see was her handsome escort who wanted her to be his mistress badly enough to make her a fabulous offer.

He smiled and reached across the table to take her hand. "You're worrying far too much. Let it go for tonight and enjoy the evening. Whatever your decision, it'll be easier to make. You'll know better whether or not you enjoy being with me."

"You and I both know already that I like going out with you," she replied, aware of his fingers rubbing her knuckles while his eyes conveyed his desire. "I wish you'd stayed that Montana cowboy you must once have been."

"Had I done that, you wouldn't be getting this offer, which should be advantageous for both of us, not just one. I won't be the only one to benefit from it," he reminded her, and she merely nodded.

They ordered dinners, and after the entrees arrived, Laurel ate only a few bites before putting down her fork. "I can't imagine eating one more bite of food. You say to let it go tonight, but how can I forget even one full minute the prospect of becoming your mistress or the financial offer you've made?"

"Dance with me and maybe moving around will get your mind off your decision." He raised her hand to brush his lips across her fingers, his warm breath sending another sizzle racing over her nerves. "You're beautiful, Laurel," he whispered.

"Thank you," she answered, pleased in spite of herself.

In his arms on the dance floor, Chase smiled at her. "So, tell me about growing up in Montana and where you went to school and what you did."

She tried to focus on answering his question and get her mind off his proposition for the time being. "We lived here in town most of the time so we could go to school here," she said, telling him about her early years. Chase was an attentive listener, adding tidbits about his boyhood, and soon she forgot for long moments the problem at hand as she laughed with Chase about their childhoods.

"I mentioned before that my dad was always ready for a party and always having groups of friends out to our place. He played the banjo and sang and taught all of us to sing and perform with him," she said.

"Do you play the banjo?"

"Heavens, no!" she exclaimed. "I learned to play the piano and to sing and dance, so I would sing while he played the banjo—we all sang."

"I can't imagine my dad cutting loose like that," Chase said. "He worked until he was exhausted every night. He was out working before sunrise and didn't come in until after sunset. There wasn't singing and dancing and we worked, too. I don't remember when I didn't work. Maybe that's why I like to play now," he stated, and she wondered about his life.

"Don't you want to settle sometime when you're older? That's a bleak outlook on life."

"Bleak? Far from it," he replied. "From my viewpoint, it's the best possible outlook."

"Are your parents unhappy in their marriage?"

"No, not as far as I know, although I certainly would be in the same situation. I've tried to give them trips, but they won't go. I don't ever want to be in that kind of relationship. Marriage looms like prison."

"I have an entirely different view," she said, realizing Chase was definitely a confirmed bachelor and still thinking it was a bleak outlook.

"We had parties, often several times a month, either in town or on the ranch in good weather. I grew up playing, but Mom saw to it that we worked, also," she said.

"Then I'm surprised you're not one of those party women. You've shouldered a lot of responsibility," he said, studying her as they danced.

Gazing into his eyes, she could see desire ignite in their depths and the moment changed. She forgot their conversation and became aware of their hands touching, their bodies pressed together lightly, and she wanted his kiss.

"Let's go back to the hotel," he suggested and she nodded.

The moment they were in the limousine, he pulled her into his arms to kiss her.

As they entered the hotel, the clerk handed a note to Laurel. Frightened, she feared any late call concerned her dad. "Chase, wait a minute," she said as she scanned the brief message swiftly. Her fears lifted when she saw it was from a family friend, and she pocketed the note. "No big deal. Sorry, but I worry about my dad, so I have to check any contact."

"Sure. No problem," Chase replied, holding her arm as they entered the elevator and rode to the top.

"Want to come in for a little while?" she asked.

"Of course," he answered in a deeper voice, and she knew they would take up with kisses where they had left off.

Inside, she turned to wrap her arms around his neck. His arms banded her and he held her to kiss her long and hard. When he raised his head, her heart pounded. She opened her eyes slowly to find him watching her with a hooded expression.

"You think about my offer, Laurel. I had a great time tonight with you," he added.

"I did with you," she confessed, although she felt a degree of reluctance to admit it to him. He had far too much self-assurance already. "I'll think about it all night," she whispered, wanting to pull him back to kiss some more, knowing she might as well give him an answer this moment.

"I'll take you to breakfast and we can talk," he said. "How's seven?"

"Fine," she said.

He gazed into her eyes and caressed her throat. "You're fantastic," he whispered, leaning down to brush her lips with his, another tormenting kiss that heightened her desire.

He turned and left, shutting the door behind him. Wanting to kiss him again, she stood motionless, her entire body tingling with awareness. She ran her hand across her forehead and walked in a daze to her bedroom. She knew there was only one answer to give him.

Agree to become his mistress and the hotel was sold. Half a million on top of it. For the first time she allowed herself to consider what his offer truly could mean to her and her family, and it made her weak in the knees.

She sat at her desk and noticed a blinking red light on her phone, which jogged her memory about the note she'd been given downstairs. She withdrew it again. *Need to talk to you tonight—Ty Carson.* She thought of the local rancher who had been a friend of her family all her life and was her best friend's father. She listened to her voice mail on the phone to hear a message from Ty asking her to return his call no matter what time she got the message.

The urgency of his calls puzzled her, and she picked up the phone and dialed the number he had left. After one ring he answered, said he was in the hotel bar and asked if she would meet him so they could talk.

With growing curiosity, she took the elevator to the first floor and saw Ty waiting near the door to the darkened bar. With the sun-toughened skin of a Montana rancher, he was in jeans, a white shirt and a western broad-brimmed hat. He spotted her and headed toward her, meeting her with a brief hug.

"Thanks, Laurel. I know it's late, but this is urgent. Where can we talk?"

"Why don't we go to my office?" she said, leading the way. Instead of sitting behind her desk, she turned a chair to face him. He tossed his hat on a sofa by the door and raked his hand through his salt-and-pepper hair as he gazed at her with a solemn expression.

Placing his elbows on his knees, he leaned forward. "I wanted to see you about Chase Bennett and his outfit. Your dad is in the hospital and he can't talk to you, and I feel responsible to try to help in his place even though I'm not family, but I'm close. Your grandmother won't and your sisters aren't able to discuss this with you."

Becoming increasingly puzzled, she smiled uneasily. "Mr. Carson, you don't need to worry about me."

He held up his hand. "Just call me Ty, Laurel. I'm worried about you—me and my family and everyone else in these parts. If things were reversed, I'd feel better if your dad talked to Becca. By the way, she doesn't know I'm here."

"I appreciate your concern," Laurel said, thinking about Ty's eldest daughter.

"That man is coming in like a whirlwind and trying to change everything he can. A bunch of us are getting together to talk about what we can do to protect ourselves."

"Mr. Car—Ty, I'm shocked," she said, frowning. "I thought Chase's business here would help Athens."

"He's out for himself, not Athens. At the same time I'm worried about you. I've heard that he's taking you out, and I know you're getting over a broken engagement. The hotel is for sale, and I assume it's to help pay your dad's hospital expenses. Whatever the problems, Laurel, we all need to band together to help each other. The man is a shark, and he's after too much around here."

"I really appreciate your concern, but I'm fine and I can deal with him," she said, thinking about her evenings with Chase and his offer and realizing it had all become more complicated because local people must be viewing him as an enemy.

"Laurel, you can't deal with a man like this. He has endless resources. He wants my ranch and he's after it however he can get it."

"You absolutely don't care to sell?" she asked, surprised that Chase wanted the Carson ranch.

"Damn straight, I don't. My great-great-great-grandfather started our ranch, and it's been in the family since that time. What would I do, where would I move? And there's no good reason to sell. Oh, Bennett has offered a huge price, more than I could get if I put the ranch on the market, but that's no incentive. My boys like the ranch and I expect them to take over eventually."

"Why does Chase want it?" she asked. All her life, particularly as a child, she'd seen her father and his friends as strong, invincible men. Now her dad was in a coma in a hospital, and here was his friend, Ty, appearing older, worried and sounding vulnerable—it gave her heart a painful twist.

"My ranch is adjacent to the field he's discovered, and I have water—more abundantly than anywhere else—and my place would give him the easiest access from Athens. Let me show you," he said, reaching into his hip pocket and pulling out a folded, tattered paper. It had been torn out of a book and she saw it was a map of Montana. He had circled Athens, and beyond Athens Ty had drawn a red circle around his ranch. Beside his ranch, with a yellow marker, he'd circled the field where Chase would drill, and instantly she saw that the best access from Athens would be across Ty's ranch.

"Oh, heavens!" she exclaimed, looking over the map. The best town for him to center his activities in was Athens because other towns were farther away from his new oil field.

"He's pressuring me something fierce and thinks he can run me off my own land," Ty said.

"Well, in this day and time, he can't do that," she said, irritated again by Chase's selfish actions.

Ty shifted uncomfortably and scowled. "He can't run me off, but he can make life harder for me if I stay."

"How? I can't imagine he would do anything like that."

"He would in a flash. He's already bought the Higgens' place, and he can divert water that I get. He can boggle up a couple of entrances to my place where it's not as convenient for me to come and go. It's little things mostly—so far," he added darkly. "Bennett can buy up some of the local supply places and raise prices, which will hurt all of us. His people have made it clear that he's determined to get my ranch, and what's worse is there's a huge chunk of the ranch I took a loan against three years ago, and there are rumors that he's considering buying the bank. Mitch knows if he doesn't sell to him, Bennett will start his own bank here."

She shivered slightly with a cold chill. How ruthless was Chase? How far would he go and how much would he hurt local people to get what he wanted?

"I just hoped to make it clear to you that we'll all give you assistance if you need help," Ty said and she nodded.

"Thanks. We're all right, and with Dad's health I do want to sell the hotel and the ranch. The doctors have told me that Dad may not be able to take care of any of it again the way he did. If we still own it all, he'll try."

"You can't know that for certain, Laurel. I think you ought to hang on until he recovers—a bunch of us are willing to try to help you. We'll support him, too."

"Thanks so much, Ty," she said, touched by his offer. "That means a lot, and I wish Dad could know what you're willing to do."

"The Durbins, the Malloys, the Dubinskis. I could keep giving you names—we're all banding together to protect each other from Bennett. I don't know whether we can because he is already putting too much pressure on us." Ty stood. "It's late and I need to get home. Molly worries when I'm gone. Stay away from Bennett, Laurel. Be careful. The guy doesn't have your interests at heart."

She walked to the door with Ty. "Thanks again," she said, patting his arm. "I'll think about what you've said. Please tell Molly and Becca hello."

"Sure. You be careful. Call anytime you want me. Don't let him pressure you, Laurel. And don't let him sweet-talk you, either. You know my cell number."

She nodded and watched him walk down the hall and turn the corner. Then she closed the door, leaning against it to think about what he'd said to her.

How ruthless *was* Chase? she wondered again. If she moved in with Chase, would townspeople be angry with her and feel as if she were siding with the enemy?

When she'd heard about the new discovery of the Montana field, she'd thought it would be a windfall for Athens and all the ranchers in the surrounding area. Evidently, some people would be hurt in all the change. Yet if she accepted Chase's offer, it would be a windfall for her.

She switched off the lights and went the back way to her floor. A light shone beneath Chase's door, and she wondered what he was doing. She went to her suite and stepped inside, moving automatically while she contemplated her choices.

Debating both sides, she pulled on a long nightgown and cotton robe and switched off lights, curling up in a chair to gaze outside into the darkness and consider Chase's proposition.

Two hours later she came to the same conclusion she had every time she considered various possibilities.

Tomorrow she would have breakfast with him, and she needed to give him an answer. If she waited much longer, he would seduce her anyway and his offer would be beside the point. Then she would lose not only the sale of the hotel but also the bonus of half a million dollars. Too, too much for her to turn down, and he knew it.

The next thing was to decide whether there were any concessions that she wanted to try to wring out of him.

After tossing and turning, Laurel woke early the next morning. Following her usual morning routine during summer, she slipped into her bathing suit and went down to the pool to swim. It was locked at that time of day, but she had a key. She placed her things on a chaise and dove into the cool water, swimming laps and trying to work off some energy and worries. Breathless, she bobbed up at the deep end, catching the side and tossing her head back to get water out of her eyes.

"Good morning," a deep voice said, startling her. Chase sat on the edge, his feet dangling in the water.

"You're not supposed to be out here!" she blurted. "How did you get in?"

"Bribery," he replied easily. "And now I'm glad I did. I like a morning swim. It gives me a chance to think. I suspect we share that."

While she was annoyed to find that an employee had been talked into letting him in early, her attention was taken by broad shoulders, a stomach like a washboard, with a well-sculpted chest and firm biceps. In spite of bobbing in cool water, heat ignited in her, spreading, playing havoc with her pulse. Dark curls were a mat across the center of his impressive chest. In his clothes he had looked good, but out of them he was breathtaking.

He dropped off the edge and bobbed in the water by her, placing his hands on her waist and lifting her slightly as he looked her over leisurely. When he did, the hot pink suit that she had pulled on so casually this morning suddenly seemed skimpy and revealing.

"We can skip breakfast," he suggested, his gaze returning to hers, and she knew what he was asking.

"No, we can't," she answered breathlessly. "You promised breakfast, and I'm holding you to it."

"I want to hold you to something else," he said in a deeper tone, and every nerve came alive. She twisted free and swam away, aware that he followed and kept up with her. At the shallow end she stood, water running off her. His gaze moved over her again in a slower, more thorough study down to her thighs.

He inhaled. "I think I better let you go in ahead of me," he said and flung himself into the water to swim away from her. She climbed out of the pool with her back tingling, sure he was watching her whether or not he was swimming. She scooped up her towel and headed to the gate. As she stepped through, she glanced back to find him standing on the side of the pool with his towel in his hand while he stared at her.

She turned swiftly but not before feeling another wave of heat in her lower regions. He was a magnificent hunk, making his offer even more tempting. She hurried the back way to her room and headed for the shower, unable to shed the images of him, too easily imagining him without that last scrap of clothing and knowing he was probably doing the same to her.

She bathed and dressed carefully, selecting an indigo cotton suit, a matching blouse and high-heeled matching pumps. She combed, looped and pinned her hair at the back of her head.

Promptly at seven he appeared, wearing a charcoal-colored suit with a fresh white shirt. He smiled as he looked at her and stepped inside.

"You're breathtaking. So far, this is starting out to be the best day I've had in Montana."

She laughed. "I know better than that!"

"Soon I hope I get to take down your hair," he said in a husky tone that added to her anticipation. He was more desirable each time she was with him—clean-shaven, hair combed, a scrubbed look about him. His aftershave was another enticing scent. He looked dressed for a photo shoot, which he could have done easily with great model potential. All that thick brown hair made her want to run her fingers through it, and she tried to keep her gaze away from his mouth. His heavily lashed, fascinating green eyes were doing enough damage to her self-restraint already.

He stepped closer to touch the corner of her mouth. "I like your smiles," he said. "Even though so far there haven't been many of them."

"These are not the happiest of times."

"I'm sorry to hear that, and I know it's because of your dad."

"My dad, selling the hotel, being away from my business—mostly Dad."

"Any chance you want to give me your decision this morning?"

She noticed that he watched her closely. She smiled again as she shook her head. "Let's wait until after breakfast and let me have a few more minutes of public time with you before we get down to business."

"Down to business—not really. This is something else."

"Down to lust?"

"Still something else," he said. "I like being with you. Lust can be easily satisfied."

"I guess I should be flattered," she said, still reluctant to give him her answer and knowing she was putting it off. She'd already resigned herself to what she was going to do. "I'm ready to go to breakfast," she said, gazing up at him and feeling as if he were on the verge of kissing her and beginning to want him to even though she was angry with him.

He crossed the room to hold the door and the moment was gone, but she was excited by merely thinking about his kisses. In the hall he took her arm, his fingers a faint pressure, yet she was conscious of it.

"An old family friend came to visit me last night after I left you. It was Ty Carson," she said.

"Wasn't that a little late for a friendly visit?" Chase asked. They entered the elevator and she saw speculation in his expression.

"He's worried and wanted to warn me about you. He said you're after his ranch, which he doesn't want to sell. His great-great-great-grandfather established that ranch, and Ty loves the place. He was raised there and his kids grew up there."

"I'll admit, I'd like to buy it. I've tried to make him an extremely good offer," Chase said, running his index finger along her collar and distracting her.

"He's adamant about it, Chase. He doesn't want to leave his ranch."

Chase shrugged. "That's his preference. Whatever he wants to do." The elevator doors opened, and she was quiet until they were seated and had ordered breakfast.

"Ty seems to think you'll force him to sell or make life unpleasant for him," she said, watching Chase, but he had no reaction to her statement. Seated across from her, he looked every inch the executive he was, as well as still looking as if he were ready to model. The man was handsome, but there was a cool look in his eyes that indicated the power he wielded. Already she was certain she would have to guard her heart well or he would break it far worse than any hurt inflicted by Edward.

"How on earth can I force him to sell?" Chase asked.

"I guess by making ranch life a little more difficult for him. He said something about limiting the availability of his water. He mentioned that you've already bought a ranch that borders his place."

"That doesn't have anything to do with him. It's a business deal," Chase replied in an offhanded manner.

"Ty's a good man, Chase," she said quietly. "I've known him all my life. I've known the whole family, and his daughter is my best friend. He said you want to buy the bank, too."

"I might," he replied with a faint smile, "but I think that also falls under business and shouldn't make me villain of the year. I really expect my company to help the town of Athens."

"I hope so," she said with sincerity. "One last note before I leave the subject of Ty's visit—he warned me to avoid you. By being seen with you, I may test friendships."

One of Chase's dark eyebrows arched. "I'll admit that's bad news, and I'll have to work on my image with the locals. I don't want to hurt you or cause you trouble."

She shrugged. "I'll worry about that. You don't need to. Just try to avoid riding roughshod over people or hurting someone needlessly," she added.

"I don't intend to, but there are things in work that have to be pursued—you're self-employed, so you should understand."

"I comprehend firm dealings and fairness and honesty, but I don't want to hurt anyone or take their home from them."

"You make me sound like Simon Legree," he said, smiling and leaning forward to touch her chin. "If the townspeople are getting down on me and want you to avoid me, perhaps we should spend our time together away from Athens."

She reached across the table to take his hand. "We'll keep a discreet distance when we're in public. Now, let's enjoy breakfast and then we can go talk in private."

Instantly his eyes darkened, and he inhaled. "Want to go now and have breakfast sent up?"

"Do you think we'd really eat? We have some wonderful strawberries that I've been drooling over."

"There's only one thing in this hotel that I'm drooling over, but I'll wait if I have to," he said, gazing intently at her.

"That's good. It's a glorious morning and I've had a refreshing swim and worked up an appetite."

He smiled and reached out to take her hand again. "I won't mention my appetite," he said, yet she knew what he wanted.

"You just did," she reminded him and they both smiled. Was he really the ruthless monster Ty had described? Would Chase help or hurt Athens? He expected to help the town and she couldn't imagine that he wouldn't, yet she worried about Ty almost as much as if he were part of her family.

The waiter came with their order and refilled sparkling goblets with orange juice before he left.

"Tell me about Athens and the people who live here," Chase said.

"Nearly everyone knows everyone else," she said. "Until my generation most people didn't move away and the town grew. But that's not true currently—most high school grads go to college, on to jobs and never return. I'm an example of that, and I don't expect my sisters to come back here to live. I don't care for ranch life—neither do my sisters. I think my grandmother is tired of dealing with the ranch, and I don't think any of them will mind moving to Dallas."

Chase asked her about specific people he had met, the local lawyers, various business people, until breakfast was finished and they left to go to her suite.

The one subject he didn't broach was his offer.

"I have an appointment at nine this morning, and sometime today I'm going to the hospital to see Dad," Laurel told him as they rode in the elevator. Her palms were damp because it was time to give him his answer and at this moment she could still change her mind. Was she making a decision she would regret deeply? Or one that would be a relief to her later when she looked back on it? With each minute tension coiled tighter in her.

Once inside her suite, he closed the door and the lock automatically clicked, sounding loud in the silence.

He shed his coat, loosened his tie and strolled to her, placing his hands on her shoulders. "I think it's time I hear your decision on my offer. Will you be my mistress for the next month?"

Five

"I have a counteroffer," Laurel said quietly. "I don't know how much you'll bargain to get me to accept what you've proposed. I've been warned that I'll be hurt, that you're ruthless. Also, I think if I have a close relationship with you, folks around here are going to be unhappy with me. Therefore it has to be worth my while. And you are well able to afford more than you offered, and you know it."

Amusement lit Chase's eyes. "I can guess—you want more money."

"That's right," she replied, hoping he couldn't hear her pounding heart. "I want another quarter million on top of what you offered."

He nodded. "Fine. Do we have a deal?" he asked.

She realized she could have asked for a million and he probably would have agreed as swiftly. "Also," she added, her heartbeat racing as she tried to blank out what she was committing to. "There are two more things. I'd like to be able to continue to live in my suite until we move to Dallas."

"Certainly. I would have offered that anyway. I want you living here, hopefully closer than this suite. What else?"

She took a deep breath. "I can't imagine jumping into bed in the next few minutes. I want until tonight at least."

As he smiled, triumph sparkled in his eyes. "Excellent," he whispered. "You have a deal."

All the time she'd talked, an inner voice had screamed to avoid accepting, but she knew she couldn't. She had way too much to gain and not much to lose, if she could only remember to guard her heart. That would be the biggest danger to her well-being. She might be ostracized by locals, but she could weather their hostility and she would move back to Dallas eventually.

"Can you clear your books and go away for the weekend with me? Locals are getting hostile over how much I'm seeing you—actually over how much you're seeing me. Let's get out of here for a weekend. If anything changes with your dad, I'll fly you back immediately," Chase said.

"Where are we going?"

"I have a home on the California coast."

"Very well," she answered, knowing the chances of having to get to the hospital in a hurry seemed slim, but she didn't want to be too far away.

"Then we have a deal. I'll get my attorney working on the purchase this morning and we'll close as quickly as possible. I'll see if I can't have the closing moved up. We need to get the inspections done—the usual routine."

"It's a little difficult to accept that this is actually happening," she said, feeling stunned as she began to think about the sale and the money she would have.

"I'll put the money into an account for you today," he said.

"Since I'm going to be living with you, I want you to meet my family. Can you go to the ranch with me tonight?"

"Meet your family?" he asked with a frown. "This isn't a long-term arrangement," he reminded her. "If you take me home to meet the family, won't that be an implication that our relationship is serious?"

"Whether it is or not, if I go off for the weekend with you and then move in with you, I want them to know you," she said flatly, trying to retain her patience. "I don't want them to hear I'm seriously involved with you when they don't have a clue who you are."

"We're not going to be 'seriously' involved," he remarked dryly.

She bit her lip and her temper rose. "If I'm living with you for a month, I'm seriously involved, Chase."

"That's fine," he said, rubbing her upper arms, "but when the month is over, I'm gone."

"You've made that abundantly clear," she snapped.

"Why do I suspect your grandmother won't like me at all?"

"What do you care?" she retorted, surprised that he even brought up the subject. Or were some of his old Montana values still alive? Why was he so opposed to marriage? His parents were still together and she hadn't heard him say any dreadful thing about their relationship.

"I'm not worried," he replied in an unconcerned tone. "I'm surprised you wanted to introduce me to them. Your younger sisters will probably find the whole idea exciting that you've got a new man in your life so soon after Edward."

"I'm sure you're right. Also, I want you to meet them anyway, because even though the entire family has agreed it's for the best to sell the hotel and get the responsibility for it off my father's shoulders, this hotel is our heritage and has been in our family since the first Tolson settled in Montana. The sale is probably the most difficult for my grandmother. I'd like my family to meet you and get to know you a little so that won't seem so cold and impersonal."

Smiling, he rubbed his knuckles lightly on her cheek. "Softie. Sure, I don't mind. I'll be happy to meet them. I can't guarantee that they'll approve of whatever I do with the hotel."

"That's all right. In time, it won't matter so much. If they move from Montana, it won't be important at all."

"I remember your sisters are Ashley and Diana. What's your grandmother's name?"

"You have a good memory. It's Spring Tolson. I call her Gramma."

"Your sisters are seventeen and fifteen. It won't be long until Ashley will be going to college."

"Yes, and now I'll be able to send her."

He smiled at her. "Hopefully, you'll never regret your decision to accept my offer."

"Time will tell," she said, her thoughts on business at hand. "I'll call my real estate agent, inform Brice and let my family know. I'll tell them we'll get there about six. How's that? We'll have to leave here about half-past four."

"Fine," he replied, sliding his arm around her waist. "At last," he whispered. Her heartbeat quickened and her lips tingled in anticipation as she slipped her arms around his neck.

He kissed her possessively, and she returned his passion with her own. Fires built deep and low inside, and her hips arched against him, his arousal evident. His arm tightened around her waist, pulling her closer.

Thoughts spun away as her temperature soared and desire became torment. She ran her hands across his broad shoulders and felt his hands moving on her as he pushed away her suit jacket and it fell around her ankles.

Then his hands were in her hair, pins spilled out and blond locks tumbled around her face.

Her desire flared, hot and intense. Wanting him more each time they were together, she knew she soon would be able to let go of constraints, to touch and kiss him as much as she desired. Eagerly, she combed her fingers through his thick hair, then she slipped her hand down to caress his nape and the strong column of his neck while she arched against him. Above the roaring of her pulse, her moan was dim.

His hand cupped her bottom, crushing her against him. He shifted, his fingers twisting free her buttons and reaching beneath her blouse to shove away the flimsy lace and lightly rub her nipple.

Desire escalated and she wanted to toss aside waiting, but caution prevailed.

She pushed away. "Chase, not so fast. We both have appointments soon. Not yet," she said.

His eyes clouded with desire. "I want you," he said in a husky voice, looking at her mouth.

Her heart pounding, she stepped out of his embrace. "It's early morning, Chase, and we have so many things to do today."

He nodded, but his gaze stayed on her mouth and then ran hotly over her, as tangible as if it were his hands caressing her. His dark hair was tangled, locks falling over his forehead, always reminding her of the biker she'd first met. His fresh, immaculate shirt was slightly rumpled, and his slacks bulged from their kisses.

Chase came closer, sliding his hand behind her head. "It will be amazing between us, Laurel. You'll see."

"Watch out, Chase. You might fall in love."

"I might fall in love, but I won't marry. When the month ends, so will our relationship."

Even though she knew he wouldn't wed, his words were cold and harsh and gave her a twist of pain along with stirring her anger.

"You've made it clear you're a bachelor for life because of your parents' dull marriage," she answered coolly, determined to avoid losing her heart to him but equally resolved that if she did, to never let him know or show it.

He picked up his suit coat and slipped into it, straightening his tie and putting himself back together so he looked as neat as he had when he'd arrived. "I'll call my attorneys and get everything started. The sooner we begin, the quicker everything will be done. Do you want to meet me at your bank to make this deposit today? You should call your bank president and make an appointment for us."

"If you want to wait, I'll do that right now."

"Sure, it'll save time," he replied and followed her through the suite to the bedroom, where she crossed the room to a desk and in minutes had an appointment set up for eleven.

When she replaced the receiver, she gazed at Chase. "None of this seems real."

"It will," he replied, reaching out to lightly caress her nape again. "I'm counting the hours," he whispered, leaning down to kiss her. Standing on tiptoe, she placed her hands on his chest and kissed him back. In minutes he raised his head.

Dazed, as usual, she looked up to find him watching her intently. He put his finger beneath her chin and tilted her face. "This is going to be a long day," he said. "You're making me wait, which is what I was trying to avoid."

"You're getting what you want, Chase. Everything is the way you wanted."

"Soon I'll get what I desire—you, Laurel. I want to kiss each sweet inch of you," he whispered, brushing another kiss across her lips. "I have to go," he said, striding toward the door. Following, she watched him with mixed feelings until the door was closed behind him.

For the first time what she was acquiring from Chase and what it would mean to her and her family sunk in, and she wanted to jump in the air and shout with delight. She thought about what she would receive—almost one million dollars today! She would be able to do so much for her family. She thought about telling her grandmother, but the minute she announced she was leaving for the weekend with Chase, the questions would commence and she dreaded answering them.

The hotel was sold. This was a monumental date in the

history of her family because the hotel would no longer belong to the Tolsons. The loans with the bank could be paid off fully. She felt as if a crushing weight had lifted from her shoulders.

No more pacing the floor until wee hours of the morning, wondering what they would do if the hotel didn't sell or if the medical bills kept climbing. No more worrying over how she would get the proper care for her father. So many problems that Chase's money would solve easily. Joy bubbled in her, and she relished the relief that buoyed her and made her want to laugh and dance and sing. Her father's debts would be totally eliminated. Maybe someday he would recover and know all was taken care of and he had no worries.

The one thing to aim for as a goal was to come out of this arrangement with her heart intact. She dashed to the phone to call Brice to ask him to meet her in her office, then rushed to grab her jacket and look in the mirror. Her blouse was wrinkled and her hair tumbled over her shoulders. She changed into a fresh white blouse, combed and pinned her hair up, yanked on her suit jacket and left.

By the time she reached her office, Brice was standing outside the door. "What's happened? Is your dad better?" he asked. "You look like you've had good news."

"It's not Dad, but the next best thing right now."

"You sold the hotel?" he asked, following her into the office.

She spun around, hugged him and stepped away. "Yes! Chase has bought the hotel. I made a deal with him, Brice."

He smiled. "Congratulations! I'm happy for you, Laurel. You deserve this. You've really earned it. You've worked harder than any of us."

"I don't know about that. I had a big personal stake," she said. "Thank you, though."

"It's fantastic!" he exclaimed. "We'll celebrate officially soon when it's convenient for you."

"I can't celebrate too much with Dad in the hospital, but

I'm happy, Brice. Thanks for all your help on this. You're getting a bonus for your part."

"Thanks, beyond words. I have a feeling I had nothing to do with this sale," he added dryly. "I'm beginning to hear rumors from various places that some are less than happy with Chase Bennett's heavy-handed approach and his taking over everything he chooses, so I'm glad you got what you want."

"I'm happy, Brice. Be sure you always remember that."

He gave her a quizzical look and his eyebrows arched. "Did you get the price you wanted?"

"I got my asking price, plus a generous bonus."

"That sort of boggles the mind," he said, his eyes narrowing as he studied her. "He must have really wanted the hotel."

"He did," she answered smoothly, becoming uncomfortable with the turn in the conversation. "I have to let Lane know. I'm sure Chase's people will call him if they haven't already."

Her cell phone rung. "Speaking of our realtor—here's Lane Grigsby."

Brice walked away while she talked to Lane and agreed to an appointment to sign the contract.

"Chase's realtor had called Lane, and we're meeting this afternoon in Lane's office."

"Again, congratulations!"

"I'm taking Chase home to the ranch for dinner tonight so he can meet Gramma and the girls."

Brice frowned. "Is it getting that thick with you and Chase?"

She nodded. "I guess it is in a way. I simply wanted him to meet them."

"You've had dinner with him and been with him constantly since his arrival. Now you're taking him home to meet the family. Laurel, be careful. You just got over Edward."

She smiled. "It's not serious and I'm not engaged and I'm fine."

"This conversation is a complete turnaround. I was lectured you to be nice to the man and you despised him without ever seeing him. Now that's reversed. Maybe I shouldn't have urged you so much to be nice to him. Don't get that involved with Chase Bennett. Your dad isn't here. If he were, I'd keep quiet, but I don't want to see you hurt again."

"Brice, everyone wants to take care of me because Dad's in the hospital. He's let me take care of myself since Mom died. I'll be fine, and Chase Bennett isn't going to break my heart. Not at all. He's not the marrying kind, and I'm not ready for that either. Especially to a playboy. I've been there and done that—at least an engagement—and I don't want to do it again."

As he walked toward the door, Brice held up his hands. "Okay, okay. Don't take my head off. I merely don't want to see you hurt by a man who is well known as a womanizer. I've watched him pass through the lobby and every female in sight drools. And I promise you, he won't marry."

"I'm not going to get hurt."

"I'll see you later. If you need me, call," he said. As he left, she stared after him with an uncomfortable feeling, postponing telling him that she was going away for the weekend with Chase and wishing no one would ever know. But the whole town would learn about it soon.

She called her grandmother to tell her that she was bringing Chase to the ranch for dinner that night. Next, she spent over an hour taking care of hotel business. At twenty minutes before eleven, she left to go to the bank. Chase was waiting. He watched her cross the lobby, and her insides churned beneath his gaze. Nothing seemed real about the moment, including the huge sum of money he intended to deposit into her account. Self-conscious beneath his steady gaze, she was also aware of Chase; she could easily look at him for hours on end. He stood, one hand in a pocket, the other at his side, looking as if he owned the bank. It was also a shock to realize that soon she would be living with him.

For a panicky moment she realized she still could back out without complications. The money hadn't been put into her account, and her anger over his arrogance still simmered. Chase had a ruthless streak, and she thought of Ty's and Brice's warnings—both justified. She could turn around right now, walk out and her life would be her own. She halted, looking across the bank into Chase's eyes, and then he sauntered toward her.

He didn't hurry, crossing the room as if she weren't his destination, yet he never took his gaze from her. As she walked to meet him, her heart drummed.

And then he was only a few feet away. "Ready?" he asked, but she suspected he was aware of what she felt.

One last chance. She debated once more, angry with him for his expectations, that damnable certainty that he could get what he wanted one way or another. Yet, she knew he would. The money and what it could do for her family was too fantastic. And so was Chase. She nodded. "I'm ready."

"You don't have to look as if I have a gun at your back," he said.

She smiled and moved on and he walked beside her.

The slender, graying bank president, Mitch Anson, a longtime family friend, could barely contain his curiosity while he ushered them into his office and chatted briefly. He continually studied Laurel as if she'd worked some sort of magic spell on Chase who seemed relaxed, no more disturbed than if he'd been depositing a couple of hundred into her account.

Chase wrote a check to her and she stared at the figures that would forever change her and her family's lives. She glanced up to see him watching her intently, and then she looked back at the unbelievable sum that was becoming reality and would be all hers within minutes.

"This is hard to fathom," she said with amazement.

"It's yours now, a bonus for the hotel," Chase said, she assumed for the benefit of Mitch Anson.

"I can't really believe it." She endorsed the check and gave it to Mitch, who stared at it, blinked and then smiled broadly at her.

"You've received a generous payment," Mitch said, smiling at Chase. "Quite fabulous."

"I'll be moving some of it soon, Mr. Anson," she said.

"Of course. If we can help with investments or savings, you know we will," he told her.

They finished and walked out with Mitch accompanying them. He was cheerful and chatty with both of them and it took a short time to get away, but once they were alone, she turned to Chase.

"Talk will be all over town before I get back to the office."

"I assumed bankers were supposed to keep such things quiet," he said.

"Mitch is good about most secrets, but everyone will know about the sale of the hotel. Besides, I think Mitch still sees me as a kid."

"I can guarantee you that I don't," Chase remarked, and she smiled at him.

"You never knew me as a kid."

"I still wouldn't see you that way now. Let's go get lunch before we have to meet at the real estate office."

They bought sandwiches and took them to the park to sit beneath the shade of a large black walnut tree. As they sat on a bench and ate their sandwiches, she studied him, curious, but hesitant to pry into his personal life.

"Penny for your thoughts. You're very quiet all of a sudden," he said.

She debated whether to really tell him what was on her mind or not, deciding to go ahead. "I was wondering about you. You don't have to answer if you don't want. Have you ever been in love and had a broken heart?" she asked.

"Nope, that's easy to answer. Not unless you count when I had my heart broken in the sixth grade. I thought I'd never recover. Patsy Lou Jessup wouldn't meet me after school for pizza. I thought the world was going to end."

Laurel smiled. "Did you ever kiss her?"

"Oh, my, yes. Fabulous kisses, even with braces, but it wasn't meant to be and the next year she moved to Detroit. I've never seen her since."

"I wonder if she ever reads about you."

"I doubt if she remembers me. I don't think I made much of an impression on her."

"Hard to imagine," she said, and he grinned. He shed his suit coat, rolled his sleeves up and removed his tie.

"I take it you haven't made Mitch an offer on the bank yet."

"No. Actually, my staff is dealing with what we acquire in Montana. I'd just planned to come for a couple of days to look over everything, go see my folks for a few days and then fly back to Houston. I got sidetracked," he said, smiling at her. "As far as the bank is concerned, if I buy it, will that be another mark against me?"

She shook her head. "I don't care whether you purchase the bank or not. As long as you don't hurt people."

"I hope to do the opposite." He touched a lock of her hair that had come loose. "You put your hair up again. It looks nice, but I like it down."

"Sometimes you'll get what you want and sometimes you won't," she said.

"You don't care whether you please me or not, do you?"

"I'm not worrying about it, if that's what you mean. I don't recall any stipulation about pleasing you," she said and amusement sparkled in his eyes.

"I hope to try to keep you happy," he said. "You're different from other women I've known."

"I can well imagine," she said, "but you tell me. How am I different?"

"You're more direct, for one thing. I know where I stand with you. You're not as eager to keep me happy."

She shook her head. "Makes me wonder why you're interested in me."

"You're gorgeous and sexy and there's fire when we're together, more so when we kiss—"

"I get the picture," she interrupted. She folded up the papers. "It's time for me to get back to the office, and soon we'll meet to sign the contract on the hotel."

His hand closed on her wrist. "You almost stopped and walked out of the bank today, didn't you?" he asked.

She took a deep breath and tried to curb the annoyance that still simmered in her. "You're arrogant, self-willed and flamboyant," she said. "I had a moment there, but I had made my decision and I stuck by it."

"I can't seem to improve my image," he said, standing and taking papers from her. "Get your purse and c'mon. We'll walk back to the hotel."

"So, how do you see me?" she asked as they strolled back, curious about his perception of her.

"Independent, alluring, a chip on your shoulder—maybe from Edward."

She shrugged. "You're probably right, at least about being independent and having a chip on my shoulder. Alluring, I wouldn't know."

"Trust me, alluring fits."

"My grandmother is probably cooking a roast right now," Laurel said, shifting the topic of conversation.

"Sounds delicious," he said. "I'm looking forward to meeting her."

Suddenly they were back at the hotel. Since they were in public, she said a professional goodbye; then she left him to go to her room and make calls.

Chase had a meeting to attend regarding the property they needed to acquire in Athens.

During the meeting, he realized he had let his thoughts

stray from business to Laurel. Wryly, he thought that was another first in his life—several of them now with her, but all were meaningless and easy to explain. He had never had his attention shift from business because he was thinking about the woman he would go out with that night.

She was stunning. He couldn't wait to make love to her and was sure that would end the restless nights and his daydreaming when his mind should be on business. With a start, he realized he was thinking about her again, and he tried to concentrate on what was being said, too aware of Luke's frowning scrutiny. He resisted the urge to glance at his watch and see how much longer before it was time to meet her. His anticipation was building by the minute, and it startled him to realize he'd never felt this strongly drawn to a woman before.

He tried to put aside thoughts of Laurel and concentrate on what Luke was saying.

As the hour approached to sign the contract, Laurel's nervousness grew. She thought she was past that earlier, but she was having butterflies much worse than the morning because this would change the lives of everyone in her family—the Tolson legacy.

Her stomach churned and she wished she hadn't eaten lunch. How would her grandmother take the news tonight? The hotel had always been part of their family since earliest days.

Glancing at her watch, she saw it was time to meet Chase for their appointment with the realtor. One more giant step in the next hour that would change her future forever.

Six

Laurel had been quiet in the car, on the way over, and now when they were alone in Lane Grigsby's office while he left for a moment, Chase reached across the table to tilt her face up and look into her eyes. "You look solemn."

"This is a big step."

"You can still say no," he informed her.

"I know I can, but I won't," she said, taking a deep breath and knowing she had to go ahead with what she and her grandmother had planned.

Lane returned along with Chase's realtor, Sam Kilean, and both attorneys. As Chase stood to shake hands with his realtor and his attorney, she greeted Wes Hindley, her attorney.

"Laurel, you know Sam," Chase said easily, and she shook hands again with the heavyset, brown-haired realtor.

Copies of the contract were handed out at a long conference table. Lane carefully went over the contract with them, and finally it was time to sign.

She stared at the blank line for the seller's signature, the place that would deed the hotel to Chase. A shiver ran down her spine. Once more, she knew she could still stop now, return the money deposited earlier and get out of all dealings with Chase. When she signed the contract, then she would be locked more tightly into a deal with him.

Trying to reassure herself that she was doing the right thing and following the course she and her grandmother had charted, she stared at the figures written in the contract.

She glanced up to find Chase watching her. Firming her lips, she looked down again and knew there was only one thing to do. Feeling as cold as if she were in a blizzard, she penned her signature with a shaking hand. She looked up again to meet his gaze, but this time she saw triumph, which increased her anger. Once more she tried to focus on the figures.

She went through the rest of the meeting in a fog.

As they returned to the hotel, Chase took her arm. "Let's go to my suite and have champagne to celebrate. It will be hours until I drive tonight, so I can have one drink. I get the feeling that you're less than happy with me over this transaction."

"You know how I feel and you know why. And I can't keep from thinking about how the hotel has been in our family for generations until today. As far as being unhappy with you, there's lust between us that doesn't have one thing to do with emotions."

"I intend to change that," he said, and she frowned.

"You want it all, Chase. My body you're getting. My heart—no. It's as locked away as yours is from me," she declared, remembering clearly his hurtful words. ...*in a month I'll be gone...*

He studied her with an unreadable expression, yet she was certain he wasn't pleased. He was accustomed to women fawning over him. He had known he wouldn't be getting that with her, and there was nothing in their agreement about how much she liked or approved of him. Or even that she had to cooperate with him. She intended to keep her part of the bargain to the extent that she had to. She knew lust would override her anger, but she had no intention of falling in love with him.

The minute he closed the door behind them in his suite, he tossed aside his coat, reached her in two long strides and pulled her into his arms, his gaze triumphant.

"Congratulations to both of us," he said. "We're each getting what we hoped for. I want you, Laurel," he declared in a raspy voice.

Her heart thudded and she stood quietly, more enveloped in anger than desire, yet when she saw the longing in his expression, her breath shortened. He pulled her closer, his gaze lowered to her mouth, and as usual she forgot why she was annoyed with him. He brushed her lips, a warm, slight contact that set her aflame.

"Damn you, Chase," she whispered with no anger. Losing all her fury, she wrapped her arms around his neck, raising her mouth to his, impatient for his kiss.

Each time they kissed, she wanted more of him. She pressed against his marvelous body, relishing the hard planes, aware of his readiness. This was the moment to let go and accept Chase fully, and she knew it was going to be easy to do. He tugged her blouse out of her skirt, but she was only dimly aware of his light touches. Her skirt fell away and then in minutes her blouse followed. She loosened the buttons on his shirt and pushed it off his shoulders, running her hands over his muscled chest and tangling her fingers in thick chest hair. He was strong, sculpted, filled with vitality, and she wanted to touch and kiss him.

When he held her away with his hands on her hips, she opened her eyes, dazzled as she looked at him. "Chase," she whispered, tugging lightly on his hips.

His gaze moved slowly and thoroughly over her. "You're gorgeous!" he said. He held her back. "We're going to wait to consummate what we feel. I want a special moment for you, something you'll remember. I want you to desire making love as much as I do," he whispered and every nerve in her body tingled. The depth of her craving surprised her, yet reason returned and she gathered her clothes to pull them on, aware of his watchful gaze and his arousal, indicating what his body clamored for.

He stepped close to tilt her head up and look into her eyes. "Lovemaking will be special between us, Laurel. I know it will."

"You're so certain about what you want," she whispered.

He kissed her hard briefly and then released her. "I'll be back in a couple of hours, and we can go to your ranch."

She watched him pick up his coat and tie and stride out of the room, with one last look at her.

Shaken, she stared after him. She simply melted with his touch. She didn't want to and planned not to, but it always happened. How would she survive with her heart intact after a month of his lovemaking? How could she have gotten entangled with two playboys who trampled her feelings?

And when did the month start? With the signing of the hotel contract or with the consummation of their agreement in bed? She suspected the latter, so it would probably begin tomorrow and last until the eighth of September.

With Edward there had never been the fiery attraction that she had with Chase. She hated to acknowledge it, but that set him apart and there was no way to crush a running undercurrent of excitement.

Two hours later Chase knocked. When she opened the door, his gaze traveled over her beige slacks and matching blouse in a thorough study. "You look luscious," he said.

"You don't look so bad yourself," she had to admit, knowing it was an understatement. Dressed in black slacks and a black knit shirt and hand-tooled western boots, he made her pulse race.

"There's one thing we can fix," he said, stepping closer and tugging loose the beige scarf that held her hair tied behind her head.

Her blond hair cascaded across her shoulders and he smiled. "Much better," he said softly. "Now we can go."

He stood close enough that she could detect his aftershave, and when she looked into his eyes, her heart fluttered. Desire was hot and intense and she wanted to kiss him, but she didn't.

In front of the hotel, a valet held the door to a sleek black sports car. While she climbed inside, Chase walked around to slide behind the wheel. As they turned into traffic, he glanced at her. "Your grandmother does know I'm coming, doesn't she?"

"Of course. I told her I had a new friend I wanted to bring home."

"That screams a serious relationship," he remarked.

"You and I know better, and eventually my family will know that you've gone out of my life and they'll forget you."

"I'm glad I don't have a damn delicate ego," he remarked. "You would constantly trample it into the dirt."

She smiled. "I have absolutely no fear of that. You're the most self-assured man I've ever known, and I've known some champions."

"Wealthy Edward. Who else?"

"Actually, my dad. He always had total confidence in himself. Another reason it seems such a change and shock to the family. Chase, tonight I'd rather leave the impression with my family that we're in love," she said, even though she was uneasy about the suggestion.

"I can accommodate you on that one," he said, reaching over to take her hand and place it on his knee.

"I talk to at least one of them every day, and usually on weekends they come into town to go to the hospital and we eat together, so I'll have to tell them I'm going away with you."

Looking mildly amused, he glanced at her. "You're definitely a family person. If you're in Dallas, do you keep in touch like that?"

"Not that much, but it's different when I'm here, and it's not the same with Dad in the hospital."

"I can see that. Sure, that's one for which I'll be more than happy to oblige. How far are you carrying this? You're not telling them we're talking marriage, are you?"

"Good heavens, no!" she exclaimed forcefully, and he laughed.

"I should've known better on that one," he said. "You're on, then."

"Thanks, I think," she replied, dreading taking him home to the family but feeling it necessary before she left town with him. Would he have balked if she had said she wanted to indicate marriage loomed? She didn't care. She was into this and trying to make the best of it, reminding herself constantly what she was getting out of it. Her financial worries had ended and her responsibilities had lightened. She had taken the burden off her dad for when he recovered, and she refused to consider the possibility that he wasn't going to recuperate.

"I have business in the morning and I can't get away from here until about two o'clock. How's that with you?" Chase asked.

"Fine," she said, unable to believe she was going away with him for Saturday and Sunday. "That will give me time to go to the hospital and take care of things at the hotel. Until we have the closing, I still feel responsible for the hotel."

"It'll take about two hours to fly to my place, so we'll arrive in late afternoon. Your cell phone won't work there, but I'll give you a phone number for my landline, and you can pass it on to everyone."

He raised her hand to drop light kisses on her knuckles. His warm breath was the barest hint of what was to come. "I can't wait until tomorrow, although you're not as excited about the weekend as I am. I'll try to change that," he added in a low voice.

"We have a deal, Chase."

As he looked back at the road, he smiled. "I don't usually strike out so completely with a woman. Particularly if we have some kind of chemistry between us, and you and I have almost spontaneous combustion."

"I don't think it's quite that fantastic," she remarked dryly, "and you know the old saying, 'You can't win them all.'"

"I hope you're not still seeing Edward when you're with me," Chase said quietly and she shook her head.

"No. I'm seeing Chase Bennett. I'm influenced by my experience with Edward, but I know it's you."

"I'll have to keep working at this," he said.

"Don't make me a project," she told him and turned to watch the countryside, dreading taking him home but determined to do it nonetheless.

When they finally passed through the tall posts with the iron sign declaring the Tall T Ranch, her tension increased and she wondered what her grandmother would think.

Soon they could see the two-story wooden ranch house surrounded by tall pines and outbuildings and a large barn behind the house and garage.

"It's great, Laurel," Chase said. "Reminds me of my home, actually."

"Why do I get the feeling you're sizing up the place to decide whether you want to buy it?"

"I thought you'd already put it on the market."

"I have, but I plan to talk to Gramma tonight about keeping it. At the time I didn't want Dad to come home to so much responsibility, but now, with the money from you, I can afford to wait and include my father on the decision to sell or I can hire more people to help him run the place."

"Sounds like a good plan," Chase remarked.

"Tonight I want to get Gramma alone to discuss the ranch,

because whatever we do, the girls will go along with our decision. They don't have much interest in the ranch at this point in their lives."

He nodded. "This place looks first-rate and it's spectacular countryside," he said, and she gazed at the mountains beyond the house.

"It's a pretty place and a successful ranch, but it takes a lot of work. Pull up in front and we'll go in that way. I'll get a lecture if I bring you through the kitchen the first time here."

He smiled and stopped in front, coming around to hold the door for her. Dressed in jeans and T-shirts, her sisters appeared on the porch, and her palms grew damp as she went up the steps with Chase's hand on her arm.

"Ashley, Diana, meet Chase Bennett," she said. "Chase, this is my sister Ashley," she said, turning to the seventeen-year-old, who was an inch taller and had her blond hair in a clip behind her head. Ashley smiled as she greeted Chase, and Laurel turned to the shorter honey-blonde. "And this is Diana."

After they said hello to Chase, she hugged them, then saw her grandmother approaching. "Gramma," she said as the woman stepped out on the porch, her cool blue eyes on Chase, "this is Chase Bennett. Chase, this is my grandmother, Spring Tolson."

Offering his hand, he greeted her with a friendly smile. "It's nice of you to have me for dinner tonight."

"We're always happy to meet Laurel's friends. Won't you come inside," she said, and Chase stepped up to hold the door for everyone as they all filed into the wide entrance hall.

Permeated by enticing smells of roasting meat and freshly baked bread from the kitchen, the hall looked comfortable with wooden benches along its walls. Paintings of western scenes decorated the walls, while potted plants stood on the polished maple plank floor. She wondered if it was similar inside to the ranch home he'd grown up in.

As they followed her grandmother, Chase draped his arm across Laurel's shoulders casually, a gesture Laurel was certain was noticed by all three family members.

Feeling as if she were entering a haven, she walked into the front living area that held upholstered furniture and heavy mahogany pieces, some from the time the house was built. A painting of wild horses hung above the broad mantel.

When they were seated and her grandmother had served wine, lemonade and hors d'oeuvres, Laurel glanced at her sisters and then her grandmother. "I wanted all of you to meet Chase because we've become friends, but also I want you to know him because he's bought the hotel."

"Wow!" Diana exclaimed, her eyes sparkling.

"Congratulations and, I suppose, thank you," Spring Tolson said, lifting a glass of lemonade to him. "Here's to the new owner of one of Montana's oldest hotels. I'll have to admit that I have a lump in my throat to see it pass from our family, but the time has come and I know it's for the best," she added.

Her words saddened Laurel because of what had happened to her father to bring all this about. She suspected her grandmother knew the sale was the best thing to do but was hiding how deep her hurt ran over losing the old hotel that was such a big part of their family history.

Smiling and looking relaxed, Chase raised his glass in return and then sipped. "I'm glad to have it because it'll be a great place for my employees and their families to stay, and it's in excellent condition right now."

"Chase is paying our full asking price," Laurel added and saw a faint smile curl her grandmother's mouth.

"Then I definitely need to say 'thank you,'" Spring added.

"I enjoyed learning its interesting history, with two gunfights transpiring in the original bar and the tables salvaged from that original structure," Chase said.

"The hotel has a long and varied history. For that matter, so does Athens," Spring said.

"I think my employees will enjoy Athens. I certainly do."

In minutes Chase seemed to have her family charmed, and even her grandmother was laughing at his anecdotes of growing up on another Montana ranch. Laurel felt a degree better, yet it was difficult to relax because she still had to tell her grandmother where to find her during the weekend.

As she'd expected, her younger sisters were dazzled, both all but drooling over Chase and hanging on his every word. It was her grandmother's keen blue eyes that made her nervous, but as the evening wore on and Chase proved to be as attentive a listener as he was a storyteller, she felt better about bringing him to meet her family. Even so, she was anxious to have the evening end.

After dinner he joined them in cleaning the kitchen, and she wondered when he'd last done any such work, if ever. Next, they played a word game. Between rounds they paused and Laurel left to help her grandmother serve homemade peach ice cream. In the kitchen she got out crystal bowls and faced her grandmother.

"Gramma, I wanted to talk to you without the girls. I'm making enough from the hotel sale that we can take the ranch off the market if we want to."

Her grandmother's eyes narrowed and she studied Laurel intently. "How much are you making from this sale, Laurel? You said he's paying your asking price."

"I asked for more and he's agreed to it," she said, feeling heat flood her cheeks and wishing her grandmother weren't quite so astute.

"Are you certain you're doing what you want to do?" Spring asked.

"Very. And this will give us the opportunity to hang on to the ranch until Dad can give us his input on selling."

"Laurel, your father may not recover," Spring said, looking away and wiping her eyes.

Laurel stepped close to give her grandmother's hand a

squeeze. "I'm planning on his recovery and so should you," she said firmly. "What about taking the ranch off the market?"

"If you're sure you want to, fine. We can always list it again. Lane shouldn't be too unhappy to lose the listing after selling the hotel."

"That's right. There's one more thing I wanted to tell you," Laurel said, taking a deep breath. "I'll be in northern California this weekend, and I'll leave you the number before I go."

Her grandmother turned to stare at her. "What are you doing in California?"

"I'm going with Chase," she said, feeling her face flush.

Spring studied her intently. "This is soon after Edward. Are you sure about what you're doing?"

"Yes, I am," she answered. "I wanted you to meet him and to know my plans."

"I like him better than Edward," Spring said, "but maybe I'm prejudiced because he's from Montana and he's trying to help your father. I don't want to see you hurt again," she added, moving to Laurel to hug her and then stepping back. "I want you to be happy."

Laurel felt a pang because if her grandmother knew the truth, she would be protesting what Laurel was doing and would run Chase right off the ranch. Sooner or later it would be obvious that there was a windfall of money, and her grandmother was a shrewd woman who would put it all together eventually and be furious.

"I'm glad you brought him home for us to meet, and even though I'm sad about it in many ways, I know it's best to sell the hotel. The money will help your father, and now he won't have such a burden."

Laurel reached out to squeeze her grandmother's hand. "I feel so much better hearing you say all that," she said, thankful for her grandmother's supportive attitude.

"The ice cream will melt, Laurel. We better get it served,

although your sisters are probably delighted to have Chase to themselves."

Laurel laughed as she dished out scoops of peach ice cream. "I'm sure they are and I don't know which one is happier about it."

"They approve of Chase and I know they like him better than Edward, too."

"That's obvious," Laurel answered with amusement. Both girls had fawned over Chase all evening, and she knew when they learned she was going away with him for the weekend, they would be filled with questions.

By eleven Laurel could tell that her grandmother was tiring, and it was time to leave. The girls followed them to the car and were still waving as they drove away, but her grandmother had already turned and gone back inside the house.

Chase reached over to take her hand. "Nice family. We could've accepted your grandmother's invitation and driven back early in the morning before daylight."

"No. I wanted to get back and we accomplished what I went for. It would simply have been a few more hours of my sisters fussing over you. You do have a definite effect on women—of all ages."

"Your grandmother wasn't dazzled, but she seemed to accept me."

"She accepted you and approved and told me she liked you better than Edward."

"I'm not sure that's a big plus. I think you're the apple that doesn't fall far from the tree—you're like her. I suspect if you'd turned everything over to her, she could have stepped in and run it all the way you have."

"You're right and she has in the past. She's running the ranch right now."

"You have a nice family. Be thankful your dad knew how to enjoy life. I take it you talked to her about keeping the ranch."

"Yes, I did and she agreed, so I'll call our realtor in the

morning and take it off the market," she said, watching Chase. "I hope you've decided to back off on Ty's property."

"Actually, I haven't. I doubled my price and offered to let him keep his house plus ninety acres. That's a generous offer."

"I don't think it matters what you offer," she said. "He doesn't want to sell."

"He wouldn't have to move or stop ranching there. Every man has a price."

For the first time in the evening her anger toward Chase surfaced. Another glimpse of the arrogant, affluent man, she thought. "For his sake, I hope it's a deal he will accept because I know you won't stop until you get what you want. I've looked at the map and I saw why you want it. What I don't understand is why you're in such a hurry about all this, Chase? You'd think you'd sunk every nickel you own into developing this new field and have to have results immediately. But then, I don't really know you. Maybe that's the way you work."

He chuckled and caressed her knee, pulling up the leg of her silk slacks until his hand was on her bare skin while he kept his gaze on the road. "It's because of a bet."

Surprised, she turned to stare at him. "What on earth does a bet have to do with it?"

"A lot. I told you my mother has sisters. They were Texans and when they were in college, each of them married northern men. Mom married my dad, a Montana rancher, and moved here. Aunt Mercedes married a rancher from South Dakota and moved there. Aunt Faith married a man in the drilling business and moved to Wyoming. I've grown up seeing my cousins, Jared Dalton and Matt Rome, often and we're close friends."

"That's really nice, Chase," she said, having difficulty seeing him as caring about anyone else except himself. "I'm surprised. You seem so self-contained."

"We went to different colleges, but all were in Texas and we played football, so we competed and saw a lot of each other those years. Financially, we've all done well, and we get together once a year in Texas for a weekend-long poker game. After the last one in April, we made a bet. Whichever one of us can make the most money in the next twelve months wins. We each put in five million, so the winner gets his five back, plus ten million from the other two. In addition, the winner treats the others to a weekend."

"Good heavens!" she exclaimed, stunned by the high stakes and the reason for his rush. Again, all she could see was a wealthy, frivolous playboy. "This is because of a bet! That's an enormous amount!" she exclaimed, aghast.

"Don't look as if I'd just admitted to robbing banks! It's only a bet with my cousins. I don't gamble otherwise." He grinned. "It adds spice to life. So, I'm interested in getting that field developed and bringing in a profit as quickly as I can. Right now, the only thing I'm doing is spending money, but all of it is an investment that I expect will pay off royally."

"I'm sure it will," she said, wondering about the kind of high-stakes life he led, suddenly feeling as if she had discovered a chasm between their lifestyles. How could she ever have any common ground with him? She thought about Chase playing the word game with her grandmother and sisters. What a dull life he must think she lived.

"Where are your cousins now?" she asked after a period of silence.

"Jared works in Dallas and Matt headquarters in Wyoming and has several homes. Actually we all have homes in various places."

"You're trying to make the most money, yet you paid me a fortune."

He smiled again. "Not really," he said quietly, and she realized she could have easily gotten more from him, that he viewed what he was paying her as a paltry sum.

"That's decadent," she said, thinking he had two sides, the charmer and the arrogant mogul.

"Don't get in a huff over my money," he said with amusement lacing his voice. "It's doing us both good."

Clamping her lips together, she turned to stare into the darkness beyond the highway. At night, out of the city lights, she could see myriad twinkling stars, a sight rarely seen in town. Chase's life was far different from her own, yet he had the same kind of background, so they had similarities.

Tomorrow she would leave with him. Could she weather the weekend with her heart intact? She knew she'd better because she had the whole month to go.

He reached over to caress her nape, his fingers warm and light, causing tingles and making her want to touch him in return. "Tomorrow night at this time, you'll be in my arms," he said, and she knew that's what he was envisioning, while she was deliberately avoiding speculating about it.

Finally they arrived back at the hotel and at her door she turned to him. "It's late—actually early in the morning. I won't ask you in tonight and our month can start tomorrow night."

"I'm not rushing you now," he said in a thick tone that always indicated he was having erotic thoughts. "Until tomorrow night," he whispered and took her into his arms to kiss her. His kiss lengthened as she returned it passionately.

She was tempted to ask him in and start the month tonight, but she wanted to wait until they were away from the hotel to commence this relationship. Finally she pushed against his chest and he released her.

"I need to go in," she said breathlessly. "I'll see you tomorrow. Actually, in a few hours."

"Thanks for tonight, Laurel," he said solemnly. "I'll see you in the morning."

Nodding, she turned and entered her suite, leaning against the door and closing her eyes, relieved she didn't have to invite him in tonight yet wanting to at the same time. She ached for more kisses and was too aware of how badly she wanted him right now.

Feeling exhausted by all the events of the day, she thought she'd fall asleep instantly, but she tossed and turned most of the night, dreaming of Chase.

Saturday morning, as she dressed in a tailored white shirt and a straight, blue cotton skirt, slipping on high-heeled sandals, she thought about all the things she had to do before she left with Chase. The most onerous chore was to talk to Brice.

She had managed to deal with her family. Now she dreaded telling Brice about leaving for the weekend with Chase because Brice would know she wasn't the least bit in love with Chase.

She didn't get an opportunity to talk to Brice until after ten o'clock, when she called and asked him if he would come to her office. Seated behind her desk, she thought about Chase moving into her office soon.

She heard a light tap at the door and Brice appeared, smiling at her. Clean-shaven and dressed in a tan suit, he looked refreshed and energetic and brimful of his usual optimism. His blue eyes held curiosity.

"You wanted to see me?" he asked.

"Yes. Close the door and have a seat."

"This sounds serious," he said, sitting across from her, waiting expectantly with a faint smile still on his face. "What's up?"

"I guess in a way it's sort of serious," she said. "I'm taking the weekend off."

He shrugged. "I'd say that's good news because you've earned it. You've worked like crazy getting this hotel ready to sell and dealing with Bennett and his entourage. You've gone daily to see your dad, and if you're where we can reach you—and I'm sure you will be or you wouldn't be telling me this—we can get you back here soon if it becomes necessary."

"I want you to promise to call me if there's the least little reason that I should return."

"Sure, I will. You know that," he said and his smile faded as he studied her with curiosity.

"The girls will go see Dad tomorrow and Sunday, so they'll be around."

"There you go. You're not needed here. The hotel should be fine."

"Thanks, Brice," she said, wishing she could let it go at that, but she knew he would find out anyway from Chase's employees.

"My cell phone won't work. I'll have my BlackBerry and I can give you a landline number to call."

"Sure. I hope you have a great time. So, where exactly are you going?" The question hung in the air.

"I'm going with Chase to the northern coast of California."

All the blood drained from Brice's face and then flooded back, and he turned so red that she was frightened he might have a heart attack. "Brice—"

"Dammit to hell," he said quietly, clenching his fists. "This is why the hotel sold like lightning, isn't it? It's none of my business what you do, but if your dad were well, none of this would be happening."

"Not you, too!" she exclaimed. "Stop trying to protect me because my dad is in the hospital. I've been on my own a long time now."

"Dammit," he repeated. "If your dad were well, you wouldn't have sold the hotel and you wouldn't be going away with that bastard. You traded the hotel for the weekend," he said bitterly and jumped to his feet to jam his hands into his pockets and pace.

She stood, unable to sit still either. "Brice, it isn't that bad."

"The hell it isn't!" he exclaimed, spinning around. "I've known you since you were three years old. I should've guessed he didn't fly in here and buy the hotel as easily as it appeared. I should've prevented this."

"No, you shouldn't have," she said firmly. "First, I'm an adult. Second, I gave it thought. Third, I'm doing what I want to do. I guess I can add a fourth—he has more than made it worth my while. He's not repulsive, either, Brice. We get along."

"He's Edward all over again only a lot worse. Dammit, I hate this. And I know there's nothing I can say or do to change things now. The hotel sale contract has been signed."

"I don't want to back out of the deal. Brice, besides the sale of the hotel, he paid me personally three-quarters of a million dollars," she said quietly. Brice spun around to stare at her, his jaw dropping.

"Three-quarters of a million plus buying the hotel in exchange for a weekend?"

"A little more time than a weekend. And remember, he's a charmer and I enjoy being with him."

Brice combed his fingers through his hair. "How much more time?"

"One month."

He closed his eyes and rocked back on his heels. "I should have stopped this from happening. Ty talked to me the other night and said if Bennett gives you any trouble to let him know, that he felt terrible with you having to deal with Chase Bennett without your dad around."

"Ty Carson talked to you about me? I think there are some old-fashioned attitudes here," she remarked, feeling less defensive and slightly exasperated. "I did what I wanted to do. A month with Chase is not an unpleasant prospect."

Brice studied her intently and she gazed back at him as steadily. "He'll break your heart the way Edward did," Brice said finally.

"No, he won't," she replied firmly, aware she had recovered rapidly from Edward.

"I shouldn't have let this happen. The whole town will be talking about it and speculating."

"The whole town won't know that it's anything other than I've fallen in love with Chase on the rebound."

"I think you'll hear from Ty."

"I won't unless you tell him some of this. I wish, for my sake, you would keep the conversation we've had confidential."

"I damn sure will if you want me to, but people will talk and it'll get around that you two are together. You know that."

She shrugged. "Yes, I do, but that's okay. I've grown up with that going on in this town," she said, glancing at her watch. "There's constantly gossip about someone or something."

He gazed at her. "I feel as if I really let you down."

Walking closer to pat his shoulder, she smiled. "I'm fine, Brice. Now, please don't worry. It's time for you to meet with one of the inspectors."

"I should've done something," he repeated as he walked beside her. He opened the door and Chase was striding toward them.

Brice glowered at him and moved so swiftly that she didn't realize what was happening as he threw a punch and struck Chase.

Seven

Chase staggered back into the wall, and pain shot through his jaw. He stared at Brice in surprise, not having any idea what had brought on the rage.

"What was that for?" he asked, getting out a snowy handkerchief to dab at a cut on his cheek.

"You're bleeding! Brice, for heaven's sake, apologize!" Laurel exclaimed, as she stared at her employee.

Brice clamped his jaw closed and looked at Laurel and then back at Chase; Chase guessed what had Brice hot under the collar. Chase waved his hand. "Forget it. No hard feelings on my part," Chase said.

"Brice, please," Laurel pleaded, hanging on to Brice's arm as if she feared he would attack Chase again.

"Sorry, Laurel, if I've upset you," Brice said to her, clearly indicating that the only person who would receive an apology would be Laurel. Scowling, Brice spun on his heel and stomped away.

She moved to Chase to take him by the arm. She smelled

delectable, like flowers. "Your cheek is bleeding. Come into my office and let me give you something to put on it," she urged, and he was happy to go with her, wanting to pull her into his arms.

She closed the door behind them and Chase said, "I didn't see that coming until he was in my face. I take it you told him about going away for the weekend with me," he added dryly.

"Yes, that was why," she admitted, looking worried and biting her lip. "I assured him that I was doing what I wanted to do, that I enjoy being with you."

Chase shook his head. "I'll be a little more alert around here. Anyone else going to take a swing at me over taking you away with me?"

She took a deep breath. He tilted his head and stared at her because she hesitated before she answered. "I don't think anyone else will resort to violence, but I never would have thought that about Brice."

"Who else? You do think so or you would have answered instantly. Is it Ty Carson?" Chase asked as he followed her into the bathroom adjoining her office. She reached into a cabinet and withdrew a bottle, then fished out cotton and a gauze pad.

"I don't need all that," he said, wanting to chuck all the first aid and pull her into his arms. "Just let me get the blood off," Chase said, retrieving a washcloth to run water on it and dab at his cut. "Is it Ty?" he repeated, naming the most likely person.

"I don't think he would get in a fight with you, but I'm shocked that Brice did. And I know Ty is unhappy with you. Let me clean that cut the right way," she added, taking the washcloth from him.

She dabbed at his cheek, and Chase rested his hands on her waist as he inhaled her perfume and admired her clear, flawless skin. When she reached up to touch his cheek, the vee of her blouse revealed enticing curves.

"I'll have my guard up around the local men. Jealousy, I

can understand. This came out of the blue. You aren't being forced to go away with me," he said, thinking more about undressing her tonight and wishing the hours would go faster until he could have her all to himself.

"That's what I told Brice," she said quietly, putting down the washcloth. "There. That should do. I'm sorry, Chase."

Feeling foolish, he grinned. "Brice caught me totally off guard. I was getting ready to shake his hand." He watched her. "You could kiss it and make it well."

She shook her head. "I'm glad you're making light of it. You won't hold it against Brice, will you? He's wonderful about managing the hotel."

"I won't do anything to cause him the least bit of trouble," Chase answered, not caring whether Brice ran the hotel or not. His staff would make those decisions, yet for a time he would pass the word to leave Brice where he was because if they removed him, Laurel would think Chase was doing it to get back at the man.

"I have an appointment in twenty minutes," he said, glancing at his watch, "and I'll be busy until we leave at two o'clock, but I wanted to see you."

"Well, we've finished cleaning you up. Let's get out of here," she said.

He followed her back into her office, then pulled her into his embrace for a kiss that grew steamier until her phone rang and he had to release her.

On fire with wanting her, he watched her as she hurried to her desk and bent over to grab the phone. Mentally undressing her, he perused the length of her and her trim backside and long legs, and his arousal responded to his erotic thoughts. She was reluctant to go to California with him, almost backing out of signing over the hotel yesterday, dreading last night. He intended to seduce her tonight, to wipe out every shred of reluctance until she was as wildly passionate as possible.

She was hot and tempting, and he was going to enjoy this month beyond measure. He suspected there would be tears and anger at the end of the thirty days, but she knew full well what to expect and he would be gone quickly. No woman had ever held him longer than he'd planned and Laurel wasn't going to either. Thoughts of the dull routine of marriage always loomed as a prison. He wanted no part of it. Yet how he wanted her! His nights were a torment because of dreaming about her and during his waking moments, thinking about her. Chase walked up behind her and ran his hand up her bare leg beneath the cool cotton material of her skirt.

She felt fabulous with her smooth, silky skin, good muscle tone, and shapely long, long legs. He wanted to be on top of her, both of them bare, his hands all over her, and by night that's what he expected.

She turned to glare at him and stepped away. He smiled, leaning forward to trail light kisses across her nape.

The tone of her voice thickened, her breathing became erratic and she gave him another glare. He knew he was distracting her, but she was talking about a food order for the hotel and he didn't care. He wanted to touch her in the few short minutes he had left before his meeting.

Finally she finished the call and spun around with fire in her eyes. "Chase, for heaven's sake! I was making a business—"

He stepped closer, wrapped his arms around her and kissed her, silencing her lecture. His tongue thrust into her mouth; there was a moment when she was still and unresponsive, but then her arms wrapped around his neck. Her hips pressed against him. She kissed him back with passion and fire and he groaned, knowing he had to stop and cool down for his business meeting, but she was too tempting.

Finally he released her and she opened her eyes slowly. Her full lips were redder, parted, and she looked up at him with a dazed expression.

"You make me want to chuck this meeting, but it's important. We're trying to make arrangements to use a trucking firm that's located north of here, and the owners are coming to talk to me. As much as I hate it, I have to run," he said, heading toward the door. "I'm late right now. See you at two, darlin'," he flung over his shoulder.

Outside her office, Chase began to cool down. He thought about the night before and her family who had been nice, yet it had made him nervous because he usually didn't get taken home to meet the family of his mistresses. All evening her grandmother had given him cool, assessing looks, and he suspected she was a shrewd woman who was sizing him up. It was done and over and he'd never see them again, unless he bought the family ranch, which he didn't expect to do.

That family visit was a first with her, and tonight would be another first. He kept his California home solely for a getaway for himself, and he'd never taken a woman there before. With her father in the hospital in the shape he was in, Chase knew he'd never get her to go too far from Montana, so the California house seemed best. And it was a good escape from hostile locals. He had never wanted to take a woman there before, yet he looked forward to having Laurel with him, which made him surprised at himself and his own reactions.

In so many ways she was the kind of woman he had always avoided—tied to family and old-fashioned values, aimed for marriage and children. She was too independent, too self-willed and too much of a take-charge person to suit him, one of those capable women who were probably descendants of the pioneer stock that settled Montana and could endure all sorts of hardships and manage well. He preferred a sophisticated, uncomplicated beauty whose biggest worry was her pedicure and hairdo. Yet Laurel was incredibly beautiful and luscious. She took his breath away, and his body reacted swiftly to her slightest touch or the rare moments when she flirted with him.

He rushed into the meeting room to find only Luke. "The others have been delayed by a tie-up in traffic on the highway. They'll be here in about ten minutes," Luke said, his gray eyes assessing Chase.

"Damn, I didn't have to hurry after all," Chase said.

"I wanted a moment with you. We've set a closing date for the hotel for the fourth of September.

"Fine. That should suit Laurel, too."

Luke eyed him. "What happened to your cheek?"

"Brice threw a punch."

"I'll be damned. Doesn't he know you're his new boss?"

"He doesn't care. There's a streak of independence in people around here. Must be something in the Montana air," Chase remarked lightly.

Luke's scowl grew. "That isn't funny. Why did he hit you? Let me guess—it's over Laurel Tolson and you. Brice must have found out you're taking her away with you tonight."

"She told him. I didn't even see it coming. They stepped out of her office as I walked up, and next thing I knew, I'd been hit. I never expected it."

"You went home with her last night, and then one of her employees slugs you today. This isn't your type of woman, and she isn't one for you to fool around with, Chase. She isn't the love-'em-and-leave-'em type you like that has the same attitude about relationships as you. This one practically has a bridal bouquet in her hand."

"She knows I'm not the marrying kind. I've made that abundantly clear."

"You're getting her on the rebound from Edward Varnum. Frankly, I don't know how you talked her into going with you except you probably won her over by buying this ancient hotel for an exorbitant price. Let me introduce you to someone else."

"No. Don't bother bringing it up again. Thanks for the kind advice," Chase said, "but I'm doing what I damn well please and the lady is spending the weekend with me."

"You're taking her to California. Is there special significance in that?"

"Only that she won't go far away with her father in the hospital."

"Ah," Luke said, still frowning. Chase tried to hang on to his patience because besides being a valued employee, Luke was his friend and he knew that he meant well.

"Stop worrying. She'll be in my life awhile, and then she'll be gone and there will be another woman."

"I suppose. It's just that she's a ravishing babe and she's different, and you're doing things you've never done before with anyone else."

"Babe? That description doesn't exactly fit Laurel, but ravishing does. And there's no particular significance to what we're doing. I told you why we're going to California. She wanted her grandmother to meet the man who bought the hotel. No great meaning in that either."

"Did you have a good time last night?"

"I know you're asking that to see if you can discern something special in my visit with her grandmother, but there wasn't," Chase replied, struggling not to lose his temper. "Sure I had a good time. Grandma can cook beyond belief— too bad you can't hire her, although the chef here is damn good."

"That's the truth! I've already gained four pounds since I started staying here."

"Don't worry, I won't fall in love with Laurel and she knows this is temporary."

"Women like that never know a relationship is temporary. They always think they're different."

"Listen, Dad," he joked, "you're so damn full of advice, let me give you a clue—I can take care of myself where women are concerned. End of conversation."

"Sure, sure. On the business side, we gave your offer to Ty Carson about keeping his house and ninety acres and doubling the price, and he said no deal, but we told him to think about it and give us an answer in two days."

"Dammit," Chase swore, touching his sore cheek. "Stubborn old codger. Driving from Athens across his ranch to the oil field is the easiest and shortest way, and this town is the most convenient for me to use for a headquarters." Chase rubbed his forehead and thought about Laurel telling him about Ty; he knew that if he pressured Ty too much, she would be furious. He clamped his mouth closed and tried to think about how to get Ty Carson off his land. "Money doesn't tempt him, but there must be something. I want that damned ranch of his and we could use the water."

"He's stubborn as hell. I've talked to him twice now."

"Ty Carson may be the next one who'll try to slug me over Laurel. He's known her all her life, is the father of her best friend and is protective of her."

"Oh, hell," Luke said, looking glum. "I still say that she's not the best woman for you."

"Luke—" Chase said, a warning note in his tone.

Someone rapped on the door. Three men in suits poured into the room, and Chase smoothed his shirt and raked his fingers through his hair as he turned to greet them, trying to get his mind on business.

Halfway through their meeting, Chase realized someone was speaking to him and his thoughts had wandered. He tried to cover for it and didn't look at Luke. The men didn't know him and seemed unaware of his hesitation and switch in topic, but Chase knew Luke had noticed and hoped he didn't hear about it later because it wasn't the first time his mind had wandered.

Ten minutes later he found himself surreptitiously glancing at his watch. Time was dragging and it was still only eleven-thirty. He wanted out of this meeting and to finish his other business. Two o'clock couldn't come soon enough.

* * *

Laurel finished the hotel chores by half-past eleven and intended to leave for the hospital. She stopped by Brice's office to give him the phone number where she could be reached. He looked up, his features impassive as he stood, closed the door and faced her.

"Brice, please don't worry about me."

"I'm sorry if I caused you grief this morning, Laurel. I was so damn mad at Chase Bennett. I don't want to see you hurt, and I know you're doing all this for your family. If you didn't have any family, you wouldn't be going away with him."

"I do have family, so I've never even looked at it in that way," she said gently. "I can't."

"That makes it all the worse."

"I don't *have* to go."

"Oh, hell. Who could turn down almost a million on top of selling the hotel at a price you never dreamed you'd get? Lane is ecstatic and celebrating like crazy."

"I'm not surprised and I'm glad, because I had to tell him that I've taken the ranch off the market."

Brice frowned. "I thought you wanted your family to be free of the responsibility."

"It's different now," she said gently. "I can hire all sorts of people to run it and none of us have to deal with the problems, yet we can keep it—at least until Dad can make a decision about it."

Brice's scowl grew and he rubbed his jaw. "I guess it's good that you can take the ranch off the market. By the way, I've accepted a job with the Barclay Champion Hotel. I won't start until Bennett's outfit takes over here and you don't need me."

"Oh, Brice!" she exclaimed, hating to hear he was leaving the Tolson. "I know you have my best interests in mind and I appreciate that. I'm sorry to see you go, because you've been great. I think Chase will want to keep you."

"Maybe he'll offer me a million dollar bonus to stay," Brice stated with sarcasm, and she had to smile as she shook her head.

"I'm sorry it worked out this way. I felt better about leaving the hotel in your hands."

"You're leaving it in Chase Bennett's clutches. It's for the best for me to move on. I won't work for him and I'm sure the animosity is mutual. I'll be even angrier if he hurts you."

"That's sweet, and I appreciate your concern." She glanced at her watch. "I need to go to the hospital, and then I'll come back and leave at two with Chase."

"You take care of yourself and don't fall in love with him. This one won't offer you an engagement ring."

"He's made that more than clear, but I don't want one from him, either," she said quietly. "I really haven't changed my feelings about wealthy playboys."

Brice clamped his jaw closed and clenched his fists; she hugged him lightly and he patted her back in return. "I feel as if I've failed your dad and you. You take good care of yourself," he repeated.

"Stop worrying. I'll be back Sunday night."

"Sure. Call me if you want me to come get you."

She laughed and nodded. "Will you stop worrying, please!" she repeated and turned to go, still hurting that he was leaving the hotel yet warmed by his concern for her welfare.

At the hospital, she sat beside her dad and talked quietly, telling him about the sale of the hotel, Brice's leaving and taking the ranch off the market. Finally she kissed his cheek, chatted with their private nurse and left, catching the doctor in the hall and talking briefly. There was no change.

When she returned to the hotel, she packed a few things and looked through her clothing, trying to select what she wanted to wear tonight.

Opening a wide drawer, she gazed at her undergarments,

wondering whether she wanted to look seductive to turn him on or look cool and aloof and remind him that her heart was not in this endeavor. Either way she expected to make love with Chase as soon as they were at his house.

She eventually selected pristine white lacy underwear and a matching bra, deciding she would go for cool and remote, but suspecting she could wear a tent over her head and it wouldn't cool Chase. Gathering her belongings, she went to take a shower.

At ten minutes before two she was ready with her bag by the door. Five minutes later there was a knock. Opening the door, she drew a deep breath. Wickedly handsome, Chase was in chinos, a white shirt, a navy sport coat and snakeskin boots. A black Stetson hat shaded his face. Adding to her pleasure at seeing him, she noticed how his gaze warmed with appreciation when he looked at her red silk blouse and matching slacks. She had let her hair fall loose, which she knew pleased him.

"You're beautiful," he said in a husky tone.

"Thank you and likewise to you," she replied, smiling. "Incredibly handsome."

He caressed her nape, then shouldered her bag. "I'd like to delay leaving a few more minutes, but I won't. The sooner we go, the quicker we'll be there—and I'll admit, I can't wait to get you to myself."

"Aren't you taking anything?" she asked as they stepped into the elevator.

"I've already had my carry-on picked up."

Her anticipation climbed because she knew they would make love when they arrived at their destination. They were driven in a black limo to his waiting plane and then flown to his home in California, where he had a runway and hangar on his land. When a car met them, Chase slid behind the wheel to drive them the short distance to his house. For the entire trip Chase was being his most charming, and she bubbled with excitement, which she knew she couldn't bank. For this weekend—and in many ways for the next month— she had to let go of her anger toward him and her resentment that he was another strong-willed man who had to have his way in life. The only thing she needed to use was caution to guard her heart or this billionaire would break it far more than Edward had. Now, when she looked back at her engagement, she wondered if she had been in love with Edward at all.

She unbuckled and scooted close to Chase, to rest her hand on his thigh. Speeding along the private road, he put his arm around her.

"You're living dangerously, unbuckling now."

"I trust you totally to take care of us," she said, laughing. "Besides, we have the road to ourselves."

He gave her a quick searching glance. "This is damn good, Laurel. I knew it would be," he said.

The winding road followed the ocean, and she watched waves break over boulders that thrust up and out of the water. Windswept cypress branches stretched skyward.

"This is a spectacular place and an awesome view," she said.

"I think so. I'm glad you're getting to see it for your arrival because at the moment it's a clear day. Later, the fog may come in and hide our surroundings. Either way, it's peaceful here and I can relax." Ahead she saw tall wrought-iron gates, which swung wide on Chase's approach. "I have a privacy fence except on the ocean side, and none of the help will be at the house, but they live nearby. I have some people who handle security and they're around. You just won't see them."

"You seem totally isolated here."

"That's what I like. I don't bring people here with me." He glanced at her. "You're a first."

"I'm flattered but curious," she said, stroking his thigh lightly. He inhaled and rubbed her arm where his hand rested. "Why did you bring me here?"

"I knew you wouldn't go far away, and I want to be alone

with you where we won't be disturbed by business or family or anything else," he said, glancing at her. "I have plans for us for the weekend," he added in a thick voice that caused her heart to beat faster.

"Your family has been here, haven't they? Your cousins?"

"No. You really are the first."

Startled, she stared at him. "I'm learning all sorts of things about you. You must like being alone, don't you?"

"Yes. A lot of the time," he answered. "I've told you that I had a house filled with brothers and sisters growing up—six of us, four boys and two girls and I'm the oldest. Thankfully, I had hiding places on the ranch where I could get off to myself." She studied his profile, his thick eyelashes and prominent cheekbones.

"Amazing you're so social and yet so solitary. You can be quite charming, even though I shouldn't tell you, because you already know it too well."

He laughed. "I'm happy to discover that you think I can be charming."

"You know women find you captivating. You even won over my grandmother. That takes a bit of doing, particularly when she's not happy with us about this weekend."

"She's a shrewd woman, and frankly I'm glad I don't have to see her often. It's been a long time since someone made me feel as if I were sixteen again and needed to watch my manners."

Laurel laughed softly. "That's Gramma. She has that effect on people, but she has kept us all in line much more than my dad. Or mom, too, for that matter."

"I'm surprised your dad was so into enjoying life if she keeps a tight rein on the family."

"I think he charmed her, just as you did."

"What about your mom? Was she a stern force?"

"Sometimes with us, but never with my dad. She was so in love with Dad and charmed by him that he could do no wrong in her eyes," Laurel said, gazing outside but seeing her parents. "I hope I'm never that much in love with any man!" she exclaimed.

"That's a little scary for any man to hear," Chase remarked, bringing her back to the moment.

"You needn't worry. It will never apply to you and me."

"I don't want to marry and you don't want to be wildly in love with someone. Seems to sum up our feelings about relationships. I'm surprised."

"I want to remain my own person and be able to see the other person as human, not invincible. Mom thought Dad could do no wrong. That wasn't the case."

"You sound as if you don't approve of his lifestyle."

She shrugged. "My dad could be frivolous and maybe flighty. There were times Mom should have said no."

"That kind of love is admirable, though. My folks are in love, I suppose. I've never thought much about it. They stay together and they seem compatible, but each has created his own life and they don't spend time together except for a couple of hours at the end of the day."

She glanced at him. "I haven't told anyone this, Chase. Even Gramma doesn't know. After Dad went into the hospital, he told me that he got deeply into gambling debts."

"Oh, damn," Chase remarked under his breath. "That's why you were selling everything," he said and she nodded.

"Yes. Dad took out loans to pay off the debts. He's longtime friends with Mitch Anson, so Mitch approved the loans. For years Mom used to go with him to Vegas, so I knew he gambled. He told me he never played for high stakes while Mom was alive. After she died a few years ago, he piled up big debts. He mortgaged the ranch and took out loans against it and the hotel. Thank heavens he paid off the gambling debts with the loans and I don't have to deal with those people. I accepted your offer to pay off his loans."

"You've been able to, haven't you?"

"Easily, now, thanks to you," she remarked dryly. "That's

all confidential, but that's part of why I couldn't say no to you."

"You've made a lot of sacrifices for your family. That's commendable," he said and she shrugged.

"I love them and they love me, and I have some responsibilities for them." Laurel turned to look out the window as a sprawling, clapboard house came into view. Outbuildings were farther in the distance, almost hidden by tall cypress. "This is a spellbinding place," she said, "with the ocean and the cypress."

"I've always liked it," he said. They parked in back and in minutes she stepped into a large living area with a vaulted ceiling that ran above the second floor. Light poured through skylights high above them as well as through two-story-high panes of glass along one wall. Extending from the kitchen was an area that held a breakfast table and hutch. Adjoining the informal dining area and kitchen was a sitting area that held maroon leather sofas and chairs and where a massive stone fireplace filled one corner.

"This is spectacular, Chase," she said, looking around. "The view is awesome!" She gazed at the ocean and its whitecaps as the waves rolled in.

"Thanks," he replied. "Come upstairs and I'll show you where we'll be."

He tossed his hat on a chair as they entered an expansive hallway that had a wide, curving staircase. She followed him into a sitting room bathed in light through floor-to-ceiling glass windows. One wall held a large stone fireplace, and two area rugs were on the maple floors. Through an open door she could see the adjoining bedroom with a king-size bed. "This is a wonderful place," she said, gazing through the tall windows and getting an even better look at the ocean. The house sat on one side of curved land, and she could see the waves washing against the rocks and cliff on the other side of the curve.

"Laurel," Chase said, his tone entirely different. "Come here. I have something for you."

He held out a box wrapped in blue tissue and tied with a blue satin ribbon.

Though she knew it wasn't an engagement ring, her heart still soared at the prospect.

She was in deeper trouble than she thought.

Eight

Her heart thudding, Laurel opened the box to find a huge diamond pendant surrounded by smaller diamonds. "Chase, it's fabulous!" she exclaimed, amazed he would give her such a gift.

Chase stepped around her and fastened it behind her neck. "You're what's fantastic. I want you to remember today."

She turned and modeled it for him, then wound her arms around his neck. "Thank you! It's dazzling and how could I ever forget this day? And I intend to see to it that you don't forget it either," she whispered.

His gaze consumed her. "I've waited for what seems like an eternity. I want you more than you can ever know," he said.

He leaned forward to kiss her, drawing her more tightly into his embrace, and his expression grew solemn.

He kissed her until she forgot the gift and could think only about Chase.

His sizzling kisses sent her temperature soaring. Desire heightened and she moaned softly. Her breasts became sensitive and tingled. For now she would seize what she could from these moments with him because there was a fabulous hot chemistry between them.

This weekend, as well as the entire month, she could remove both physical and emotional barriers. Eagerly, she wanted to explore his marvelous body, to discover every inch of him. She intended to see to it that he didn't walk away easily at the end of the month, and she wanted to feel that he would never forget her.

"Laurel, my love," he whispered, and she knew the endearment meant nothing to him, that he merely mouthed it in the throes of passion.

"Love me," she whispered, wanting his hands and mouth and body on her. His tongue stroked hers and his hands roamed over her. She didn't notice as he twisted buttons free, but her blouse fell to the floor, followed by her red slacks. She kicked away her shoes and impatiently tugged off his shirt and unfastened his trousers to let them drop. Keys jingled and his belt buckle clinked. She paused to frame his face with her hands.

"I hope you never forget this afternoon," she whispered, and his eyes changed to the color of a stormy sea. He held her away to let his gaze run over her.

"I want to kiss every inch of you. You take my breath away, and I want to look at you endlessly—I want to touch and caress and kiss you. I intend to see what excites you and make you lose all that cool control," he said.

His words were an aphrodisiac. She simmered beneath his gaze, eagerly reaching for him. Gasping with pleasure as she arched her hips against him, she felt his thick arousal. She hooked her fingers in his briefs and freed him from them.

All reason and resolutions were demolished, and she relished his loving. Showering kisses on her throat, he unclasped her bra. It fell on her feet, but she gave no heed.

He cupped her breasts in his large, tanned hands, and his thumbs lazed back and forth across her taut peaks, making her gasp. She grabbed his strong forearms, inhaling and surrendering to the intense pleasure streaking from his touch.

"You're perfection," he whispered in a rasp. "You don't have any idea what you do to me," he said, leaning closer to circle her nipple with his tongue. Hot and wet, each stroke increased her need for him. Deep and low inside her, heat burned, heightening desire. He was male perfection and she drank in the sight of him. She kissed him hungrily and then scattered her kisses down, kneeling to circle his thick manhood with her hand. As he wound his fingers in her hair, he inhaled deeply.

With a pounding heartbeat, she ran her hands along his strong legs slowly. At the same time the tip of her tongue traced circles on his belly and his fingers clenched handfuls of her hair. Pleasure grew as she stroked his thick rod and then took him into her mouth, running her tongue over him.

With a gasp he pulled her to her feet, wrapping one arm around her and leaning over her to kiss her hard. Their mouths fused, he swept her up into his arms and carried her to bed, flinging back covers and placing her on the bed. She was on fire with need, her body clamoring for him.

He moved to her foot and ran his tongue upward along the inside of her shapely leg, and she writhed with pleasure, her fists knotting the bedding. She opened her legs to him and his hand dallied over her intimately, rubbing and caressing her.

"Chase," she whispered, watching him as he knelt between her legs. He was thick and ready. She couldn't get enough of looking at his superb body. She memorized the sight of him. His broad shoulders and chest always stirred her desire.

He caressed the inside of her thigh, his fingers drifting lightly to her soft folds.

Closing her eyes, she arched beneath his touch, raising her hips for more, wanting him inside her with an urgency that was becoming unbearable.

Soon he lay beside her, tangling his legs with hers as his

fingers continued touching her intimately, rubbing her and driving her wild, making her thrash beneath his touch. "Chase!" she cried out and he kissed her, silencing her.

With a cry she broke away and pushed him down. "Let me love you," she said, turning him over and moving astride him, starting at the backs of his knees to trace wet kisses up the backs of his legs, stroking his firm bottom and then sliding up to caress his smooth, muscled back until she reached his nape. He turned, wrapping an arm around her while he kissed her and his other hand explored her as thoroughly as she had him.

Still kissing her, he rolled over, taking her with him, and then he climbed off the bed, pulling open a drawer in a bedside table to get a condom.

"I'm on the pill," she said, clasping his wrist to stop him.

While he moved back between her legs, she drank in the sight of him, running the tips of her fingers over his strong legs, caressing his manhood. Kissing her, he lowered himself, and she wrapped her arms around him and closed her eyes.

She slid her hands down to cup his bottom and pull him toward her. "Love me, Chase," she whispered until he kissed her again and her words were lost.

Thick and hard, he eased into her and she gasped, wrapping her long legs around him and arching beneath him as he withdrew.

"Chase!" she cried. "I want you!"

He eased in again, slowly filling her, and she arched again to meet him, writhing with longing for his loving.

He was covered with a sheen of sweat. She stroked his back, wishing she could drive him to lose his iron control the way she'd lost hers. She moved wildly, clinging to him as her head thrashed and she moaned with pleasure and need. "Love me!" she gasped.

Still he held off, tension steadily building. And then his control disintegrated and he pumped furiously, filling her, hot and hard. Lights exploded behind her closed eyelids. Her thundering pulse drowned all sounds as together they moved frantically until she felt him shudder with release.

"Laurel! My love!" he exclaimed.

She cried out when the release burst inside her in a dazzling climax enveloping her in rapture.

While she tried to catch her breath, she floated back to reality. She could feel his heart pounding as violently as her own.

Relishing touching him, she ran her hands over him feeling a closeness and union that wiped out all constraints and differences. He was marvelous, breathtaking, handsome. At this moment he was united with her and she basked in satisfaction and satiation.

Turning, he showered her temple with light kisses, trailing them to her ear. "You're fabulous," he whispered, his breath hot.

"I can say the same about you," she purred, opening her eyes to find him watching her intently. The moment was aglow and his expression held joy and satisfaction.

"You're more than I dreamed of and hoped for," he whispered, trailing kisses on her cheek to her mouth to kiss her lightly. He raised his head again to look at her. "So much more," he whispered. "I feel like I was empty until you came along."

She trembled, his words the first intrusion of reality and the world they'd temporarily left behind. She wanted to believe the fabulous things he was saying, but he was a charmer and she knew better, and now she wished he had kept silent and held the moment between them with its euphoria.

"The loving is fantastic," she said softly, knowing that she was being truthful with him. She wouldn't mouth endearments she didn't mean, empty lies that he might believe although he should know better, since he did such things himself.

He rolled over, taking her with him and turning on his side, still holding her close. "I could hold you for the entire night. I don't want you out of my arms."

"I would like it if you did," she answered, winding her fingers in his chest hair, feeling the short, crisp hair tickle her breasts.

"You said you're opposed to marriage because of your parents. Is that really the whole reason, Chase?" she blurted out, surprising herself.

His jaw firmed and he gazed beyond her. "It's more than enough reason I've watched my dad spend his whole life working like crazy for his family. He married young and started a family, so Dad has been bogged down with responsibility his entire life. He's tied to the ranch. He's never traveled, never partied, never developed hobbies because he took care of the ranch and his family."

A sharp pain twisted her insides while her anger flared. She thought of Edward and how he'd broken their engagement the moment she'd taken responsibility for her family. Chase was the same, wanting to avoid anything that interfered with his life and what he wanted to do. She knew she had to let go of her anger for now, forget that Chase was so focused on himself. She tried to turn her attention back to what he was saying to her.

"Mom and Dad have never done anything except work. Only Dad is worse than my mom. She at least gets out and meets her sisters and goes back to Texas to her family. Dad and my Montana grandparents have spent lifetimes working and being tied down. They've never traveled, never had a social life, nothing. All the years I was growing up, I saw marriage as a trap. I still get claustrophobic when I contemplate it, and I've never, ever been in love." He looked down at her.

"You got it with both barrels," he added softly, his voice changing as he smiled at her. "You touched a nerve, as you can see. Most women don't believe me and don' t ask or they feel the way I do and view marriage as a trap or they've been married and it went sour and they don't ever want to do that again."

"You sound bitter," she said, aghast at his view of marriage. He was no more a man to love than Edward had been, in spite of how wonderful a time she had when she was with Chase. She touched his jaw. "My parents were happy, and no one could ever describe my dad as being 'tied down.' He didn't travel a lot, but they went places, with and without us, and my dad loves people and parties. He made the most of being married, and I think he loved Mom deeply and she loved him."

"That wasn't the view of marriage I ever had, and you couldn't possibly have been describing my parents. It makes my blood run cold to consider being trapped for the rest of my life the way my dad is," Chase said, nuzzling her throat and then kissing her lightly.

"Perhaps he doesn't feel trapped. Maybe he would have lived that way had he been single all his life," she said, and Chase's eyebrows arched.

"I guess he would have, but it's hard to imagine. I'll never know, but I know what I don't want."

"You don't find it better to be with someone, more exciting, more entertaining? Reassuring when life takes a bad turn? But then, your life must not take bad turns."

"Of course it does, at least occasionally. And yes, it's definitely better to be with you right now than off by myself. I would never have the excitement I do now if I weren't with you." He leaned away and let his hand slide down over her breasts, and she pressed her hips against him as a tremor of desire rocked her.

His eyes darkened and he kissed her, brushing her lips first and then kissing her more passionately. She could feel him stir.

"Chase!" she whispered, running her hand along his hip, feeling the short hairs on his thigh. "You're supposed to be exhausted and quiet and not aroused."

"Parts of me don't know that, and all of me is responding to you," he answered as he kissed her throat and caressed her breasts.

"I should shower."

"We can do better than that. Don't move," he said, extricating himself and crossing the bedroom. She watched him, relishing looking at his strong body, feeling a pang over the circumstances she was thrown into with Chase.

In minutes he returned and picked her up. She wrapped her arms around his neck and smiled at him, and he paused as he looked into her eyes and smiled in return.

"We're going to shower?"

"I told you, better than that," he said, carrying her into a large bathroom with a huge marble Jacuzzi tub, partially filled with water. He walked down steps into the tub and sat, holding her on his lap.

She could feel his arousal pressed against her and her desire rekindled. She twisted around and the minute she looked into his eyes, she saw the desire she felt, mirrored there.

She wound her arm around his neck and pulled his head down to kiss him, her heartbeat speeding. He lifted her easily so she sat astride him and then he thrust into her and she moved on him. He fondled her breasts, cupping them as his tongue circled her nipple, first one and then the other until he groaned and held her, moving his hips against her.

Wildly she thrashed on him until she climaxed again as he did. Draping herself over him, she gasped for breath while pleasure filled her. She felt boneless, warm and satisfied, pressing against him until she climbed off to sit between his long legs and lean back against him. He held her and nuzzled her neck, kissing her ear.

"Best bath ever," he whispered.

"I'd agree with that," she replied, running her hand along his legs. "You're a fantastic lover."

"Thanks," he said. "I'm glad you think so. This is good, Laurel. Damn good. It's better than I thought it would be, because you're fantastic."

"Thank you, kind sir. Pure flattery but delightful to hear," she said, feeling giddy and realizing that she was going to fall head over heels in love with this man and there was no way to stop it from happening unless she walked out on him today. And *that* was impossible. She would have to back out of their deal to do that. He was too likable. She thought of the reasons she should avoid falling in love, first and foremost, knowing that he would never return her feelings.

"This is the way a bath should be," he said, his hands caressing her breasts.

She inhaled and captured his hands, holding them in hers. "What will you do with my hotel, Chase?"

"Use if for my people who won't be living in Montana on a more permanent basis. It'll be there for employees who will come and go. Probably let Brice continue to run it, since he's done that for years and is competent and recommended by you."

"He's excellent, but he told me this morning that he's taken a job with the Barclay Champion Hotel and he'll leave when I no longer need him and I turn things over to you and your staff."

"Although I'm not surprised, I'm sorry to hear that, because I'd just as soon keep competent people and the transition smooth."

"He's a great manager. Our employees have been with us a long time. They hire on and stay."

"That's a tribute to your dad, then."

"Dad and Brice. My dad didn't ever stay at work 24/7 the way you've said yours does, and Brice takes over when he's gone. Without Dad there, we need someone who is totally reliable. Anyway, I hope you do forgive Brice."

"I'm thankful we weren't in the front lobby and on the evening news."

"I hadn't even thought of that," she said. "How awful that would have been! I would have never heard the end of it about this weekend."

"Well, it wasn't, so we don't have to worry. When we get back, Laurel, will you move into my suite with me?"

"That's the deal we made," she remarked dryly.

"I hope the time comes when you can stop focusing on the deal we made and you don't sound so bitter about it. Even more, I'm looking forward to reaching a time when you don't have any anger toward me," he whispered, his breath warm on the back of her neck as he toyed with locks of her hair.

Her anger had vanished from the time they walked into his house. It might return, but she doubted if she would ever be as annoyed as before. She would have to deal with hurt later because after one month of his loving and charm, she couldn't guess how long it would take her to get over him.

How many broken hearts did he have in his past? She suspected a large number, and she hadn't intended for that to happen to her.

"So, do we get to eat around here?" she asked, putting her head back against his shoulder.

"If I can stop loving you long enough to get food on the table."

"Maybe I should get our dinner on the table," she said.

"Let me see if I can get your mind off food," Chase said in a husky voice and then lifted her around to kiss her.

It was past midnight before they were wrapped in robes, seated on a sofa in the sitting room in front of a roaring fire Chase had built. He raised his glass of wine. "Here's to the best night of my life," he said quietly.

Smiling, she shook her head. "That's absurd, Chase! Probably the best night was the time you made your first million. Why do I suspect you've made the same toast other nights in the past?"

"This is the best night," he replied solemnly. "Making money is always fine, but it can't give me the high you have in the past few hours."

Unable to believe him, she looked down and swirled her

wine. "This is better than I expected, I will admit that." She glanced around. "I can see why you like the solitude and to come up here alone, yet at night this must be a lonely place."

"I love it here. Since this is the first time I've brought anyone, I'm glad it's you, and I'm happy you accepted my offer and that we came here."

She realized she wouldn't be back, but everything with Chase was temporary.

"You've sold the hotel and taken your ranch off the market. Have you decided what you'll do now?" he asked. "Go back to Dallas for a time? Go back and forth? You have more choices."

She nodded. "I'll stay around here because of Dad, although I'll go back sometime soon for a couple of days. I'll stay in touch better than just by fax and e-mail and phone, as I've been doing."

"I'll fly to Dallas with you soon, and we'll look at lawns you've done. Maybe I can hire you."

"I'm expensive."

"I'm rich," he said, smiling at her as she laughed.

"Very well. I have a portfolio if you want to see."

"Sure," he replied, sipping his wine. "I can't wait to look at your portfolio and whatever else you'll show me," he said in a suggestive tone.

"Strictly business, Chase. I didn't mean here—I don't carry it with me," she said. "When we get back, you can come to my office and I'll show you."

"For this next week I want to clear my calendar. I'd like to stay here with you. Can you do that?"

"The whole week here?" she asked in surprise. Eagerness flared over the prospect of spending that much uninterrupted time with him. She thought about the responsibilities in Montana and Texas. "I suppose I can because anyone who needs to get in touch with me will be able to," she said.

"Excellent," Chase exclaimed, placing her wineglass on a table beside his. He moved closer and pulled her on his lap and wrapped his arms around her. "I want you here where we can make love day and night."

Her heart skipped a beat, and she ran her fingers through his hair. "I'll second that suggestion," she said and he grinned. She had tossed aside reluctance, worries and resentment for now, suspending caution and enjoying Chase, determined that she would see to it that he wouldn't forget her easily and allow her to fade and blend into his memories of other women who had briefly passed through his life.

He pulled loose the tie to her robe and shoved it off her shoulders, cupping her breasts in his hands. "You're gorgeous," he whispered and leaned closer to circle her taut peak with his tongue.

Gasping with pleasure, she tangled her fingers in his hair, tossing her head back and letting him love her until the torment became too intense.

Hours later, after a snack, as she was once more in his arms in bed, she caressed his bare shoulder. "You are an insatiable animal," she whispered, and he chuckled softly as he traced the shape of her ear with his finger.

"I think I can say the same. You're a tempestuous woman, even more passionate than I expected, and you respond to the slightest touch, which sets me on fire."

"I hope so," she purred with satisfaction. "I want to drive you to lose your strong control and torment you as you do me."

"Sounds good to me. We'll work on that tonight," he said, sitting up. He stood and picked her up to carry her to his shower, where he set her on her feet. As he turned on warm water, she ran her hands over his marvelous body, and in minutes showering was forgotten.

Light, gray and dim, spilled into the room. Laurel lay against Chase in the crook of his arm with her leg thrown over his. "Are you ever going to feed me a real meal, or am I simply a sex object?"

"You are definitely a sex object," he replied with amusement, toying with locks of her soft hair. "A wanton, torrid, red-hot lover. How can I think about food if you're around?"

"You better think about it before I starve and waste away and can't make love to you. The last time you told me we'd eat, I had about three sips of wine and that was it."

"Waste away, huh?" he teased, running his hand over her hip and then cupping her breast while his thumb circled her nipple and she inhaled. "I don't think you're exactly going to disappear. You feel solid, soft, warm—definitely enough of you there to set me on fire again."

"Will you stop," she said, laughing and catching his hand as she lay back against his shoulder. He rolled on his side to look down at her.

"I can't stop making love to you, but I'll try to get something for you to eat. You better cover up from your chin to your toes, though, if you want me to leave you alone while you cook breakfast. Or if you prefer, since you missed dinner, I'll cook a huge breakfast."

"I will do exactly that. Even better," she said, wriggling away from him and sliding across the bed to get out on the far side. "I will shower *alone* and you can go cook. I got in a rush yesterday to get ready to go and missed lunch."

"I wish I thought you'd done that because you were so eager to begin this weekend," he said, and for once she didn't hear the teasing note in his voice. Startling her, she looked at him and saw he was watching her with a sober expression.

"I was eager, Chase," she answered in a tone as solemn as his, and he slid off the bed to step toward her. She held up her hand.

"Just wait—"

"After you say something like that to me, I can't keep from reaching for you."

"You're not coaxing me back to bed until I've had food."

"Now that is a challenge," he said, approaching her, but now his eyes were twinkling, so she scooped up her robe to yank it on and turned and ran. Behind her, she heard his chuckle. She knew if he really wanted to catch her, he easily could. When he wanted, he could move like lightning, but he let her go. She rushed to shower and get into some clothes, wondering if she would even be able to keep them on through the meal or get more than a couple of bites down before they made love again. And for a minute there he'd sounded as if he'd meant what he'd said.

In the shower she was wrapped in euphoria, daydreaming of Chase's marvelous body, his strong muscles and his untiring energy. He was a marvel in bed and she tingled, thinking about their lovemaking. She also blushed while re-membering moments with him.

She gave vent to erotic images until she was hot and wanting him again as if they hadn't made love again and again since the first moment they walked into his house.

She dressed in a black bra that was a wisp of lace and a matching black thong. She pulled on red silk lounging pajamas, the top tight and very low cut. She'd never worn the pajamas before, but for now, shut away alone with Chase, it suited her.

She found him outside on a lighted redwood deck, a fire burning in a large cast-iron chiminea as he stood grilling sausage and ham. Food smelled enticing but not half as tempting as Chase. With her pulse speeding, she looked at him in his tight jeans, black knit shirt and loafers. She walked up quietly behind him and wrapped her arms around him, her hands on his chest.

"You handsome devil," she said in a throaty voice. Turning, he wrapped her in his embrace, leaning down to kiss her thor-oughly until she pushed against his chest.

"Chase, don't burn up breakfast."

"Why not? I'm already on fire," he said quietly and then

noticed her clothes, holding her away slightly to take a more thorough look. "You look red-hot and I'd like to take you right back to bed."

"Don't you dare! Feed me first or I'll get really surly."

"Surly? I don't believe it," he said. He pulled her up against his chest. "I'll feed you and then I'll seduce you."

"Sounds like a deal to me," she drawled in a breathy voice, and she ran her hand lightly over his manhood, which was already aroused. He inhaled and his eyes darkened.

"Laurel," he cautioned. "You keep that up and breakfast is postponed."

"I think you'll keep it up," she said softly, twisting out of his arms and walking away.

She heard the fork he'd been holding clatter on the cooker, and as she started to look over her shoulder, he caught up with her and pulled her into his embrace to kiss her fervently again until she pushed against him.

"You go cook and I'll leave you alone," she said breathlessly. "Can I get anything on the table?"

He took a deep breath and shook his head, turning away without a word and she knew he'd lost all interest in food. Smiling to herself, she walked away. She'd rather be in his arms and wanted to make love, but she hoped to make him want her to a degree he had never felt before. Also, she was almost faint with hunger.

Finally, breakfast was served. They devoured only about half when he stood, and picked her up and carried her to the bedroom where the next hours were spent in lovemaking.

By Monday morning, after they'd showered together, she lay in bed in Chase's arms again. She wound her fingers in the thick mat of curls across his chest as she listened to his deep breathing. "Chase, we've spent all our time since arriving either in bed or making love, with just a few minutes between to shower or eat. That is truly decadent."

"Is this a complaint?" he asked, his voice laced with amusement.

She rose up to look at him, tracing the line of his jaw that had a night's growth of dark stubble. "Definitely not a complaint, only amazement."

He grinned. "It's been damn great." He twirled a long lock of her hair around his finger. "I can't think of one better way to spend my time," he added, his voice becoming solemn as his gaze traveled over her features and then lingered on her mouth.

"I know that look. I do want to eat breakfast because there's no telling when I'll get to eat again."

"You seem to require regular feeding."

"More or less," she stated dryly.

He propped his head on his hand to look at her. "You're beautiful. I want you more each day, instead of less," he said, once again a rare moment when he sounded earnest and convincing, yet she knew she shouldn't give much heed to such words.

That was the way she felt about him and his marvelous body, but she wasn't going to tell him. "Today, I need some time to call the hotel and check on things and talk to Gramma and see about my dad."

"Sure," he said, leaning the last few inches to kiss her senseless.

It was almost noon before she got away to the study, where she closed the door and called the hotel to talk to Brice, writing a list of things he told her and listening to problems— *a lot* of problems.

Then, lost in thought about the weekend, she stared at her reflection in a mirror without really seeing herself. She had dressed in jeans and a blue shirt, with her hair in a ponytail, and it amazed her to realize it was the first time she'd put on her regular clothes since her arrival Saturday. "Is your heart still intact?" she whispered to her image. "Are you falling in love with him?"

She thought she could honestly say no and walk away when the month was over, yet at the same time she had to admit she was having a wonderful time with him. "I hope not," she whispered, feeling hollow inside at the thought of parting from him.

When the month ends, I will be gone. She could remember him saying that to her, and she shivered. No matter what she did, he wasn't going to fall in love.

She looked at the notes she'd made and left the study to find Chase, to tell him about Athens' news. It wasn't good. He sat in his office with papers spread in front of him.

"Ready for an interruption?" she asked and he motioned for her to come in. Through the window behind him, she could see that fog had rolled in and it was difficult to see far, yet she could make out the breakers crashing against rocks. "I need to talk to you," she said, wondering if their euphoria was about to come to an end.

Nine

Laurel sat across from Chase, and her breath sped as she looked at his broad shoulders in a knit shirt that still revealed his muscles. As her gaze traveled over him, she thought about him naked, holding her. Desire stirred and momentarily she forgot why she had come to see him.

"Yes?" he asked, his eyebrows arching with curiosity, bringing her back to the moment. Her cheeks flushed over her erotic daydreams.

"I was thinking about something else," she said, rattling a paper in her hand.

"It must have been interesting," he said, one corner of his mouth curling in amusement.

"Chase, I called the hotel to check on things, and Ty has called twice, so I returned his call."

"And I assume he's unhappy with me. Or more accurately, with my people."

"That's right. They are really pressuring Ty to sell and buying out land around him and threatening him to make it more difficult for him if he doesn't cooperate. Those are horrible tactics." As she talked, his expression remained the same except a coldness filled his eyes.

"Look, Laurel, I don't tell you how to run your business. I need that land. You said yourself that you could see why it would be more convenient for me to own the Carson ranch."

"Chase, for a brief time can you stop viewing the world from the standpoint of what you want? Think about the Carsons and their family place. You're not a sentimental man, obviously, so it's a stretch, but for once put aside your own selfish wants and take a good look at the situation to see if you can find another solution," she said heatedly. She knew she was losing her temper with him, which wasn't going to help matters and could make things worse. She suspected people close to Chase seldom corrected him or told him what he should do. "Do it another way besides owning his property."

He clamped his jaw closed and glared at her and she glared back.

"Is this going to make a difference between us?" he asked quietly.

"Not really. My emotions aren't all tied up in my relationship with you anyway, and yours aren't with me," she snapped.

His eyebrows arched. "You run roughshod over my feelings, and as I've told you before, I don't usually bomb out to this extent with a woman. Particularly not after spending time with her."

"You're charming and handsome and ever so appealing," she said. "You're not bombing out, but I'm not so gaga that I can't think straight."

She thought she saw the corner of his mouth twitch, but she wasn't certain. While she couldn't tell what his reaction really was, she suspected he was less than happy with her. Silence stretched in the room, and tension wound tighter as she stared back at him and wondered what was running through his mind.

Finally he picked up the phone and made a call, leaning back in his chair.

She listened as he talked to Luke Perkins.

"Luke, stop dealing with Ty Carson. Make an appointment for me to see him a week from today. I'll talk to him. I'll see if we can lease some land from him and pay him to get water from his place. That way his damn ranch will stay intact and still be his." Chase swiveled his chair around and spoke softly and she couldn't hear the conversation. She suspected Luke wasn't happy with Chase's decision, but she was thrilled that he had backed off buying Ty's ranch.

Knowing that he had done this solely for her, she stood impatiently, bubbling and happy.

"That's right," Chase said emphatically into the phone. "Thanks."

As he broke the connection and turned to replace the receiver of his phone, she rushed to sit in his lap and hug him. "Thank you!" She kissed him hard.

Quickly, his arm circled her waist and he kissed her in return. His fingers went to the buttons of her shirt to unfasten them, and she tugged his shirt out of his jeans and pulled it over his head. In minutes he carried her to the sofa to peel off her jeans and shed his.

It was an hour later after lovemaking that she lay in his arms on the wide sofa and remembered the phone call. "Chase, thank you for planning to go see Ty and deciding to ask him if you can lease part of his ranch. Thank you so much!"

He smiled at her. "You're too softhearted, darlin'."

"I know you're doing that for me. Don't make me fall in love with you."

His smile broadened. "That would be bad? I'm head over heels in love."

"No, you're not," she replied, combing locks of hair off his forehead and running her fingers down to his jaw. "You're head over heels in lust, and there is a monumental difference."

"Back to the marriage theme," he said in a resigned voice. "I can be in love."

"You told me that you never had been in love in your life."

"Not the kind that leads to marriage, like you're talking about," he answered dryly.

"There, see. You're not in the kind of love now that leads to long-term commitment or marriage. Therefore, you do mean lust."

"Call it want you will—to me, I'm in love and I want you."

"Yet not permanently," she repeated in exasperation. "The more we talk, the more I realize I can stop worrying about falling in love with you."

"In that case," he said, rolling over and picking her up, "we'll go shower and stop this discussion. I want you grateful, wanting to please me and thank me and in love with me."

"You want it all, don't you?" she asked him, smiling at him, yet knowing he was definitely deep in lust and nothing more. But she was grateful to Chase concerning the Carson ranch, and it made her feel better toward him to find that he wasn't as hard-hearted and cold as she had thought.

Early on Sunday morning, Chase stirred first and looked at Laurel, sleeping against him. He turned carefully on his side to see her better. Her blond hair was spread across the pillow. This past week with her had been fabulous, so much more than he'd expected and he didn't want to go back to work tomorrow and give up having her to himself.

He had no illusions; she wasn't in love with him. Far from it. He couldn't think of any woman he'd ever spent time with and given so much attention to who had been as cool as

Laurel. He suspected that if their deal was declared off today, she'd be packed and gone, which he had to admit bothered him. Women he was interested in were usually in love with him and he had always been the one to walk on the relationship. He knew he wouldn't be the one in this case. It would be Laurel.

She stayed because she was keeping her part of a bargain with him, yet there was a hot chemistry between them that had grown hotter with each passing day. That was what amazed him.

He'd expected to spend a weekend away with her, enjoy his month with her and walk away forgetting her totally, as he had from affairs in the past. He still thought he'd feel that way at the end of the month, but he didn't want to think about leaving California today. In spite of work piling up in Montana and Texas, he wondered whether he could talk her into staying longer because when they returned to Athens, there would be demands on his time as well as hers and they'd never get the opportunity, intimacy and privacy they'd had here.

He pushed down the sheet, letting his gaze drink in the sight of her nude. He was already aroused and wanted to wake her and love her, but he also liked looking at her. He traced a circle on her breast, and she stirred in a slow, sensuous move. He leaned down to trace around her nipple with his tongue and then raised his head to look into her eyes, which were sleepy yet filled with desire.

He ached to possess her. Wrapping her arms around his neck, she pulled him down to kiss him. As he embraced her and moved above her, he kissed her and desire escalated.

Tangling one hand in her hair, he stroked her silky skin. She was all softness and curves, bewitching and seductive.

She pushed him over and straddled him, shifting to lavish kisses over him. He watched her while his temperature climbed and need built until he could no longer wait and moved over her to spread her legs and enter her. Wanting to make it last and draw out ecstasy, he thrust slowly.

"Darlin', you're awesome," he whispered.

"Come here, Chase," she said, pulling his head down to kiss him, and words were gone as he filled her and withdrew to fill her again, soon pumping until he climaxed with her, crashing over an edge and sinking down to hold her tightly.

As they lay on their sides with their legs entangled, he stroked her damp hair from her face.

"Laurel, this is good between us, really good. Let's stay two or three days more. I can move my work around, and you've sold the hotel, so you don't have the responsibilities you did."

She frowned at him, and as he waited for her to answer, he realized he badly wanted her to accept. At the hotel she'd move in with him anyway. He thought about his calendar, which was packed with appointments for the coming week, but Luke could juggle them around, postpone them or attend in his place in some cases.

"This is something special, darlin'," Chase admitted, surprised by the depth of need he had. He traced his hand along her throat.

Her blue eyes darkened and he saw desire stirring again, marveling at how easy it was to arouse her and how much she liked to make love.

"You know I might have to get back quickly."

"Same deal as when we first came—I can get you back on a moment's notice, and at the most we're only a little over two hours away. Let's stay two more days."

"When's the last time you took off more than a week?"

"Probably back in March," he said, knowing full well that it was less than a week and he planned for it months ahead of time. He took off a lot but not for long periods of time. Weekends, a few days during the week, usually were the most he'd do at a time.

"I've missed so much in Texas, Chase."

"You can miss a bit more," he said firmly, amazed at

himself for pushing her and wanting her to say yes. He wondered how important she was becoming to him. Although every moment together he was becoming more emotionally entangled, he plunged ahead. "Stay and let's have the moment," he said.

"Very well," she said, sighing, and he had to laugh.

"There you go again, smashing what's left of my ego."

"No worries there," she add dryly, running her fingers along his bare shoulder. "I'll call home later and tell them when I'll return. So, how will you entertain me?" she asked, stretching with a teasing sparkle in her eyes and he laughed.

"How's this for a start?" he asked, leaning down to kiss her.

That evening as they sat eating grilled snapper fillets, Laurel sipped her wine and turned to look through the floor-to-ceiling windows. Fog rolled in over the ocean, and she knew it soon would envelope everything and visibility would be gone.

"I'd think it would be frightening and dangerous to be out there in a boat."

"Nowadays everyone has radar and sonar equipment and therefore they know where there are obstacles, but once upon a time it was probably damn frightening. I can show you some of the lighthouses along the coast, if you'd like."

"Yes, I would. Chase, I'll admit, I love this place."

"Me, too. This is my haven, more than the other homes I have." He stretched out his arm to caress her nape.

"I called the hotel. Brice was beside himself that I'm staying with you longer. I doubt if your people were happy either."

"I don't give a damn," Chase remarked. "Luke was shocked. I don't usually take this much time off at once," he said, raising his wine glass to her in a toast. "You're causing me to do things I've never done before. Here's to you, Laurel."

Thrilled by his statement, she raised her glass in return, toasting with him and wondering why he wanted to stay, because she'd be with him whether they were in Athens or California.

Brice had wanted her to return, and her grandmother's skepticism and disapproval were clearly discernible over the phone. She knew Ashley and Diana would think it was great because they had both been agog over Chase.

"This is a wonderful home," she said. "It's so quiet that you wouldn't know there's another person within a hundred miles."

"Actually, there are some people down the road and around the bend, but it seems that way and that's what I like."

They both sat quietly eating, but when they finished, Chase wanted her on his lap; soon she was wrapped in his embrace while they made love.

Tuesday afternoon, they packed and flew back to Montana. On the plane Chase took her hand. "I'll get someone to move your things to my suite. You can show them what to take."

"We're only across the hall," she remarked with amusement. "I'll bring my belongings when I need them. I can go back and forth."

"You can stay naked and I'll be happy."

"I'm sure you would be," she stated, laughing. "Forget that one, Chase. We'll have so much work to catch up on."

"I want to go back to California next weekend. Will you go?"

"Perhaps, let me see if I get caught up, but I won't stay another week."

He nodded. "I'll need to see if I can get away, too."

She looked out the window of the plane. The first part of her month with him had passed so swiftly she was amazed. Not even three more full weeks and they would tell each other goodbye.

Reflecting on the past week, she studied Chase, acknowledging to herself that she had fallen in love with him. Love with such a charmer was never her intention, but it was impossible to prevent. She didn't want him to know it. She would have to get over it just as she had gotten over heartbreak with Edward. The nagging thought plaguing her was that she was in love with Chase, perhaps forever.

* * *

Wednesday morning Brice called and wanted to see her; Laurel could tell from the tone of his voice that he was unhappy.

Striding into her office and looking neat as usual in his brown suit, he raked his fingers through his hair. When he closed the door and sat facing her, his worried frown indicated the problem was large. "Laurel, I'll get to the point. Chase called me in this morning. He offered me triple my salary if I'd stay to work for him."

Joy for Brice was her first reaction. Once more Chase had been a good guy and had surprised her. Puzzled about Brice's scowl, she sat back in her chair. "I'd say that's wonderful news. He's not holding a grudge, and he recognizes the quality work you do. I'm glad he can afford to pay you more. I don't exactly see the problem."

"That's why I need to talk to you," Brice said, rubbing his hands together. She wondered what could be making him distraught when he'd had such a fantastic offer. "Soon your month with him will be over. If he breaks your heart, I couldn't bear to work for him."

Relief flooded her. "Brice, he won't break my heart. I promise," she said, feeling uneasy over making statements that weren't truthful. Each day she was growing more accustomed to having Chase in her life. Telling him goodbye would be a huge adjustment.

"You can't promise any such thing," Brice said as he studied her. "You're glowing right now, which means you've had a wonderful time with him. You stayed longer with him in California than you'd planned to. Whether or not you'll recognize it, Laurel, I think you're in love with him. I was there when you both came in last night, and anyone can see you're in love. You never looked like that with Edward. Frankly, he looks as if he's in love, too, but I doubt if the man can fall in love with anyone except himself."

She felt her face flush and bit back, telling Brice that he assumed too much. "I'm not going to fall in love. And even if I do, that has nothing to do with whether you accept his job offer or not."

"If he hurts you, I can't work for him. I'd hate him and feel responsible in a manner I never would have when your dad was here."

"Stop worrying. It's absolute foolishness," she stated, exasperated that people were worrying over her yet reminding herself they simply cared about her. "If you want to stay with the hotel, accept his fabulous offer and continue the wonderful job you do. Why go to a new place and start all over? Here you have the staff and conditions you like and your family seems happy. Have you and Deb talked it over?"

"Of course, and she wants me to accept and stay, but she understands my worry."

"Stop fretting needlessly." Smiling, she stood and walked around her desk to him. He came to his feet and she hugged him. "Accept the job. Grandmother, all of us, will feel better if you do. And don't worry about me. I'm not going to fall in love. He's still a wealthy playboy, and I haven't changed how I feel about that."

"You're not convincing me, but I may go ahead and accept."

"I'll be so happy if you do," she declared truthfully.

He clasped her lightly. "Thanks, Laurel. You take care of yourself. You just said it—Chase is another Edward."

"I know. I'll take care," she said and watched Brice leave.

She hurried down the hall to the office Chase had temporarily turned into his own. She walked through the outer office and knocked at his door.

Dressed in a tan suit, he looked up from his desk and came to his feet; her heartbeat quickened while business became secondary.

"I'll only be a minute because I have an appointment, but

Brice came to see me," she said. Chase closed his door, then put his arms around her waist.

"That was a fabulous offer you've given Brice, and I know he'll take it. That's wonderful—and once again, you're a good guy," she said, smiling.

"I wish you wouldn't always sound so damn surprised," he said solemnly. "I've missed you like hell."

"I'm not that far away," she reminded him. She reached up to kiss him, breaking away soon. She was breathless, filled with desire, and Chase was aroused.

"I have to go and you do, too. I'll see you tonight," she said.

Nodding, he inhaled deeply. As she left, her back tingled because she was certain he stood watching her.

Midafternoon, Chase called, saying he would be delayed and wouldn't be in until late that night.

With each hour her anticipation grew, and early in the evening she began to get ready for his arrival. She bathed and pulled on a new sheer black nightgown. Turning on soft music and building a fire, she was eager for him.

When he opened the door, she hurried to meet him. Lights were low in his suite, and as she entered the front room, he dropped his coat on a chair and turned.

His gaze roamed over her, and in quick strides he reached her, pulling her to him. "Damn, you look good enough to eat," he whispered, and her answer was lost when he kissed her, picking her up to carry her to bed.

On the last Monday in August, Laurel met her grandmother at the hospital, and after an hour with Laurel's dad, they left for lunch together.

Halfway through lunch, her grandmother set down her glass of water. "How's Chase?"

"He's fine, Gramma. I've been with him to see the field his company is developing, and their plans sound impressive. The oil will make a difference in Montana's economy."

"That's all well and good, but it's you I want to know about. Are you happy?"

"Yes," Laurel answered honestly. "I am, except for worrying about Dad."

"We're all doing that. I don't want to see you hurt, and Chase doesn't seem like the type to marry."

"At this point in my life, I'm not ready for marriage either, so that's okay," Laurel replied, feeling nervous about the turn in conversation.

"I hope. Edward hurt you and I can't help feeling that a second time with someone as charming as Chase—if you fall in love with him—will end with you hurt badly. Just be careful."

"Sometimes it's difficult to be careful where your heart is concerned," Laurel answered, smiling and reaching over to squeeze her grandmother's hand. "Thank you for worrying about me, though," she added.

"When your dad recovers, you'll go back to Dallas. What then with Chase?"

"I'll face that problem when it happens," she answered, knowing that she would have to tell Chase goodbye. Her grandmother continued to study her with a slight frown. "Gramma, don't worry. I'm fine."

"I pray you are, sweetie. He's far too likable."

She laughed, thinking her grandmother was right. "I'll tell him you said that. I think you scared him a little."

"Nonsense! That young man wouldn't be scared of the devil himself!" she said, and Laurel laughed again, knowing that would make Chase laugh, too.

When lunch was over, she kissed her grandmother goodbye and headed back to the hotel, deciding to start early getting ready for her dinner with Chase. She had only one more week with him and then they'd part. Forever.

On the desk in her office she kept a calendar that she watched carefully, aware of how swiftly August had ended and September had come. The closing came and went on September fourth. And suddenly it was the seventh of September, the night before their time together was over. She dressed with care in a long, backless, black silk dress with a plunging neckline. She left her hair down, and when he came through the door, she flew into his arms and dinner was promptly forgotten until long after midnight.

While he held her close against him in bed, Chase turned on his side to look at her. "Laurel, things have come up in my business, and I have to leave tomorrow and get back to Houston. I'm turning all the business here over to Luke, who can manage well without me."

Something twisted deep inside, but she was determined she wouldn't let him know.

He stroked her hair away from her face. "I want you to go with me. I can move your Dallas business, or you can keep it and I can open another one for you in Houston. I want you there. Will you go with me?" he asked, and her heart thudded because she wanted desperately to say yes.

Yet how could she?

Ten

Laurel looked at the handsome face that had become so important to her, his thick eyelashes and crystal-green eyes that darkened in passion, his sensual mouth, his prominent cheekbones and dark brown hair. Aching to accept, she stroked his cheek, knowing too well that later Chase would end their relationship and she would be hurt even more.

"Chase, it's been wonderful, but you said it all long ago—I'm geared for family. I don't want to go to Houston and be your mistress."

He inhaled and hugged her tightly. "I want you there. What we've had has been fantastic, Laurel," he said roughly and her pain deepened.

"You know that part of me wants to say yes," she answered truthfully, fighting tears, wanting to stay with him, "but the moment when we'd part would come, so I'll be hurt less if it's now," she stated with a knot in her throat.

"At least, give me another month," he said solemnly.

She slipped out of bed and pulled on her white silk robe.

"I think we're finished, Chase. It's been fantastic, but it's over. I can't go to Houston with you. I have responsibility for my family. I've got a business in Dallas I can't go back to either because of my dad. I'm looking for a house in town to move my grandmother and the girls. They prefer that to moving to the hotel, and thanks to you and our month together, I can afford a house. When Dad recovers, he'll be there." She gazed into Chase's eyes, which were unreadable, and she had no idea how deeply he felt about what he had asked her.

"I need to stay here, and you have to go," she continued. "I won't be your mistress indefinitely, but this past month I've loved being with you," she added, unable to stop tears. She turned away and left, hurrying toward the door. Grabbing her purse, which still held the key to her suite, she rushed inside and closed the door, switching on a light. There hadn't been any footsteps behind her, and she realized that Chase had let her go and it really was over.

Blindly, she walked to a chair to sink down and put her head in her hands and cry, giving vent to her anguish. She had done exactly what she had promised herself she wouldn't do—fallen in love with him—and it hurt beyond any distress she had felt in parting with Edward. Chase had been the love of her life.

Even if she wanted to go with him to Houston, she wouldn't leave her family; yet questions tormented her. Would it be a way to hang on to him? If she went, would he eventually want to make the relationship permanent?

She knew she couldn't deal with his kind of temporary arrangement on a long-term basis, and she had responsibilities here.

She spent a sleepless, tearful night, finally falling into a restless sleep when it was almost dawn.

In the morning, there was a knock, and when she opened the door, Chase stepped inside. She could smell his aftershave, and it was difficult to resist putting her arms around him and kissing him.

"I wanted to see you before I leave," he said, gazing at her solemnly. "I'm flying out right away. I don't expect to be back here for a while." He handed her a key. "Here's the key to one of the suites, the one I never used. You and your family can use it whenever you want."

"Thank you," she said, taking the key. "I'll miss you," she added softly, trying to maintain control of her emotions and hating to see him leave.

"I still would like you to go with me to Houston. I can fly you back and forth to see your family."

She shook her head, fighting the knot in her throat and the tears that threatened. "Thanks, but no. That's not the life for me, and I have responsibilities here."

While tension mounted between them, he faced her and then closed the distance between them by wrapping her in his arms and kissing her.

Winding her arms around his neck, she poured all her longing and love into her kiss, wanting to make him regret leaving and not forget her. His cell phone rang, and when he ignored it, she pushed against him, stepping out of his embrace.

"Someone wants you," she said. "You go."

As he stepped back, a muscle worked in his jaw. "Bye, Laurel. You know how to reach me."

She nodded, feeling the threat of tears and trying to keep from crying. He turned and left, closing the door behind him, and she covered her face with her hands and cried. "I love you," she whispered.

She didn't want to see anyone until she was more composed, so she left a message on Brice's phone that she was working in her suite and would be in the office later in the morning.

When she did go to the office, she shut herself in to try to pour herself into work and keep her mind off Chase.

Brice was quiet and to her relief never mentioned Chase. When five o'clock came and she could escape to her suite, she spent an hour alone in the quiet of her empty quarters. She missed Chase terribly and kept wondering what he was doing, curious if he was thinking about her. She suspected he was right now, but she didn't think it would last many days. He was a busy person, and she knew before long another woman would take her place, but at the moment she couldn't bear to think about that.

The night was long and lonely, with little sleep, and she was relieved to dress for work the next day. When the phone rang, her heart missed a beat, and she raced to answer it, holding her breath and hoping it would be Chase.

"Is this Laurel Tolson?" an unfamiliar voice asked. Disappointment swamped her.

"Yes, it is," she answered.

"Just a minute, Dr. Kirkwood would like to speak to you."

Her heart missed another beat as she gripped the phone, terrified that something had happened to her dad.

"Laurel? Brett Kirkwood. Your father has regained consciousness, and I thought you'd want to come. He's not clear, but he's awake."

"I'll be right there. Oh, thank heavens!" she exclaimed, joy replacing all the misery she'd been feeling. "Have you called my grandmother?"

"No, I'm leaving that to you."

"Thanks," she cried, shoving her feet into shoes. "I'm on my way. Thank you so much!" She replaced the receiver and called her grandmother as she grabbed her purse and rushed out of the suite.

In less than ten minutes she walked into her father's room. He was propped up on pillows and still had tubes in him, but his eyes were open and he focused on her. "Dad!" she exclaimed, rushing to him and wanting to throw her arms around him but restraining herself. She squeezed his shoulder lightly.

"Laurel. Love you," he said, sounding exhausted with little lapses between his slurred words, but he recognized her and she was overjoyed.

She held his hand. "I called Gramma and the girls, and they're on their way here. We're all so happy you're better. Just try to get well."

"You here from—?" he frowned as if he couldn't think where she'd been living.

"I've been staying here until you get well."

He squeezed her hand.

"I love you and I know you're going to get well," she said. He looked like a shadow of his former robust self, but now she was certain he would mend.

He closed his eyes and she didn't disturb him. When the doctor came into the room, she walked over to him.

"Thank you for calling me. I talked to him a little and I suppose he's asleep."

"He's come around beyond what we expected. He's a strong person. I think that in a couple of days you'll see a big difference in him. His vitals are good. His recovery will take time."

"We can hire nurses to care for him at our ranch. I've sold the hotel and financing care for him won't be a problem."

"Good. We'll just have to take it a day at a time and get him back on his feet so he can go to therapy, but one crisis is over."

"Thank heavens!" she exclaimed. "Thanks for all you've done," she added and he nodded, going to the bed to take her father's pulse.

Her father woke and the doctor talked to him briefly and then left. Laurel went back to sit at her father's side. Ten minutes later her grandmother and sisters arrived, and she was happy to see that her father was awake again and could talk a little to each of them.

The family spent the day in his room and then left for dinner together. The moment they sat at their table in a local café, Diana turned to Laurel. "Where's Chase? Want to call him to eat with us?"

"No. He's gone to Texas right now," she said and that ended the conversation, but she saw her grandmother give her a sharp look.

"He's a keeper," Diana said. "I hope you marry him."

She laughed, wishing they could change the subject but trying to avoid announcing that he was out of her life. In minutes she got the conversation on the girls' and their activities, and Chase didn't come up again.

When they parted, she hugged each one. "I'll call you whenever I talk to the doctor again," she said.

"We'll come back tomorrow," her grandmother replied. "This has been a wonderful day. I feel he's turned a corner and will get well."

"I'm sure he will," Laurel said, feeling positive about him. When she returned to her empty suite, she looked at the phone to see if the red light indicated messages, but there were none.

Trying to get her thoughts off Chase, she began to plan her father's move to Billings for physical therapy. Now with Chase's money plus the sale of the hotel, she had far more choices and more resources and they could do what they wanted without financial restraints.

Even with her joy over her father, she couldn't get Chase out of her thoughts, and at night she missed him terribly. She gazed off in the distance, wondering what he was doing at that moment and if he'd missed her much at all. "Chase—" she whispered, longing to see him.

In Houston, Chase swam laps in his pool, pouring all his energy into the swim, trying to work off the hurt he couldn't escape. He missed Laurel and couldn't forget her; it wasn't like any other time in his life when he'd walked out on a relationship. She'd never even been in his Houston home, yet he kept seeing her everywhere, especially when he glanced at his big, empty bed. During the day when he was in public, it had been worse. Every tall, good-looking blonde made him take a second look and wish it were Laurel.

With muscles aching, he stopped and climbed out of the pool. He'd worked out for two hours after getting back from the office. He'd run ten miles this morning. He'd swum laps tonight. And still he couldn't get her out of his thoughts. He was sleeping only a couple of hours at night. "I miss you, dammit," he said to no one.

His phone rang and his hopes jumped that it would be her and she'd changed her mind about moving to Houston.

He yanked up the cell phone and punched a button to take the call, his hopes plummeting when he heard Luke's voice.

"We got a contract on the office building, so now we own the next block and this one," Luke said.

"Good," Chase replied without really thinking about what Luke had told him. "How's Laurel?"

There was only a moment of silence. "She's fine. I heard that her father came out of his coma and she's spending most of her time at the hospital and getting ready to move him to her ranch or Billings. She'll have her hands full, so I don't expect to see her around the hotel. Matter of fact, I heard she's planning on moving out to be with him."

"I'm glad he's recuperating. I didn't think he would."

"You wouldn't think so, but I guess miracles happen. The entire hotel staff is staying, so there won't be any upheaval or transition. I'm going to the field tomorrow, and I'll give you a report about that. If it meets your approval, I'd just as soon put Brice in charge of the hotel and let him report directly to me. He knows the Tolson as well as a person can know a business."

"Do what you think is best," Chase said, still thinking about Laurel.

They talked briefly about business, and then Chase hung up, staring into space, seeing Laurel and wanting her badly.

He clenched his fist. What was the matter with him? He'd never been like this over the breakup of a relationship. He hadn't intended for this one to break up, and he wished again that she'd come to Houston with him.

Two more miserable nights and days of grueling workouts and he sat glumly on the side of his empty bed, reaching for the phone as he had over a dozen times each night. He wanted to call Laurel, but he knew there was no point in it because there was no future for them. No future—that was the bleakest thought of all. He rubbed the back of his neck and wondered if he had fallen in love. Really in love. Laurel had been right. In the past it had always been "in lust," but this was different and he was beginning to see that. He wasn't getting over her. If anything, each day grew worse, and if he thought about her going out with another guy, he hurt as if stabbed by a knife. Was he in love?

He shuddered and thought about his dad and his feelings about marriage and his claustrophobia over being tied down. Yet how bad would that be with Laurel? All the time he'd spent with her had been paradise, and he'd never felt claustrophobic or tied down. He'd felt more alive than at any time in his life, and he'd had the best sex life ever, plus he liked being with her and talking things over with her. She had solved the problem of Ty Carson to everyone's satisfaction.

Chase stood impatiently and paced the floor, going to his exercise room to change to shorts and running shoes. As he ran, he continued to mull over his feelings for Laurel.

Could he think about marriage? It gave him a chill, but he thought about when he had been living with Laurel. There had been nothing terrible or confining about their relationship. Far from it. He couldn't wait to get back to her each day.

Was he really in love, and could he possibly face marriage and deal with it? All he knew for certain was that he hurt like hell without her and thought about her constantly. His work was suffering and something had to give.

* * *

Each day Laurel's father improved, and she had been amazed at his progress. The third week of September, as she pored over books in her office after sundown, her phone rang and she answered to hear Diana's frantic voice.

"Laurel, it's Gramma. She's fallen and hurt herself, and we've called an ambulance from Athens. I thought you'd want to meet us at the hospital."

"How badly is she hurt?" Laurel asked, cold with fear.

"I don't know. She seems in a lot of pain. She doesn't want to move, and we don't want to move her. She had her hands filled with magazines and stuff she was bringing downstairs, and near the bottom she missed a step and fell. She said it's her foot that hurts."

"Thank goodness it's not her back or her hip! I'll meet you. I'll be waiting at the emergency room entrance," Laurel said. Next, she called Brice to tell him where she'd be, glad he was working a night shift at the hotel.

When she went downstairs, he was waiting. "I'll drive you to the hospital," he said, but she shook her head.

"I'll be fine. Ashley said Gramma is complaining about her foot, so maybe it won't be too bad."

"If you're sure," he said and she nodded.

It was well after two in the morning when she returned to the hotel. Her grandmother had a broken foot, and they were keeping her overnight for observation, but otherwise she seemed fine. Ashley and Diana stayed at the hospital to spend the night and take their grandmother back the next day.

Laurel knew they could move into the hotel. Her grandmother wouldn't have to cook, and they could have a taxi whenever they needed one. She lay in bed, mentally making plans that she would work on the next day. The weekend approached, and she dreaded it because she would have empty hours and miss Chase more than ever.

Midmorning Tuesday, the last day of September, she stood

in the lobby with Brice and froze when she turned to look at the front door. Her heart thudded and she felt for a moment as if she were dreaming, but it was really Chase Bennett.

Eleven

Breathless, Laurel could only stare. Dimly she heard Brice say goodbye, but she ignored him. Chase was wearing a navy suit, and he looked more handsome than ever—it took all her willpower to keep from running to throw her arms around him.

When she looked at his solemn expression, she suspected he was here to attend to something involving business that wasn't going the way he wanted it. As his gaze swept over her, she became aware that her hair was loosely clipped with strands falling around her face. She wore cream-colored slacks and a white shirt and wished now she'd dressed up more, even though she guessed she would see little of him.

As he walked up to her, she could barely breathe. Her mouth was dry and her heart drummed. She wanted more than anything to reach for him. Instead, she just smiled. "I'm surprised to see you. I didn't think you'd be back."

"Can we go where we can be alone and talk?"

"Sure. Let's go to my office," she said. He walked beside her. "Did you just get in?"

"Yes. I don't think anyone else knows I'm here, although they will by now," he added.

Surprised, she glanced up at him. "You didn't come on business?"

"Yes, of a sort," he answered and reached around her to hold the door open to her office.

Mystified, she stepped inside, catching the scent of his aftershave, which gave her another pang of longing. Memories tugged at her and she locked her fingers together because the temptation to reach for him now that they had privacy was overwhelming.

"You look wonderful," he said, placing his hands on her shoulders.

"Thanks, and I can say the same to you," she answered quietly, putting her hands on his waist instead of hugging him as she wished.

"I've missed you," he admitted, and her heart skipped a beat. His gaze was filled with desire and her lips parted. She leaned closer and then she was in his arms while he kissed her hungrily.

Knowing she was headed for more hurt, she held him tightly while she kissed him. She wanted to make love to him, wanted him to love her, yet she knew that wasn't going to help the situation. Finally she pushed away and gasped for breath. "Why are you here?"

"I had all sorts of plans, but I can't remember them. Dammit, I don't want to be without you. Will you marry me?"

Stunned, she stared at him—her heart took another swoop, missing beats and then racing. The swift rush of joy was instantly snuffed out because it was déjà vu and Chase's reaction would be the same that Edward's had been.

"Chase, I remember long talks about you wanting to avoid responsibility and getting tied down." She knew this would end his proposal as swiftly as he had presented it. "I'm completely tied down and have responsibility for my family. Diana and Ashley are still underage. Gramma fell and broke her ankle and is on crutches, so I'm moving the three of them here to the hotel. Dad has come out of the coma and soon he'll be moved to Billings for physical therapy; I'm looking at houses there so I can stay with him. I'm shocked you proposed," she said, feeling anguish and expecting him to back off as swiftly as Edward had, even though Chase had known some of her feelings before he proposed.

"I love you, Laurel," he said solemnly. "I've got plenty of money to help, and we can work it out," he said. "You talked about moving them to Texas after your dad finishes therapy. We can move them in with us—"

"You said you never wanted to be tied down with responsibility for a family. Good heavens!" she exclaimed, dazed by the turnaround in his attitude.

"That's before I was really in love. I don't think I'll be 'tied down,'" he replied. "I didn't feel that way when we were together. Maybe I'm beginning to see that my dad did what he wanted all those years."

Shocked, she stared at him. "You were so certain—"

"I'm damn certain I don't want to live without you. I love you," he repeated and pulled her into his arms to kiss her, and this time she let go of her worries and fears and kissed him wildly in return, joy filling her as well as desire sweeping through her as swiftly as a raging fire.

Over an hour later, as she lay in his arms on the sofa in her office, she wiggled. "This is not nearly as large a sofa as the one you had in your office."

"It's large enough for me," he said. "I don't want to let go of you."

"Are you staying the weekend?"

"I can stay or I'll take you to Texas with me so you can see my Houston house."

"I don't think I can leave right now," she answered cautiously, expecting an argument.

"Well, then I'll stay. To hell with business. Let's go up to my suite," he said, sitting up with her on his lap.

"I didn't think you'd ever be in it again."

"I didn't either," he said, looking at her. "Can we shut ourselves away for the rest of the day?"

"I need to cancel some things, and you should really talk to Luke because he'll know you're here. After that we can."

"If you insist," he said with a long sigh. "All right." He stood and pulled on his briefs and trousers while she pulled on lacy underwear and reached for her slacks.

She realized he was standing, watching her dress, and she waved a hand at him. "For heaven's sake! Look the other way."

"Not for a cool million dollars will I look the other way," he said. She wrinkled her nose and pulled on her slacks. "Laurel, you never did give me an answer. Will you marry me?"

"You don't care that I'm a family person?" she asked again.

"Haven't I made that clear?" he replied with a solemn expression.

"Yes, I'll marry you. I love you," she said, giving him a hug, and he kissed her.

"I love you and I hope to spend the rest of our lives showing you. Now dress so we can go upstairs and I can undress you again."

"As quickly as possible," she said, scooping up her blouse. He reached into his pocket.

"I brought you something from Texas," he said, holding out a small bit of pink tissue paper tied with a pink ribbon.

"Thank you," she said, smiling and taking it from him. Curious, she couldn't feel anything in the tiny package. She tore the paper open and looked at a dazzling diamond set in a gold mounting.

"Chase! This is magnificent! Absolutely awesome!" She

threw her arms around his neck and kissed him. He kissed her passionately until he stopped abruptly.

"Dammit, let's go upstairs. This is torment and I don't want another round on that sofa or the floor."

She laughed and held out her hand. "You put it on me, please."

He took the ring and held her hand, looking into her eyes. "Laurel, will you be my wife?"

"Yes. I love you and I'll marry you," she said, joy making her laugh. He slipped the huge diamond on her finger. It was dazzling, catching the light and sparkling. "I can't wait to tell my family."

"You can wait a little while," Chase said. "C'mon. Let's get up so I can undress and kiss you."

She laughed and linked her arm in his as she looked at her ring. "Now Brice will apologize for slugging you."

"That wasn't why I proposed," he said and she laughed, squeezing his waist and then taking his arm again. "Laurel, let's marry soon. I don't want to wait a long time."

"Fine with me, but I want my family present and I'd like to meet your family."

"We can call them and we'll go see them as soon as you can get away." In the elevator he pulled her to him. "I love you, darlin'. I can't believe how much I love you. And now you're making me the happiest man on earth."

Epilogue

In October, Laurel stood at the entrance to the sanctuary. Dressed in a long pink organza, her grandmother was seated in front with her crutches at her side and one foot propped up. Diana and Ashley, as well as Becca Carson and Chase's two sisters, Madison and Emma, had already walked down the aisle and were standing at the front.

It was Chase whom Laurel looked at, her heart racing with joy and eagerness. Within minutes she would become his wife. She was still surprised that he was so eager for marriage.

His three brothers, Graham, Justin and Gavin, were grooms-men, along with his cousins Jared and Matt. She smoothed her veil, and the wedding planner straightened the cathedral train of her gown as trumpets blared and the music changed to the wedding march. She took her dad's hand. He was beside her in a motorized wheelchair, and together they went down the aisle.

He gave her to Chase, and she stepped forward to repeat her vows to the tall, handsome man she loved with all her heart.

As if in a daze, after the ceremony she drifted through the

photo-taking process. Then they went to the Athens' Country Club for a reception. She removed the train from her dress and finally stepped into Chase's arms for the first dance.

"You're stunning, Laurel," he said, smiling at her as they circled the dance floor.

"And you're breathtakingly handsome, and I can't wait until we're alone."

He groaned. "Let's not talk about that, because I know it's hours and hours away before I'll have you to myself."

"This is the happiest day of my life," she said.

"I think that's my line."

"I'm still reeling with shock that you're settling down to marriage, but you're into it now, mister!" she teased.

"Hot nights with you is not 'settling down.' I can't wait. This is exactly what I want. I was miserable without you, Laurel," he said solemnly, and her heart lurched.

"When do I get to discover where you're taking me for our honeymoon?"

"I hope you like the coast of France."

"With you, I'll love the coast of France," she said as he spun her around.

"Great! After this dance I don't expect to get to talk to you again until we cut the cake, because my dad and then my brothers and cousins will each want to dance with you."

"Your family is wonderful. You cousins are delightful, and I like Jared's wife, Megan. Their son, Ethan, is a great kid."

He smiled at her. "I wish we were alone."

"Both of us do. Time will pass." The music ended and she saw Will Bennett approaching. His brown hair was streaked with gray, and he had a ruddy complexion from many hours spent outside, but he was a handsome man and attention-getting in his pearl-gray cutaway coat and dark trousers. "Here comes your dad."

"And I will go tell your grandmother we'll take her dancing when she's on two feet again."

"May I have this dance?" Chase's father asked and stepped up to take Laurel's hand as a waltz began.

"Welcome to the family," he said, smiling at her. "I'm happy to have you in the Bennett clan, Laurel," he said, gazing at her with eyes as green as his son's. "I had given up on Chase ever marrying, so this is wonderful. I can stop worrying about him now."

She laughed. "It's difficult to imagine anyone worrying over Chase, because he's so supremely confident about what he's doing."

"Even so, his mother and I are deeply thankful you have come into all our lives. You'll be a good influence on him, and he's already settling down."

Laurel chatted with her father-in-law as they danced, glancing often at Chase. She saw Ashley dancing with Chase and she was sure Diana couldn't wait for her turn—despite the fact that both girls had danced with him last night at their rehearsal party.

As the dance ended, Chase joined her briefly. He had shed his gray cutaway coat, and she was eager to change to her regular dress and leave with him. "I'll ask Mom to dance, and here comes Gavin to dance with you."

She glanced around to see Gavin, Chase's twenty-nine-year-old brother, approaching them.

"Now here is a true confirmed bachelor," Chase said, clasping his green-eyed brother on the shoulder. "My best accountant and one who will never succumb to marriage."

"True, bro. May I have the next dance?" he asked Laurel, and she smiled at him as she took his hand.

Just as Chase had said, she danced with his brothers and then with his oldest cousins, Jared and Matt.

It was early afternoon before Chase appeared at her side and took her arm, and they spent another hour telling their families goodbye. Then Laurel changed to a pale yellow silk dress. Finally, they rushed to a waiting white limo and sped away, with the bride instantly in her groom's arms.

"So, where are we spending tonight?" she asked him.

"The closest place we can get to is my coastal home, even though it's in the wrong direction for our honeymoon and will mean longer travel tomorrow. We'll spend tonight on the California coast and tomorrow night in New York City. Then we'll be in France for two weeks. How's that sound for the itinerary?"

"Paradise," she answered, smiling at him and pulling him to her.

It seemed another eternity before they arrived at the house in California. Fog had closed in and moisture dripped from trees. Chase came around the car and opened her door, sweeping her into his arms.

"Luggage. Remember, there's luggage," she said, wrapping her arm around his neck.

"You won't need it tonight," he answered, carrying her to the front door. He handed her the key and lowered her to where she could unlock the door. When they entered, he set her on her feet while he turned off the alarm. He had changed to a new black suit and had shed his coat and tie in the limo and had unbuttoned the top buttons of his shirt.

With every step her pulse sped. She couldn't resist touching him. She was eager to kiss him. His green eyes had darkened when he turned to draw her into his arms. As he kissed her, she felt his hands at her zipper and then her dress fell in a swish around her ankles.

Eagerly, she tugged his shirt out of his trousers and unfastened the buttons, pushing his shirt off his shoulders and trailing her hands over his chest as she looked at him. "I love you, Chase," she whispered.

"I'm going to spend my lifetime trying to keep you happy," he said, holding her away slightly and gazing at her. "You're gorgeous, darlin', and I can't live without you."

She caressed his jaw, thinking she was the luckiest woman on earth. She loved Chase with all her heart.

"Chase, I still can't believe you wanted to marry and that I'm your wife now. It doesn't seem real. You had convinced me completely that you wouldn't do this."

"That was before I fell in love with you, Laurel. And I'm so in love. You can't imagine. Without you, I hurt like I'd never hurt before," he confessed, and her heart thudded.

"You couldn't have hurt any more than I did," she whispered, "but that's over now because we have each other, and as long as I live, I hope you never feel tied down or have regrets."

"I couldn't possibly. I want to love you constantly all during our honeymoon and then as much as possible when we return to our regular lives. I want to be with you the rest of my life. I love you, darlin'. Love you always and forever," he said, and her heart pounded with joy as he pulled her close to kiss her again.

* * * * *

WYOMING WEDDING

BY
SARA ORWIG

To David

One

October

Matt Rome sat in one of the best steak houses in Cheyenne, Wyoming. Waitpeople moved between linen-covered tables that held flickering candles. The dim lighting cast a spell over the room. The piano player explored an old tune. Having dined earlier with the woman from his most recent affair, Matt was back for a late-night coffee —on a mission. He'd tipped the maitre d' generously to seat him in the section assigned to Brianna Costin. While he watched her wait tables, hurrying between the dining room and kitchen, he ran his fingers along the handle of his coffee cup.

Whenever he saw her, it only served to reinforce his

opinion that she was one of the most beautiful women he'd ever seen. The fact that she was a waitress was no hindrance to his plans. Just the opposite—her status and income would probably make her more cooperative. She was tall with luscious curves and flawless skin. Her black hair was always thickly coiled at her nape. She suited his future plans fine.

His time and patience both had dwindled and still, he had no more likely a candidate for a paper marriage. Once, he would have given serious consideration to Nicole, the woman he'd had dinner with, but no longer. She was too demanding of his time. Their fight tonight had been the final push for them to break off relations. It had been easy to tell her goodbye when she'd issued an ultimatum to spend more time with her or get out of her life. His thoughts shifted to Brianna as she approached his table.

Usually his waitress now that he'd started requesting her, she was efficient and courteous. Beyond that, she seemed barely to take note of her patrons. Even though Matt always gave her impersonal courtesy—as if he hadn't noticed her, he couldn't avoid watching her as she made the rounds. Sometimes she would glance his way, whether out of professional reasons to keep up with her patrons' needs, or something more personal, he had no idea.

It was half an hour until closing, yet a few diners still lingered. Holding a carafe of coffee, Brianna approached his table to refill his cup.

"Do you want anything else?" she asked. Even

though she never held eye contact long, when he gazed into her thickly fringed green eyes, the contact fueled a primitive reaction.

"As a matter of fact, yes, I do," he replied. "I'm back to see you. I'd like to talk to you after work."

"I'm sorry. I never socialize with our patrons," she answered coolly, all friendliness leaving her voice. "It's better that way," she added without a flicker of change in her expression.

Unaccustomed to rejection, he bit back a smile. "I'm asking for an hour over a cup of coffee. If you prefer, you can meet me somewhere else. I promise you, I'm safe to be with," he said, reaching into his pocket to hand her a business card. "I'm Matt Rome."

"I know who you are," she replied. "I imagine everyone in Cheyenne knows who you are, Mr. Rome." Without glancing at the card, she pocketed it.

"It won't take long," Matt continued. "How's the Talon Club?" It was an expensive private club located at the top of one of the city's tallest buildings.

She smiled. "Thanks, but I don't believe they would allow me in—I'm not a member."

"I belong to the club. If you'll meet me in the lobby of the building, after your shift, they'll let us in. Or if you prefer, since it's three or four miles from your work, I can wait and follow you home to take you from your place."

As if mulling over his offer, she paused. "I have a feeling you intend to ask me something big. I can save you time by saying no now."

Again, he suppressed a smile. "This is not what

you're thinking, I can assure you. Here isn't the place to talk. I would wager a sizable bet you'll be pleased we talked tonight."

For the first time since he'd met her he seemed to have her full attention as her eyes narrowed a fraction. He waited, his amazement increasing. Matt could usually outlast any silence at a bargaining table, though as time stretched, he decided she was sticking by her refusal. "I understand you can't talk as freely here," he said finally.

"That's for sure. My clothes might not be presentable for the club either."

"Yes, they are," he said, glad to find she was considering his offer. She wore what every other waitperson in the restaurant wore—black slacks and a black shirt, only on her, the outfit was as stylish as a high-dollar ensemble.

"Very well, I'll meet you in the lobby at a quarter before midnight."

"Excellent," he said, his eagerness making him laugh at himself. When had it ever been this difficult to get a woman to go out with him? He was more amused than annoyed.

"You don't intend to order anything else now?" she asked.

He raised his coffee. "This is sufficient. As a matter of fact, I'll take the check so they can clear this table."

She left to return in a few minutes with his bill. "Thanks."

"I'll see you in the lobby," he said, and she was gone. Congratulating himself on his victory in getting her to go out, he watched her walk away. The black slacks rode low below her tiny waist that was emphasized by the ties of her white apron. He wondered how her legs looked— they were obviously long and slender. He liked watching her, mentally peeling away the slacks, wishing for a moment this was a restaurant where waitpeople wore skimpier clothing.

Despite the fact that she was reserved, and with obvious barriers, he remained interested.

Time seemed to drag in the lobby of the building that housed the club until the revolving door spun to reveal her. The apron was gone and her straight black hair cascaded over her shoulders. As she approached him, her hips swayed slightly. His desire stirred.

"I'm glad you came," he said, lust warming him.

"I'll reserve judgment on whether I can say the same or not."

He laughed. "I'll admit, the last woman who responded similarly was a little six-year-old girl in grade school, I think. I had some hostile encounters in the first grade," he said, expecting to wring a smile from her. Instead, she gave him another solemn glance and remained silent. "Let's have a drink and then we can talk," he said, motioning toward the dark, glossy elevators

"Is this why you've asked for my section each time you've come to the dining room lately?" she probed as the elevator sped them skyward.

"Not exactly…maybe partially. You're good at your job."

"Thank you," she answered, giving him the feeling she was hoping to get this meeting over with so she could go home. Her lack of interest was beginning to bother him.

The maitre d' greeted them and escorted them to a table by the window overlooking the city. On the table, a small candle threw a soft glow on Brianna, catching shining glints in her silky dark hair. They gave their drink orders, hers a limeade and his a glass of brandy. As soon as they were alone, she looked at him expectantly.

"I've wanted to meet you," he said, and something flickered in her eyes that made him suspect that she felt the sparks as much as he did. That awareness jolted him.

"Brianna, I've had my staff look into your background so I could learn more about you," he said. This time the flash in her green eyes was unmistakable indignation.

"I'd call that an invasion of my privacy."

"Not really. I only have information that is more or less public knowledge. You're from Blakely, Wyoming, the first of your family to attend college. You're enrolled in Wyoming University in Laramie, commuting from Cheyenne—that one stumped me even though it isn't a long drive."

"I doubt if it gave the information that I found a better job here and I only have classes on campus on Tuesdays and Thursdays this semester, thanks to the convenience of online classes. So tell me what else you know about me."

"You have five siblings, two married sisters and three younger brothers. One brother is still in high school and all three of them work. You are a senior in college and you hope to go to law school."

"So far, you're right. How much deeper did you look into my private life? Do you do this with every woman you invite out?"

"Calm down," he said, noticing her words were becoming more clipped. Her irritation was showing.

"How's school going?"

"I have a suspicion you already know. I like my classes. So far, I have all A's."

"Commendable," he remarked. "And at the moment there is no man in your life. I'm surprised there wasn't one waiting in the wings. You're a beautiful woman."

"Thanks, and there isn't one, waiting or otherwise," she said with the first faint smile since her arrival.

"What do you really enjoy? Tell me about yourself," he said, leaning back slightly.

"I have the feeling I'm being interviewed for something," she said. "I like cold winter nights, roaring fires, roasting marshmallows. I like achieving my goals, living in the city." As she talked, he watched her. They were the closest face-to-face they had ever been, and she was even more gorgeous up close. Her green eyes captivated him, and he could only imagine them filled with passion. Her bow-shaped mouth and full lips made it impossible to avoid conjuring up fantasies of kissing her. She was composed, rarely gesturing when she talked with a soft voice that was as sexy as everything else about her.

"And what do you dream about doing?" he asked,

trying to get through the barrier she kept between them. For some reason, probably out of her past, she had a chip on her shoulder. Or perhaps it was because any man with a pulse would try to hit on her. He knew she had men in her life on occasion.

"I dream about being a lawyer, having complete independence, helping my family."

"But on a more personal level? Everybody has hopes and longings."

"That's easy," she replied, smiling at him. "I want to see things I've never seen in real life—palm trees, seashells, the ocean, tropics with balmy weather. I've never seen the ocean. Actually, I've never been out of Wyoming or even flown in a plane." For the first time, she looked as if she had relaxed with him. "I dream about going to Europe because pictures of foreign places are breathtaking. So, Mr. Rome, what do you dream of doing when you've probably already done everything in life you want to do?"

"It's Matt, not Mr. Rome. What do I want? That's part of what this is about," he said, pausing when their drinks were served. "I hope what I'm going to discuss is something appealing, not something threatening to you."

"Since we've been all around the mulberry bush, so to speak, why don't you tell me why I'm here?"

"I'm not certain being so direct is going to help you in law school," he observed.

"I'm not in law school tonight," she said, and he knew she was waiting for an answer to her question.

"This evening isn't going exactly the way I expected.

I'll grant that while I don't know you, I'd like to. Will you have dinner with me tomorrow night?"

When she stared at him in silence, he thought perhaps she was going to get up and walk out. "You could have asked me that when I was your waitress at dinner. It didn't take all this."

"I want to get to know you. Also, I had a feeling if I'd asked you then, you would have turned me down."

"You're right. I think there's more to this than going to dinner with you. Guys at the club ask me out often and they don't actually take me out ahead of time to do so."

"Let me guess—you've never gone out with any of them."

"You're right," she said. "You and the other men who ask me out want one thing—my body. I'm not in your social class and we both know that. I'm a waitress, you're a wealthy bachelor. Not all the men who've asked me out are even single. I've received explicit invitations when the wife is in the powder room. At least you're not married."

As she looked away, her cheeks flushed a bright pink. The color heightened her beauty, and he knew he wanted her body as much as any other man had. Every inch of her was enticing. So far, he also enjoyed being with her—all reasons to support the argument that he was making an acceptable decision.

Zach Gentner's warning floated in the back of his mind. He could recall too clearly his best friend and chief investment advisor trying to talk him out of even thinking about getting to know her. Zach had his own arguments:

her poverty-stricken background, her lack of education, her lower-class life, her large, uneducated family.

Worst of all, she was three or four weeks pregnant by a man who had run out on her. That last argument had almost carried the day for Zach, until the next time Matt had gone to the club to eat. With Nicole accompanying him, he had surreptitiously watched Brianna, finding he was still drawn to her. Because of her pregnancy she might possibly be an even more likely candidate. She would need the money—no other woman on his list of candidates did. Until Brianna, the women he had taken out since college had been almost as wealthy or wealthier than he was. He knew, too, without any doubts, that all the other women on his list, including Nicole Doyle, would not want a two-year marriage of convenience. Not at all. He and Nicole had fought tonight over how seldom she had seen him. He was tired of her relentless dissatisfaction, which made him leery of choosing her as a candidate for his proposal.

Brianna seemed the perfect choice and when the marriage ended, she would be easier to get out of his life.

Leaning forward, she propped her chin on her fist and seemed to shake off the anger in her previous comment as she smiled at him. "So again, Matt, what's behind all this really?" Brianna inquired in a coaxing voice.

Desire flared. He wondered if lust had completely clouded his judgment as Zach had declared. Perhaps it had, because at the moment, Matt knew he craved her with an intensity that surprised him.

"All right, I'll get to the point. First hear me out. I'm

going to present something to you. Before you give me an answer, I want you to think about it for at least twenty-four hours or even several days if you want. Will you agree to that?"

As disappointment took the smile off her face, she sat up straight, all of her barriers once again in place with a frosty chill settling around her. "I think I can give you an answer right now. It's definitely not."

"You're jumping to conclusions. I'm not going to ask you to be my mistress."

Her eyes widened in surprise. "I can't imagine one other possibility you'd have for wanting to talk to me. I don't have any skills or a degree, so you're not out to hire me. What *do* you want?" Now she was filled with obvious curiosity, and he was satisfied that he finally had her full attention. The first little nagging doubts tugged at him that he might be making a mistake, only not for the reasons Zach had given. Matt didn't care about her background because she could rise above that and, as his wife, she would be accepted. What worried him for the first time was finding out that she had a strong will and a stubborn streak. Sticking with his decision, he pushed away worries.

He took her hand in his. The first physical contact startled him. He was going to make a commitment. "I need a wife. I want a marriage of convenience."

Two

Shock came first. A marriage proposal from Matt Rome, probably the wealthiest man in Wyoming, a man she knew only because she was his *waitress*. Her second thought was—as his wife, she would have money. Real money, oodles of money.

A mansion and a sports car and no more struggling to put food on the table—her head spun. At the same time she was filled with disbelief. She turned icy and alternately awash in heat.

Then common sense set in. Billionaires did not propose marriage to her. Actually, only Tommy Grogan at home had ever proposed and that had been when she was sixteen years old. She knew, down to her toes, that there was a catch to this offer and it must be a whopper.

All her defenses rushed back and she was ready to end the evening and go home in spite of her promise to hear him out. Reeling from it or not, she suspected if she knew the full story, she wouldn't want any part of what he had on his mind.

"Why me?" she asked. "You have beautiful women in your life from the same kind of society background. Why are you asking me instead of one of them?"

"That's your opinion, not mine. For one thing, they bore me. For another, I want this marriage for a short time, two years max. Then I want to be able to dissolve it without an emotional hassle and walk away. I think that will be much easier to do with you than with one of them," he added dryly. The latter reason made sense to her.

"Any other explanations why you chose me?" she asked, knowing that when he found out about her secret pregnancy, he would withdraw his offer. That alone was justification for him to find a more likely candidate for his marriage proposal.

"Why do you want this?" she asked, knowing there had to be something behind his proposal.

"There's an international investment group of men I want to join. I have a couple of friends in it. I'm a likely candidate except for being a bachelor. They're concerned about a bachelor's lifestyle, even though mine is far from wild. If I marry, they'll view me as settled."

She had mixed feelings: caution vied with temptation. She couldn't imagine it was as simple as he presented, yet he was bound to reward her generously. Two years as Matt Rome's wife? The thought made her giddy. Dreading telling him about her pregnancy, she knew she should end this.

"Why would you want to be in the group? You're enormously successful now. You don't need money."

When he smiled, her heart skipped. He was irresistibly handsome with his curly black hair and thick lashes that emphasized his clear blue eyes. She, along with all the other females in the vicinity, had always noticed him when he'd come to the dining room where she worked. Fortunately, she'd never made an issue of it and he didn't seem aware of her reaction to him. She'd heard everyone talk. In a club filled with wealthy members, Matt Rome stood out because he was the richest. And probably the youngest. He was hands-down the best-looking, with a smile to die for.

He had seemed attentive to the different women he brought to the steak house, although she knew earlier he and the woman with him had had a heated, drawn-out disagreement.

"I'd like to get into the group because they're far more successful than I've been. They're international and will open doors for me that won't be opened otherwise. I'll make more money faster."

"You have more money than you can spend. Why would you want to make more?" she persisted, and his blue eyes twinkled with amusement.

"Maybe it's the challenge of making it. There's never such a thing as too much money," he added as she shook her head.

"I can't imagine wealth like yours. If I had that much, I think I'd want to quit striving for more."

"You'll see someday. If you become a successful lawyer, you'll want more money."

"That wouldn't bring me anywhere close to your wealth." She sipped her limeade and put it down. "You don't want me. Even if you may have checked me out, there's a very big reason you will want to look elsewhere."

"Your pregnancy?" he asked.

She stared at him for a moment, at a loss for words. "I thought medical records were private."

"They are. There are other ways to find out."

"One of my friends must have talked," she said, narrowing her eyes and remembering only two of her closest friends, plus the father, had been told what she thought had been her secret. "I suppose once you tell someone, it's no longer a secret."

"A pregnancy is something you can hide for only so long. It might actually be a plus. I understand you're not very far along."

She shook her head, amazed by all he'd learned about her. "No, I went to the doctor two weeks ago and found out. I'm barely a full month."

"It definitely doesn't show," he said.

"No, not yet."

"What about the father?"

"He's out of my life. He's gone and he left no for-warding address, so to speak—which suited me. He legally signed away all privileges and rights." She con-tinued, "He came from a big family and he never wanted kids. Actually, he turned out to be a jerk. He is on a full scholarship, so he's intelligent, which may be a good biological trait for the baby. But he and I didn't part on the best of terms," she answered, giving Matt the same information she'd told her two closest friends. She'd been devastated when the doctor told her she was pregnant. One of her friends had had a party and she remembered how much fun she'd had that night with a guy she saw there and had known from school. She tried to focus on what Matt was saying to her, looking at his blue eyes, eyes the color of the Wyoming sky on a clear summer day. She knew she had to get away from his influence, to think over his proposal with a clear head.

"You've told me what you'll get out of this marriage of convenience. What will I get from the union?"

He smiled, that captivating smile that had probably set too many female hearts fluttering. He was handsome. Handsome and rich beyond dreams. "You'll get half a million dollars when we marry, the other half when we divorce."

"A million dollars!" She gasped. She stared at him, unable to imagine having such money.

"That's right," he confirmed his statement.

"And a divorce later—won't they boot you out if you divorce?"

"They have two men who have divorced and the group let them remain, so I think I can weather that scandal. We'll keep a divorce low-key. I'm willing to take the risk to get this marriage and join the group."

"You expect to get your way, don't you?"

"Why not?" He smiled at her, conveying a cocky self-assurance. "Now back to discussing what you get out of this union. In addition," he continued, "I'll take care of the expenses of your pregnancy and the baby's birth. I'll give you a weekly allowance of a thousand dollars, that's yours for however you wish to spend it. You can buy a new car with my approval of your selection. It's yours when we part. You can get a new wardrobe now with my approval—no mink coat at this point. I want a real marriage as far as sex is concerned and I want you to move in with me."

In spite of trying, she couldn't stifle her laugh. He cocked one dark eyebrow as he surveyed her with curiosity. "You don't know me—you may not be able to stand me after I move in with you," she said. The money kept dangling in her thoughts. A million dollars for her!

"We're doing all right so far. Granted, the past hour has been a little cut-and-dried. But don't worry, I'll move you out if I don't like it," he replied.

She shook her head. "You must want in this group desperately."

His amusement vanished. "Joining this investment bunch is important and I intend to get an invitation from them. If it means I have to marry to do so, so be it."

"I can't imagine any amount of money making it worthwhile to get locked into a loveless marriage."

"That's why you're the perfect selection for me," he said, leaning forward to grasp her hand. "You're gorgeous," he said, and her pulse jumped to a faster speed.

"You're intelligent. You're sexy. You work hard. You're honest."

"You don't know that at all. Sorry, I guess that didn't sound so good on my part," she added hastily and knew her face flushed in embarrassment. "There has to be something to this besides more money."

"No, there isn't. Money is enough."

"Then why the rush? Why don't you wait? In another few months you might fall in love. Why rush into a paper marriage?"

"I'm in a rush because my two cousins and I have a bet that ends next May. It's to see which one of us can make the most money before that May deadline. I want to win the bet. If I join this group, I think I can."

"All this is over a bet?" she asked in disbelief, beginning to wonder if he was as smart as she'd heard and read. "No bet is worth getting married for."

"Ahh, this one might be. I'll win that bet, I think, if I join this group."

"Then it must be for an enormous prize. How much money is at stake?"

"We each put in five million dollars. In May winner gets all and the winner treats for a weekend getaway where we can all be together."

"Five million each!" she echoed. She had always heard about his wealth, to actually deal with it left her dismayed. She counted pennies. He didn't even count thousands. "That's astounding you toss money around like that."

"It isn't exactly tossing. I intend to win, I promise you."

"You're driven," she declared, staring at him and wondering about his life that seemed totally focused on making money.

"The pot is calling the kettle black. You're ambitious yourself."

"On a tiny scale compared to you. And our reasons are light-years apart. My goals are meant to get me out of a life of poverty. Your goals are to achieve a whim."

She smiled to take the edge off her statement, feeling sparks ignite between them. He certainly knew how to charm women.

"How do those terms sound to you?" he asked.

"Like a dream. They don't seem real to me. I've never even been alone with you until we came here," she said.

"So far, so good, I'd say. I'm enjoying the moment."

"To my surprise, I am, too," she said. "How could I not enjoy being proposed to and offered so much money?" she asked and they both smiled.

"It has happened, though. I want you to think about it for a few days."

"Where will I live if I marry you?" she asked, thinking the moment was turning surreal.

"I live here in Cheyenne. I have other homes and I have a ranch near Jackson Hole. Does it matter?"

"Not really. When I finish school, I had expected to move out of state to get a job. Now I'll stay near my family because of my baby."

"You may want to rethink your future. If you marry me and I pay you a million, you won't need degrees. I

don't want you laboring over college texts when I need
you at my side for parties and travel."

She pursed her lips and ran her finger along her cold,
empty glass as she shook her head. "That's a problem
because I don't want to give up my education. I can take
classes in the mornings when you're at work. Also, I can
juggle things and make arrangements with professors to
make up the work when we travel."

Now he sat in silence, turning his empty brandy glass
in his fingers. He had well-shaped hands, broad shoulders and she knew enough from newspapers that he had
once been a champion bull rider. Beneath the slick billionaire façade was a tough cowboy, she suspected and
guessed that was why he'd kept the family ranch and
still remained based in Wyoming.

Feeling their clash of wills, she wondered how often
they would disagree. Even if it would be easier to get
her out of his life, he was taking a huge chance by
asking her to marry him when he didn't know her.

"I was thinking," she voiced her thoughts aloud,
"you'd be better off marrying someone in love with
you because she'd do everything you want to try to
keep you happy."

"If we agree to this marriage, I think we'll work out
our differences," he said, and she could detect the supreme confidence in his tone.

"If this marriage is for two years, you'll have a baby
on your hands," she reminded him.

"With my money, I don't see that as a problem. I'd
claim your baby as mine as far as the public is con-

cerned. That will make me appear even more settled and reliable to this investment group."

Her indignation flared—he would view her baby merely as a means to achieve his end he wanted. She bit back a retort because she wanted to think about possibilities. He wanted to look married and settled and respectable. Reliable. That might give her leverage for bargaining for more for her baby.

"I can see the wheels turning in your head," he said, looking mildly amused. "What do you want?"

"I'm thinking about what you just told me. You'll look terrible if you walk out on a wife and baby."

"So I will, but I'll probably get some sympathy if you walk out on me and take the baby, leaving me because of the long hours I work."

She shook her head. "I suppose that would bring you some sympathy, especially from men who work as long and hard as you."

"So this all looks viable to you?"

"I'm torn between walking out right now or staying and giving consideration to your proposal. It's the coldest, most hard-hearted marriage proposal ever. On the other hand, you know I need what you're offering."

"So you'll think it over?" he asked.

"Of course I will. In some ways, it's the opportunity of a lifetime."

"Maybe if we can get past the proposal, we can find we're good company for each other. Sooner or later, I would have gotten to know you anyway."

She smiled at him. "I find that one a real stretch. I

don't think I would have been in your future if you hadn't needed this."

"We'll see how it goes between us." He leaned forward and reached across the table. "Let's let it go for now. You can mull it over later."

She glanced at her watch, looking up at him in surprise. "It's after one! We need to get out of here so they can close."

"The club is open until two," he said, coming around to hold her chair. "You need your sleep for the baby. We should go." He walked with her out to her car. "I'll follow you home. It's late."

"I drive alone all the time. It's a wonder I survived before I met you."

"I'll follow you," he said in a tone that ended her argument. He put his hand on the car door to stop her from opening it and she looked up at him.

"Tomorrow night, would you prefer to go out to eat, or to eat at my place where we can have a little more privacy to discuss my proposal? You can see where you might live soon."

"I can't believe this is actually happening to me."

"You'll believe it before long."

"Can I look up anything about this investment group you want to get into?"

"Yes." He pulled a card out of his pocket and wrote on the back of it. "Here are some names. Start with these. This group is real."

"I'm sure it's real. I want to know about it."

"I'll pick you up tomorrow night about seven."

"You know common sense tells me to say no to you."

"I don't see that. You stand to gain a lot and lose very little unless you hate being with me."

"You know full well there isn't a female on this earth whose heartbeat doesn't speed up when you're around, so there's no danger of any woman not being able to stand being with you," she said.

"Until this moment, I was beginning to wonder about you. This is the coolest reception in my adult life."

He stretched his arm out again, placing his hand on her car door and blocking her from opening it. Leaning closer, he lowered his voice. "I've proposed to you tonight and we've never even kissed. That's a giant unknown when there's a marriage proposal."

While her pulse had raced all night, now her heart thudded and she looked at his mouth. "I can remedy that one," she said, tingling at the thought of kissing him. She stepped closer to slide her arm around his shoulders, feeling the soft wool of his suit jacket and beneath it, the warmth of his body.

She moved even closer, stood on tiptoe and placed her lips on his. She had started the kiss as if she were tackling a math problem, yet the moment his tongue slid into her mouth, the kiss changed. Heat suffused her, spiraling down to pool low within her and build a fire of physical longing that burned with scorching flames.

His arm banded her waist, pulling her tightly against him, his fingers tangling in her long hair. He leaned over her, his tongue thrusting deep and exploring slowly, a hot, sexy kiss that intensified desire. She would never again be able to view him as dispassionately as she had prior to this moment. His kiss was melting her, stirring longing for so much more with him, surprising her because never had any man's kisses affected her the way Matt's did.

His fiery kiss made his proposal infinitely more inviting. She suspected she wouldn't think straight in the next few minutes about any decisions.

How long they kissed she didn't know. She ran her fingers through his hair, down the strong column of his neck. His tight embrace pressed his arousal against her, hard and ready.

It was late; the restaurant would close and other patrons would come out into the parking lot. She and Matt weren't kissing in a private place. All the dim arguments nagged, though they were faint inducements to stop.

Her pulse roared and she wanted to unbutton his shirt and place her hands on his chest. Realizing what she was about to do, she gathered her wits and pushed lightly against his chest instead.

Pausing, he raised his head as they both gasped for breath.

"Marry me, Brianna," he said and she opened her mouth to answer. Instantly he shook his head and put his finger on her lips. He seemed to pull himself together.

"Don't rush an answer. Your kiss made me ask you again," he said, his blue eyes focused intently on her with a searching look as if he, too, had been surprised by his reaction to their kiss.

She hoped he had been. She didn't want to fade into

the long line of women in his life—all of whom he seemed able to ignore and get rid of sooner or later. In that moment, she knew if she accepted his offer, she would have to guard her heart with all her being to escape falling in love with him.

Moving his hand away, he took her keys to open her car door, holding it for her before returning the keys. As soon as she slid behind the wheel, he closed the door and leaned down as she lowered the window. "Go to dinner with me tomorrow night."

"Of course I will."

"Thanks for meeting with me tonight. I know you didn't want to when I asked you at the restaurant."

"It's been interesting, to say the least. I'll go home and think over your proposal and see you tomorrow night."

"Sure," he said, stepping back away from the car and heading to his own. Turning on the ignition, she drove out without waiting for him. In minutes when she glanced into the rearview mirror, beneath streetlights she saw him following behind her in his sleek gray Jaguar. She drove to the old apartments that were near her work. She parked in the graveled lot and hurried to the side door, turning to wave at him as he waited nearby in the parking lot where he could see her go inside.

Smells of old fast-food boxes and mildew permeated the halls, the sour odor a permanent one. Climbing the steps to the second floor, she entered her apartment that was on the front of the complex. She shared a cramped two-bedroom apartment with Faith Wellston, one of her closest friends and a classmate.

As she shed her clothes and pulled on a heavy nightgown, she considered Matt's proposal. She assessed her surroundings and wondered how she could question the answer she would give him. He was sexy, handsome and appealing. Yet, from all he had said, money was his first love. Maybe his only love. He was going into a paper marriage that, except for sex, was a coldhearted business deal. Yet what difference should that make to her?

His proposal included sex. After his kiss, the mere thought of sex with him made her temperature soar. She shoved aside a stack of textbooks and papers on the scarred kitchen table and pulled out a blank sheet of paper, drawing two columns to represent the pros and cons of accepting his proposal.

His love of money was number one on her con list. And the only thing on the con side. The pro side, she could fill the page. She heard a key turn in the door and Faith walked in.

"Studying this late? Quiz tomorrow?" Faith asked, raking her fingers through her thick red curls.

"Nope. Did you have fun tonight?"

Faith tossed down a stack of textbooks and her purse, then headed for the fridge, her flip-flops flapping with each step. She leaned over to get a cold bottle of water and wiped it on the tail of her gray T-shirt before coming back to the table to pull out a chair and sit facing Brianna. "No, I didn't have any fun tonight. Cal and I went to the library and studied for an exam we have Friday. So what did you do?"

"You wouldn't guess if I gave you all night," Brianna

said. The excitement that she'd tried to stifle all evening made her wiggle and grin. "Ever heard of Matt Rome?"

"Sure. You've said he comes to the restaurant." Faith narrowed her light brown eyes. "He hit on you?"

"Oh, no. Better than that. He wanted me to meet him after work."

"Wow!" Faith let out a squeal and sat up in the chair. "Tell me about it. So he wants to take you out again?"

"Yes, he does, only there's more—a two-year marriage of convenience!" she announced, excitement bubbling up as she threw the paper in the air.

"Marry him! You've got it made! The baby will be paid for and provided for completely," Faith cried. Springing up, she pulled on Brianna and they both danced wildly for a few minutes, Brianna enjoying the moment and letting go all the restraint she'd struggled to exhibit with Matt.

When Faith sat finally, she leaned forward. "How soon? He must be paying you."

"He's made me an offer and told me to think about it before I give him an answer."

"So how much?"

"Half a million now and the other half when we divorce. And we will divorce."

Faith screamed again, throwing up her hands. "A million dollars! Why didn't you accept tonight?" Instantly, her smile vanished. "Did you tell him about the baby?"

"Yes, I did, although he already knew, Faith, from someone," Brianna said, staring hard at Faith, whose eyes widened.

"Not from me." She raised her hand. "I swear, I haven't told anyone with the exception of Cal and he promised to keep quiet. I'll ask him if he talked to anyone."

"It doesn't matter so much now. Matt knows about it and is okay with it."

"Why does he want a paper marriage?" Faith asked.

"Now you're getting to the point. I'm making a list and giving my reply some thought," she said, retrieving the list she had started and waved it at Faith. "My pros and cons list. His life revolves around him acquiring more money all the time. He wants an in to some international investment group and they're leery of letting in a bachelor, hence the marriage."

"That's okay," Faith said, seeming to think about it.

"Maybe. I think his attitude is cold and hard-hearted and material."

"So what are you? You're as driven as anyone I've ever seen and you want your education with a vengeance. The only reason you had a one-night stand was because you finally let your hair down and had too many drinks and had some fun."

"And accidentally got pregnant," Brianna said.

Faith grabbed the pro and con sheet and ripped it in half. "Marry him and stop even thinking about pros and cons. I've seen the guy—he's gorgeous. All of us in Advanced Statistics got to go to a seminar where he was on the panel. He was engaging and magnetic. He's the most moneyed man in Wyoming, maybe. How could you possibly bicker about that? Two years—spectacular. Marry him, use the money and your life will never be the same. It'll mean care for your baby, no worries for you and all the education you want. You'll get out of the dumps like this," she said without pausing. "Forget arguments. Go for it. I would have said yes on the spot."

"I started to and he stopped me and said to think it over."

Faith snorted, puffing out her cheeks. "What's to think over? If he had a kinky lifestyle, it would have already been in the news, so no problem there. Say yes tomorrow night. What'll you wear? Let's go see."

The following night Brianna was all nerves. Faith had already left the apartment. Taking quick breaths to calm down, Brianna walked to the mirror to look again at her image. Studying her plain, black cotton dress, she recalled the few clothes she'd brought with her when she'd graduated from high school and arrived in Cheyenne with a scholarship to college. She'd had few clothes. One formal dress that was bright blue and yellow, several pairs of worn jeans, flip-flops, T-shirts, one plain brown skirt and one white cotton blouse that she'd worn to job interviews. She wondered how many details of her past Matt knew—if he'd known she'd gotten the job at the ritzy steak house in her junior year. No one could know except Faith, whom she'd told, how she'd studied the female patrons to notice their clothing and she began to change her home wardrobe accordingly. While she assumed Matt would find her clothes too cheap, at least she knew they weren't tacky.

When the doorbell buzzed, she grabbed up her purse and her list of what she wanted if they married. Glancing

at it one more time, her heart raced. Would this list
cause him to revoke his marriage offer? That's what
Faith feared, but Brianna kept telling herself to stick by
what she wanted. Matt Rome needed this marriage.
Now she'd see how badly.

Three

When she opened the door, the first thing she saw was a smile that made her knees weak. How could she argue with Matt over anything? She wondered if he had a clue about the dreams that now filled her life.

"Hi," he said. "You look great."

"Thank you," she replied. "I'm ready. You can come in if you want. I'll warn you, my place is pretty plain."

"If you're ready, we'll go," he answered easily. His charcoal suit jacket was unbuttoned and while dressed for something fancy this evening, there was an aura of earthy sexuality about him that his suit couldn't tame.

After she locked her door, he took her arm to walk with her to his car, holding the door until she slid inside. As she watched him circle the front of the car, she

slipped her hand over the luxurious tan leather uphol-
stery. The Jaguar's walnut paneling in the interior had a
beautiful sheen and she marveled at the world of money.
This was the most elegant car she'd ever ridden in.

Yet she couldn't shake Faith's warnings. Faith had told
her repeatedly not to make demands on Matt, to accept
what he had offered and enjoy life because it was far
better than she would ever see otherwise. Too true, except
she had no doubt he could afford what she was asking.

As she watched him walk in front of the car, her concerns of money and needs and marriage ebbed. Wind
caught dark locks of his hair, blowing them away from
his forehead. He was incredibly handsome. Her heart
pounded and she remembered their passionate kiss that
had filled her with longing. They would be together all
the rest of the evening. The excitement made her bubbly.
She knew she should get her feelings under control so she
could think clearly. She was the only advocate she had.

As he sat behind the wheel, he glanced at her. "Ready?"

"Of course," she answered, smiling. "Drive me to
dinner in the most opulent car I've ever ridden in."

He laughed. "We're going back to the club—the main
dining room tonight. They have good food, only where
you work is one of the best restaurants in the state."

"That's good to hear from a customer."

"Have you thought about my proposal?"

"I haven't been able to think about anything else," she
admitted. "When I went to classes today, I gave up my
front-row seat in each of them to sit at the back because
I knew I wouldn't hear one word of the lecture anyway."

"I'm glad to know you're thinking about it."

"My friend is blown away by it."

"And I take it you're not," he said, smiling. There was speculation in his gaze as he glanced at her.

"We can talk about it when you're not driving. I need your full, undivided attention. In the meantime, tell me about your day."

"Today was mostly business as usual." While he talked about projects and investments, she gazed at him, thinking she could look endlessly at him. She still couldn't believe what was happening to her. It was a Cinderella story, only the prince was in love with money and she was merely the means to an end. Still, there were such promising prizes for her—she would be worth a million dollars. She couldn't get that out of her thoughts and again, the list in her hand was a fiery torch. She didn't want to get burned by it.

Soon he was relating funny anecdotes, and she relaxed slightly, despite the electric current bubbling in her since she first sat to talk to him last night.

When they walked into the darkened dining room of the downtown club, she wanted to pinch herself to know it was all real. She never had evenings like this and she knew she would remember every detail for the rest of her life. A pianist sang the lyrics to the slow song he played while several couples already circled the small dance floor.

They chose a martini for him and milk for her after they were seated. As he gazed at her, the flickering glow of the candles highlighted his prominent cheekbones. He reached over to hold her hand. "Let's dance."

She walked to the dance floor to step into his arms, and it sent her pulse into overdrive. His legs brushed hers lightly, and every touch stirred a riveting response. Just as his car had been an extension of his fortune, she was aware of everything else that proclaimed his wealth—from his fine wool suit to his inviting aftershave, something men she'd known had seldom worn.

She knew she had to accept his proposal. As fast as that thought occurred, she reminded herself to hold out for her most important demands. When he heard her requests, would he get angry? Could she fit into his world of power and money? So many questions about a future which had spun off into the unknown.

"You're deep in thought tonight," he said, his voice quiet as he held her close to slow dance.

"I'm wondering if I can ever get accustomed to things you take for granted. I've never ridden in a car like yours before. I don't have the table manners or the background to go the places you'll go."

"You'll learn. It won't be a problem, I promise. And my world is filled with regular people, the same as your world."

"Our environments aren't the same at all," she said, thinking now more about their kiss last night. She looked at his mouth, a slightly full lower lip. Two years and then marriage to him would be over. One thing she was absolutely certain about—life in the future would be all new to her and she should avoid ever trying to make him the center of it.

"So what else is on your mind?" he asked, watching her intently.

"I'm still thinking about your proposal," she answered.

"Good. That's what I wanted you to do," he said.

When the music changed to a fast number and couples melted away around them, Matt continued to hold her hand. "Let's keep going."

As she watched his cool moves, she forgot contracts, bargaining and wealth. All she could think about was Matt and how attractive he was. She wanted to kiss him again, wanted him to kiss her. Every move of his was sensual, heating her and causing erotic fantasies, images she tried to banish.

Tossing her head, she circled around him and then met his gaze and she knew he wanted her in his arms. If they had been alone, she thought, by now they would have been in an embrace.

There would be no problems with the physical part of their relationship. She worried about her requests for more money and wondered if she should abandon her demands.

When the song ended, he took her hand to return to their table. A couple approached them from Matt's side and he paused. Brianna stopped to wait and recognized a woman Matt had brought to the steak house in the past. The tall, slender blonde glanced at Drianna and then turned her attention to Matt. She was stunning in an intricately embroidered and beaded black dress and the tall man with her was almost as handsome as Matt. They stopped and the men shook hands, exchanging greetings.

"We're leaving," the tall, black-haired man said.

"Nicole, Ty, this is Brianna Costin. Brianna, this is Nicole Doyle and Ty Bookman."

"I barely recognized you out of your waitress uniform," Nicole said acidly to Brianna. "I believe we already know each other. You work at the steak house, right?"

"Yes, I do," Brianna answered.

"The food here is almost as delicious as it is there," Nicole added, turning to Matt. "We've eaten and are going. It's good to see you again, Matt," she said in a warmer tone.

Ty echoed her greeting and they moved on.

"Ignore her, Brianna."

"She didn't say anything that isn't so, although if looks could kill, I'd be a goner."

"There's nothing between us. Nicole is out of my life," he said, holding Brianna's chair for her.

He sat facing her again, opening his jacket. Dark locks of hair had fallen on his forehead and he looked more appealing than when he was buttoned up with every hair combed into place.

"That was better. You're more relaxed tonight. Last night, I felt as if I were standing outside castle walls with the drawbridge up."

She laughed. "If you're comparing me to a princess in a castle, that's a first. No one has ever drawn that comparison. Cinderella in ashes wouldn't be as wild an exaggeration. I came from nothing. My sisters and I all shared one room."

"Are they all as pretty as you?"

"I don't know about that. We resemble each other and

look like my mother, thank heavens. My brothers look like my dad, who was a charming man, merely unfaithful and unreliable and unable to hold a job. Actually, I don't think my dad liked to work."

"Some people don't. Evidently, he stayed inside the law, so that's commendable."

"Yes, he did as far as anyone ever knew. He liked bars and women. I wasn't getting into that trap. My sisters married early and young. I got scholarships. When I got to Cheyenne I got part-time jobs and here I am."

"I've noticed you since the first time I ever saw you at the steak house. It was a June night last year and I ate on the terrace and I don't even remember who I ate with."

"You remember that?" she asked, feeling her face flush and her pulse jump because she couldn't imagine him noticing and remembering a waitress. "Actually, I remember the night. I was new on the job. When I was assigned to your table, one of the other waitresses who had befriended me gave me the scoop."

"What did she tell you? Not that I'm demanding, I hope."

"Of course not. Not to me anyway," she said, and he smiled.

"You've never given me any indication that you've noticed me more than you do the busboys or the maître d' or anyone else there. Had I but known," she said, fanning herself and teasing him, getting another smile from him.

She kept waiting all through dinner, over her roasted pheasant and his lobster, for him to bring up his proposal. By the time they had finished eating, there still had been no mention of the offer. Soon they returned to the dance floor where she stopped thinking constantly about his proposal until finally a dance ended and Matt held her hand as they returned to their table.

"Let's go out to my place and have something to drink and talk about my proposal. Is it too late for you?"

"No," she said, thankful she didn't have any early classes.

In minutes they were in his car and she turned in the seat to watch him drive. He glanced at her and back at the road. "What do you think so far? We're getting along."

"I agree. I'm still surprised you're interested. You've never given the slightest indication."

"I'm interested," he said. "And I've spent all day and most of tonight wanting to kiss you again," he said in a husky voice that stirred heat in her.

"We'll kiss, but I'm going home tonight. Alone. I'm not staying over," she said.

"I hadn't planned that you would," he answered easily. "I'm patient."

"I don't know where you live."

"I don't make much of an issue of it because I value my privacy. I won't give interviews at home or let the media photograph my house. That's another reason I like living here. I can maintain a certain degree of privacy without too big of a hassle. I can drive myself sometimes and I don't feel as if I have to have a bodyguard everywhere I go."

She hadn't even given a thought to limos or bodyguards.

He drove through tall iron gates that swung open when he punched a small handheld device. They wound up a drive to another iron gate that was opened by a gate-keeper. Matt spoke to the man before continuing on his way. She turned to look back as the gates closed. "How many people work for you here?"

He shook his head. "I'm not sure. I don't deal directly with my staff. I have someone who oversees the house-hold for me."

With each passing second, she became more amazed as she suspected Matt had intended she would be.

They rounded a bend and the forest vanished, re-placed by immaculate grounds with tall stately pines. "My word! You live in a castle," she said, awed by her first view of a palatial mansion with wings, balconies and a wide portico. A circular drive in front created a border for a well-lit garden of fall flowers. "I didn't know there was anything like this in the state. You guard your privacy well."

"That's right. I don't bring people home with me. There are other places to go and few women I see even live here in Cheyenne. It's easier that way."

"You may be making the most colossal mistake in asking me to be your wife," she said, letting out her breath. "This lifestyle is totally foreign to me. I knew you were wealthy. Now this makes it seem tangible."

"I'd think my offer to you would make it seem sub-stantial," he remarked dryly.

"No, your proposal still has a definite dreamlike quality."

"Your kiss last night didn't. It was very real," he said. "And so were the effects of it."

She smiled. "Maybe I can try again later," she flirted.

As Matt stopped in front, a man had come out to open the door for her. When she emerged from the car, the employee greeted Matt, who introduced her.

Matt took her arm and led her into the front hall. Beneath a sparkling crystal chandelier, water splashed in a fountain. Farther along the hall, two staircases spiraled to the second floor.

"I'll show you around later. First, let's relax in front of the fire where we can talk. What would you like to drink?"

"Hot chocolate sounds tasty."

"That's easy. Come with me," he said and they walked across the hall and into another spacious area with a fire roaring in the fireplace, floor-to-ceiling glass doors that opened onto an enclosed room that held a pool, fountains and flowers.

After placing a drink order on the intercom, Matt led her to a brown leather sofa. As he shed his jacket and tie and unfastened the top buttons of his shirt, she momentarily forgot her surroundings and was ensnared in watching Matt. When she was with him, longing was a steady smoldering fire that now fanned stronger. He looked casual, more approachable, his appeal intensifying.

"If you accept my proposal, this is where we'll live when we're in Cheyenne."

She looked around at one wall lined with shelves with an assortment of books, oil paintings, vases, bronze statues. The room was filled with leather furniture, a hickory floor, the huge stone fireplace, a plasma television. Had he brought her out here to intimidate her?

She faced him squarely. "I can't believe that I could ever be a part of this, even for a brief time."

"All you have to do is accept my offer."

"Did you bring me out here so I'll drop my conditions? It seems ridiculous to ask anything more of you when you're doing something that would enable me to live in this house."

He sat on the leather sofa. "Let's hear what you want."

She reminded herself that the worst he could do was refuse. In reality, the worst he could do would be to withdraw his proposal and tell her to get lost.

There was a light rap at the door and a maid appeared bearing a tray with cups of cocoa and a china pot with a lid, plus a plate of cookies.

"Thanks, Renita," he said. "Brianna, this is Renita, who has worked for me for several years now."

After Brianna greeted the woman, Renita turned to leave them alone, closing the door behind her.

"Now back to our subject," he said. "Your requests."

"I have a list," she said, getting out the paper and he smiled.

She held the folded paper in her hand. "Look, Matt, I'm the oldest child in my family. You are in your family, right?"

"Yes, I am."

"From the time I was about twelve years old, I pretty much had to run things at home for all five of my siblings. My mom has cleaned businesses all her life and she's worn out. When my dad was alive, he drank too much and he cheated on her all through the years. I could never be with someone who cheated."

"You won't have a problem with me on that score."

"Good, can we put it in a prenup agreement?"

"I don't think you need to write that one down," Matt said dryly. "I'll be faithful. By the way, once we marry, and I get into the investment group, I won't necessarily hold you to two years. If you want out sooner, a divorce wouldn't affect my role in that group. They have some members who are divorced."

"Seems a little inconsistent to me, but acceptable. Two years maximum, though, right?"

"Right. That will do."

"No problem there. Now the next thing. You're a very wealthy man. So much so that half a million up front and half a million later seems paltry by your standards."

A smile flitted over his face and disappeared, but amusement still danced in his eyes. "How much do you want, Brianna?"

His name rolling off her tongue gave her a tingle. And she felt a momentary panic for trying to wrest more money from him when a million dollars was a fantastic fortune she couldn't imagine earning on her own. Taking a quick breath, she looked him squarely in the eyes. "Two million up front and two million when we part. In addition, I want you to pay for a nanny for my baby as long as I need one. And put some money in trust for the baby's education."

"That's a lot of money. You're going to make some

more by being married to me, plus the car I promised and the clothes and you'll live in a manner you don't now have. I'll think about it. Anything else on that list?" he asked.

She held it closer to her as if to keep him from seeing it. "That covers it. I have a preference about waiting to sleep together until we've said vows," she said, her palms growing sweaty because he didn't appear to be willing to accept her terms about money. "I want to know each other better."

He looked amused. "I won't push that on you anytime you don't want to. Married or not," he answered easily.

She felt her face flush hotly and wished she could control her blushes. "You might consider that a strange request when I'm expecting. I'm pregnant because I partied and let go, celebrating exams being over. Otherwise, I've had one other guy in my past and that was in high school."

"I'll wait until you're ready."

The hot chocolate sat forgotten and she felt the tension increase. What she wanted and what he wanted were different. There was no mistaking which one of them had the most power. If he took back his proposal, she wondered whether she would ever get over letting a million dollars slip through her fingers. Her heart was pounding so hard and fast, she thought he surely could hear it.

He gave her a long look and she almost blurted out to forget what she had requested.

"While we're into demands, I have one more that we

didn't settle last night when we talked. I want you to drop out of school."

"Now?" She was aghast and he asked the impossible.

"Now. In two years you can pick up where you left off."

The thought of losing momentum on her education set her back. It was the one thing she most wanted. Her degree and a nanny. She'd never had any substantial cash in her life, always living hand to mouth, but school was tangible and she had almost achieved part of her education goal.

"I want to finish this semester," she said. "It ends in December. That's not very long."

"Withdraw from college this week. I'd like to take you on a honeymoon. I'll want you to accompany me to Europe often. Your grades will suffer. You can pick school up again when we divorce and you'll be better off than trying to juggle classes *and* marriage *and* a baby. The baby will be two or more when you go back. Easier to handle."

The prospect hurt of giving up a goal she'd had since she was old enough to realize a degree would get her out of the poverty she'd been born into. Two years and she could go back. She would have a nanny, help and money, which would be infinitely easier.

"All right, I'll drop out," she said, feeling as if she were ripping part of herself away.

"Good. As for my part—I'll pay you *one* million up front and *one* million when we part and I'll provide nannies and that education trust fund," he said flatly.

"Thank you," she said, drawing a long breath as relief

filled her. She would still get two million dollars! Her heart was in her throat over wresting so much money out of him. She and her baby—and the rest of her family—were fixed for life, she was sure. There would be more than enough for all of them to go to college or trade school. Matt would provide a nanny for her baby. Financial worries fell away and she was giddy with excitement she couldn't contain.

Smiling at him, she scooted the distance that separated them to throw her arms around his neck. "I accept your proposal, Matt. I'll marry you!"

Four

The minute Brianna voiced her acceptance, her green eyes sparkled. Reaffirmation that he'd made a good choice swept Matt, sending his own enthusiasm soaring. She looked as if he had handed her the world on a silver tray—and well she should, he knew. It was also a look he never would have received from any other woman he'd considered wife material.

Wrapping his arms around her, Matt pulled her closer as they kissed. Soft, sweet-smelling and eager, she pressed against him, her tongue thrusting deep into his mouth as she poured herself into her kiss and set him ablaze. He wanted her more than ever. The thought that soon she would be totally his fanned the flames already raging in him.

He pulled her onto his lap to embrace her as he kissed her, slowly and thoroughly. Her soft moans, her hands running over his neck and shoulders, heightened his passion. Remembering that she wanted to wait for consummation rose dimly in the back of his mind, but her kisses sent another message.

He wound his fingers in her silky hair and longed to bury himself in her. Thought vanished and only the pounding of his heart and roaring of his pulse enveloped him. Holding her, he ran his hand down her back over the thin cotton of her shirt, lower over her cotton slacks to follow the curve of her bottom.

Continuing to kiss her, he cradled her against his shoulder. All of his senses were steeped in pleasure and she was turned in his arms to where he could caress her slender neck. His hand went lower, lightly across her breast. The instant he caressed a taut peak, she moaned and twisted her hips slightly, clutching his shoulders. Her softness and instant responses inflamed him.

He freed her top button to slide his hand beneath her shirt and bra to cup her breast while his thumb circled her nipple. She moaned again, a sound of enjoyment that heightened his own.

Raising her head, she grasped his wrist and pulled on his hand. "Wait, Matt," she whispered. Her plea halted him and he moved his hand, raking his fingers through her hair to comb it away from her face.

"This is too new," she said. "Slow down a little."

"Whatever you want," he said in a deep, husky tone that happened in passionate moments. His pulse still raced and he was hot with desire that he tried to cool. Her lips were red and swollen from his kisses, her face flushed. Her response to his kisses had been intense and he had to curb the impulse to pull her close again and try to kiss away her protests. If she would even protest further.

Scooting off his lap, she pulled her clothes in place and faced him on the sofa. "We have plans to make."

She retrieved her cup of cocoa and sipped it, holding the china cup with both hands.

"We're not in love, Brianna, so I think a small, quiet wedding would be more appropriate. Family and only close friends."

"That's all I would have anyway," she said.

"I'll pay for the wedding, so you'll have no worries there. Get the dress you want, but not formal. This won't be that big a deal. I'd like to marry as soon as possible. This is Friday. Can you marry a week from tomorrow?"

Her eyes widened and she seemed to be thinking about it. "I don't see why not," she replied.

"Excellent!" His pulse jumped again. He'd get into the investment group before the year was out, he guessed. "I'll clear my calendar and we'll take a week for a honeymoon." He pulled out his wallet and gave her a card. "Here, use this to buy clothes. If you can't find the wedding dress you want here, tell me and I'll fly you to San Francisco, Dallas or wherever you'd like to look. Monday we can open an account for you and transfer money."

"You don't waste time, do you?"

"Quit your job in the morning. You don't need it any

longer and they can get a new waitress. Not one as beautiful, though," he said, smiling at her.

She licked her lower lip and inhaled and he was sidetracked. He knew she was thinking about something besides her job. He slipped his hand behind her head to comb his fingers into her long hair. "We'll both benefit, Brianna. You'll see."

"I know it'll be a miracle for me," she said. Her ongoing wonder pleased him because it continued to confirm his choice. Nicole, or any other woman he'd known well, would never be awed. They'd be asking for more of his time and his attention, plus money.

"If you'd like, you can move in here right away," he said, hoping she'd accept.

Her eyes widened again and she looked around. "I can't picture living here."

"It's a home and comfortable and why not? After we marry you can move into my bedroom with me. There are twelve bedrooms in this house, so there's no lack of space," he remarked dryly.

"Maybe I'll move in Monday. It won't take long to pack my things."

"Do it tomorrow. Brianna, you're so early in your pregnancy that we can tell everyone the baby is mine."

She bit her lip and looked lost in thought. "I'd like that, but what happens if we stay together until my baby is a toddler? This baby will see you as Daddy by then. Besides, the baby will have my last name."

"I hadn't thought about that," he said, realizing this wasn't going to be as simple as he'd envisioned and he hadn't given enough attention to the prospect of a baby in his life. "Let me talk to my lawyer and accountant and I'll see what I can do."

She nodded as if satisfied by his answer.

"Maybe I can work it out where your baby has my name. If it reaches the media that it's not my baby, the news won't be earth-shattering anyway."

"Because by then you'll be in your investment group," she said and that cool tone she'd first used returned to her voice.

"That's right. This decision is up to you," he said. "I'd think you'd prefer it, too."

"I do, even though it may complicate our lives later."

"We can call our families right now so they can start making plans," Matt said.

"Are you going to leave the impression that we're in love, or are we going to tell our families this is a temporary marriage?" she asked.

"I'd just as soon say it was the real thing," he replied, having already given thought to what he wanted. "That way, when the press gets wind of this, there won't be a big scandal. Will that be a problem with your family?"

"No. I'm close with my mom and sisters and we'll talk. I'll need to bring them here a few days early so they can buy clothes for the wedding that I will pay for with your money," Brianna said.

"Unless you have a preference, we'll marry here at the house," Matt replied. "I'll get the minister. That way, I can keep this private."

"That's reasonable," she said. The more they talked,

the more he longed to pull her back into his arms and kiss her and forget their planning or waiting.

"Sunday morning I'll take you to church with me and you can meet the minister."

Matt pulled out a card and gave it to her. "Here's a card from the owner of a shop that has pretty dresses. It's a small shop and you see the address. Go look there tomorrow. She'll help you and you might find what you like for the wedding."

"I've seen their ads," Brianna said, taking the card from him, her fingers lightly brushing his. The slight contact added to his yearning to hold her in his arms again. "I couldn't ever afford a dress from this shop."

"Now you can, so go look and buy something if you see what you want. I'd like to have both of my older cousins as groomsmen and my two brothers as grooms-men, also."

"That will work for me because I'll have my sisters and my two closest friends," she said. "We've got our plans set for now, and I can feel the evening catching up with me. I should go, Matt."

"Certainly," he said, wondering if their plans would blow up in his face or work as smoothly as he hoped. Was he letting lust kill all his business judgment?

As if she guessed his thoughts, she gazed at him with a somber expression. "We're both jumping into this as if into a dark well."

"No, we're not," he said, his self-assurance kicking in full force. "I've given this thought. I know my pro-posal and my plans are new to you, but I've been living with them for a while. I think we'll both come out ahead."

"You're being driven by greed and love of money."

"And you're not?" he asked lightly, amused that she could see her own motives in a better light than his.

"This marriage has to make life better for my baby, me and even my family who'll benefit, too."

He hugged her. "Stop worrying and dwelling on the negative possibilities. We're into it now."

"Not absolutely until we say wedding vows," she said. Before he could reply, she spoke quickly. "I still want to go ahead. Don't misunderstand me. I'm glad you selected me."

He held open the door for her and walked to his car with her. "It's natural to have wedding jitters—and in this case, even more expected."

He closed the door and walked around the car, glad he'd planned to marry soon. If he could whisk her to a justice of the peace tomorrow, he'd do it, but he wanted this to appear to be the real thing for now and a big deal for both of them—which it was.

He drove her home, giving her a light kiss. "Think about the money, Brianna, and forget the rest. It's going to be worth your while and mine."

Matt's words rang in his ears early Monday morning when he went to his office. He'd only been there half an hour when his closest friend arrived and came in to see him.

As soon as Matt announced Brianna's acceptance of

his proposal, Zach glared at him. "You'll regret this more than anything you've ever done. You can pick stocks, but choosing a woman as you would a stock is going to be a disaster." Beneath a tangle of wavy blond hair, Zach's pale brown eyes filled with irritation.

Matt calmly faced him. "It's a done deal. We're engaged."

"You can get out of that and you know it. Get out fast. Marry Nicole. She's gorgeous, a socialite who moves in your world. She's wealthy in her own right, so she won't be after your money and she's not pregnant with another guy's baby. Another guy who may show up when he gets wind that the mother of his baby has landed a rich guy."

"The minute I get into that investment group, I don't care. I'm not worried about him, anyway. They went to an attorney and he signed away all rights to the baby. He's long gone from Wyoming."

"That can be broken in court and you know it."

"That's their fight. Not mine. But if it'll shut you up, we can have him found," Matt said, entering his schedule for the day into his BlackBerry.

"As your friend, I'm pleading with you not to marry this woman. She isn't in your social class. She only has waitress experience. She won't know how to deal with your lifestyle."

"Don't be ridiculous," Matt said with amusement. "You think I was born into this lifestyle?"

"You weren't as far removed from it as she is. She's from a tiny little town and plain."

"Her family is honest, aren't they? Never been in any criminal trouble?"

"No, but that's about all you can say for them. That's not the kind of person to lock yourself into a marriage contract with. She'll want more, I can promise you."

"She already has. She demanded more money."

"You've got to be kidding. And you agreed, didn't you?"

"Yep, I did. It's done, Zach. Now, get me a list of places she can put the money I'm about to give her. I'll meet with her later this morning and discuss what she wants to do."

Zach raked his fingers through his hair that sprang back in thick waves. He shook his head and threw his hands in the air. "I give up. I've said all I can say. I suppose you've told Nicole goodbye."

"She walked on me. She was unhappy that I wouldn't give her more of my time. I don't expect those demands from Brianna. I promise you, she's not going to bore me," Matt replied, smiling at his friend. "Think you can have a list in an hour?"

"Sure. I'll get someone working on it right away and I'll go over it… I wish I could dissuade you."

"I'm grown, Zach. I know what I want. She's perfect."

"I'll try to avoid saying 'I told you so' later," Zach grumbled and left the room.

Matt gazed at the empty doorway and wondered if Zach would prove to be right. He couldn't imagine being bored by Brianna. At the moment, he couldn't wait to be with her. He picked up the phone to call his chief attorney.

***

Twenty-four hours later, seated in a quiet, high-priced restaurant, Matt glanced at his watch impatiently. After Matt's lunch appointment with Zach, Brianna was going to meet him at the restaurant at one. If Zach didn't show soon, Matt realized he was going to run late for Brianna. Zach was already ten minutes behind. Zach had asked for the lunch appointment away from the office and Matt couldn't imagine the reason. It was uncharacteristic of Zach, who was as much of a workaholic as Matt.

"Matt?"

He heard the familiar voice and glanced around to see Nicole slide into the seat facing him. She looked as gorgeous as ever in a white designer suit with bright red accessories that complemented her pale blond hair. She smiled at him. "Don't get angry at Zach. I asked him to do this because I want to talk to you."

Matt kept his temper in check over Zach's high-handed interference, wondering how much of the blame Nicole shared.

A waiter appeared with glasses of water, took their order and left.

"I ought to walk out now," Matt said easily.

"Please don't. I want to talk to you. I really am responsible for this. I heard from someone that you're thinking about getting engaged to that waitress."

"Nicole, we're through."

Nicole shuddered and gulped. "I suppose I deserve this for getting in such a huff the last time we were together, but I know you're not in love. I know the only thing keeping you out of that investment group was your bachelor status."

"Not any longer."

"Matt, don't do this. You can break the engagement. We had a wonderful relationship for a while and we can have it again," she said, beginning to sound desperate. He wished Zach hadn't set him up for this encounter.

He shook his head. "You should have just phoned me, Nicole, and saved yourself the trouble. I intend to marry her. It's over between us. You made that abundantly clear."

"Matt!" she cried, interrupting him. "I'm sorry if I demanded too much of your time. Stop and think how wonderful we were together. She means nothing to you. You barely know her."

"This is my decision," he answered patiently, wishing lunch were over and he could escape. He looked at her flawless skin and wide eyes. She was a stunning woman and once upon a time, she'd set his heart pounding, but she didn't mean anything now, nor did he find her desirable. He realized it was finished—if he'd ever truly cared for her at all. Idly, he wondered how long it would be until he would feel that way regarding Brianna.

"Give us another chance," Nicole urged, leaning across the table to caress his hand lightly while she talked. "It was incredible between us—you know it was."

"Nicole, this is an absolutely useless conversation." Matt stopped talking as the waiter approached with a tray of food. He placed a salad in front of Nicole and a sandwich in front of Matt.

She smiled at him and raised her water glass in a toast. "Then here's to the happy bridegroom. May your future be filled with joy."

"I'll drink to that one," he said, touching her glass with his and sipping the icy water.

As they ate, Nicole was her most charming, switching totally from the subject of Brianna, yet Matt knew she was deliberately trying to entertain and charm him as a reminder of how good things could be between them. He struggled to pay attention to her conversation and tried to avoid being obvious when he glanced occasionally at his watch. He had to get rid of Nicole before Brianna appeared.

To his consternation, Nicole selected a dessert. Matt asked the waiter for the check and then as soon as they were alone, Matt faced Nicole. "I'm sorry, I have an appointment. I'll get the lunch and you can take your time. I have to leave."

She smiled at him. "That's all right, Matt. I still wish you'd think about what I've said to you. It's not too late to get out of this engagement. You'll be incredibly bored with her."

"That's for me to worry about," he replied easily.

Their waiter returned and Matt settled up.

As the waiter turned away, Matt glanced across the dining room and saw Brianna approaching the table. As he started to stand, she looked from him to Nicole and then back at him and he could see her surprise. She stopped and then turned, rushing away from him.

"Nicole, I have to go," Matt said.

"*She's* your appointment?" Nicole protested, stepping to block his path as she grasped his wrist.

"Move out of my way, Nicole," he said quietly.

"Don't leave. Stay here, Matt. Give us another chance together because what we had was great."

"Goodbye, Nicole," he said.

"Matt—"

In spite of her calling his name, he rushed through the restaurant and outside, to watch Brianna climb into her car. He ran across the lot in the warm sunshine. When she backed out of the parking place and turned, he stepped in front of her car to prevent her from leaving. She honked as he stood with his hands on the hood of the car. Certain she wouldn't hurt him, he had no intention of letting her drive away until he talked to her.

In seconds, she opened her window and thrust her head out. "Matt, move out of my way."

"No. I want you to promise to listen to me."

She glared at him a moment and then cut the motor. He knew she could start up and race away and he wouldn't be able to stop her, but he wasn't going to get anywhere by standing in front of her car. He walked around to climb in on the driver's side. "Move over," he ordered.

With another glare at him, she did as he asked, climbing over the gear shift to sit on the passenger side. He slid behind the wheel, started the car and pulled back into a parking place, where he cut the motor once again and turned to face her.

"That wasn't what you're thinking. You pay attention

to my explanation," he said, determined to get her to listen to the truth. He had no intention of allowing an unwanted encounter with Nicole to harm his future.

Five

Brianna locked her fingers together and nodded. She had feared all along that Matt wouldn't be faithful to her, but she hadn't expected to find him with someone else before they were married.

"I didn't plan that lunch with Nicole," he said firmly, gazing into her eyes. "I thought I was having lunch with Zach, a guy who works for me."

Brianna didn't believe him and waited in silence.

"Nicole said she asked Zach to get me to lunch so she could talk to me. I was already there when she appeared and we went ahead and ate lunch. That's all it was."

"I find that difficult to believe. You forget I've waited on your table when you're together."

"Brianna, do you think I'd make a lunch date with

another woman when I knew I was meeting you at the same restaurant? I've got more sense than that if I'd intended to do any such thing."

She gazed at him, realizing that was probably true. As she began to believe him, her hurt eased. She had been shocked and furious to discover him with Nicole, but she knew what he'd said was logical. Now she really looked at him without a haze of fury. Black curls tumbled on his forehead and his jacket was un-buttoned, revealing a crisp white shirt. His navy tie was slightly askew. Otherwise, he appeared as com-posed as ever.

"All right, Matt. I believe you," she said. "It shocked me to see you together today. I know she's been a big part of your life."

"That's past. I promise you, she's out of my life now and she won't be back in it."

"But she wants in it, doesn't she?" Brianna asked, hoping she was wrong. Disappointment surged when he nodded.

"Yes, she does. I told her, and I promise *you,* it's all over with her. You and I have a deal. I feel nothing when I'm with her."

Brianna studied him, wondering if he would be say-ing the same words about her someday. It was decided that their marriage would be over in a maximum of two years. In the future would she be referred to as casually as he dismissed Nicole now?

He leaned forward to tilt her chin up so she looked into his eyes. "You're the woman in my world. By this time next week you'll be my wife. I don't want any other woman. Okay?"

"Okay," she said, her gaze lowering to his mouth. He was only inches away now and her irritation had been replaced by desire. "I don't intend to share you," she said.

"You won't have to," she dimly heard him say, but her pounding heart was dulling his words and she raised her mouth to his as she slipped her arm around his neck. His mouth came down on hers and her lips opened beneath his. His kiss was hot, demanding, confirming that she was his woman in a way words never could.

Worries and concerns about other women in his life ceased to exist. Now all she wanted were Matt's kisses. They were leaning over the gear shift of her car and she realized they were still in the parking lot of the restaurant, so she pushed lightly on Matt's chest.

"We're in public," she whispered. "And this is less than the perfect place to kiss," she added, scooting away from him.

"We have appointments this afternoon, but I would like to cancel all of them and take you home with me."

"You can't," she said, smiling at him. "Not if you want to stay on schedule for a wedding this weekend."

"There's something else, Brianna. We will honeymoon in Rome because there's a charity ball I want to attend. I'd already agreed to appear and I'd still like to go because members of the investment group will be there and I'll have a chance to chat with them and introduce you as my wife. I'm telling you so you can buy a dress for the occasion. Get something elegant and don't worry about expense."

"Rome…?"

Intimidated by the thought of participating in a charity gala with him and meeting his investment acquaintances, her smile vanished. She knew she would be out of her element.

"Matt," she said hesitantly, and his eyes narrowed. "Are you certain you want me to accompany you to something like that immediately after we get married? I haven't ever attended a charity ball."

"You'll dazzle them," he said. "And I'm very sure about taking you. I want you there with me. If you need someone to coach you, I can get someone."

"Not at all," she answered, trying to cover her uncertainties and fears. As soon as possible, she knew she should start getting ready for the ball and practicing her Italian.

She reflected that he would also be working in Italy. As carefully as he'd charted his marriage to help him get into his investment group, so his honeymoon would give him a chance to promote his marriage and show her to the European investors. His constant eye on his goal jarred her until she reminded herself that she had a contract with him. There was no love in this union, so why wouldn't the honeymoon be a business trip?

Brianna glanced at her watch. "We're going to be late for our meeting at the bank today. After that, I see the wedding planner."

"Given the amount I put into accounts for you yesterday, the banker won't mind if we're a few minutes late," Matt said, his heated expression conveying his fervor. "I'll drive and we'll come back to get my car."

Gazing out the car window, she thought about having to stop by the university again today. Even though she'd dropped out of her classes, she wanted to figure some way by next semester to continue her education because Matt would be often occupied with his work. She suspected after their honeymoon, she would have huge chunks of time when she could study. He might want her out of his life as soon as he was accepted into his investment group. She intended to get all she could out of this brief union.

Wednesday, she stopped at Matt's office.

She stepped into the lobby that had enormous planters with tall, exotic greenery, palms, banana trees, tropical plants that were at least eight feet tall. A fountain splashed in the center of the lobby.

First she had to deal with security, but her name was on a list and she was ushered toward the elevators.

As she walked away from the security desk, she heard the low voice of the employee telling someone that she was headed toward the top floor and Matt's office.

When she stepped out into a thickly carpeted hallway, light spilled through the glass walls. More potted plants and leather benches lined the hallway. A stocky blond man stepped out of an office and approached her.

"Miss Costin?" he asked, his gaze raking over her as he frowned. "I'm Zach Gentner. Matt has been momentarily detained in a meeting. If you'll come with me, I'll show you into his office. You can wait there."

"Thank you," she said, smiling and relaxing slightly beneath his friendly smile.

They walked through a large reception area where she met a receptionist and then through a smaller office where she met Matt's private secretary.

She followed Zach into a spacious office with light spilling through two glass walls. The carpet was plush, the dark walnut paneling a complementary backdrop to the brown leather furniture with oil paintings of Wyoming landscapes on the walls and the two tall bronze statues of a stalking mountain lion and galloping horses on tables.

"Congratulations on your engagement, Miss Costin," Zach said.

"Thank you," she said, feeling uncomfortable in spite of his congratulations.

"Your family should be extremely proud of you— you have money now for your baby, a comfortable future and endless opportunities. I hope you can always remember the sacrifices Matt has made to take a total stranger as his wife, in a less than satisfying business arrangement that locks him into a loveless marriage."

His sarcastic words hit her with the pain of a knife thrust. Her smile vanished and she chilled. "It was his choice," she replied stiffly.

"I know it was. I heard you made even greater demands, which he caved to. I hope you don't ruin his life. Of course, if he doesn't get in that group, he'll dump you so fast your head will spin. How long this fake marriage will last anyway, is anybody's guess. Until he tires of your body or you are quite large with child."

She clamped her hands together and bit her lip, trying to keep calm and think before she replied to his hurtful words. "You obviously don't approve of me," she said, forcing her voice to stay low and controlled, determined she wouldn't let him goad her into losing her temper.

"Not at all," he said, "but it isn't my choice. While I've told him what I think, he's stubborn. I hate to see him hurt or watch you ruin his life. You're pregnant with some other guy's baby from a one-night stand, not the best recommendation for marriage. Only you know if that guy is really the father or if it's someone else."

"He's the father," she said quietly, livid with fury that she was determined to keep in check. "Are you overstepping your bounds as an employee, Mr. Gentner? Aren't you afraid Matt will be furious to learn about this conversation?"

"Not at all," he answered coldly. "He'll know I did it for his own good. We go back a long way. Almost as far back as those cousins of his whom I almost called to see if either of them could talk sense into him. That confounded bet is the reason for this ridiculous proposal you have.

"Of course, they're so competitive, they'll see this marriage as a way of eliminating Matt from the running. They'll know he'll get out of this marriage eventually. I hope it doesn't cost him too much money. I know it won't cost emotionally because he doesn't have one shred of love for you. I'm sure that's no secret. Matt is up-front about business deals he makes and that's all this sham marriage is."

"I don't want to listen to this," she said, heading toward the door. "You tell—"

Matt strode into the room. "Brianna, I'm sorry I'm late." He broke off his words as his eyes narrowed. Looking back and forth between Zach and her, he focused on her. "Is something wrong?"

"Maybe for him—"

Zach spoke in a slightly louder tone, drowning her out. "I was congratulating your fiancée on her engagement and upcoming union. I'll leave you two alone," Zach said, leaving the room in haste.

Matt watched him go and then turned to study Brianna. He walked to her to place his hands on her shoulders and continue to gaze at her with a probing stare. "What's happened? What did he say to you?"

"He hopes I don't ruin your life," she answered quietly. "I simply assume you're doing what you want to do and you've given your proposal thought."

"Damn!" Matt said softly. "Forget Zach. Damn straight I've given it thought and I'm doing exactly what I want. Don't think about him or what he's said. I'll talk to him about it later."

"Don't get into a fight over it. I'll forget what he said," she stated, knowing in reality she would never forget.

As she looked up at Matt, it was easy to forget the past few minutes and Zach's hurtful words because Matt gazed at her with such desire in his expression that Zach no longer mattered.

"Brianna, there's something else. I've talked to my lawyer and thought over what I want to do. I'll adopt your baby so the child will have my name, the same as if it were my own."

She gasped with surprise. "You'd do that?"

"It seems the best way. Sooner or later, we'll divorce, but the baby will have my name and I can pay child support."

"Matt!" The enormity of how badly he wanted this marriage made her weak in the knees. "You'd do all that to get more money?"

"I'm doing a lot of it to get you," he said in a husky voice, drawing her closer to him.

She couldn't believe that he really meant what he said. They weren't in love, but whatever his reason, she was going to accept before he had time to reconsider. There was no way his adopting her baby would be bad. "Matt, I hope you really know what you're doing," she said. "It's acceptable to me."

"I thought it would be. I don't see how else we can deal with your baby."

Once again, she wished love was in the mix. Matt's words should have been thrilling, but his offer sounded too businesslike to give her a deep joy. Even so, she was glad for her baby's sake, and his offer gave her another degree of security.

"Now don't worry about Zach or your baby or our future," Matt said.

She wound her arms around Matt's neck. "This is what's important. If you're content, then I'm satisfied."

When he picked her up, she tightened her arms around his neck as he gave her a long kiss that shut out the world.

* * *

Before the rehearsal dinner Friday night, she took deep gulps of air and tried to relax as she waited in her suite for her family to gather before leaving for Matt's. His family was staying with him. She had moved to the hotel where she had booked suites for her family and herself. Members of both families and friends in his wedding party and their spouses planned to gather at Matt's home for hors d'oeuvres and to get acquainted. Then after the wedding rehearsal, they'd leave for an extravagant restaurant.

She was incredibly nervous over Matt meeting her family for the first time. Her family had never been far from Blakely, where they'd grown up. She was the first and only to finish high school, the first to attend college and they knew little about etiquette or table manners. She had spent the past three days getting them new clothes and haircuts, which Brianna could easily afford now. At each meal she had coached them on table manners, with an etiquette book open in front of her for quick reference.

Her family was to meet in the sitting room of Brianna's spacious suite and her mother was the first to arrive.

Adele Costin had been transformed and Brianna gazed at her mother with joy. "Mom, you look great!"

"I have you to thank for it," she replied, smiling at her daughter. "Look, my first manicure. I can't recognize my own hands or my hair or my image in the mirror, for that matter," she said, laughing and holding out her hands. Her mother had spent a lifetime cleaning and Brianna could remember her red, chapped hands.

Now they looked lovely with a pale pink polish on her well-shaped nails.

Her mother's tailored navy suit was attractive and flattering. Her black, slightly graying hair was cut short and combed straight to highlight the soft contours of her face.

"You look wonderful, Mom," Brianna said again and kissed her mother's cheek.

"I hope you are pleased, Brianna, although at the moment, I don't see how you could possibly keep from being joyous. But money isn't everything."

"Mom, I'm happy," Brianna said. "I'm doing what I want to do. We're alone for a minute now, and there's something I want to tell you, but it's not for the rest of the family yet."

"What's that?" Adele asked.

"I'm expecting a baby."

"Oh, Brianna! A baby!" her mother exclaimed, smiling at her and hugging her briefly. Stepping away, she frowned and then leaned closer to study Brianna intently. "Are you happy about the baby?"

"Oh, yes! Of course. And now I'll be taken care of so well and I can help the whole family."

"The whole family isn't what you need to be concerned about. I want you to be really pleased," Adele said quietly.

"I am," Brianna replied, smiling at her mother. "I really am, Mom. I wouldn't be getting married if I didn't want to."

Her mother studied her as she nodded her head. "I hope so, and I want you to tell me if you need me."

"I will, I promise," Brianna said. "Now you'll be a grandmother again."

Appearing to relax, her mother had a faint smile, and Brianna was relieved that the worried look had vanished, at least for now. "A grandmother!" Adele said. "Ah, Brianna, that fills me with more hope for the future and gives me another purpose in life."

Brianna laughed. "You have plenty of purposes in life because you already have grandchildren."

"Each one is precious. Is Matt happy about the baby?"

"Yes, he's okay with everything," she answered carefully, trying to stick as close to the truth as she could. "Now don't start looking worried," Brianna said. "I'd rather not tell the rest of the family until after we've had the wedding. I'll tell them soon afterward, but I wanted you to know."

"That's fine. I can keep the secret, and you don't look as if you're pregnant. How far along are you?"

"Not far at all. The baby is due next summer—late June. We'll announce it soon."

"I understand. I want to meet this man who'll be my son-in-law."

"I think you'll like him," Brianna said, knowing Matt would probably charm her mother and all the rest of her family. "I'm nervous about tonight and meeting his family," Brianna admitted.

"You look beautiful, and he's lucky to get you as his bride."

Brianna smiled and brushed a kiss on her mother's cheek. "I love you, Mom."

"Your sisters are probably going to guess anyway, but your brothers never will. They won't say anything to me about it, though, nor will I to them."

"That's fine," Brianna said, feeling better now that she'd shared her news with her mother and wishing she could tell her everything about this marriage that was really a loveless union.

A knock at the door interrupted them, and Brianna's sister Melody entered with her children in tow.

Brianna smiled broadly, holding out her arms to hug the children. "Everyone looks so great!" Melody's hair had been cut as well, hanging straight with blond streaks, and her plain black dress was short enough to show off her long, shapely legs.

"So do you, Brianna," Melody replied. "Thanks for the dresses, the hotel, the haircuts. Everything is a dream."

Dressed and subdued, Phillip, who was four, and three-year-old Amanda, as well as the other children, would have two nannies to watch them after the rehearsal while the rest of the family went out to dinner.

"You think I look good," Melody said. "Wait until you see the transformation of the guys. You won't know them."

"I hope so," Brianna teased, "since they're usually working on cars in overalls covered in grease."

When her brothers and brothers-in-law entered, she saw what her sister had been talking about. Shaved, shorn and attired in conservative suits with white dress shirts and navy ties, the men had been transformed.

"Mercy! You guys do clean up well."

"So does everyone," said her youngest brother, Josh,

whose black hair was spiked in the front and combed down smoothly otherwise.

"I'm so proud of my family," she said, smiling at them. "And I want all of you to have a good time. Matt is a wonderful guy. Now, if everyone is ready, let's go."

"I can't wait to see this place," Melody said. "I've threatened the kids to behave and not touch anything."

"She's not kidding," Melody's husband, Luke, said. "She threatened me, too."

Laughter followed his announcement and more joking until Brianna raised her voice.

"Matt has limos waiting to take us to his house. Shall we go?"

As they rode through Cheyenne in the limousines provided by Matt, her nervousness returned. Once again, she experienced the same trepidation that she'd felt upon arriving in Cheyenne and again, on her first visit to the university campus. She was too aware of the limitations of her early years, her lack of cosmopolitan experiences or experience with a polite, more sophisticated segment of society. Momentarily, she envied Matt his background and his colossal self-assurance. Yet if they'd been born into the reverse circumstances, so Matt had come out of the backwoods, she couldn't imagine that he wouldn't carry off the transition to an urbanite with the same confidence and aplomb he exhibited daily now.

Her stomach churned with something worse than butterflies. Her palms were damp and she wondered if she could get herself and her family through this evening intact, or if Matt would rescind his proposal.

A uniformed man opened the door, but the minute she stepped inside, Matt was there to greet her. As soon as she saw him, her worries evaporated. Her heartbeat raced for a different reason and eagerness replaced worry.

"Am I glad to see you," he said softly, walking up to her to smile at her. "You are breathtaking and I wish we were alone for the night."

"Matt, I'll confess, I'm so nervous about tonight. You know this entire week is new to my family."

"Relax, Brianna, my family won't bite. We're here to have a good time and get ready for a wedding. Let me make an announcement to everyone and then we can do the introductions."

"Sure, whatever you want to do," she said, thankful to turn the moment over to him.

"Folks," Matt said in a deep, authoritative voice. To her surprise, he got everyone's attention and the room became silent.

"I'm Matt Rome and welcome to Cheyenne and to our rehearsal dinner. I want to thank you for coming to share this time with Brianna and with me. Now, why don't we go around the room and say our names and what relation we are. Brianna, we'll start with you."

When each of Matt's relatives spoke, she paid close attention, noticing Jared Dalton and Chase Bennett, the cousins she'd heard so much about. As her family introduced themselves, she watched each one, assessing her handiwork. Again, she focused on Danielle, whose brown hair was twisted and pinned at the back of her head. Danielle's three-year-old, Hunter, and two-year-old Emma, were as subdued as their cousins.

Finally the last person spoke, and then everyone's attention returned to Matt.

"Thanks again for coming and let's all enjoy the party! Help yourselves to drinks and hors d'oeuvres. In about an hour we'll have the rehearsal. Dinner will follow at a restaurant," Matt announced and then turned to her and people began to talk.

"Brianna, meet Megan and Jared Dalton and Laurel and Chase Bennett."

"Ah, the famous cousins," she said after greeting each in turn. Jared and Chase grinned.

"And our infamous bet," Chase added. "I think some family members are taking bets on who'll win," he said. As the men began to talk and joke about their bet, Megan took Brianna's arm. "You come with us. We've heard enough about that bet to last a lifetime," she said, pulling Brianna aside while Laurel nodded and joined them. "I suspect Megan and I wouldn't be married if it hadn't been for that bet," Laurel added dryly. "Whatever happens, the winner treats the rest to a weekend getaway, so we'll all have a wonderful weekend together."

"Those three are so competitive, yet they are truly close," Laurel said, glancing at her husband, who was nearby. The love in her gaze gave Brianna a pang, because she didn't feel that way with Matt, nor did he love her. This marriage simply secured her future. A future alone with her baby.

"This is exciting," Megan said, "and a big surprise to us. Jared didn't expect Matt to get married ever."

"Nor did Chase," Laurel added with a smile. "But then not too long ago, neither Jared nor Chase expected to marry. Life is filled with surprises."

Brianna listened as the two women talked and it was obvious that they were becoming friends although they seldom saw each other. She was glad to be included in their friendship, even though she knew it would be short-lived.

Soon she excused herself and began to circulate, going to talk to Faith, her friend who would be a bridesmaid.

"I'm so happy for you," Faith said, her light brown eyes sparkling. "This house is a dream home! I can't believe this is your house now—except I know it is."

Brianna laughed at Faith's exuberance, a relief after the tension she'd felt around her family who didn't really know the whole story.

"This is it," she said, realizing she was losing her awe about it since she'd moved in with Matt. "My first time here, I felt overwhelmed—as you should remember."

"This is the best thing that could possibly happen."

"I don't know so much about the best, but it will be good."

"Good. Stop being so pessimistic and such a worrier. He'll fall in love with you. And how could you possibly keep from falling in love with him? He's charming."

"He is that," Brianna agreed. "I'm glad you're here. I hope you're always close by. And I hope we always stay friends."

"I'm going to love having a friend like you. Have me over for a swim sometime. I've seen that pool. Mercy!"

Brianna laughed. "Wait until the honeymoon is over, and I'll call you and we can swim. Weather won't matter. Thanks for being in my wedding."

"I wouldn't miss this for the world. Thanks for inviting Cal to this, too. He likes your brothers."

"I'm glad. I hope Matt does. And vice versa, but then I expect all my family to like him. Let's get together soon. I've missed seeing you."

"Just call."

"I better go talk to Matt's family because I haven't yet."

"Get going. I'll see you later," Faith said, smiling at Brianna.

Moving through the guests and relatives, Brianna stopped to meet and talk to Matt's mother. Penny Rome put her arms around Brianna to hug her lightly. "Welcome to the family!" she said warmly. "We're so happy to see Matt marry. His dad and I'd given up on him."

"Thank you," Brianna said, smiling at Matt's tall, slender mother.

"You must be good for him—he seems more relaxed now. He's too much like his dad—constantly working whether it's necessary or not. Both of them are driven, as I guess you know about Matt by now. This marriage is good for him and we're thrilled."

"I'm glad," Brianna answered. Guilt assaulted her for the fake marriage, but she pushed it aside in her mind. If it hadn't been her, it would have been another woman.

She met and talked with his father—seeing instantly that was where Matt got his handsome looks as they both had the same coloring and features. "Welcome to our family. Mom and I are happy to see Matt settle and marry. He needs that in his life."

"Thank you," she replied politely.

"I hope you'll bring him to see us. We don't see much of him, but I understand that better than his mother does."

"We'll do that, Mr. Rome," she said.

"Brianna, you're in our family now. Call me Travis, or call me Dad if you want."

"Yes, sir. Thank you." She chatted a few minutes longer with him and then they were joined by one of Matt's sisters and Travis Rome moved away. His relatives seemed to accept her into their family and they were all friendly enough that her nervousness ebbed.

She discovered her own relatives were also enjoying themselves and at ease with Matt's side of the family. To her delight, she realized that the men in both families had a down-to-earth common thread of being cowboys, which cut across all levels of society.

Time passed quickly until they boarded limousines and were driven to dinner at an elegant restaurant. As she sat in the restaurant, she gazed at the array of silver cutlery and the crystal and was thankful she had bought an etiquette book and had been studying and coaching her family. Reaching for a shrimp fork, she felt more relaxed and assured than she would have a week earlier.

The one flaw in a perfect evening was Zach Gentner. He shook hands with her, greeting her with a coldness that mirrored her own. She hadn't given any thought to Zach being present, but if he was as close to Matt as he'd said, then he would be included in the wedding party.

During the evening, there was never a moment alone with Matt and she returned to the hotel with her family, going to her suite where she was finally alone. Long into the night she sat up. The next morning would be her wedding, and she was already too far in now to back out of the agreement even if she had wanted to. To her relief, her family had made it through the evening without too many obvious blunders. Hopefully, Matt's money would help give them the opportunities they needed to better their lives.

Tomorrow night the wedding would be over and she would legally be Mrs. Matt Rome. Merely thinking about it gave her a flutter of anticipation.

Finally the moment arrived to step into the large room where they were to be married. Both families and a few close friends were standing as an organist played and Brianna walked in with her arm linked with her youngest brother's. She met Matt's gaze. In a navy suit and tie, he looked handsome, confident and pleased. She felt assured about her appearance—having checked a dozen times before leaving the room where she dressed. Even though her knee-length white silk suit was plain, she liked its simple lines. A diamond and sapphire necklace wedding gift from Matt sparkled around her throat and a gorgeous diamond engagement ring sparkled on her finger. Tiny white rosebuds bedecked her pinned-up black hair.

Her brother placed her hand in Matt's and then she turned to gaze into his eyes as she said vows that she knew would be broken eventually. How hollow the words rang in her ears! For an instant guilt assailed her over the farce they were perpetrating, but then she remembered what each one was gaining. If it hadn't been her, it would have been another woman. She reminded herself again of the things she intended to do to care for her mother, the things that she would be able to do for herself.

After a brief kiss from Matt, they walked out of the room together as newlyweds.

The party commenced in one of his large reception rooms. Outside, flakes of snow swirled while fires blazed in each big fireplace and a band serenaded them.

When Matt drew her into his arms for the first dance, he smiled at her. "For a small wedding, we gathered quite a crowd. We each have sizable families."

"I can't imagine what a large wedding would have been like. This one is huge to me," she said, barely aware of her conversation because most of her attention was on the handsome man dancing with her. Her pulse raced and she was eager to be alone with him. She was conscious of their legs brushing, of her hand enclosed in his warm grasp. As she gazed up into his eyes, she could see the change from the polite smile he had been giving friends and family all day. Desire blazed in the depths of his crystal-blue eyes.

"This is great, Brianna," he said.

"Yes, it is. I'm still overwhelmed and overjoyed. Matt, you've been so good to my family. You were nice and patient with them."

"They're friendly people," he answered.

"Unless they get snowed in, they're all leaving tomorrow morning to drive home. This snow is supposed to stop soon, so it shouldn't amount to much."

"Have you told any of them about our arrangement?" he asked and she shook her head.

"No one. They've heard of you and now they've seen your house and had this weekend, but they don't know the extent of the wealth. They think I'm fortunate, but they have their lives and they'll return to their routines tomorrow. This weekend will be a memory."

"I thought maybe they'd want a bit more after this weekend."

"No. I don't think they've guessed quite what I can do."

"My family is staying here and we can leave before the party breaks up. Why don't we in an hour?" he suggested, and her heart missed a beat. They were leaving here and tonight this marriage would be consummated. She tingled with anticipation.

"Whenever you say," she whispered. "We still need to cut the—"

"I'll come get you at an opportune time," he broke in. He moved on in the crowd and after cutting the cake, for the next hour, she chatted and smiled constantly and hoped she didn't say anything that was nonsense because her attention was half on the handsome man she had married. She had never liked the Cinderella fairy tale because it seemed the antithesis of real life. Prince Charming didn't come along and transform the life of his love, someone poor and uneducated. She didn't expect that to happen, couldn't even imagine it happened. Yet today, the moment she became Mrs. Matthew Rome, it had occurred. She now had money, a hefty savings, investments and a large bank account plus more cash in her purse at one time than she'd ever had in her life.

She watched Matt with a circle of friends, women gazing up at him adoringly, men laughing and joking with him. A beautiful brunette stood close to him with her hand on his arm while she told him something and the group laughed. There was no reason for any jealousy. Married or single, Matt would always have other women after him, but she expected him to keep his promise to remain faithful as long as they were married.

As she watched, Matt took a cell phone out of his pocket and walked away from the crowd to head toward the hall. A couple came up to talk and then a friend appeared who asked her to dance and she lost Matt in the crowd.

Matt listened to one of his analysts discuss an acquisition while he threaded his way through the guests and into the hallway. Replacing the phone in his pocket, Matt heard a familiar voice and turned to face his cousin Chase.

"I thought you might like a drink," Chase said, handing Matt a glass of wine.

"Thanks. One glass of champagne is about all I can bear."

"You have a beautiful bride."

"Thanks, I think so. So do you."

"Thank you. The difference is, I'm in love with mine," Chase said quietly.

Matt gazed into his cousin's green eyes that were steady and filled with what looked like pity. "How'd you know?"

"When you know someone as well as you and I and Jared know each other, it shows," Chase said, flicking his head slightly so stray locks of his straight brown hair would go back into place above his forehead.

"My folks have been fooled."

"They probably don't want to know the truth. I think I can guess why you did it. Jared told me he asked Megan for a marriage of convenience, but she wouldn't have any part of it, and then later they fell in love all over again."

"So Jared knows, too," Matt said, wondering how many others in his family realized the truth.

"Yep, and I didn't tell him. We both came to the same conclusion before we ever said anything to each other. In some ways maybe this bet wasn't such a great idea. If our wager thrust you into a loveless marriage—"

"Whoa," Matt interrupted. "I'm delighted and she's thrilled. She's getting two mil for this marriage and I'm having a dream affair that I would have pursued anyway, wedding or not. We're very content."

"You may be pleased, but you're not in love. There's a vast difference. Even so, it's good to hear that this isn't quite the business arrangement Jared and I assumed it was."

"It isn't remotely a purely business arrangement. I think she's fantastic."

"She's a beauty and very charming. Maybe before too long you both will be in love. Here's hoping you are."

Matt smiled. "Don't count on that one."

"I'm glad she's getting money out of the deal, and I hope that she thinks it's worth it to be hitched to you."

"If I do say so myself, I think the lady looks happy."

"That she does. And may you both be fulfilled in your bargain." Chase held out his drink. They touched glasses and sipped their wine.

"Where'd you find her? What debutante list? She looks younger."

"She's twenty-three. She's been going to college, she's from a tiny backwoods town, she's never been out of Wyoming and she's never flown in a plane."

Chase laughed. "So both of you are in for big changes."

"One of us is."

Chase chuckled. "You may be caught in a bramble bush of your own making. She told me she wants to get a law degree."

"I have no doubt that she will. Now she can easily afford to enroll."

"No problem there. She could have a zilch IQ and with her looks and as your wife, it wouldn't matter." Chase's mouth curled in a crooked grin. "Unless—"

"Unless what?" Matt narrowed his eyes, knowing he shouldn't even ask.

"Unless she's really smart and gives you a run for your money." Chase chuckled. "That would be fun. At least for Jared and me to watch, although you'll never let us know if you come out holding the short end of the stick. Or if you fall in love and she dumps you. 'Course that one, we might know."

"Right. Quit wringing your hands with glee—it won't happen. And I intend to win our bet."

Chase had a wide grin this time. "Sure, coz. We all aim to do that. And one of us will. We each have our own idea about who it will be."

"Speaking of my wife, I want to find her. Where's Laurel?"

"Dancing with an old friend the last I saw. I wish you luck, coz," Chase said with a grin as the two men went in search of their wives.

Brianna listened to someone who was speaking in the cluster of people around her, yet her mind was on Matt.

Soon now they could escape the party, get away to themselves. Anticipation continued to grow. A dark cloud loomed on her horizon—this marriage was as loveless as it was temporary.

She knew the one thing she had to constantly re-member was Matt's true nature and love of money.

And then she caught his gaze and her pulse jumped. Across the large room, too far apart to communicate, someone who had been a stranger to her only a short time ago, now could exchange a glance with her and send her pulse into overdrive.

Still watching, she knew when he excused himself and began to move through the crowd toward her. Soon her life would really begin as Mrs. Matt Rome.

Six

That night, Matt carried her over the threshold of his Manhattan penthouse overlooking Central Park, a mere private jet flight away. Setting her on her feet, he wrapped his arms around her waist. "Welcome home, Mrs. Rome," he said and her heart thudded and she wished with all her heart that they had a real marriage.

She struggled to let go of all worries about his cold heart in order to try to make this wedding night a thrilling memory, untainted by reality.

She wanted to love him, to have him make love to her, wondering if this night would be any better and not the disappointment that lovemaking had been in the past. She stood on tiptoe to kiss him.

His arms tightened around her, crushing her to him

while she combed her fingers into his thick mass of
curly hair and wrapped her other arm around his neck.
Leaning over her, he kissed her possessively, groaning
with longing, his tongue a slow, hot exploration.

She thrust her hips against him, knowing they could
take hours, certain he was the kind of consummate lover
that would be deliberate, tantalizing, infinitely sexy.

Each kiss and caress heightened her appetite for him.
She poured herself into her kisses, wanting to obliter-
ate the stream of women that must have been in his life.

Shoving away his jacket, she unfastened the studs of
his shirt. His fingers tangled in her hair, sending pins
flying and he combed out her long locks slowly while
he continued to kiss her.

She pushed away his shirt and ran her hands across his
broad shoulders, sliding them down to tangle in his soft,
dark chest hair. She freed him of his trousers that fell away.

As she traced kisses over his muscled stomach, he
groaned and lifted her to her feet. Unzipping her dress
and pushing it away, he held her hips while lust darkened his expression.

He stood in his low-cut, narrow briefs that couldn't
contain him while he looked at her leisurely, a heated
gaze that was as tangible as a caress.

"You're gorgeous," he whispered, unfastening the
clasp to yank away her lace bra. Cupping her breasts in
his hands, he rubbed his thumbs over her nipples lightly
in an enticing torment.

She gasped, gripping his narrow waist and closing her
eyes while streaks of pleasure streamed from his touch.

"This is a dream," she whispered, winding her fingers in his thick curls as he bent down to take her nipple in his mouth, to kiss and suck and tease, his tongue circling where his thumb had been.

"No dream," he said, the words coming out slowly as his ragged breathing was loud. Hooking his thumbs in the narrow band of her thong and her pantyhose, he peeled them away and she stepped out of the last of her underclothes. He held her hips again, straightening and leaning away to look at her as she stood naked before him.

"I've waited too long for this moment," he whispered.

"There should be more to it," she whispered, unable to refrain from letting her bitterness slip about this loveless night. If he heard, he didn't acknowledge it. She peeled away his briefs and he stepped out of them, leaning down to pull off his socks.

As he straightened he picked her up and she raised her face to his, winding her arms around his neck, without looking to see where he carried her.

Still kissing her, he placed her on the bed. He was astride her and he leaned over to shower kisses to her breasts, his tongue stroking each pouty bud. His fingers drifted across her belly, down over her thigh and then so lightly, back up between her thighs. Her cry was loud in the silence, the tantalizing need building in her. Matt was loving her and she could make love to him in return, man and wife for tonight at least.

Reaching to caress him, she opened her legs to him. She kept her eyes closed as Matt explored and teased slowly, his caresses feathery touches, his tongue hot and wet, her need intensifying swiftly.

Driving away her thoughts about a loveless union, he moved lower, raining kisses down the inside of her leg, holding her foot as he caressed her and his hands played over her. Beneath his touch, she arched her hips and writhed.

His muscled thighs were covered in short, curly black hairs that gave slight friction against her skin.

"Turn over," he whispered, rolling her over without waiting. And then he moved between her legs, his fingers playing over her, touching, caressing and exploring, discovering where he could touch to get the biggest response from her. His tongue followed where his fingers had been and when he slipped his hands along the inside of her thighs, sliding higher until he touched her intimately, she gasped and attempted to roll over, but he placed his hand in the middle of her back.

"Lie still, Brianna," he ordered, his fingers driving her to dig her fists into the bed and spread her legs wider.

She moaned, crying out, attempting to turn until finally he allowed her to and then his hand was back between her thighs, touching, rubbing, exploring, another constant tease.

Losing all awareness of anything except his hands and mouth on her, she arched wildly, spreading her legs so he had full access to her.

"Brianna, love, you're beautiful!" he gasped, but she barely heard what he said and paid no heed. She had to have him inside her, wanting his heat and hardness.

With a cry, she raised her hips higher. "Love me!" she gasped as she fell back and he kissed her deeply. She returned his loving, but then pushed him away and down on the bed to climb astride him and pour kisses down across his belly as she stroked his hard rod.

She shifted to take him in her mouth, her tongue circling the velvet tip while he clenched his fists in her hair and groaned, letting her kiss and caress him for minutes until he sat up suddenly to pull her to him and lean over her, kissing her thoroughly.

She kissed him in return until he placed her on the bed and started the loving anew, his hands playing over her lightly, caressing while her need climbed to a fever pitch.

He moved between her legs, hooking them over his shoulders to give him access to her as he kissed and stroked her.

Her eyes fluttered open and she saw him watching her when she gasped with gratification.

"Do you like this?" he whispered, his tongue flicking over her and she moaned softly.

"Yes, yes," she whispered, caressing his strong thighs, stroking his manhood. "Love me, Matt," she whispered, placing her hands on his hips, to tug him closer as he continued to caress and kiss her.

When he moved between her legs and she opened her eyes to look at him, her heart thudded with longing. He was handsome male perfection, ready and poised. Tangles of black curls fell on his forehead and his face was flushed. His body was lean, hard muscles and his manhood thick and ready.

She held her arms out to him. "Love me, Matt. Become part of me."

He lowered himself, wrapping an arm around her as he kissed her passionately again.

Slowly, he entered her, the hot, hard tip of his manhood plunging into her softness, making her cry out with longing. Still kissing her, he withdrew. His kiss muffled her cry as he entered her again, hot and slow, filling her and withdrawing, tempting and stirring desire to white heat.

The teasing heightened enjoyment while driving her wild with wanting him to love her, reaching a point she'd never known where she was desperate for his loving.

She tore her mouth from his. "Matt, I want you!" she cried, arching against him, her hands sliding over his firm bottom trying to draw him closer, her legs tightening around his waist.

He entered her slowly and she moved beneath him, and then they rocked together.

With her blood thundering in her ears and her eyes squeezed tightly closed, she held him, crying out for him to keep loving her. When she climaxed, spasms shook her and ecstasy consumed her. Lights burst behind her closed eyelids and she couldn't stop moving with him until she climaxed again and heard him cry her name.

As she clung to him, he thrust wildly in her. Enjoyment she'd never known before rippled with aftershocks of pleasure.

Finally, they quieted, their ragged breathing returning to normal as he showered light kisses on her face and shoulders and murmured endearments she couldn't believe.

Turning his head, he kissed her fully on the mouth, a long, slow kiss of gratification. They had shared the time with a mutual pleasure but love was missing. Even though he acted like a man in love, she knew he wasn't.

Holding him close, she caressed him while they continued to kiss until finally he raised his head. "You were worth the wait, Brianna. My decision is justified."

Once again he focused on himself, reminding her she was locked into a businesslike bargain. "I can say the same." She was unwilling to think beyond the present moment.

This time with him was fleeting and false. On the plus side, if they had been wildly in love, she couldn't imagine they would have had better sex. He truly was the consummate lover she had expected.

Finally, holding her close against him, he rolled onto his side.

"I don't want to let you go. I can't believe my good fortune in finding you," he whispered.

"I suppose we can both feel fortunate," she said lazily, enjoying being held in his arms and feeling euphoric, trying to keep at bay all the hurt over the lack of love in their relationship, yet feeling an emptiness behind the pleasure.

His hands played lightly over her and he showered kisses on her temple, throat and ear, all faint touches that rekindled her desire.

"Ah, Brianna, you're the best," he murmured, yet

she paid little heed, assuming he was repeating what he'd said before. Deep inside, along with desire for sex, was a hungry need for a true relationship that she couldn't dissolve. She should be more like Matt and focus on the money involved in this arrangement, but it was turning out almost from the first that she couldn't.

"Come here, darlin'," he said, leaning down to scoop her into his arms. Wrapping her arms around him, she combed locks of his hair off his forehead.

"Where are you taking me?" Without waiting for his answer, she pulled him closer to kiss him.

When he raised his head, he crossed the room with her and entered a huge bathroom that held a sunken tub. Matt set her on her feet and turned spigots. "We'll bathe together," he said, testing the water and then turning to pick her up again and carry her into the tub.

Setting her on her feet, he kissed her while water rose and swirled around their legs. Finally, he stopped and took her into his arms again to sit down, holding her close against him.

"You've got an insatiable appetite," she whispered. She could feel his manhood, thick and hard and ready for her again.

"What can I say? You make my blood boil."

"I can do something about that right now," she said in a sultry voice, turning and sitting astride him to lower herself onto him. Desire ignited again, a hungry need that she couldn't believe had been so totally satisfied only a short time earlier, yet now she wanted him with a desperation that seemed fiercer than ever.

He kissed her as she moved on him and in minutes she cried out when she climaxed and felt him shudder from his own orgasm.

Soon she was seated between his legs in a tub of hot, swirling water.

"Better and better," she murmured and felt a rumble in his chest when he laughed softly.

"Before the night is over I'll show you better and better," he promised and her pulse jumped at the prospect.

"This is temporary," she said without thinking.

"Shh," he commanded. "It's not temporary tonight and it won't end anyway, not until we want it to end."

"Until you want it to end," she corrected. "But no matter. Tonight I don't want any angst. This is the best ever," she said, trying to ignore that nagging inner voice.

When they climbed out and toweled each other dry, as she lightly rubbed the soft terry cloth over his body, she looked into his hungry blue eyes. A flame started low inside her.

While he continued to watch her, he rubbed her nipples lightly with a dry towel. Then his towel slipped between her legs as he stroked her.

She gasped, closing her eyes, and he tossed aside his towel to pull her closer, one arm circling her waist and his other hand stroking her soft feminine bud while he kissed her.

In minutes she had her eyes squeezed tightly shut as she held him and moved, his hand driving her wild.

"Matt, I want your love," she said, meaning it literally, knowing he would think only in terms of passion.

He picked her up to carry her to bed and finish what he'd started. Midmorning while they lazed in each other's arms in bed, he combed her hair from her face with his fingers. Caressing his chest, she curled the tight hairs around her forefinger.

"Matt, I'm beginning to have hunger pangs. I think the meal yesterday on the plane was the last time we ate."

"Could be," he drawled in a lazy, satisfied voice. "The only hunger I have is for you," he said, his voice thickening as he rolled on his side and gazed at her. "A penny for your thoughts."

"You'd have to pay a lot more than that. Besides, you can probably guess my thoughts," she drawled in a throaty tone and saw his eyes darken. Could he possibly surmise what she was contemplating, or what she really wanted? If she could, would she trade his money for his love? The question came out of the blue and was one she didn't want to pursue. Why did it matter so much to her? Yet she knew exactly why, and the closer she drew to him in physical intimacy, the more she wanted an emotional relationship. Love was never part of the equation, she reminded herself.

He drew his finger along the top of the sheet where it curved over her breasts, a faint touch that stirred tingles and aroused her again.

She caught his hand. "You wait. You're going to have to feed me before you have me again, mister."

"You think?" he asked, sounding amused. "There's a challenge that I might have to rise to."

"You've already risen and you need to cool it," she

said, knowing she was fighting a battle she didn't even want to win. "How easily you can manipulate me," she said. "Shameless!"

"I'll show you shameless," he retorted, rolling her onto her back and moving over her to lick and kiss until she forgot about food and only wanted him.

"Matt, come here!" she cried, pulling him over her and wrapping her long legs around his waist.

He lowered himself into her, thrusting hard and fast this time as she rose to meet him.

With another burst of satisfaction, she climaxed. Rapture enveloped her while she continued to move with him until he climaxed and called out her name.

"Brianna! Love! My love!"

She knew the endearments were meaningless and she should ignore them, but for today, she relished knowing he wanted her.

Later, she curled against him in his arms with her hair spilling across his chest. She could hear the steady beat of his heart, feel the rhythmic thumping beneath her hand. She was satiated, lethargic.

"I can't move," she whispered, running her forefinger in slow circles through his thick chest hair.

"We'll bathe and then go eat."

"I think we had the same plans earlier, but they went awry. Perhaps we shouldn't bathe together this time."

"Perish the thought. A simple bath and food. The simplicities of life."

"It doesn't seem to work out that way. This time, I'll tip the scales in favor of getting to eat," she said and slipped out of bed, gathering a sheet around her as she hurried away from him to the bathroom to shower alone. She locked the bathroom door behind her, certain if he came and pounded on it, she would open it at once.

To her surprise, he let her go and she showered and dried in total silence. Wrapping herself in a thick maroon towel, she went to find him.

She located Matt with glasses of orange juice, a pot of coffee, a tall glass of milk and covered dishes, some on the table and some still on a nearby cart. He wore jeans and a T-shirt and his hair was wet.

She walked up behind him to slide her arms around his waist. "You're a fast cook."

"I used my powers of persuasion to get room service to deliver on the double. Now feast away, my love. I ordered everything I could think you might like."

His "my love" stung. She wasn't his "love" and it bothered her more than she'd expected it would. She tried to focus on all she was gaining, but love was turning out to be far more important than she'd expected.

With her appetite suddenly diminished, she sat down, opening dishes and discovering tempting omelets, scrambled eggs, hot biscuits, slices of ham, strips of bacon, bowls of strawberries and a fruit plate with grapes, melons and pineapple slices.

"This is the ideal way to start the day," he said, and his tone took her attention from food. She looked up to see him seated, watching her with his head propped on his fist.

"Aren't you going to eat?" she asked.

"Yes, but I was thinking about last night."

She waved her fork at him. "Do not think lusty thoughts until I've had breakfast. I really forbid it!"

"Yes, ma'am, sexy wench."

She laughed. "Not really. What's our schedule?"

"Tomorrow we fly to Rome," he said.

"I hope I see it. I haven't seen anything of New York City. Not even the park, which is right across the street."

"We'll be back here soon, I promise. Then I'll take you anywhere you want to go."

She set down her fork and took a drink of milk. "You've given me paradise and allowed me to do things I could only dream about before."

"It's a good arrangement," he said. She hoped she hid her disappointment, because he could have been discussing a business transaction he'd made.

In minutes she forgot her disappointment as she returned to eating breakfast, determined to get a glimpse of Central Park before he carried her back to bed.

With each passing mile of their flight to Rome, Matt was pleased to see she was captivated. She hovered at the window, looking at little more than clouds and water, yet she seemed totally engrossed. "Flying is the best possible means of travel!" she said.

"If you'll save all that enthusiasm until we're in bed, this will really be a memorable day."

She smiled. "I'll remember this flight always," she said, and he wondered how long they would stay together. Right now, he was unable to imagine tiring of her, but he always eventually grew bored with women. Yet he suspected Brianna would last longer than any of the others ever had.

"I'll bring you back plenty of times, Brianna, so you'll be able to fly more often than you'll want. You'll see Europe to your heart's content."

"I can't envision such a thing. You take this for granted. Even if I moved here to live, I can't imagine ever being that way."

"You'll be a jaded traveler, I promise."

"Don't make promises you can't keep. We'll never know who's right, but I feel certain I am."

"I'll tell you what I want—I want you in my arms in bed."

"Later, later," she said, waving her fingers at him without tearing her gaze from outside the window. "I want to see everything."

"I figured you would," he answered with amusement. "Enjoy it. Rome will be more fascinating than ocean and clouds."

"I'm scared to even think about Rome," she said.

"You—scared? I don't believe it. You'll be fine, and as my wife, you'll be totally accepted."

"I want to see as much as possible in the short time we'll be there."

"I'll repeat—I promise to bring you back, so you don't have to try to see and do everything this time," he said. He suspected he was going to have to do the tourist things sometime this week for her sake, but he'd be thinking about how he couldn't wait to make love again.

* * *

In Rome, they moved into a luxurious suite in the hotel where Matt usually stayed. She gawked only slightly at the elegant lobby, and then they were locked in their suite and could have been in a tent as far as the outside world was concerned.

Matt had intended to show her Rome, but his intentions were lost in lovemaking until Friday, when he left her a limo and driver while he attended a meeting.

She had a whirlwind tour, stopping at the Colosseum and at St. Peter's. As she stood in St. Peter's Square and admired the beauty of the ancient Basilica, she thought how some of her dreams had become empty and disillusioning.

All through the years of growing up with hardships and only hopes of becoming affluent, and then through the generous bargain with Matt, she had thought riches would give her all she wanted. Matt's money would give her, her baby and her family comfort, education and security—but the rest was empty.

She had been thrilled over the prospect of a honeymoon in Rome, but now that she was here, it was not the pleasure she had expected. She wished she had someone with her to share each discovery—there would be no great memories to take home from this trip. She'd brought her camera, yet she didn't care to keep any pictures. Love was missing and it made a difference.

The real disappointment was Matt. There were moments he was charming company. How easily she could fall in love with him if only—

She stopped that train of thought. Matt was who he was, and she had to accept it. He was at a meeting today, working to get even more wealth. Yet she had been guilty, too, of placing too much importance on money.

She stood in the square, combing her breeze-tussled hair away from her cheek with her fingers, and realized she would never feel quite the same about what was truly important in life.

Strolling around, she only half looked at her surroundings, still lost in her thoughts and hurting because she had locked herself into a situation where she lived with a charming man who didn't even know she existed except in bed.

Finally, she turned away to head back to the limo, wanting to stop her sightseeing for the day, wondering if she would ever return to Rome with someone she loved.

Later in the afternoon, Matt arrived, sweeping in the door and kicking it closed as he pulled her into his embrace.

"How did you like Rome?" he asked, and her half-hearted answer was lost in his kisses, her sightseeing report forgotten.

Getting ready for the charity ball, Brianna took her things to the large bathroom. She knew Matt had already showered and was dressing which would take him no time. When she finished bathing, she expected to have the bedroom and bathroom to herself. She didn't want distractions from Matt while she got ready and she continually ran through the list of names of the investors and facts about them.

As she dressed, she wondered if Matt had concerns about his new wife's inexperience. So far, he'd expressed absolutely none. She felt as if anyone could glance at her and sense her background, her lack of experience and sophistication, yet she reminded herself that Matt's monumental self-assurance would cover a lot.

Repeatedly during the trip, she had been thankful for the honeymoon being in Italy and the ball being in Rome, because for the past two years she had been studying Italian in college. Since she felt she might be interested in international law, she wanted a minor in languages. The day she learned about the ball, she'd even gone out and bought a crash course in "Teach Yourself Conversational Italian" to practice further.

Finally, she went to find him at his desk, poring over something. The desk light caught glints in his thick black hair. She wondered how he could tune out the world and concentrate on business when he had only minutes before leaving for a glamorous evening with people he intended to impress. Her palms were damp with nervousness and she felt the same as she had on the first job interview in Cheyenne.

"Matt," she said softly.

"One minute, Brianna," he answered, his head still bent over figures. "I want one more minute to finish this list," he said. "I'm in the middle of—" His words died as he glanced up at her and he stared at her. "You're gorgeous," he said, his voice becoming husky as it did when he was aroused.

She let out her breath. One hurdle passed. Her pulse speeded when he circled the desk toward her, never taking his gaze from her.

When he crossed the room, she tingled. Fighting the urge to smooth her skirt, she knew she was dressed as flawlessly as she could in a scarlet sleeveless dress that was the most expensive dress she'd ever owned with the exception of her wedding outfit. Cut in a low V neckline, the skirt split up one side to an inch above her knees and she wore matching sandals.

"You look too beautiful to waste the evening at a ball," he whispered, walking up to her and slipping an arm around her waist. As he leaned toward her, she pushed lightly against him, wiggled out of his embrace and stepped away.

"Not so soon. You don't know how long I worked to achieve this look. Let's go. When we return tonight, you can do as you please and I promise I won't protest."

He groaned. "You make things so difficult."

"You'll manage," she said, smiling at him while her pulse raced.

"Shall we go?" he asked, offering her his arm. She nodded and stepped close to loop her arm through his.

The streets of Rome were congested. Traffic was busy, and her case of nerves returned, but not as threatening as before because now she was at ease with Matt and he was the one person who mattered.

"This city is beautiful," she said, knowing this

night would remain a vivid memory for the rest of her life.

"Yes," he answered, smiling at her. "Did you enjoy the sights? I haven't heard about your day."

"Of course I did. I hope yours was successful— whatever your meeting was about."

"About an investment I have. Yes, I had a productive meeting. And now we're going to impress some people tonight," he said, still smiling.

"Rome seems incredibly noisy. Scooters are everywhere," she said, barely aware of her statement, trying to stop reflecting on Matt's ambition.

"Here we are," he said. "I want you to have a memorable evening."

The limo halted in front of the canopied door of a luxury hotel where lights blazed. As she emerged, her nervousness climbed. She inhaled deeply, glancing at Matt, who looked drop-dead handsome in his tux. Smiling at her, he turned to hold her hand. Squaring her shoulders, she decided to simply enjoy herself and to stop worrying over the impression she might make.

Her heart twisted because he was still thinking about work and the investors.

They entered the large ballroom, where a waltz played and couples danced.

From the first moment in the door, Matt greeted people and introduced her to too many to recall. The names of the investors she finally had firmly in mind and within minutes she saw the first one approach. He was a tall, black-haired man with a beautiful black-haired woman was at his side. His dark gaze was on Brianna. "Here comes—"

"Signore Ruffuli and his wife, Letta," Brianna said quietly to Matt. "And his wife doesn't speak English."

"Very good!" Matt smiled broadly, turning to greet the couple.

"Buona sera, Signore Rufulli e Signora Rufulli," Matt acknowledged his friend and his wife. *"Vorrei presentarle a la mia sposa,"* Matt said in fluent Italian, turning to make introductions to Brianna.

"Buona sera, Signori Rufulli. Piaciere di fare la loro conoscenza. Che bella serata." Brianna smiled as she greeted them.

While the men talked, the two women conversed until Matt took her arm as they walked on to meet others.

"You surprised me," he said. "You didn't tell me you speak Italian."

"It's very limited. In college I had two years and I studied a little in one of those crash courses on a CD, 'Teach Yourself Conversational Italian,' before we came tonight."

"I'm impressed," Matt said as he gave her an appraising study and she wondered what he was thinking.

"I intended you to be," she said, turning to smile at a blond man who approached them and shook hands with Matt as he greeted him.

"Brianna, please meet Sven Ingstad. Sven, I want you to meet Brianna Rome."

"I hoped to meet your lovely wife," he said in a courtly manner while he smiled at her.

Gradually, they circled the fringe of the dance floor and she met all the men from the investment group who were present. She knew from beforehand that three wouldn't be present at the charity ball.

Finally, she was in Matt's arms to dance, and as they whirled across the floor, he studied her. "You have facets to you I know nothing about. I may have to reassess my expectations."

"If you think that, from my standpoint, the evening just became a success," she said, flirting with him.

"Then I think we can both count tonight as a big accomplishment. You've captivated them."

She laughed. "I hardly think 'captivated' is the correct description. I hope they like and approve of me," she said, refraining from adding that he was the one whose opinion of her was important.

"There isn't another man on this earth who wouldn't approve of you," Matt said, and his voice dropped a notch lower. "Wait and see, as the evening wears on, who wants to dance with you."

Except that approval by others was important to Matt, she hardly cared about his business acquaintances. Matt was pleased with her because it moved him closer to his goal, but she still had the feeling that he saw her only in those terms—and through desire. Matt never seemed to miss the women who had gone out of his life. Why did she expect to be different? Was there any way to break through that total focus he had on wealth and make him see her as part of his life? And since when had she started wanting to? Was she already falling in love with him in spite of fully knowing what he was like?

"How long do you think it will take before they invite you to join?" she asked.

"I can't answer that. I don't think they will for a couple of months at the earliest. Anxious for this marriage to end?" he asked and she wondered how much he was teasing and how serious he was.

"Not at all," she said. "Why would I be? I'm doing the Grand Tour. I don't want this to end."

"That wasn't the answer I hoped for," he said, gazing at her with a questioning speculation. "I wanted a reason that included me," he said and, again, she wondered at his statement.

"So do you want to hear that I think you're the sexiest man on earth and I can't wait to be back in bed with you?"

His blue eyes darkened. "The first possible moment, we're out of here," he said.

The music ended and Sven Ingstad appeared to ask her to dance, followed by another Italian acquaintance of Matt's who was widowed.

Wide doors were opened on an adjoining reception area where long tables were covered in fancy dishes of caviar, foie gras, truffles, brandied fruit, crepes, tempting chocolate extravagances and other exotic dishes she couldn't recognize. Throughout the evening, talking with wives, or in clusters of people she had met tonight, it was her tall, handsome husband who took her attention. Even when separated, she was aware of where he was, glimpsing him while he danced one time with each of the investors' wives and she knew he charmed each one and probably impressed on them how delighted he was to be married.

Most of his time was spent at her side; he poured the attention on her and she suspected it was for the benefit of those investors he hoped to convince that he was happy in his union. Who would think a man on his honeymoon wasn't wildly in love with his new wife? Whatever his motive, she enjoyed Matt's undivided attention, his flirting, his amusing anecdotes.

When the band took a break for an intermission, a dignitary stepped to the microphone and introduced the planners of the ball. Then awards were made to the six largest contributors and Matt was called forward to receive a plaque, which he placed on their table.

"Matt, that's terrific!"

He barely glanced at the plaque. "It was a good cause and it's tax deductible," he said and she guessed he contributed to impress the investors.

In a short time the band commenced playing again and Brianna was swept back up into the fray.

Later, dancing with Matt, Brianna was surprised to discover it was midnight. "The evening has flown, Matt. I'll always remember this night and every detail of it."

"I'm glad. And I think we've stayed as long as newlyweds should be expected to. We're leaving," he said.

Her pulse jumped because as successful as the evening had been, the prospect of making love with Matt was vastly more exciting. She'd had her night in Rome, but now it was time to return to the privacy of their suite with a man who had to be the most fantastic lover possible.

Seven

When they were seated in the limousine and on the road with the partition to the front of the limo closed, Matt pulled her onto his lap.

"You were an asset tonight," he said, thinking she had been. She had surprised him and he was certain charmed many others. "I've been waiting to do this." He removed the pins from her hair and dropped them into his pocket.

Her green eyes were clear, fringed with thick black eyelashes, her lips full and soft. He wanted her with an intensity that seemed to increase each day.

"You wait until we get home. This is far too public and we might have to stop for some reason."

"I won't wait to kiss you," he said, knowing that would be an impossibility. For hours he had been ready to leave the ball, but he had known he should stay to shmooze with the investor group. He wanted them to know Brianna and to see that he was happily married.

He wondered if he would be invited into their group soon. If so, what about Brianna? He wasn't ready to dissolve their marriage. She was looking out the window of the limo, lost in her own thoughts. He toyed with long locks of her hair. "I haven't heard much about the places you went today. All you said was you enjoyed the sights."

"St. Mark's was beautiful." She studied him. "I'd guess that when you look at it, you are simply trying to estimate the value of it."

He smiled. "I'll have to admit, I've given thought to its monetary value because the amount would be staggering."

"Not to you. And if you could turn a profit, I think you'd go after even a famous landmark."

"Never a sacred one. No, I don't think I would. Usually, famous landmarks are national treasures or otherwise off-limits or not financially feasible. Is something bothering you?"

She gazed impassively at him. "Marriage, even a businesslike paper one, is complicated. Living with another person is a big change."

"I take it that's a convoluted yes. Is this because I haven't taken you sightseeing?"

She shook her head. "Just little adjustments. It's good between us, Matt," she said, smiling at him. "You know it is."

Puzzled, he appraised her. "It's spectacular between us," he answered.

"Watch out, you'll get accustomed to having me in your life," she said with a twinkle in her eyes, and he smiled at her.

"I know I want you here now for damn sure," he replied. "Don't tell me you're getting emotionally tied up in this marriage?" he asked.

"I know better than to do that," she answered easily, running her hand over his knee, and he forgot their discussion.

Matt wrapped his arms around her and nuzzled her neck. She smelled sweet and was soft and he wished they could get home faster because he wanted to take her to bed. He raised his head to gaze into her eyes, seeing desire dance in their depths.

"Brianna," he said and she looked into his eyes. He leaned the last few inches to kiss her, a long, lingering kiss that she returned with fire.

"This damn drive is too long," he said, once, and then bent to kiss her again. His fingers sought her zipper, but she caught his wrist.

"I'll remind you. We wait until we get back to our suite. This limo isn't the place."

"It is for me," he said. "I'll do what you want, but once we're in our suite, then I get my way." He pulled her close, cradling her head against his shoulder as he returned to kissing her.

The moment they entered their suite, he caught her to pull her into his embrace.

"Now, beautiful, I get to make long, slow love to you." He kissed her again and stopped thinking.

* * *

Around noon the next day, Matt gave Brianna a list of stores she might like and she left in the limo to go shopping.

The phone rang and he answered to hear Zach's voice.

"We acquired the property you wanted in Chicago," his friend said. "The contract is on your desk and you can sign when you return. They know you're on your honeymoon."

"Good."

"How'd the ball go?"

"How do you think? She wowed them," he answered without waiting for Zach's reply. "She was stunning, brilliant, charming the investors. She even conversed in Italian."

"I'm glad," Zach said. "Matt, if I'm wrong, I'll admit it. You know that. Maybe I underestimated her."

"I think you did," Matt said quietly.

"Be funny if you fall in love with the little woman."

Matt laughed. "No danger. And the 'little woman' has her own plans for the future."

"Sure," Zach said as if Matt had stated that Brianna could fly to Mars. "No morning sickness?"

"Nothing. If I hadn't heard her talk about her doctor's appointment, I wouldn't believe that she's pregnant. It doesn't show yet even slightly and she feels great. She's pumped up about the travel because she's never been anywhere, so that makes it fun."

"Will wonders never cease," Zach muttered.

"Matter of fact, Zach, see if you can clear my calendar next week. I think we'll stay longer. We might as well take one more week."

"Am I talking to Matthew Rome?" Zach asked, suddenly sounding puzzled.

"You heard what I said. Clear my calendar and I'll be in touch. Let me know if anything urgent develops."

He broke the connection and waited with his hand on the phone, lost in thought about Brianna and the night before. His gaze went to the empty bed and he wished she were still here. He wanted her as if they'd never made love. He couldn't concentrate on business for thinking about her, and he was thankful he'd taken another week off, but he wanted her back in his arms immediately. Recalling their conversation on the drive back to the hotel from the ball, he reflected on her warning to watch out, that he might get accustomed to having her in his life.

He gazed into space, wondering if such a thing could happen. And her remarks about her sightseeing had carried a slightly jarring undercurrent. It was obvious she recognized his life was focused on making profitable deals. He had more money than he could spend, but he liked the challenge of competing and acquiring lucrative assets. When she agreed to this marriage, she had known that much about him. So why would it disturb her now…unless she was becoming accustomed to his commitment and wanted it to continue?

His entire being was dedicated to acquisition and success. If she couldn't cope with that, she knew the conditions of the bargain she'd made.

Tossing aside worries about their relationship, he swore softly and looked at his watch, counting the hours until he'd be alone with her. His cousins, Zach, no one close seemed to think it was going to work out between them in this temporary marriage. Ridiculous. His union with her was already dizzying in its success, and any negative feelings on her part were insignificant. Her slight disapproval of his lifestyle would have no effect. Yet even as he came to that conclusion, he had an uncustomary ripple of dissatisfaction. Surely he wasn't getting bothered because he didn't have her one hundred percent approval. He refused to consider such a possibility.

On Saturday, daily life returned as they flew home, only her real life had changed forever. The first of the following week she spent two days drifting around his mansion while Matt flew to Houston to work and by the third day, she had already looked into online courses for next year. She was restless, bored and didn't have a circle of friends who had time on their hands.

Within five minutes after Matt returned home Friday night, they were naked, making love and she forgot boredom and loneliness.

The next morning she was in his arms listening to business deals he had transacted while he was away.

"Matt, you talk about your Texas ranch and property in Houston and Dallas, your property in Chicago and New York, and your Wyoming ranch. Other than the block your office is in here in Cheyenne, do you own any other Cheyenne property?"

"No. There's never been any particular reason to want any."

"I'd think you'd want to invest in more in Cheyenne since you live here. It's sort of an investment in the future."

"You might be right," he drawled in a lazy voice as he combed his fingers through her long hair. "I'll get someone to look into it."

"There are some old areas that could be fixed up and utilized and you have a lot of interest in cowboy life— it might be nice if you'd look into building a museum."

"I'll think about it. You look into museums and see what we have. I don't even know. Here's what I'm far more interested in," he said, his hand drifting along her slender throat and then lower.

"There's something else I want to discuss with you. While you were gone I looked into some online courses for next year." His hand stilled.

"I thought we'd settled the school situation. You'll go back after we part ways."

"You were gone three days. You'll be away a lot on business. I've worked all my life since I was eleven years old. I'm bored just sitting around here."

"There are charity jobs you can do that will keep you as busy as a full-time job, if that's what you'd prefer. I don't want you tied into something where you can't travel with me. I'd think you'd want to travel with me when I go to Europe or interesting places."

"Whether you are in Europe or here, you work. But I have a lot of time on my hands until the baby comes and charity work—a little will go a long way. Even after the baby is born, I'll have some time to myself and if I don't, I can drop the course. What's wrong with an online course if it doesn't interfere in any way with you?"

He rolled over to prop himself up on his elbow. His blue eyes had darkened and this time she recognized irritation. A muscle worked in his jaw that was thrust out stubbornly.

"We had an agreement. You're backing out of it and next thing I know, you'll be too involved in school to do what I want."

"I did agree. But I didn't realize how much time I'd have. I promise to drop classes instantly if they interfere in any way. Otherwise, what's it to hurt if I enroll?"

Scowling, he opened his mouth, but she put her finger over his lips. "You wait," she urged. "Think it over and then tell me your answer. If I make sure it doesn't interfere and you never even know I'm doing it, then what's the harm?"

"It's the principle."

She smiled. "That's ridiculous, Matt. That simply means you want your way in this whether it's sensible or not. You think about it calmly and rationally and then give me an answer. You have excellent judgment."

"How long am I supposed to give this thought?"

"How about until this time next week?" she suggested.

"Very well, but I can't imagine changing my feelings on it."

"We can both change our minds if it's mutually agreeable, don't you think?"

He glared at her. "All right, you get your way. I'll think about it."

"That's all I want you to do. And in order to keep you happy in the meantime," she said softly, running her hand down his smooth back and over his bare, hard bottom, letting her fingers play on him. "I'll do my utmost to please you," she whispered, wrapping one arm around his neck and pulling him closer as her tongue flicked out to trace his lower lip.

With a groan he rolled over on top of her, sliding one arm beneath her to hold her while he kissed her and ran his other hand along her bare thigh.

In minutes she knew his annoyance with her had vanished and she did her best to pleasure him until he rolled her onto her back again. Lowering himself between her legs to enter her, he filled her swiftly and then pumped as if driven and unable to take his time while she cried out with pleasure, moving with him.

Later, when they lay in each other's arms, he showered her with light kisses and caresses. "This is great, Brianna," he said.

"But not as great as a business deal and making money. You get a high from gaining more wealth, don't you?"

He studied her with a penetrating look. "Thank heaven I don't have to choose between sex or making money," he replied.

Solemnly, she shook her head.

As snow swirled and fell outside, they spent the weekend in bed together and Monday, the last week of October, when she kissed him goodbye, she had a pang because she was going to miss him badly.

Watching him drive away, she wondered if he would consider her enrollment in online courses. She thought he was being ridiculously stubborn simply because he wasn't accustomed to anyone telling him no or even giving him bad news, much less wanting to go back on a promise.

She hoped he thought about it. In the meantime, she had plans for now. Her entire family was coming to town and this time she would put them in the mansion.

It was time to get them enrolled in colleges or trade schools, as she'd intended. If they wanted to return to the life they'd had before, they always could, but she suspected each one of them would move on to something better than they'd had in the past.

She planned to talk to her mother and set up an account for her. She could afford it easily and she knew her mother was accustomed to a simple life and would keep confidential what Brianna did.

That night, she sat at the large informal table in the breakfast dining area and gazed around the table while everyone ate and talked. Her mother sat at the other end of the table and was talking to Brianna's youngest sister, Danielle. She watched Danielle laugh, her eyes sparkling while she and their mother took turns helping Emma and Hunter, Danielle's children.

"I still think this bubble will burst and I'll find out it never was true," Melody said.

"It's very true," Brianna replied. "Matt has been liberal with my allowance and about letting me do what I want to do," she said, having no intention of telling any of them the actual situation at this point. So far as she could tell, both her family and Matt's had accepted their marriage and thought they were in love, which suited her fine.

Through the weekend and into the next week, they pored over college catalogs, made calls, sent e-mails and contacted schools, searching for places for her relatives to attend school. All the men except her youngest brother enrolled in the University of Wyoming. Both sisters had picked two-year schools in Laramie, solving their search quickly and were looking for places to live in Laramie.

Wednesday night as they all sat in one of the large recreation rooms, Matt called and said he'd arrived in town and was on his way home.

Brianna excused herself and met him at the door when he came in. Snow dusted his topcoat and flakes melted in his hair, drops glistening in the light. He stomped his booted feet.

Rushing to throw herself into his arms, she pulled him close for a long, heated kiss.

Finally he raised his head. "What are all the cars out there? Do we have company?"

"Yes, as a matter of fact—"

"Damn, I've been waiting to get home to you. Who's here and when are they leaving?"

"Actually, they're not leaving for a while. My family is here. I invited them and I'm getting them enrolled in colleges."

"Brianna, they're not *living* with us, are they? You have a nice family, but I don't want them underfoot while they get an education."

"I know you don't," she replied coolly, stepping away from him. "They came when you were away."

"I'm back and they're here now."

"They are. If I remember correctly, you are going out of town again Monday morning."

"Right. But my house is mine and I like solitude. I'll be glad to put them up in any hotel they want, but I want our house to ourselves."

"I hope you're not saying to get them out of here tonight," she said, growing angrier with him by the second. "It's snowing."

"No, I'm not," he replied with a long sigh. "But I hope you can have them moved when I return from the next trip."

"Matt, this is a huge, enormous mansion."

"Right. I like space, solitude and privacy. That's why few people have ever been here. I have guards, gates, high walls, a privacy fence and a gatekeeper. That's it, Brianna. I asked you to marry me. I did not marry your family or intend to share my home with them. Frankly, I'd feel the same about my own family."

"Matt, you're a coldhearted man with only one love."

"So be it. You knew that much when you married me. Your family goes. I can tell them or you can."

"I'll tell them because I can do it in a nicer way than you will."

"True enough. I hope you put them in a wing other than the one we're in," he stated, giving her an intent look.

"Of course I did. I could have hidden them in this castle, and you'd never even see them and you know it."

"Mentally, it isn't the same as having the place to myself."

"You are really unreasonable on this subject. I can't believe you would do this to your own family."

"I certainly would. Ask my dad which hotel he prefers. Enough said on that subject. I'll go greet them, but first, come here," he said, slipping his arm around her waist and drawing her to him to kiss her.

The minute his mouth touched hers, her annoyance with him evaporated. She kissed him in return.

Finally, she pushed away. "Right now, I'll admit, I wish we were alone. But I'm not tossing my family into the cold in the middle of the night."

"I didn't ask you to do any such thing. Come on and I'll go see the family," he said in a resigned voice and she shook her head.

"Heartless cad," she said under her breath, and he turned to smile at her.

"Although lovable, right?" he teased and she glared at him, but she knew she couldn't stay irritated with him. She could move her family and they'd be so excited over hotel life they wouldn't care. They'd probably think he was giving them a great welcome.

Matt charmed her mother and sisters. He played with her little nieces and nephews, counseled her brothers and brothers-in-law on schools and courses and performed a convincing act of enjoying being with everyone.

It was eleven o'clock when they finally closed the door to their bedroom suite and had complete privacy and hours later before she turned on her side to run her fingers over him while she talked to him.

"You charmed my family tonight, I'm sure. They don't have a clue you're the coldhearted reason they will be moved out."

"So be it, Brianna. A person knows what he wants."

"I'm reeling in shock from how nice you can act when actually, you're not in the least bit friendly."

"Your family isn't going to mind if you'll find a really fine hotel," he said, smiling at her.

"No, I know you're right. A hotel will be delightful for the little kids. Actually, all of them except Mom enjoy a pool."

"Your mom might, too. Buy her a swimsuit."

Brianna made a mental note to take her mother shopping.

"Come to town tomorrow and meet me for lunch."

"It's a date," she said.

The following day at eleven, Matt heard a small commotion outside his office door. His door swung open and Nicole entered his office a step ahead of Tiffany, who was protesting loudly. "I'm sorry, Mr. Rome," Tiffany said.

"Don't worry, Tiffany. It's fine," he said, although it wasn't fine at all and he didn't want to see Nicole.

As the door closed behind her, leaving them alone, Nicole smiled at him. "Don't be angry with her or with me. I was in the area and I thought I'd see if you wanted to do lunch."

"No, I don't. Or anything else, Nicole. I thought I made that clear last time we were together. My wife is meeting me soon and I'd as soon she didn't find you here in my office."

Still smiling, Nicole sat in a chair facing his desk. "Don't be such a bear. I'm sure she really doesn't care what you do. Come on, Matt. You and I know each other well and I know why you married. I also know you don't want me to talk to the press about it." She smiled at him.

"Don't try in any manner to blackmail or intimidate me," he said in a quiet, cold voice. "It isn't going to work."

"Sit down and relax, Matt," she said. "I seem to have a knack for picking the wrong days."

"Wait until you're invited and then you won't have that problem."

"I might have a long wait," she said, standing. Relieved that she looked as if she were going to leave, he lost some of his antagonism. He glanced at his watch.

"Don't worry about the little wife. She isn't going to raise too much of a fuss. I'm sure she never wants to go back to being a waitress."

"She won't ever have to do that," he said, waiting for Nicole to leave and aware of the passage of time. "Nicole, this is pointless. It's time for my appointment," he said, growing more impatient with her because he didn't want to have to explain her presence once again to Brianna. They'd had enough of a disagreement over her family at his house and she was due to arrive soon.

* * *

Brianna stepped off the elevator and a door opened. Zach emerged, stopping when he saw her. "Good morning."

"Hello, Zach," she answered coolly and hoped her wariness didn't show.

"You look very nice this morning."

"Thank you," she answered in a cold tone, waiting.

"I should admit to you that perhaps I made judgments too swiftly. I thought your marriage to Matt would be a disaster, but to the contrary, he seems happier than I've ever seen him. I think you're a good influence on him. It's only fair to tell you."

Surprised, she stared at him. She wondered if Zach actually meant what he was saying or if there was some ulterior motive. "Thank you," she answered quietly. "I'm glad to hear that, although marriage is a big uncertainty, whether it's one like ours or a real one."

He smiled at her. "I wanted you to know."

"Thank you," she reaffirmed cautiously, still wary of the turnaround in his views toward her. "I appreciate that and I hope you're right."

"I'm right about Matt. I've worked with him almost since the day he went on his own. Of course, life is filled with change and I know this is a temporary union. If you ever need me, call," he said, handing her his card.

"Thank you," she said again, more warmth in her voice this time. "A friend is always a good thing to have. I'll go now. I'm a little early, but I may as well get Matt and maybe we'll beat the lunch crowd."

"Brianna," he said, and she paused. "I heard you carried off the ball in Rome quite well and impressed Matt and others."

This time she gave him a full smile. "I'm glad to hear that," she said, feeling better and deciding Zach meant what he was saying. Surprised and pleased, she walked away.

The moment she stepped into Tiffany's office, she knew something was amiss. Tiffany's eyes widened and she knocked over a stack of books.

"Mrs. Rome," she said.

"Please, Tiffany, call me Brianna," she said patiently, wondering how many times she was going to have to ask his secretary before she would relax and address her by her first name.

She headed toward his office. "Is he in his office?"

"Yes, he is. If you'll wait, I'll announce you."

"You don't need to, thanks," she said, wondering what was the matter with Tiffany, who was growing more flustered and nervous as she crossed the room. Had Zach merely been trying to stall her, too? Brianna knocked and opened the door, coming face-to-face with Nicole Doyle.

Eight

"I'm going now," Nicole said, smiling broadly at Brianna.

She glanced past Nicole at Matt, who approached her with impassive features but blazing blue eyes. "Nicole is leaving, Brianna. Come in," he said, taking his wife's arm and brushing a kiss on her lips lightly. He draped his arm across her shoulders.

"Goodbye, Nicole. Please close the door as you go," he added in a cold tone.

Blowing him a kiss, she left, closing the door behind her.

Brianna couldn't keep from being annoyed, but common sense told her that it had to be like the last time.

"I didn't know she was coming," he explained.

"Then we'll drop the subject. I have a feeling if you wanted her around, I'd never have seen her at all."

He smiled, kissing her lightly. "Thanks and you're right. You're the woman for me, and I'm busy trying to get you to myself before I leave town."

When she chuckled, his smile faded. "You look gorgeous today, except when you entered my office, I wished there was absolutely nothing beneath that leather coat."

"In this weather?" She laughed. "It's a cold November day and I'm not visiting your office naked beneath my coat."

"I can still imagine. Let's have lunch," he said, taking her arm. "I want you. If we go home, your relatives are all over the place. This office is as private as the street outside."

"It's difficult to work up a lot of sympathy since we made love half the night last night. Besides, I'd guess you have appointments later today and we should have lunch and let you get on with your work."

In his secretary's office, she paused. "Tiffany, what time does he have to be back?"

"Actually, not until two o'clock."

"Thank you," Brianna said sweetly, smiling up at him. "We should go before every restaurant gets crowded."

She left with him, noticing Nicole's perfume still lingering in the air and wondering how persistent Nicole would be in trying to get back into Matt's life. And how successful.

When they were in his car, Matt watched the road. "Brianna, have you told your family about moving?"

"Not yet. You're leaving Monday and you'll be gone the rest of the week. I'll tell them then and they'll be gone when you return."

"Not sooner?"

"I'm afraid not. That would be difficult."

"How difficult to make a hotel reservation? I can do it and they'll like it."

She didn't answer and rode the short distance to the restaurant in silence, wondering about him and how solitary he was and how little he seemed to care for anyone else or anything else except money.

When they were seated in the restaurant and had ordered, she took off her coat and looked up to see Matt watching her and desire had ignited in his gaze. A tingle jolted her from her reverie and made her aware of her tight-fitting, plain navy sweater and skirt.

"You look gorgeous as usual. If I didn't have that appointment—"

"But you do," she finished. "I'll make you a deal. If you're not going to let my family stay at your house, the least you can do is help my brothers by giving them job advice. You have a lot of contacts, so you should know places to send them."

Matt groaned. "Brianna, I don't do job placement. I pay people who work for me to deal with hiring."

"Then it will be a good experience for you and broaden you to look beyond yourself a little. You're kicking them out of your house—so this is the least you can do," she persisted, knowing she was badgering him, but determined to get him to help her family.

"I didn't help my brothers—Lance works for me, but that was different, and Christopher is off playing football and doesn't give a rip what I'm doing. Your family will manage. Heaven knows, you do."

"They will manage much better with your help and you owe them."

"I don't think I owe them anything when I'm footing a giant hotel bill for six adults and four little kids."

"The little kids cost nothing. Now look, Matt, your mansion will easily hold all of them and they can stay out of your sight."

"Don't go back to that. They're out and I'll get Zach to look into helping them with jobs. How's that?"

She only hoped Zach would do his best for them. "I hope Zach will," she said, wondering whether he would actually help or merely go through the motions. He had seemed sincere in his compliments to her, but she didn't know him well, so she had no idea if he had been truly sincere.

As Matt drove, she stared at his long, lean frame and knew she was falling in love with him. He had been good to her and kind and generous to her family. He was the most fantastic lover. She thought she'd be able to guard her heart so easily and never fall in love with him because she still thought he was heartless when it came to work and money. And whatever happened, their union was temporary. She had no illusions about Matt changing his mind regarding the length of their marriage.

* * *

True to his word, Matt talked to some of her family about their future plans and gave them his business card, telling them to call his office to set up appointments to talk to Zach, who would help direct them where to turn in applications and resumes. Also, Zach would see about having their resumes professionally done, something Brianna had planned on doing herself, but she was relieved to see Matt take this on.

Again, that night when they finally were alone in the east wing of the house and closed in their bedroom, she wound her arms around his neck. "Thank you for today and all you're doing."

"If I can keep you happy and showing me how grateful you are," he said in a husky voice, "it's worth it to me."

"I wish you didn't have to go Monday and be gone so long. I'll miss you."

"I miss you more each time we're apart," he said.

"Have you ever thought about not traveling quite so much?" she asked, knowing even before she finished her sentence that business came far ahead of everything else.

"I'm doing what I have to do, but it's not quite the same," he said in a solemn tone that made her heart miss a beat. Could she possibly be growing more important to him?

He tightened his arms around her, leaning down to kiss her, and ending conversation and her curiosity.

* * *

Monday she kissed him before he left for Chicago and then she turned her attention to her family. As she had expected, news of the hotel move excited her family.

She began to plan a nursery, drawing sketches and studying magazines. Her pregnancy still seemed unreal to her because she couldn't see any change in her shape. Trying to stay fit, most days of the week she walked on Matt's track in his exercise room and swam in his indoor pool.

If she could take even two courses each semester, she would get four out of the way in a year. She was a senior and needed eighteen more hours for an undergraduate degree. She suspected after a few months, Matt wouldn't care what she did. His fascination with her would surely dwindle and she could take more than two.

She looked into some local charities that she could give a day to and miss when Matt wanted her to go with him, finally agreeing to give a day each week to helping in the local food bank.

When it was nearly ten o'clock Friday evening, Matt arrived. She'd spent the late afternoon and early evening getting ready for his return and had her black hair pinned up on either side of her head, to fall freely down on her back and on her shoulders. She'd selected new red silk lounge pajamas and matching high-heeled sandals and her excitement mounted with each passing hour. They'd talked half a dozen times during the day and she knew he was anxious to get home. Her pulse rate increased when she heard the beep of the alarm as a door opened and closed.

She rushed to meet him when he swept into the hallway bringing cold air with him. At the sight of him, her heart thudded even faster.

Dropping his briefcase, he shook off his thick, black topcoat and let it and his charcoal suit jacket fall on the floor with his briefcase. Hurrying toward her, he shed his tie.

She ran the last distance to throw her arms around him and he caught her up, crushing her in his embrace and kissing her hotly.

Beneath his cotton shirt and wool pants she could feel the warmth of his body. Running her fingers through his tangled curls, she kissed him. As her heartbeat speeded, her desire was a blazing fire. "I've missed you so!" she gasped and returned to kissing him.

"Not anything like the way I've missed you, Brianna," he declared. "Love, you look luscious enough to eat," he said and kissed her, scooping her into his arms to carry her to the bedroom.

Saturday she lazed in his arms. "Matt, look at the sun coming through the windows. It has to be midmorning. I have things to do, and so do you."

"You're complaining?"

She rolled on top of him, smiling at him. "Hardly. I'm euphoric and lusty, but I need to eat for the baby."

He smiled as he wrapped locks of her hair around his fingers and pulled her to him to kiss her.

His cell phone rang and he continued to kiss her until she broke it off. "Answer your phone. Only a select few have your cell phone number."

"It better be important," he grumbled, picking up his phone and saying hello. In moments, he sat up and she rolled away, grabbing her robe and going to shower, guessing it was a business call. She dressed in jeans and a T-shirt and went to the kitchen to get breakfast.

Soon he joined her. He had showered and dressed in chinos and a tan knit shirt. His damp hair was in tight curls. His eyes were bright with excitement and she realized the phone call had been something that pleased him. As she poured orange juice, she said, "You look like that cat who caught the mouse. What's happened?"

"I'm meeting with four members of the investment group Tuesday, so I'll fly to France Monday. They all but told me outright they want me to join their group."

First she felt excitement that he had achieved his goal. That quick flash was replaced by cold fear that he would be through with her and ask her to pack and go.

"Congratulations!" she cried, hugging him, letting him have his moment and wanting to avoid any dissonance.

"It'll only be overnight, they said. Come with me. They told me to bring you along."

He continued talking about Paris, but the joy at hearing he wanted her along was immediately crushed. He was taking her because they'd told him to.

He leaned down to look her in the eyes. "Are you with me? Paris? You look like you're thinking about something else."

"No, I'm delighted for you, and yes, I want to go."

"You don't sound as if you really do. I'm not twisting your arm," he said, studying her.

Smiling, she hugged him. "I'm just wondering if you join their group now, if you'll tell me goodbye," she said, but that wasn't really what had made her joy disappear.

He hugged her. "Hardly," he said, winding his fingers in her hair and pulling her head back to gaze into her eyes. "I want you in my life for a lot longer," he said and kissed her.

And she intended to be, she thought as she kissed him in return. She would make him want her for a long, long time—long enough that he might not ever want her to go.

In spite of his all-important drive for wealth, she loved her handsome husband. She reminded herself no one was perfect, but Matt's flaw was a gigantic one that could affect everything he did.

She pushed away from him. "We should eat and then let me plan what I have to do to get ready."

"They're taking us to dinner Tuesday night and I'm sure it'll be a celebration dinner."

She shook her head over his exuberance and absolute confidence. "Matt, I've never known anyone who has the self-assurance you do. My word, you believe in yourself!"

"I suppose I do, but why else would they be calling and asking me to meet with them and bring you and plan on dinner? It stands to reason. Go buy a new dress and we'll stay Wednesday. I'll take you out for our own little celebration the following night."

She took a breakfast casserole from the oven. As

they ate, she listened to Matt talk about his plans, but her mind was still on their future together and if she was important to him in any manner other than as a means to get him into this group, or in his bed.

She realized he was telling her about problems at work with acquisitions he wanted and the difficulty he was having with one of his vice presidents, and she began to pay close attention, pushing aside her worries as she absorbed what Matt was saying.

It was three in the afternoon when he left for an errand and she went shopping for a dress for her Paris dinners.

She arrived back home before Matt and began to pack and sort through clothes, knowing Matt could take all of her time when he returned home.

She finally heard him at six-thirty when it was dark outside and a cold wind howled around the house.

He rushed inside and her heart thudded, desire instantly igniting because he looked irresistible. His broad-brimmed black hat was pushed to the back of his head and his thick leather and lambs-wool lined jacket swung open. He carried two huge boxes and she wondered if he'd purchased a suit for himself.

"So you've been shopping, too," she said. "I'd hug you, but I can't get close to you."

"Let's go to the family room," he said and, though he had four rooms the description would have fit, she knew which room was his favorite.

She already had a roaring fire blazing in the mammoth fireplace. She turned, waiting for him to set down his packages, and then she was in his arms and the world vanished.

It was hours later when she stirred and sat up in front of the fire. "I'm burning on one side, cold on the other and this floor is hard."

"It's not all that's hard and that's your fault," he said with amusement, pulling her to him to kiss her.

"Stop and let me move to higher ground. A bed and a warm shower first. And tonight, I get dinner at a decent hour. You know, it isn't healthy for a pregnant woman to miss meals."

Matt looked stricken. "Darlin', I'm sorry. I swear you won't miss another one—"

She placed her fingers on his mouth and smiled at him. "Stop. I feel fine. But food would be good right now."

"Steak it is. You go upstairs to shower and I'll shower in another bath and get dinner on the table."

Smiling at him, she left to do what he suggested. It wasn't until after dinner and they had moved back to the family room that she remembered his packages. He knelt to get the fire built up again, the scent of the burning logs filling the room. His jeans pulled tightly on his muscled legs and he straightened, setting the screen in place.

"Did you buy yourself a new suit?"

"I shouldn't have forgotten all about this," he said, picking up a long, narrow box that was the smaller of the two. He brought it to her to hand it to her.

"I should have had that sent out, but they were on the verge of closing and the truck had gone for today."

Curious, she opened the box to look at dozens of red and white and yellow roses. "Matt, these are gorgeous!" she said, taking out the card and pulling it open swiftly to read. "Thanks for helping me reach my goal. Love, Matt."

She set down the box and kissed him, pushing away from him in a moment.

"Wait now. I want to put these in water. They have them in those little vials, but I need to get them into a vase."

Rushing to get them in water before he tried to stop her, she had seen the look in his eyes and his thoughts weren't on the flowers.

He followed her into the kitchen, talking to her about Paris, and when she finished her arrangement in a large crystal vase, he carried it back to the family room for her.

As soon as he set it on a table, he crossed the room to pick up the largest box to give to her. It was tied with a red silk ribbon.

"I thought this was a suit for you," she said.

"They don't tie my suits up with silk bows. I have them custom-made by my tailor."

He placed the box on a leather sofa and she leaned down to untie a beautiful bow. She raised the lid and pushed away tissue paper to gaze at a box filled with dark fur.

Startled, she glanced at him.

"It's your present," he reminded her.

Burying her fingers in the soft, silky fur she lifted out a full-length mink coat. A card fell out and Matt picked it up off the floor to hand it to her. "Thank you, love, Matt."

"Matt, this is beautiful," she said, running her fingers through the thick fur. Yet instantly she wondered if the coat was a bribe to smooth the way and get her to go quietly when he told her they were through.

"It's elegant," she said, slipping it on, but feeling stiff and cold, knowing she should steel herself for what was to come. She turned to face him.

"You look gorgeous, but I really like you better with nothing," he said, smiling and walking up to slip his hands beneath the coat and wrap his arms around her.

Putting her arms around his neck, she stood on tiptoe to kiss him, a thorough, heated kiss. She wanted him and didn't want to be tossed out like old shoes, yet she couldn't believe that wasn't the exact reason for the gift.

She leaned away. "You don't even know for certain that they'll invite you to join. If they don't, do I lose my coat?" she asked in a teasing tone, trying to cover the chill she still suffered and the dread that had consumed her.

"You'll keep the coat no matter what, but I'm sure I'm in."

"Congratulations, again," she said quietly. "This is an extravagant gift."

"I want you to have it," he said, drawing her back into his embrace and leaning down to kiss her, yet even his hot kisses couldn't drive away the demons that tormented her.

Arriving in Paris late Monday afternoon, they checked in to another luxurious suite in a hotel near the Arc de Triomphe.

Matt had attributed her sober manner to jitters about dinner with the group of foreign investors and their wives again. Letting him continue to think that, she smiled politely at his reassurances that she shouldn't worry about Tuesday night.

While she unpacked in their bedroom, Matt walked up behind her and took clothes out of her hands.

"Stop working the instant you arrive. We have the rest of the day. I'll show you some sights and take you to dinner," he said, nuzzling her neck.

She turned to wrap her arms around him and kiss him passionately, still certain the mink coat had been a farewell gift and a bribe.

Matt's arms tightened around her, and sightseeing and her fears were all pushed aside.

After making love far into the night, they slept. Brianna woke after only a couple of hours and couldn't go back to sleep. She kept thinking about leaving Matt and it hurt. She loved him. There was no turning back and reversing her feelings for him, yet she was certain he would end their sham marriage soon now that his goal had been achieved.

She wrapped herself in a robe and moved to a window to look at the twinkling lights of Paris, knowing this wasn't the way to see or remember the city. How soon would he tell her they were through?

Sometimes she wished she had never met him. She rubbed her stomach, thinking about her baby. Matt was good with her little nieces and nephews. She had thought he would be around for a while for her baby.

She knew she needed to adjust and pick up and go on with her life, but Matt was dynamic and had swept into it, changing her world. He wasn't going to fade away or be forgotten easily.

She pulled her robe closer around her and closed her eyes, wanting sleep to come so she could stop worrying about her future.

"What are you doing, Brianna?" Matt asked, his deep voice a rumble in the dark room.

"Enjoying the city at night," she replied.

"I want you here in bed with me," he said sleepily. "I'm glad you like Paris," he added. "I can't work up the same enthusiasm."

"You miss a lot in life," she whispered, torn between annoyance that he was so totally focused on what he wanted and hurting because she had fallen in love with him in spite of it. She didn't receive an answer, but she went back to bed, slipping beneath the covers. He reached out and pulled her close against him, holding her tightly. For now, she held him, reassuring herself that she would be in his life a while longer.

The following afternoon, she shopped while Matt met with the investors and she was the first to arrive back at the hotel.

When he walked into the suite and tossed aside his topcoat, she knew he was in the group. Looking triumphant, he scooped her up into his embrace to kiss her passionately. "I'm in," he finally said. "We did it, Brianna. With thanks to you, who made this possible. I'll take you out for our own celebration tomorrow night, but tonight, they're taking us to a very expensive, very exclusive restaurant."

"Congratulations!" she said, wondering again how long their sham marriage would last now that the reason for it had vanished.

The evening should have been a warm memory in a restaurant with exotic French fare. She enjoyed sitting beside Signore Rufulli. All seemed happy to have her join them and everyone celebrated Matt becoming part of the group.

Flying home on Thursday, she had memories stored away, but along with them was the chilling knowledge that Matt no longer needed their union.

Before sunrise Friday morning, his cell phone rang and Matt stretched out a long arm, picking it up and flicking it open. He answered in a sensual, satisfied tone while she continued to run her fingers lightly over his chest and lower.

He listened such a long time she looked up. When she saw he was scowling, she guessed he was hearing bad news. Had a stock market somewhere in the world dropped during the night?

"How bad is it?" he asked quietly.

She rolled away and sat up to look at him, her curiosity growing.

"When did it happen?" he asked in a solemn voice and she wondered what calamity had transpired.

"How's he doing now?" Matt asked.

She wrapped her arms around herself and waited. It was worse than she'd imagined because someone was hurt and from Matt's tone, it was someone important to him.

"Thank God for that," he said, glancing at her and she wondered if he wanted privacy for his conversation. She grabbed a robe and slipped out of bed, leaving the room for a few minutes.

When she returned, he was propped in bed, still talking, but his voice sounded normal and he smiled over something. She let out her breath because it evidently wasn't too dreadful.

She had put on a red lace gown and, shedding her robe, she slipped beneath the covers and saw him watching her. He pushed away the sheet, but she immediately pulled it back and sat up cross-legged to stare at him, holding the sheet to her chin.

Finally, he broke the connection and looked at her. "Sorry to wake you with that call. It was Lance. My dad has had a heart attack."

"Oh, no! I take it he's doing better."

"Yes, he is. It was mild. He had chest pains and Mom took him to the E.R. From what I understand, Lance indicated there were changes in Dad's EKG and he had elevated enzymes. They want to keep him for observation, so he'll stay in the hospital for now. The prognosis is very good. Later this morning I can talk to Dad. In the meantime," he said, reaching out to pull on the sheet she grasped beneath her chin.

"Wait a minute!" she said, keeping the sheet waded tightly in her fist. "Aren't you going to Miami?"

"No. Lance said Dad's doing fine now and I don't need to come."

"You've got to go," she said, aghast that he was brushing aside his father's rush to the E.R. "Your father had a heart attack and you have a plane at your disposal. You can drop everything to do as you please."

"I need to work. There's no need for a trip to see him, Brianna," Matt restated patiently. "I'll see Dad at the next family gathering. In the meantime, there is someone I want to see," he said, reaching out again, but she scooted back quickly and pushed away his hand.

"Matt, that's the coldest attitude I've ever known. You go see your father."

"I'm all grown up now and have my own life and he's supposed to have a full recovery. It wasn't that serious."

"No wonder you don't want any children!" she snapped, staring at him intently.

He scowled at her. "Brianna, my dad is doing fine. There's no reason for me to go traipsing off to Florida to see him when he's okay."

"He's had a *heart attack*. He's older. My word, Matt, don't you care?"

"Of course I do, but I cut the apron strings when I left home for college. I don't go running home to them with every little thing, nor do they with me. We're not that kind of family."

"Well, thank heavens, mine is," she said, thinking how they all rallied around whenever there was a crisis. "We may not have money, but we love each other."

"I love my parents," he said patiently, but she could hear

the note of irritation in his voice and knew she was aggra-
vating him, but she couldn't stop. His parents seemed
warm and nice and had welcomed her into the family.

"Brianna, I am not going to Florida, so drop it," Matt
said forcefully.

"You really don't have a heart, Matt," she said and left
the room, going to the bathroom where she could shut
him out. He didn't care about family, not his or anyone
else's. He was nice and generous and giving to people as
long as it didn't involve him too intensely and personally.

Her first assessment of him as heartless, in love only
with money and perhaps himself, had been accurate.
That's all he was about. She was in love with him and
she couldn't stop loving him, but she knew it was time
to move on. She had money now, enough to do as she
pleased. What was the point in remaining with Matt?
Their philosophies of life were poles apart. She wasn't
going to change him, wasn't going to influence him. He
knew what he wanted and went after it with a ruthless
determination that shut out the rest of the world. And he
really didn't care about anything else except success and
the acquisition of wealth. She didn't even think he truly
cared around the trappings of wealth or the power it gave
him. He lived for the sheer accumulation of money.

It was a cold way to be and he would never love
anyone in the fullest sense of the word. Nor would he
be a good father. She knew he would shower a child with
gifts and give a child some attention, but that all-
accepting love that she already felt for her baby was
something Matt could not attain. Nor did he want to.

He was selfish to the core and the sooner she moved on, the better off she would be. The cold realization hurt and tears stung her eyes. She thought about her future. If she stayed he would shower her with care throughout her pregnancy and childbirth. She knew he would be at her side for that—unless some crisis arose in his business. Then he'd be off and gone and return with presents for her to make up for his absence.

Did she want to give that up this early? Stay and enjoy his attention and help. It was tempting because it would be lonely and more difficult on her own even with money to buy whatever she wanted. Also, his very generous allowance would end if she walked away.

Yet the thought of making love to him had soured. Could she turn off her feelings about his coldness? She rubbed her neck, torn between going and staying, knowing she shouldn't rush into a decision she would regret later.

She recalled the night she'd met his parents and his father, Travis, saying to her, "I hope you'll bring him to see us. We don't see much of him, but I understand that better than his mother does." As far as Brianna was concerned, that meant that they'd like to see a lot more of their son than they did.

She heard a knock at the door and went to open it, looking up at Matt. Her heart thudded and for an instant, all her thoughts of leaving him vanished. How could she walk out when each time she saw him, she wanted to kiss him?

"Come in, Matt," she said, stepping back.

"I thought I'd see if you'd like to go downstairs with me to get something to eat. I think we were headed that way when we were interrupted by the telephone."

She nodded. "I'm going to shower. I'll be down shortly," she said, noticing his jeans and T-shirt and knowing she should shower and dress.

"Fine. See you downstairs. I'll get breakfast."

Closing the door, she waited for him to leave and then she stepped out to go to the closet, where she selected jeans and a blue sweater, got underwear and went to shower.

Downstairs she found him in the kitchen with egg casserole, ham, oatmeal and a platter of fruit on the table. He had orange juice and milk poured for her. While snow fell outside, they sat at the table near the fire. "If I go to Florida now, it's close enough to Thanksgiving that they'll want us both to come and stay."

"That wouldn't be the end of the world," she said, picking at her food and still thinking about her future, feeling cold and forlorn. "You can take some more time off."

"Look, if it would make you feel better about my dad, we can call Lance and you can talk to him."

She lowered her fork. "You don't get it. If your father was going to be released from the hospital tonight and go home and I could talk to him right now, I would. Or to put it another way—if this were my mom, I would be packing right now to go and I'd probably leave within the hour to see her. So talking to your brother really doesn't matter. I know your dad is going to survive this and I believe you when you say that the prognosis is good. But people are more important to me than money. You've always known that. Family is way more important than career."

"Brianna, you'd do anything short of a criminal act to get that degree. You wouldn't let your family interfere with you getting it and you didn't stay home with them. You moved to Laramie to get an education and you've stuck with it."

"I'd go home to see Mom if she had a heart attack," she replied, knowing she was being stubborn with him, but still aggravated by his cavalier attitude.

"Admirable, but in my case unnecessary. And I would understand if the situation were reversed."

"I recall your dad telling me that he was happy to see you marry and maybe now they would see more of you," Brianna replied.

"My dad said that?"

"Yes, he did."

"Mom I can understand. She would be happier if none of us had ever left home. She likes having us around, but we all grew up and moved on and it would have been odd if we hadn't."

Brianna turned to look at the fire and think about the coming week when he would be gone. She could take her time to contemplate her future and decide what she should do. She was tempted to tell him it was over now, but she knew that would be foolish. She had too much to gain by staying if she could get a better grip on her emotion and let go some of her affection for him.

They ate in silence until she thought she couldn't get down another bite. "Excuse me, Matt," she said, getting up and carrying her dishes to the sink to rinse them and put them in the dishwasher.

"You don't need to do that," he said.

"I know. It's habit and I don't mind." The room became silent again and she suspected their quasi-marriage was over.

"Dammit, Brianna, I'm not going and that's the end of the matter. Dad doesn't need me."

"Watch out, Matt. If you're not careful, someday, no one will need you," she said softly and one dark eyebrow arched.

"As long as I have a fortune, a lot of people will want and love me," he said in a cynical tone.

"Yes, that's true and you'll always know your fortune is exactly why." Her hurt deepened at his self-absorbed, callous attitude.

"I'm such an ogre?"

"Of course not. You're charming and irresistible in too many ways, and you'll always have women who love you and men who like you, so you'll never be lonely," she said, thinking all his relationships would be as shallow in the future as they had been in the past.

"Your arguments are contradictory," he stated, assessing her intently. "Someday you plan to be an attorney. You need to get your argument tight and to the point."

She smiled stiffly. "I'll remember that bit of advice. I know you'll find as much happiness in your future as you have in your past."

Something flickered in the depths of his eyes and a muscle worked in his jaw while he clenched his fists. "I'm not going to Florida. My dad doesn't need to see me, nor has he asked me to come."

"You've made that more than clear," she said and watched him turn and leave the room.

Tears threatened, but she fought shedding them, knowing they had been headed for this moment from the start, but never expecting it to hurt so badly.

In many ways she wanted to give his money back to him and walk away, feeling free from a bad bargain. Yet she knew that would be foolish and hurt not only herself, but her baby and her family. Too much was at stake, and Matt's money would secure the future for all of them. And he would never miss it because he had already amassed enormous wealth and was primarily engrossed in the acquisition of more, not the enjoyment of having it.

That day as she went about her exercise routine, she considered her decision. She loved Matt and she wanted to be with him, but it was ridiculous for her to stay and hope he'd someday change his basic nature. As much as it hurt, she wanted out of the fake marriage, wanted to tell the truth to her family, wanted to go on with her life. A life that had been transformed by Matt.

She knew he would protest and she was equally certain he wouldn't want her to go despite the temporary nature of the whole arrangement. And how much harder it would be to leave after the baby came. Yet that might be the time when Matt would have grown tired of them. So why wait until there were two hearts to break?

She had to get out of this fake marriage now.

Monday morning, she was determined to get up before he was out and gone so she could break the news to him that their marriage was over.

Matt had already showered and gone down to breakfast. She showered and dressed quickly, hurrying downstairs to catch him before he left.

She found him in his study, poring over papers in front of him at his desk. His suit jacket was tossed on a chair and he hadn't tightened his navy tie. A fire blazed in the fireplace and the crackle and pop of burning logs was the only sound in the room. In spite of her thick blue sweater and jeans, the heat from the flames was welcome. She was chilled to the bone.

"Knock, knock," she said as she entered and he looked up, tossing down his pen before he leaned back in his chair. "Matt, I want to talk to you," she said, crossing the room to stand by the fire. "I'll be brief. I know you have to go soon."

"Come in. You look upset. What's up?" he asked. He leaned back with his hands behind his head and his long legs stretched out in front of him.

"I've given thought to the future and to us," she said. "I guess it started when your father had his heart attack. We married with an agreement and we've both fulfilled our part of the bargain. I helped you get into the investors' group and you paid me the money you promised—part of it still due. Therefore this marriage has accomplished its purpose. It was never intended to be a permanent arrangement. Right?"

"Right," he said, lowering his hands and coming to his feet to rest his hands on his hips. Thick curls fell on his forehead and he was handsome, sexy and appealing. Her heart gave a twist, but this was inevitable. Better to get it done and over.

"When we discussed a marriage of convenience, I recall you saying that once you're invited into the investment group, you wouldn't hold me to two years. You told me that I can stay that long, but if I wanted out sooner, I could go."

"You're walking out?" he asked in disbelief, and for once, his total self-assurance looked shaken.

"Yes, I am," she answered, hurting and hoping she wouldn't cry in front of him. "I see no reason to stay longer. You've achieved your goal and got what you wanted. You're through with me—"

"Not really, Brianna. We have a good thing going here—and you've acted like you thought it was great."

"The physical relationship between us is fine, but my emotions are tangled up in it. I haven't had enough relationships to make comparisons. It's been wonderful, Matt, and you know it, but it's time to go. Look how distant you are with your blood relatives. If I stay, I'll fall in love with you and then it'll be the same way with me and with the baby."

"I can't believe you want to do this."

She ran her hand across her cheek. "Thanks to you, I have sufficient money to live comfortably and provide for my baby. My family will be with me for the baby's birth. I find it difficult to imagine you being interested in a baby or wanting to go through this pregnancy with me."

"I think you're jumping to conclusions," he said quietly. "I don't want you to go," he said, walking closer.

"All we're having is an affair. A legally contracted affair. It isn't a real marriage and you never intended it to be," she said softly as if she were explaining something to a child. Tears still threatened, and she swiped her eyes again as she gazed up at him.

"You don't even want to go—"

"Of course I don't want to go!" she cried, finally losing her control. "I'm probably in love with you and even though you're charming and sex is the best, there's no future here. I don't want to end up like Nicole, dragging around after you and trying to recapture your attention."

"That's entirely different. You're unique and maybe we'll both fall in love. Isn't that worth waiting to let happen?"

"Maybe? *Maybe?* No. I think I'll get hurt worse and I don't want to have all the upheaval of moving when I have an infant to care for. It'll be much easier now to find a place, get settled and get ready for my baby."

Closing the distance between them, he wrapped his arms around her and kissed her for a long time. As she remaining stiffly in his arms, her resistance melted until she responded, aware of the salty taste of her tears.

He raised his head, wiping away her tears with his thumbs. "Don't cry. Stay with me. We're happy together and have a good thing going. If it makes you feel better about it, I'll promise to keep this marriage together for the full two years and then you won't be so worried about the future. How's that?"

She shook her head. "Not enough. I guess you made me want it all, Matt. I want a real marriage and if I can't have a real one, I don't want one at all."

His eyes darkened and he clamped his jaw closed. "There's not going to be a real marriage. You've known that from the start."

"Yes, you've made it abundantly clear," she replied, gazing steadily into his eyes.

"You know what you want. I'm not going to stick around and argue. If you want out, you're free to go," he said and the words cut with the sharpness of a knife. "I'll help you move any way I can and do what I can for you about the baby. I'll still pay for nannies when the time comes. We should part friends, Brianna."

"Thank you," she said quietly, once again fighting to keep from crying.

"You can call me whenever you want anything." He slipped his hand behind her head to caress her nape, moving closer again. "If you change your mind, let me know. I'll welcome you back into my life—anytime in the near future."

He looked handsome, appealing, as irresistible as ever and she wanted him to tell her to stay and let it be a real marriage.

Instead, they stared silently at each other, each one wanting something different, each one with conflicting desires that were impossible to resolve. Suddenly, he pulled her into his arms again for another passionate kiss.

Leaning over her, he held her tightly while his tongue thrust deeply into her mouth and he kissed her long and thoroughly.

Her heart thudded and she clung to him, kissing him in return, knowing this was his goodbye. She ran her hand across his broad shoulders that felt warm through the thin cotton of his shirt. She was tempted beyond measure to cry out that she would stay and take her chances on the future with him. She didn't want to go. She loved him and might forever.

Finally, she pushed against him. He released her only a fraction. Breathing hard, he gazed at her. "Don't go," he said.

"I love you," she whispered and he flinched. The gesture was harsh and cut as much as his words had. He shifted away a few inches, tucking her hair behind her ear.

"I can't do the permanent marriage, Brianna. I'm not into long relationships, much less a lifetime commitment. You've known that from the first night."

"I know. Saying that it's been wonderful sounds woefully inadequate for all you've done. I hope you make back your investment and oodles more. May you make another billion or so, Matt." She slipped her arm around his neck and kissed him again, long, heated and final. When she drew away, she was crying.

"Don't pay the rest of the money you and I agreed on. There's enough invested to take care of me, my baby and my family sufficiently. We have a fortune now."

"Don't be ridiculous. We have an agreement—a written contract. You've lived up to your part of the bargain."

"If you give me more, I'll send it to charities."

"That's foolish, Brianna," he stated. "Spend the money on yourself and your family. With a child to raise, you can use it. Charity begins at home."

"So does love, Matt," she said solemnly. "You're missing what's important in life."

"I'm not certain you would have made that statement when you first met me. With a couple of million, your perspective has changed."

"Not my basic feelings about family and love."

"Remember, you can change your mind about this. All you have to do is let me know," he said.

"This is officially goodbye," she said, hoping she could be out of his house when he returned from his New York trip.

"Sure. But I intend to keep in touch."

She nodded, letting him think what he wanted. He gave her a long, hard study and then turned to pick up his jacket and leave, closing the door behind him.

"Goodbye," she whispered again. She had no intention of turning into another Nicole, someone pursuing him when he didn't want to be pursued.

Shaking and cold, she walked to the fire to warm her icy hands, knowing flames probably couldn't remove the chill that enveloped her. Matt had gone out of her life. Would she ever stop loving him? How long before he replaced her and forgot her?

She suspected it wouldn't take him long at all. All

week he would be taken up with business and making more money.

When she entered her enormous closet and looked at the array of clothes she now owned—a mink coat, designer dresses and shoes, purses that at one time would have paid her rent for months—she had another pang for the life she was tossing aside.

She would need help moving her belongings. Her brothers and brothers-in-law could do it without difficulty. The first and most important thing was to find somewhere to live. The next thing was to let her family know that she was leaving Matt.

She wanted out of Matt's house immediately and finding a comfortable hotel suite became top priority. Wiping her eyes, she went to the computer to check out hotels.

Since Laramie was where all her family would be, she thought about looking there later for a house. Melody had already purchased a house and was moving in another week.

Brianna got down the one small suitcase she'd brought when she'd moved in with Matt. Now she owned so much it would take an entire set of luggage and probably more than one trunk. She wanted him home and in his arms and their lives together to go on the way they had. This time when tears came, she gave vent to them, leaning against the doorjamb and crying, knowing it was over with Matt.

Matt immersed himself in business and stayed busy every night in New York. Even so, he couldn't get

Brianna out of his thoughts. Occasionally he would spot a tall, leggy woman with black hair like hers, and his heart would skip a beat.

Too well, he remembered being there with her and the first time she had seen Saint Patrick's, her first trip to Central Park. He saw her too many places, too often, and he couldn't shake thinking about her.

He called her each night, but she never answered. For the first time he realized she really might be gone out of his life completely. She wasn't predictable or like any other woman he'd ever known. If she wanted to vanish out of his life, she would. He was sure he could track her down, but as far as seeing her socially or even taking her out again, he faced the fact that might be impossible now.

The realization she had really cut all ties hurt. He'd had her final check deposited into her account at the bank and he expected he would hear from her about it. Matt wondered if Brianna would ask his suggestions about investing the money. Or would she stick to what she'd said and give her final payment to charity? He couldn't imagine her doing any such thing.

Wednesday evening his cell phone rang and he answered instantly, hope flaring that he would hear Brianna's voice.

Instead, it was one of the investors discussing an opportunity that had arisen. Matt's attention was taken by the prospect and he worked into late hours, sleeping little and getting up to check on the market.

By Friday, he had made over a million from the investment. That night in the hotel he wrote down the figures, staring at them. For the first time the return gave him no great satisfaction. What he really wanted was Brianna in his life—even more than money. The realization shocked him, and he wondered when she had become so damn important to him that everything else diminished.

Had she been right that money wasn't the all-important facet of life, less meaningful than love? He couldn't answer his own question except for that in this case, he would have given not only the million but more to have her with him again.

He'd never thought anything could be as great as the accumulation of wealth, the challenge and success of making a big deal, but now it wasn't his prime need. He had a huge fortune. Even the bet with his cousins had lost its priority.

Disgusted with life and with himself, he pushed away and paced the room impatiently. He strode to the window to look out over the city. Lights sparkled in every direction. What was she doing now?

He missed Brianna and her exuberance and enthusiasm. She was a good listener and he'd grown accustomed to talking freely to her about business—something he didn't feel would be wise to do with anyone else, even Zach. He wondered if she'd ever know that he'd taken her suggestion about investing more of himself into Cheyenne. Now he wished he had told her that he'd asked Zach to check into some particular properties.

Matt knew he'd get accustomed to life without her, just as he always had after a breakup, but at present, it bothered him.

Turning to his usual solution after a breakup, he intended to immerse himself in work. Tomorrow, Saturday morning, he would fly to London and work there all next week.

Late Thursday he returned home, where he worked until he fell asleep over his desk before he finally went to bed. He was exhausted, yet still unable to sleep peacefully, dreaming about Brianna and waking to want her in his arms.

It jolted him the following week when he received the first thank-you from a nonprofit literacy group. Any donations he made went through the foundation set up in his name. He realized this was Brianna's doing, and she was giving the last payment to charity just as she had said she would.

Staring at the note in his hand, he stood a long time wondering about her and the depth of her feelings. He hadn't really thought she would turn down his money under any circumstances. Had she done this to emphasize to him that love was more important and he was far too material?

He spent long hours at his office and exercised several hours each day, but nothing filled the emptiness he felt. He hated missing her and reassured himself that with time his longing would fade away.

One night in his office at home, he sat thinking about

Brianna. He missed her dreadfully and he'd never missed anyone before. She had changed his life and he couldn't get his old life back. She was everywhere he looked, yet not really there, only a phantom of a memory. He missed her and wanted her and realized he had fallen in love with her, something he had never expected to have happen. Through affairs and friendships, women had been secondary in his life. Even his family had always faded to the background, but Brianna wouldn't fade away or diminish or get out of his thoughts.

He began to wonder if her family was settled in Laramie, going to school as they had planned and if she had moved there to be near them.

He'd been to the steak house where he'd first found her, but no one there had seen her. He knew he could hire someone to find her, but there wasn't much point in it. Unless he wanted to make a permanent commitment. Wouldn't that be far better than this hellish misery he was going through constantly?

Brianna tried to keep her mind on the booklet in front of her. She was trying to decide on courses for the spring semester at the University of Wyoming. She sat at a desk, poring over brochures and selecting classes, trying to get a schedule that would work. Because of her marriage to Matt, she would be behind schedule now on graduating, but only by a semester. She wanted to make certain she got her degree and she knew the baby would throw her timetable into upheaval.

Now because of Matt, she would have all the help she

wanted to hire and her mother lived here in Laramie and would be available and eager to help.

Her thoughts wandered to Matt. She missed him more than ever and wondered how long it would take her to get over him and to stop thinking about him constantly. She was lonely, hurting and missing his vitality and loving.

She had told her mother everything about her marriage and agreement with Matt.

There were moments she wished she had stayed until he walked out on her, but she knew she was better off making the break now.

She finally talked to a counselor about the courses she wanted to take and left to return to the sprawling condo she had purchased in a gated area that was in a relatively new area of Laramie.

When she turned onto her street, she saw a sleek black car parked in front of her house. As she turned into her drive, she wondered whose it was. Glancing over her shoulder, she saw Matt step out of the car.

Her heart missed a beat. He looked handsome in a leather jacket, jeans, western boots and a wide-brimmed Stetson. She stopped her car and climbed out to go meet him while her racing heart speeded even faster.

"What are you doing here?" she asked, watching him approach, snow crunching beneath his boots.

Nine

He walked up to her and she threw her arms around his neck at the same time he pulled her into his embrace. And then he kissed her.

Holding him tightly and forgetting all her resolutions, she wanted him more than ever.

She longed to push away his thick coat and heavy clothes to run her hands all over him. She kissed him hungrily while Matt tightened his arms around her.

He picked her up. "Door key?" he asked and then kissed her before she could answer him.

He held her while she unlocked the door and then carried her in, kicking the door shut behind him.

"Why are you here?" she asked, refusing to think about telling him goodbye all over again.

"I missed you," he said, glancing beyond her. "Where's your bedroom?"

She pointed as he kissed her again while he walked where she had directed.

An hour later she stirred in his arms as he rolled on his side and propped his head on his hand to look at her.

"I wasn't going to do this," she said quietly, gazing up at him solemnly and brushing his jaw lightly with the tips of her fingers as if to reassure herself that he was real.

"I wasn't, either. I've tried every way I could think of to forget you."

"Every way?" she asked, wondering if there had been a woman in his life.

"Maybe not every way," he said in a husky voice. "I want you back. What do I have to do? We're already married."

"Not really," she answered. "That's a technicality and our contract was for two years only."

"Will you marry me for real?"

Her heart missed a beat as she gazed up into his blue eyes. "Is that a proposal?"

"It is. I'm asking you to be my wife now and forever. I don't like being without you. I think about you constantly and miss you all the time and I don't want to go on like this."

"Do you mean it?" she asked, sitting up and tugging up the sheet beneath her chin.

"Will you marry me?"

"Forever?" she cried.

"Forever," he stated emphatically.

"Yes! Of course I will. I already have. I love you!"

"Darlin', I love you."

"More than money?" she asked, squinting her eyes and looking intently at him.

"Much more than money," he mused. "I found out that you were right about so many things, particularly what's really vital. Now let me see. What advantages are there to you over money? Soft, curvaceous, best kisser on earth, sexiest woman, a necessity for me to exist and function. Should we have another wedding?"

"I don't think so. Just another honeymoon."

"I'll vote for that one," he said. "You name where you want to go and I'll take you for as long as you want. I'll do anything to keep you happy."

She brushed his thick black curls away from his forehead and let her fingers slide down his cheek and along his jaw, feeling the faint stubble. "I didn't think you'd ever be back."

"I didn't, either. It was as big a surprise to me as to you to find out that I can't get along without you," he said solemnly and she smiled.

"I'm glad. I wasn't doing so well myself."

"Speaking of how you're doing. You still don't look pregnant. Are you sure you didn't make all that up?"

"Absolutely. I've been to see the doctor and I'm fine. I don't show yet and I guess part of it is because I'm tall. I don't know. He said everything is okay. I'll get bigger sometime so enjoy my skinny looks now."

"I intend to. Every way possible."

She held his jaw. "What about the baby? Do you mind?"

"I'll adopt the baby and it'll be mine. This baby will know me as its daddy. A daddy who loves it very much."

"Do you care whether I have a girl or boy?"

"Nope. As long as everyone is healthy and if you're happy, I'm happy."

They gazed into each other's eyes and she smiled at him, joy bursting in her. "I can't believe you're here and I'm so happy you are."

"I love you, Brianna, love you with all my heart."

She turned to kiss him, pausing to look up at him. "I never thought I'd hear you say that."

"I love you, darlin'," he said. "My wife. Decide where you want to go for a real honeymoon."

"Anywhere with you will be paradise," she said, pulling him closer to kiss him.

Epilogue

The following October...

"Bye, Mom, thanks," Brianna said, completing her call home to her mother. "Matt, will you stop a minute!"

He chuckled as he nuzzled her neck and she turned in his arms to hug him. "Let me talk on the phone, for heaven's sake!"

"All I was doing was holding you and kissing you a very little bit," he said innocently. "How's Jenna?"

"Jenna is fine and Mom is having a wonderful time with her and my sisters are there now so everyone is happy." She held up the baby's picture and they both looked at it.

"Brianna, I'll swear if I didn't know better, I'd think

this is my own flesh and blood. She's got my black curly hair and my blue eyes."

"Indeed, she does, but she also looks like me," Brianna said, smiling at him and looking back at their daughter. "She's beautiful. It was wonderful of your cousins to put off this weekend until Jenna was a couple of months old."

"We're great guys," he declared smugly and she laughed. She glanced around their large bedroom with bamboo furniture and plank floors. A ceiling fan turned lazily overhead. "This is really grand, but only because you're here," she said. Her smile faded as she gazed up at him. "Thank you for getting out of your investors' group so you'd be home more."

"You were right about what's important in life. And I'm glad you postponed law school indefinitely."

She kissed him lightly. "We have enough money for a good life in Cheyenne."

"That's a little bit of an understatement," he remarked dryly. "But it is good, and so was spending a week with my folks last month."

"Speaking of spending time with someone—it's past when we were supposed to join the others for the dinner party. We're already twenty minutes late," she said, glancing at her watch.

"They won't care," he said, continuing to nuzzle her throat and shower kisses on her temple and ear.

"I care. Now come on and let's join them."

"Sure," he said, straightening up and watching her cross the room. "You barely ever looked pregnant and now no one can guess by appearance that you had a baby a few months back. You look gorgeous."

She glanced in the mirror. "Thank you. You look good yourself," she said. "C'mon, Matt, and we'll go see your friends."

He groaned. "And listen to Chase crow over winning this bet."

"That's what you get for making such an extravagant bet," she said as he caught her hand and they left their island house for the large community building they all shared. Music carried on the night air from the band and outside flames danced beneath the grilling meat being turned by a cook.

Holding her hand, he led her up the steps into the large open room where a band played and the others danced.

The music ended and Brianna and Matt joined the other two couples. Brianna felt lucky to be Matt's wife and to be included in this group. From the first moment she met them, both Laurel and Megan had been friendly. Their handsome husbands had been, also.

"Finally, the newlyweds join us. A waiter should come by with drinks," Chase said.

The music commenced and Matt turned to take her into his arms to dance as the other couples paired off to dance.

Later in the evening the women sat in a cluster while the men stood nearby.

"This is a wonderful weekend," Brianna said.

"Wonderful and wacky," Megan added, "with their crazy bet, but it got us all together and that's good."

"They'll think up some new scheme," Laurel stated.

"I guess we can be glad for that bet though. I think that's what got us all together with our husbands. Right?"

"You're right," Megan said.

"What's happening?" Matt came up to join them and pulled a chair close to Brianna while the other men came to sit by their wives.

Matt raised his glass in a toast. "Here's to the winner of the bet—Chase. I never thought you'd win," Matt said. "I have to tell you."

"My oil beat out your investments and your businesses," Chase said, smiling at his cousins.

After a slight cheer, they all touched glasses and sipped their drinks.

"We were thinking about another possible bet this next year—" Jared began, but the women shouted and finally he looked at his cousins and threw up his hands.

"No more wild bets!" Megan declared, and they all laughed.

The band commenced playing again and Matt asked Brianna to dance. He wrapped his arms around her to dance slowly. "I love you, darlin'. My life is complete with you in it."

"Chase rented this island for the weekend and all this came with it?"

"Not all. The winner had to take care of the weekend, so this is Chase's deal. It's been fun, but I'm ready to go back to our own place. I want you to myself."

He waved to his cousins as they left and in minutes they were in the privacy of their bedroom, where Matt drew her into his embrace. "I love you with all my heart."

She pulled him closer to kiss him, holding him
tightly, filled with love and joy for the man she would
adore always.

* * * * *

A sneaky peek at next month…

By Request

RELIVE THE ROMANCE WITH THE BEST OF THE BEST

My wish list for next month's titles…

In stores from 21st March 2014:

❏ For the Greek Tycoon's Pleasure – Abby Green,
   Lucy Monroe & Lucy Gordon

❏ Kings of California – Maureen Child

3 stories in each book - only £5.99!

In stores from 4th April 2014:

❏ Las Vegas: Seduction –
   Marie Ferrarella, Gail Barrett & Cindy Dees

❏ His Little Miracle – Nicola Marsh, Shirley Jump
   & Victoria Pade

Available at WHSmith, Tesco, Asda, Eason, Amazon and Apple

Just can't wait?

Visit us Online

You can buy our books online a month before
they hit the shops! **www.millsandboon.co.uk**

0314/05

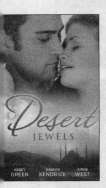
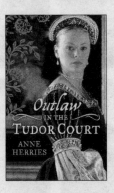

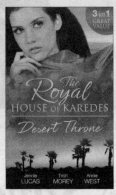

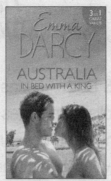

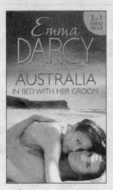

The World of Mills & Boon®

There's a Mills & Boon® series that's perfect for you. We publish ten series and, with new titles every month, you never have to wait long for your favourite to come along.

By Request
Relive the romance with the best of the best
12 stories every month

Cherish™
Experience the ultimate rush of falling in love
12 new stories every month

Desire™
Passionate and dramatic love stories
6 new stories every month

n o c t u r n e™
An exhilarating underworld of dark desires
Up to 3 new stories every mont

M&B/WORLD4a

Discover more romance at

www.millsandboon.co.uk

- ❤ WIN great prizes in our exclusive competitions
- ❤ BUY new titles before they hit the shops
- ❤ BROWSE new books and REVIEW your favourites
- ❤ SAVE on new books with the Mills & Boon® Bookclub™
- ❤ DISCOVER new authors

PLUS, to chat about your favourite reads, get the latest news and find special offers:

- 🔲 Find us on facebook.com/millsandboon
- ➤ Follow us on twitter.com/millsandboonuk
- ❤ Sign up to our newsletter at millsandboon.co.uk